CW01260888

Of The Good Hereafter

Published in 2008 by YouWriteOn.com

Copyright © Text Heather Pitt

First Edition

The author asserts the moral right under the Copyright, Designs and Patents Act 1988 to be identified as the author of this work.

All Rights reserved. No part of this publication may be reproduced, stored in a retrieval system, or transmitted, in any form or by any means without the prior consent of the author, nor be otherwise circulated in any form of binding or cover other than that in which it is published and without a similar condition being imposed on the subsequent purchaser.

Published by YouWriteOn.com

For Beulah,
My Mum

*Glimpses through the smoke discern
Of the good hereafter*

*Knowing this, that never yet
Share of Truth was vainly set*

                    John Greenleaf Whittier
                    'Barclay of Ury'

CHAPTER ONE

I continued to read Aunt Catherine's 'letter'.

… …Well before one o'clock I stationed myself on the landing. As an extra precaution I had secreted a copy of each family tree in the lining of my cloak. In addition I also stitched an old fob watch into the hem of my skirt to at least give myself a chance of ensuring the correct time should I be able to return. I heard the clock strike one and, with my heart hammering, waited: in a state of rising tension. Slowly the old door swung open once again and cautiously I stepped through. All was still and as my eyes became accustomed to the gloom they were greeted with the same images as before. A sudden gust of wind and the door slammed shut behind me.

I took several minutes steadying myself, my back resting against the rough stonework of the walls – yes, I was really here. Once I had assured myself nobody had stirred I soon located the spiral staircase in the wall corner which would take me to ground level. I lifted my skirts and cautiously made my way down as quietly as possible. Having reached the bottom I groped for the handle only to find the door was locked. This had never occurred to me and as I contemplated what to do next my hand knocked against something cold and bulky. Thankfully the key was protruding from the lock below. Turning it I opened the door, trying with all my might to lessen the inevitable creaking of the hinges.

The cold October air stung my cheeks as I stepped from the building out into the dark abyss beyond. My plan was to hide in one of the outbuildings until first light then make my way across the fields returning later in the morning in order to minimise suspicion. Through gossamer cloud the moon floated in a watery sky, shedding her veiled light over the ground ahead enabling me to take in my surroundings. Everything went like clockwork. I found an old cow byre at the rear of buildings close to the Hall and being too excited to sleep, set off as soon as dawn's light crept over the horizon: I needed to be well away from the hall before the household stirred.

Around mid morning I returned, having muddied my clothes and generally given myself a dishevelled air. I wandered up to the barmkin. This was a defensive surround aimed at keeping out unwanted guests and extremely effective against any border raids. In this case it was constructed of timber palings with a covering of clay. The gate was open as it had been last night (defeating the object one would think) and as I passed through and approached the hall I tried, as inconspicuously as I could, to take in as much detail as possible.

The pele tower was situated in the top left hand corner of the enclosure, several wooden buildings abutted the barmkin wall and in the centre of the cobbled 'courtyard' was a large well. In general everywhere looked tidy. A youth was leading a horse towards the stable that fronted my recent hiding place and from within the building could be heard the sounds of a blacksmith's hammer being pounded on an anvil. Almost immediately a large wolfhound came bounding towards me with its tail wagging and a ferocious bark issuing from its jaws. From the corner of my eye I noticed a young woman struggling to carry a bucket of milk from the byre. She was tall and slim with muscular arms and appeared to be in her late teens. Turning towards me she deposited her heavy load on the cobbles and absent-mindedly tucked a curly, auburn strand of hair behind her ear and into her hood, an action I was to see her do many times over the coming months.

I noticed her take in my dishevelled appearance and as she turned to face the dog she shouted "Down Lupus, stop that barking!" She looked at me suspiciously and continued "If yer stand still he won't hurt yer. What be yer business? Sir Anthony an' M'lady be away at present."

However, as I clutched my throat and croaked "Attacked ... thieves ... left for dead," she softened and putting the bucket down ran towards me with a look of concern on her face.

With her support, slowly we climbed the stone steps rising in front of the building. Here I leaned against the wall while she pulled open the metal grill and with difficulty managed to move the old, heavy, oak door. This opened onto the Hall and we stumbled inside.

"Yer seat yerself there while I fetch Master Anselm. He mun know what to do."

I looked around the room I had entered last night and had time to take in my surroundings. This was obviously the main hall of the property. Between the sconces were wall hangings and although the furniture was sparse the pieces looked of good quality. On the floor amidst the rushes were strewn dried alder leaves and wormwood, a remedy I knew was thought to deter fleas. After several minutes Anselm entered from the stairs wearing a full-length gown with broad, padded shoulders, full sleeves and a girdled waist. Had he sported a tonsure I would have assumed him to be a monk but he had a full head of dark brown hair, flecked with grey. His classical features put me in mind of a marble statue, accentuated by the pronounced cleft in his chin. As he crossed the room I could read a look of compassion in his eyes and I instantly warmed to him. I made to stand.

"Please, remain seated. Thou wouldst appear to have undergone severe trials and I beg of thee to rest," his voice was mellow and tinged with concern. "Margery has informed thee of the absence of Sir Anthony but we shall be more than happy to offer thee hospitality until his return and any assistance we can in order to relieve thy distress."

I began my explanation but Anselm insisted I rest and take some hot broth to ease my throat before any explanations were made. He helped me up the spiral staircase and we emerged into a room similar to the one we had vacated. It contained two chests, a curtained bed and a pallet by the end wall. Shortly afterwards Margery brought me a bowl of steaming liquid, which I consumed avidly, realising how hungry I was.

I spent the majority of the time looking out at a landscape that had changed little in four to five hundred years, noticing as I did, two young boys riding a pony in the fields behind the hall. Again I rehearsed my story in order to be as word perfect as possible and retrieved the family trees from the lining of my cloak to discover that a Sir Anthony Rutherford had lived from 1452 to 1486 when he had died from wounds received at the Battle of Bosworth. He had married a Margaret Noble in 1475 and, thankfully, appeared to be the only Sir Anthony on the tree. This certainly narrowed the dates and I reasoned the year must be somewhere between 1475 and 1485. I quickly absorbed the names of the Fitzroberts and de Raisgills for the same period and then awaited events.

Late afternoon Anselm came to enquire after my wellbeing and I accompanied him back down to the great hall. Laid out for us was a meal of cheese, bread and what I assumed to be watered down ale. After a few niceties on his part I could see he was intrigued to know my story. Consequently I embarked upon my tale, advising him that I was nursemaid to one of Sir Anthony's distant relatives, the Fitzroberts, who lived in Oxford but it had been arranged that I should travel to Carlisle to assist the de Raisgills who had an extensive 'nursery'. I had been travelling with two servants and had reached the outskirts of Kendal when we were ambushed. The robbers took my money, horse and belongings and attempted to throttle me in the process. I had fainted during the assault and upon regaining consciousness had found that the servants had fled. Knowing of my Master's relations in Overthwaite, I had determined to reach the Hall and although it had taken me several days to arrive, I felt sure I would recover fully given sufficient rest. I feigned a bad throat in order to cover any discrepancies in my tongue. I was *aware that during this period dialects varied greatly and indeed a southerner could easily think somebody from the north a Frenchman. Consequently I felt confident that I would become accustomed quickly to the local manner of speaking and hoped any discrepancies in my tongue would merely be put down to my 'foreign' accent.*

Anselm seemed to accept my story and was most solicitous that I rest. "Mistress Phillips," (I had introduced myself by my real name), "Sir Anthony and Lady Margaret return in a few days. Rest assured their hospitality shall be extended to thee. Additionally I trust Sir Anthony will insist that thou remain at Overthwaite until fully recovered and art able to journey on to Carlisle."

I suspect my 'grand age' assisted in convincing him of my need for rest and recuperation and shortly I returned to my upstairs bed where, utterly exhausted from the day's events, I was soon sleeping soundly. ……

I too felt exhausted. My aunt's temerity left me speechless: to have crossed into such unknown territory was an amazing feat and I could not imagine how she had fared. I was beginning to realise that this aunt, of whom I had precious little knowledge, was an intrepid lady.

But how had the letter come into my possession?

CHAPTER TWO

I had crested the hill on a memorable day in early January. The valley stretched out before me, its rugged beauty etched in white with a wintry covering of hoarfrost. It was my first visit to the area and, after a long and tiring overnight journey, all I wanted was to arrive at Overthwaite Hall and sink into a soft bed for a couple of hours. Nevertheless, weary though I was that first glimpse of Sleadale took my breath away.

Putting the car in gear I pressed on down the winding lanes, frequently glancing at the passenger seat where I had spread the map and directions to the Hall.

I use the word memorable because that day heralded the start of twelve months that would change my life completely. During the year an amazing quirk of fate would take me to dimensions I never dreamed could exist; provide me with experiences I could never have imagined.

Recently I had discovered I was the owner of a 17^{th}C property in North Cumbria. I was now on my way to meet Adam Knowles, my late aunt's personal secretary, who had undertaken to show me around as his one last service to Aunt Catherine.

Four months ago as I answered the telephone I had no idea what lay ahead. The call was from my aunt's solicitor and I learned that, after a short illness, she had died from leukaemia at the age of 61. Having no other relatives she had left the majority of her estate to me. Because of a rift in the family I had neither met my aunt nor visited Overthwaite Hall, the home bought by my grandfather during the 1950's. Consequently, I was extremely curious and rather excited at the prospect of reclaiming my family's heritage.

By now I had reached the lane leading to the house and, swinging the car round, I caught my first glimpse of Overthwaite Hall on the opposite side of the hill. It was a stone building and its two wings, one at either end of the property, extended towards me, almost beckoning me to approach: immediately, I felt a warmth for the old place. A central courtyard was flanked by windows and as the sun came out a myriad of light twinkled from every pane. Behind the Hall rose High Scar and, framed as it was by the brilliant blue of the sky, it looked an enticing climb even in my present tired state. To the right, a short distance away, lay the village of Overthwaite. I say village but it was little more than a hamlet with only three dozen or so properties, mainly stone-built with one or two being rendered and whitewashed.

Taking all this in I turned to my Chocolate Point Siamese who had been stretched out on the back ledge of the car for almost the entire journey.

"Well Tenzing, here we are." He gave a small yowl of response: something he did virtually every time I spoke to him. I stopped the car, opened the gate and pulled up at the front of the house. Before I was out of the car the old front door swung open and a man whom I presumed to be Adam Knowles crossed the cobbles, arm outstretched in a friendly greeting.

"You must be Miss Harvey? Adam Knowles ... pleased to meet you at last."

He looked to be in his early forties, was of medium build and approximately 5' 10" in height. His sleek, dark hair was greying at the temples and a 5 o'clock shadow was visible on his chiselled features.

"Please call me Emma," I said, shaking his hand and finding my gaze drawn to the defined dimple in his chin.

"Did you have a good journey? I hope it was not too tiring but at least you have had good weather for the trip north." His voice was soft and deep and his diction precise, having an old-world charm about it. He ushered me through the large front door.

"Yes, there were no hold-ups but I'm beginning to feel weary now I've stopped driving."

"Well, I shall be brief," he said, showing me into what I imagined was the living room. "Perhaps I could just show you around and then leave you to settle."

"Please don't think me rude or ungrateful, but I'd just like to get my head down for an hour or so before trying to take anything else in, if that's O.K. with you?"

"But of course. I should have known you would be tired," he said in a sympathetic tone. "The rest can wait until tomorrow. I have made sure there are one or two necessaries in the kitchen and if you need anything else, the local post office sells basics. I will return in the morning at 10 o'clock if that is agreeable?"

"That'll be great," I said, sidling towards the front door, "and once again, thanks for everything."

I brought Tenzing and my overnight bag out of the car, leaving the rest of my luggage and a few small boxes of personal effects in the boot until later. I climbed the ornate staircase leading to a landing which ran the full length of the house. Doors opened on either side and choosing the first I found myself in a chintzy room evocative of country cottages. After his long sleep during the journey, no doubt Tenzing would have preferred to investigate but for the time being he could sleep here with me. The bed felt firm and smelled fresh, and fully clothed I collapsed onto the duvet and soft feather pillows. Within two minutes I was fast asleep.

When at last I awoke, the pale, winter sun was low in the sky and I realised I had been asleep for several hours. Tenzing was curled up in a ball in the crook of my arm and my movement caused him to purr like a motorbike. My first priority was a cup of tea and making my way quickly downstairs, Tenzing following like a shadow, I turned away from the living room hoping to find the kitchen.

It was a large room with lots of character and although it had had a makeover in the not too distant past the result was tasteful and, I imagined, retained almost all of its original charm. An enormous oak table accommodated the eating requirements and an Aga nestled in the far corner. Systematically I went through the cupboards, familiarising myself with the layout and soon had some tea brewing in the pot. Whilst I waited, I glanced through the window overlooking the back of the property and in the quickening gloom saw a beautifully laid out garden stretching towards a limestone wall which encircled the house. Presumable my aunt had been a keen gardener, but I would investigate the outside tomorrow. With a mug of tea in hand I began a tour of the inside.

The room I had seen with Adam Knowles was, as I expected, the living room. This led to a conservatory or sunroom which had been added to the back of the property and which I felt sure caught the late afternoon and early evening sunshine due to the orientation of the house. Retracing my steps through the kitchen I entered the north 'wing'. The smell of must was unbearable and I surmised the rooms had been little used. Upstairs were three large bedrooms and a vast bathroom, which evidently were in need of modernisation. I realised that luckily I had picked the bedroom in which I would remain, with its marvellous view not only of the garden but also of High Scar.

By now the evening was drawing in and it was growing dark. As I had only managed to explore part of the house I decided the remainder could wait until tomorrow. After unpacking my meagre box of provisions and providing a saucer of cat food for a noisy Tenzing, it was time to light a fire in the living room and open a celebratory bottle of wine.

The room soon felt snug and warm and, wandering around, I noticed Aunt Catherine's books mirrored my own interests – British history from the Middle Ages through to Queen Victoria. On an old escritoire a silver frame housed a faded photograph. Picking it up and turning it towards the light I found it to be of a young woman, perhaps in her late twenties.

I presumed it was Aunt Catherine, as the resemblance to my mother was striking; however, Catherine's eyes looked sad and again I mused on this aunt I should never know.

I turned the key in the lock of the writing desk and two bulging foolscap envelopes almost fell onto the floor. They were sealed and gave no indication as to their content. Curious though I was, I decided that as I was tired, I would leave opening them until tomorrow. Sinking into an armchair I relaxed for the remainder of the evening, with Tenzing curled up on my lap.

I awoke to the sound of sheep and cattle in the surrounding fields and climbed out of bed to see the clock registering 7.15 a.m. Through the window I could see a fine day was in prospect, auguring well for outside explorations and after a light breakfast I donned my boots and duffle coat and headed off.

It was a beautiful morning, mild for January with a clear blue sky and a crisp feel to the air. I made my way around the back of the house and although I had glimpsed the garden yesterday evening in the dusk, I had failed to appreciate its beauty, even at this time of the year. I, too, was a keen gardener and my little cottage in Cornwall which backed onto a wooded ravine had an informal garden, reflecting the wild Cornish landscape. Here, Aunt Catherine had gone for a more formal plan with a small parterre containing low box hedges and roses, a heather garden with conifers and a delightful little pond still containing the remnants of last year's lily leaves.

Coming round the south wing, towards the front of the Hall, I could imagine this had originally been a separate barn, at some stage incorporated into the living accommodation. The opposite wing mirrored its twin and was possibly a later build. In addition several outbuildings were dotted around the house, perhaps one time stabling for horses. I was beginning to appreciate I had inherited a substantial property.

I decided to walk into the village and set off at a stride down the lane, my breath like a dragon's, billowing out before me. Soon I arrived at the post office and wandered in, to be met by several curious glances.

"Good morning. Do you have The Guardian?" I asked in my friendliest tone.

"No, we dun't have much call for it in t' village but I could git it if yer gan't be here fer any length o' time," replied the woman behind the counter. She was in her sixties, with dark hair and a cheery manner and I took to her instantly.

"Actually I *shall* be here for some time. I'm staying at Overthwaite Hall."

"Oh, yer must be Catherine Phillips's niece. We heard yer'd be arrivin' this week. Mi name's Claire and if there's owt I can do t' help, well, yer know where t' ask." She warmly continued, "Yer aunt wus a reg'lar customer here fer her daily newspaper an' eggs, but apart from that she kept hersel' to hersel' ... but listen to me, gan on. Whativer will yer think?"

"Well actually, I never knew my aunt, or this part of the country but I must say it is a lovely area."

"We like it. An' I'm sure yer'll enjoy bin here too. Ha long're yer stayin' fer?" she enquired.

"Oh, about six or eight weeks. I had some holidays owing and decided to get to know the place. Well I must be going. I am meeting Adam Knowles at 10 o'clock and I shouldn't be late," I said, moving towards the door. "So if you could order The Guardian for me ...? By the way, my name's Emma."

"Fine. Liv it wi' mi. It'll be here the morrer."

I meandered back, taking in most of the details of the village on my way: the church with its square tower; the meandering river and nearby pond; and the inevitable village pub. Back at the Hall I had just enough time to change out of my boots before Adam arrived.

"Hi. Come in. What a lovely day," I greeted him.

"Have you settled in? I hope you found everything in order. I did arrange for your Aunt's cleaner to prepare the rooms before you arrived," he explained.

"Everything is just fine. Tea or coffee?"

"Oh, hello. And what is *your* name?" Adam enquired. He had seen Tenzing by my leg and bent down, hand outstretched. Immediately the cat arched its back and let out an eerie wail.

"Tenzing, behave!" I scolded and bent down to stroke him. "I know you're a one-woman cat but I've never known you be rude before, even to strangers. What will our guest think?"

Over coffee we began to go through the papers and documents. It appeared Adam had been my aunt's secretary for only a couple of years. She had run a successful business in genealogical research and he had helped with her business affairs.

"She worked from home. From the studio in the south wing," Adam informed me, pointing over his shoulder at a door in the corner of the room. "Have you viewed the entire house yet?"

"No, not fully, I saw some last night. By the way, I hope you didn't think me rude. After you'd gone I slept for about six hours solid. And this morning I had a look around the outside. If you've got time I could do with the company?"

Passing through the door we entered the 'south' wing – such a grand name – nevertheless, I was still surprised by its dimensions. From the outside the wing looked only average but this room belied my earlier impressions. Adam advised me it was Aunt Catherine's sitting room, a place where she had spent a great deal of time. Unlike my bedroom the furnishings here were extremely modern, with minimal furniture and hard, stark lines. Everything was in black and white and although the effect was striking it was certainly not to my taste. From one corner rose a wrought iron, spiral staircase and I followed Adam as he climbed to the floor above. We emerged into a room mirroring the one below but this was furnished as an office, presumably the studio to which Adam had alluded earlier. The walls were lined with shelves containing box-files, rolls of microfilm, boxes of microfiche, CD ROMs and a number of books. The room was dominated by a huge desk, on which stood the inevitable computer and against the walls were machines for reading the microfiche and films.

"Although I didn't know her, I feel Catherine and I would have been kindred sprits – we seem to share the same interests. I'm absolutely mad on genealogy and history," I confessed as I worked my way along the shelves, browsing through the titles of the books.

"Oh, she was passionate about her work," Adam informed me. "She would become involved greatly with her clients and I think she enjoyed finding out about their ancestors just as much as her own. I would be ready to leave for the day and know that she would work on, well into the evening if she sensed a particularly tantalising trail. Most of her work was carried out here but in addition she travelled frequently to Carlisle, to the library and the archives office. On occasion she invited her clients here to discuss things and go through her findings with them. It had almost become her life – that and the gardening!"

"Yes, I noticed the garden. I imagine it's beautiful later in the year. That's another thing we have in common, I spend lots of time in mine." I wandered towards a door on my left. "What's through here?"

"Catherine's library. You spoke just now of your liking for history. Well your aunt was obsessed with the subject. Were you aware that she had a degree in Mediaeval English History?" We had moved through to a cavernous room approximately twenty five feet square. The walls were lined from floor to ceiling with books of every shape and size. I was speechless as Adam continued, "She had an excellent memory and although I cannot say that she had read every volume, I would not be surprised to learn so."

"I do wish I had met her."

We spent another hour or so in the studio, going through more papers, with Adam giving me a quick run through of my aunt's systems. Most of her cases had been finalised since her death and Adam agreed to wind up the last few before severing all connections with his old employer.

"I think it's time for a drink." I stood up and stretched. "I'm just going to the bathroom so I'll see you downstairs." Making my way towards the library I was through the door before Adam spoke.

"I regret there is no access to the remainder of the house from up here."

"But there's a door over there," I said, pointing to the right-hand wall of the library.

"Unfortunately it is sealed."

I wandered through and despite Adam's comment tried the handle. It wouldn't budge. Standing back I noticed the door was ancient, having metal studs and old-fashioned fittings. "God, I bet that could tell a tale or two!" I laughed. Adam flinched and I presumed his reaction was to my blasphemy: I would have to watch my language in front of him.

"It is the original door from the old Hall." He seemed suddenly tense but then relaxed and carried on in a gentler tone, "I understand that it was sealed many years ago, perhaps at the time the 17th century renovations were carried out."

"My Mum told me the original pele tower was almost 600 years old." By way of explanation I added, "My mother was Catherine's younger sister you know."

"Yes, I remember her telling me that once. She only began to talk about her family during her illness. Until then, she was a private person."

"Well there had been a family rift many years ago. I'll tell you about it one day." Again I looked around me. "Was this room part of the old Hall or was it through there?" I pointed towards the main part of the house.

"This room formed the Great Hall of the tower." I sensed that same tenseness in his manner. "There were further floors above but, presumably, they were removed when the building was enlarged. More than that, I know not." He turned to gather up his papers. "Shall we progress to the remaining rooms?"

We moved through to the northern arm of the Hall. I had already seen the dining room on the ground floor but above was a large study, obviously a man's room, which Adam informed me had once belonged to my grandfather. Beside this study, at the end of the corridor and facing the sealed oak door was a large en-suite bedroom also belonging to my grandfather but taken over and refurbished by my aunt upon his death.

My tour was at an end. By then it was mid day and (not having much else in) I suggested an omelette, unless he had other pressing engagements; he assured me he was in no rush and would love to stay for lunch. And so it was that we had a pleasant couple of hours during which I learned a little about Adam Knowles.

I was surprised to find he lived in a small cottage close by which belonged to Overthwaite Hall. He seemed shy and reluctant to talk about himself but with careful manoeuvring I learnt he came from the Ludlow area and had applied for the post of personal secretary/assistant to Catherine, having seen her advertisement on the internet. He had previously worked in archive offices and consequently this knowledge had greatly helped in securing the job. They had hit it off instantly and as the cottage was empty, he had moved in immediately.

"I miss her greatly," he told me. "Catherine was a sensible and reliable person and although she could be abrupt at times, she had inner warmth that shone through. I became close to her throughout her illness. Such a terrible disease …." He left the sentence hanging in the air.

"My father died of cancer so I do have some experience of the disease," I said, instinctively.

He sat quietly, looking out of the window and I could see he was reliving past events.

"What are you going to do when you finish here?" I enquired, trying to change the subject.

"Oh, I intend to return to Ludlow. I have relations in the area and as your aunt left me a small legacy I may do some travelling before I decide on my future plans." He seemed flustered and, not wanting to seem inquisitive I decided not to pry any further.

We were just finishing our meal when Tenzing wandered into the kitchen. He made straight for the back door and tried to use the cat flap.

"No. It's locked," I called sharply to him and received an indignant chatter-like response. "I'm keeping him in for a week until he finds his bearings. Tell me, did my aunt have a cat?"

"Yes she did, a young tabby named Czar. When your aunt died the couple at the post office agreed to have him – they had taken charge of him previously, at times of Catherine's absence."

"I'm sure Tenzing would pine if he had to go to new owners and I don't know what I would do without him. I have had him four years now. He belonged to my parents and when they died I 'adopted' him, or perhaps I should say he adopted me! I don't think I had much choice once he started working his charm on me and now I think the world of him – especially as he's a tie to them." I somehow felt I wanted to talk to Adam about my parents and decided to continue. "My father died almost three years ago. Mum nursed him through his illness and it took so much out of her that when he died it was as though she had given up. Nine months later she too was dead, from a heart attack."

"I am sorry. It must have been a terrible shock for you," Adam said softly.

"Oh, it was. Especially mum's death. At least with dad we had come to terms with it. Well, as much as one ever can. With mum, it was such a bolt out of the blue. But with hindsight it's for the best. They were terribly close and she was lost without him, but it didn't make my loss any easier to bear."

"No, I am sure that that is so." He looked deeply into my eyes and continued, "My parents were not young when I was born and my mother died giving birth to me. I was only thirteen years old when my father died and I was away at the time at, er, school."

"You were at boarding school?" I enquired.

"Er, yes. I felt very lonely and the grief for my father was intense." He appeared to be in another world and I remained silent, unwilling to break his reverie. When at length he looked up I saw sadness in his soft brown eyes. The intimacy of our last few exchanges brought an odd feeling to the pit of my stomach and although I had known Adam only a few hours I was surprised to find that already I was beginning to feel an attraction towards him.

He seemed to sense the change in the atmosphere. "Please excuse me, I must be going. Lunch was lovely, thank you." He rose easily from his chair, and made to stroke Tenzing who had just entered the room. Once again the cat evaded him, vehemently hissing and spitting in his direction. "Sadly, he does not like me."

"Well, as I said before, he isn't usually like this." I shook my head, bewildered. "Normally he tends to sense warmth in a person."

"I hope you do too," he remarked, turning to face me and as he did so our hands brushed accidentally. It was as though an electric shock had surged through my arm and I could feel my neck and face starting to grow hot. To hide my emotions I lead him quickly from the room and walked as steadily as I could down the hallway towards the front door. The butterflies dancing in my stomach were starting to settle and, with my hand on the open door, I managed a semblance of calm as I bade him farewell.

"I will need to return later in the week to work on those last few cases but I will telephone beforehand," he said, as again his eyes held mine. Then glancing away he added, "Well, if that is everything I will say goodbye."

Once more my heart was beating erratically and I could sense the familiar feeling of excitement starting to grow in the pit of my stomach. All I could manage was a feeble "Yes … fine … bye."

I watched him disappear down the lane. I could hardly believe it was less than thirty-six hours since we had first met and now here I was experiencing all sorts of emotions I thought were well and truly under control. I wandered into the kitchen and idly tidied things away, my mind in a whirl but by the time I had washed the dishes I was my usual self once again. But it did not stop me thinking about him. I wondered about his early years, living without his parents. What outside influences had moulded him into such an old fashioned, courteous person?

Then I remembered the writing desk and its contents: I headed for the living room.

Two hours later I was on my hands and knees, surrounded by paper and immersed in the history of the house.

One of the foolscap envelopes contained the deeds and documents relating to Overthwaite Hall. In amongst the papers I found a plan of the present day house. This also outlined the changes that had been made over the years since the original Hall was built. Notes indicated the old pele tower, belonging to a family named Rutherford, was being improved during the mid 1600's but at that time it was suddenly sold. The new owners, named Armstrong, had amended and enlarged the project incorporating the whole of the old hall into the new build at the southern end. The plan of the old hall tied in with Adam's description: probably a standard layout for pele towers dating back to that period. The drawings helped to clarify the position of the sealed oak door. This had been the main entrance to the tower and was situated on the first floor with access via a set of external stone steps. When the enlargement had taken place in the 17th century the steps had been demolished and the two upper storeys removed. As I suspected, the south wing was originally a barn incorporated into the development but the north wing was missing: obviously a much later addition.

I turned my attention to the second envelope. This contained three bundles each neatly tied with string. Undoing the largest I found it to be pages and pages of names and dates and realised it was a family tree. Fitting it together was like completing a jigsaw and by the time I had finished the floor was covered with papers forming the Rutherford family tree dating from the 14th century. I was fascinated by the contents, which included dates of births, deaths and marriages of the family living at Overthwaite Hall. The remaining bundles formed two more 'trees' for the de Raisgill and Fitzrobert families, the first containing dates, but this time in a much less detailed form than that of the Rutherford's, and the second being a sparse affair with few details. How were these families connected I wondered?

I must have sat there for a good hour poring over the details, gradually seeming to make some sense of it all when I noticed a smaller envelope which was hidden beneath all the paperwork. On the front were written the words 'Rutherford

Family Legend' in a hand I had seen recently and surmised was that of Aunt Catherine. Looking inside I withdrew a foolscap sheet of paper, in the same handwriting, which read as follows:

RUTHERFORD FAMILY LEGEND

Below is a transcript of papers found during the 1970's whilst conducting my researches into Overthwaite Hall. The original documents were in poor condition and sadly soon disintegrated.

"This history is set down for posterity's sake, by myself Matthew Rutherford, as a true record of our family's heritage lest any gainsay our bloodline or indeed that of my half brother and sister, and records details related to me by my father, Thomas Rutherford, Knight of this county of Westmoreland.

During the reign of King Richard he bestowed on that gentleman Robert de Vere Earl of Oxford, the lordship of Ireland. During the year of our Lord 1386 that gentleman whilst in Ireland did get with child a girl being named Frances who later was brought to her confinement and gave birth to twins who be named Richard and Agnes. That gentleman was so taken with the girl that he fetched her and the infants back with him upon his return to our shores. Being a true friend of King Richard he requested that a good marriage be made for the girl and so this was done. My father being a Knight in the service of the King had already earned himself good favour and had, some few years earlier, been apportioned land in the County of Westmoreland. Being in his thirty second year and not yet having found himself a wife, my father at the bidding of his liege Lord, took the girl to his name.

The boy child, Richard Fitzrobert was taken to the house of our Lord Oxford until the untimely death of that gentleman in the year of our Lord 1392 when King Richard had the boy taken into his own household and brought up in the ways of a gentleman. When our good King Henry rightfully took the throne of England, being the honourable man he is he gave lands to Richard in Oxfordshire and made for him a good match.

The girl, Agnes Fitzrobert was sent to the household of John de Raisgill being near Carlisle and was brought up as a lady. She later married his son James who is now master of that household upon the death of his father John.

My dear mother Frances was brought to bed and gave birth to a son, myself Matthew Rutherford in the year of our Lord 1388. She was so affected by the birth that our good Lord saw fit to take her and she is now at peace and lies buried in our churchyard.

My father, God rest his soul, died in the year of our Lord 1403 fighting for our good King Henry when he defeated Harry Percy in Shrewsbury.

I, being the only child of the aforesaid union am continuing to maintain my father's land and property in good and grateful token to his memory. And furthermore, our good King in his esteem for my father's faithful service has provided for me an agreeable match and I have so taken as wife to me, the daughter of the King's trusted Master of the Household, Jane Goodman.

Perchance the time arises, we are happy to pay visit to my half sister Agnes, her living but a day's ride away, and likewise are happy to receive her good husband and family at Overthwaite – would that my half brother lived close by, so that we too were able to pay visit upon one another. Alas, there is scant opportunity to travel to Oxfordshire but his last missive stated that he and his family are well.

Written this 9th day of October, in the year of our Lord 1409, under our good King Henry."

I let the paper fall to my knees absolutely entranced by what I had just taken in. It was all so tangible, as if the characters had been here only yesterday. I felt as though I knew them. What were they like, these people whose names were boldly outlined on a sheet of paper? They had lived and breathed, loved and died: my mind was in a whirl.

At the bottom of the page Catherine had made cross reference to a file marked "Rutherford/Fitzrobert/de Raisgill Family Histories" which I presumed would detail her further researches into the families named. I could hardly wait to read the file and learn of my aunt's further findings into the family who had occupied Overthwaite Hall all those years ago.

CHAPTER THREE

Over the next few days I settled in. My meagre possessions did add a little of my own personality to the Hall and with each day that passed I was amazed at the depth of my feelings. It was as if I had always known the house – I felt completely at home.

For as long as I can remember I had yearned to visit both my aunt and the house as, my father being an only child and with his parents having died before I was born, I had no other relations. I was intrigued by my mother's family but found it difficult to ask questions in view of past events.

Many years previously my mother's actions had caused a family rift. With no other siblings, upon the death of my grandparents Aunt Catherine had inherited and taken over the running of the family home, Overthwaite Hall. Since the 1960's my mother had had no further contact with her family, hence my unfamiliarity with this part of the country. I had never met my aunt nor been allowed to speak of her or my grandparents in my mother's company, although I had managed to glean one or two details from my father. It was the usual 'love triangle'. He had met and become engaged to Aunt Catherine whilst my mother was at Leeds University. However, on her return she and my father fell in love and eloped to Gretna Green. Not surprisingly Catherine was heartbroken and vowed never to see either of them again, nor did she ever marry. My grandparents disowned my mother, so she and my father resolved to get as far away as they possibly could. My father's ancestors had come from the West Country, he thought it an ideal choice to make their home in Cornwall and there they settled. Because of our lack of relations we led a solitary existence. I had no siblings and consequently the three of us were always close. Since the death of my parents I had sometimes wondered about getting in touch with Aunt Catherine but had never managed to pluck up the courage to try to contact her. So the call from her solicitor came like a bolt out of the blue and it was an even bigger surprise to learn she had left everything to me. Perhaps she had mellowed in later years. I felt I would never know.

I read with ever growing interest Catherine's further researches on the Hall's previous occupants. The amount of detail she had accumulated was unbelievable and I thought that perhaps she had been obsessive on the subject. I determined I would talk to Adam about it. Increasingly I was finding I wanted to learn as much as I could about my aunt. Apart from the things I had already learnt, what were her likes and dislikes? What made her tick? I needed to try to build up a picture of her, to help satisfy the insatiable curiosity I was feeling about a lady whom I had never known but to whom I now felt so close.

Adam came to the house virtually every day and I could feel a growing attraction – on my part at least. I had had relationships over the years: at thirty-eight years of age who hadn't? But they had all been innocuous flings, until I met Guy Devereux. I was on holiday in Greece at the time. Four years ago I had gone there on my own and had noticed him on my first night at the hotel. He was tall and blond and every female gaze followed him across the dining room floor. I tried not to stare but that night my eyes seemed to have a mind of their own and towards the end of the meal, as he headed straight for my table, I could feel the blood slowly rising up my throat and face.

"I hope I haven't been staring, but don't I know you from somewhere?" his deep voice almost made my heart skip a beat. Of course I knew it was a chat up line but felt thankful to him, as obviously *I* had been the one to stare.

In an instant I knew I wanted him to stay and decided to take the lead. "Mmm …? You know, I was thinking the same thing myself. Please, join me. The waiter could always bring another glass."

Things progressed from there: like a whirlwind, in fact, for he swept me off my feet. What came over me, I do not know. I had always been cautious with my previous partners and sex had taken time to develop but with Guy it was different. On that first evening we made love. It was fervent and intense, as though we were both trying to assuage some deep, hidden thirst and certainly I had never known anything like it before. By the end of the holiday I was totally in love with him and desperately hoped that he too regarded it as more than a holiday romance. He was *so* good looking and *such* good company I was amazed when the phone rang on my first night home and I heard his liquid tones telling me he was missing me already. Why me, I asked myself? I'm an ordinary person: medium height, a reasonable figure (with a *slight* tendency to plumpness!), blue eyes and long, brown hair. Anyway, Guy wanted me so I thanked my lucky stars and went with the flow! I discovered he was a forensic pathologist, working and living in Oxford and over those first few months I became fascinated with the tales he told about his work with DNA. For him it was a real passion.

He met my parents before my father was diagnosed with cancer and when the time came was a tower of strength not only to me but to my mother as well. So it goes without saying that when my mother passed away, I grew to rely on him more and more. Whether that was the reason for the breakdown in our relationship, I'm not sure. But gradually he drifted away from me until that dreadful evening when he told me he felt we should part. I was devastated. Although by then my parents had been dead for over a year, the wounds were still raw and when we split up I felt, once more, my world had been torn apart. It was as if the grieving process had begun all over again. I could neither eat nor sleep and although I tried to throw myself into my work to keep my mind off him, that too was suffering. Luckily I have an understanding boss who stood by me and eventually things slowly improved. But having given my heart to Guy and having had it broken I decided to lock up my emotions and throw away the key. That was less than twelve months ago and I certainly hadn't looked at another man since.

That is, until I met Adam. Every day I listened with baited breath for his arrival and I knew that increasingly I was becoming emotionally involved. He would let himself straight into the studio and I invented all sorts or reasons to interrupt his work. But throughout, I told myself it was probably one-sided and I mustn't lose my head (or my heart) again. I told myself, but I don't know whether I was paying attention at the time!

When the 10th January dawned, little did I know what lay ahead.

It was a cold, cloudy morning and I decided to get to know the area better. I donned my boots and waterproof, threw some lunch in the rucksack and set off. I must have walked for miles and when I returned dusk was falling. Tenzing greeted me at the back door, impatiently awaiting my return and obviously in need of company after a day cooped up in the house without me. I decided on a good long soak and he sat on the corner of the bath whilst I luxuriated in the bubbles. After eating I soon felt my eyes close and resolved to have an early night.

I must have been in a deep sleep when suddenly I was awakened by the sound of a dog barking loudly. Glancing at the clock through bleary eyes I saw the fingers registering just after 10 p.m. The noise was so close and my first thought was that a stray dog must be in the garden. I stumbled towards the bedroom door to find it ajar and was amazed to hear a baby crying. Intrigued, I pulled the door open and was about to step onto the landing when the slamming of a heavy door reverberated through the stillness. I walked down the hallway and listened: everything was deathly quiet. I shivered, for a strange chill hung in the air and something else, an unusual smell. A musty, earthy sort of aroma the like of which I had never smelled before. I had a quick look around, but all seemed well and I returned to the bedroom. Tenzing was on the bed where I had left him and I was amazed to see his ears flattened, back arched and the fur along his spine bristling like a porcupine's.

"Now then, what's the matter with you?" I enquired, tentatively putting my hand out and beginning to rub my fingers along his backbone. He was emitting a deep, banshee-like wail and his gaze never left the bedroom door. As I continued stroking him I could feel the tension gradually leave his body until once again he was back to normal.

"Whatever was all that about? Come on, let's go downstairs and have a few crunchies." I picked him up and headed towards the door but he suddenly leapt from my arms, his claws drawing blood on my flesh in a frantic hurry to escape.

"Alright, alright … you stay there. I'm going to make myself a warm drink to show you there's nothing to be frightened of through that door." I hope I am not the only person to talk like that! Living on one's own has a lot to answer for.

I returned with a mug of hot chocolate and, as there were no further outbursts from Tenzing, soon succumbed to sleep.

In the morning I had virtually forgotten the incident as things soon swung into the pattern that was quickly becoming my daily way of life at Overthwaite Hall. A couple of days later I decided to explore the attics. I had bobbed my head in when I first arrived but now decided to spend some time up there. I was fascinated to find boxes and boxes of old family photographs and for the first time I could see what my grandparents had looked like.

My mother had mentioned, during one of our rare discussions about her parents, that my grandfather was a strict disciplinarian, almost a martinet. He had been born in Cheshire and gone into medicine after obtaining his qualifications at Manchester University. Whilst working at a leading hospital on the outskirts of the city he had been invited to relocate to the north Lakes when a position became vacant in Carlisle via a recommendation from one of his University colleagues. A total workaholic, he had thrown himself into the position and eventually became one of the country's leading surgeons during the late 1950s. I looked at his photograph and could imagine what a strong person he had been. By contrast my grandmother looked soft, frail and totally dominated by her husband, as my mother had recounted with a bitter note in her voice.

Delving further I found a photo which made my heart skip a beat. It showed two girls in their late teens: one was my mother and the other I recognised from the photo on the bureau as Catherine. The date on the reverse stated 'Summer 1960' – it had been taken before my father came on the scene. They looked young and close and it tore at my heartstrings to think of what was to follow.

I continued with my explorations until I came across a suitcase in the corner which, although old, looked as though it had been used and dusted recently. It was unlocked and, having lifted the lid, I almost moved on after only a cursory glance thinking it a case of old clothes, when my eye noticed a plastic bag labelled "A keepsake of Edward's" in Catherine's writing. I was intrigued and opening the bag I found, carefully folded in tissue paper, a shirt which I estimated would fit a boy in his early teens. What I found difficult to imagine was that any teenage boy would be willing to wear it; in fact it looked more suitable for a girl, having frills around the neck and cuffs. Who was Edward I wondered and why had Catherine kept this memento?

The case's other contents were items of clothing for a man and a woman (which again looked as though they had come out of the Ark), a beautiful bone comb and a small, leather drawstring purse. Emptying the contents onto my hand I found myself looking at a small pile of old coins. They appeared foreign and were so old and well used I could hardly read the wording on them. I slid them back into the purse, refolded the clothes and packed away the suitcase, all the time musing over its contents. And then it dawned on me. Mum had told me Catherine had always harboured a secret desire to act. She must have been involved in some local amateur dramatics and these were the costumes and props. I must look to see if she had kept any of the programmes or write-ups.

The remainder of the attic's contents kept me employed for the rest of the day: the room mainly consisted of the usual lifetime acquisitions and would need some prudent sorting at some stage in the future.

The days passed and I began to think about returning to Cornwall. My employer, an eminent neurologist, had been very understanding when I learnt about my inheritance.

"Emma, stay for as long as it takes to sort things out," he had said. "I haven't spent years moulding you into the perfect P.A. to lose you by not agreeing to some leave of absence. Whatever it takes is fine by me. We'll muddle along here without you but as soon as you're ready to return, I will welcome you with open arms."

Dear Jeremy, I had been with him now for almost twelve years and he had been such a tower of strength when I lost my parents. But the time was approaching when I must return. I needed time to think about my long-term future and what I intended to do with the Hall. With the money Catherine had left me I now had sufficient income to be a 'lady of leisure' if I so desired but I failed to see myself living up here, gardening all day. No, I needed to return to my little Cornish cottage and see how much or if I missed Overthwaite – but not yet. I already knew how much I would miss Adam, hence my reluctance to leave. My hope was to get to know him sufficiently well to convince him he needed to see me when he moved back to Ludlow.

With this in mind I persuaded him to take a day off and go walking on the fells. My father had taken me rambling as a child and I had retained the enthusiasm, often strolling along the coastal path in the Padstow area where we lived. I adored the rugged beauty of north Cornwall, particularly around Bedruthan Steps and a perfect day would be to find a quiet niche where I could look out to sea, spray lashing my face and the wind blowing cobwebs from my hair. But now I decided it was time to appreciate the beauty of the Lake District fells. I had found a book on Catherine's shelves about the valley of Mardale and its surrounding hills and I was fascinated at the thought of Roman soldiers marching along High Street. That was where I intended to go, with Adam as my companion.

We ensured the forecast was good and set off in the early morning in order to be back in good time before dusk. It was a cold, bright day and the car park at the head of Haweswater was deserted, as was the path up the Gatescarth pass. I had noticed that close by the route towards High Street the map mentioned a feature, 'Adam's Seat'.

"We can't miss an opportunity like that! It wasn't named after you was it?" I joked. Adam merely smiled as we made our way towards the small grassy knoll. The view across to the sea was brilliantly clear and we stood in companionable silence, the wind buffeting our faces and causing my eyes to water. We pressed on over Harter Fell then dropped down only to climb again to Mardale Ill Bell. I was less fit than I had thought, finding the fells a tougher prospect than the Cornish coast but by pausing on several occasions to take in the view an opportunity was provided to catch my breath.

The last lap of our goal was the 'march' towards the higher summit of High Street and it was exhilarating; however, as we reached the ordnance survey column my legs were telling me I had climbed over 2000 feet. I supposed with practice the Roman soldiers must, literally, have taken it in their stride. It was well worth the effort: the air was crisp and again the views were breathtaking as we rested our backs against the wall looking out towards the Helvellyn range. I was ready for my lunch and eagerly rooted through my rucksack for the sandwiches I had made earlier in the morning.

"Please, help yourself. Those are chicken and the others cheese." He had been quiet on the climb and with the exertions I hadn't pushed the conversation but I was now eager to make up for lost time. "Have you done much fell walking?"

"Not until I met Catherine. She introduced me to the beauty of these hills and I often came walking at weekends."

"She was fit then?" I enquired.

"When I first met her, yes. And she had a passion for the fells. I think it was a way of escape whilst your grandfather was still alive."

It was the first time he had mentioned my grandparents and I was intrigued. "Did she talk about them much?"

"The first time was during her illness. I think that after years of being on her own she needed to bare her soul. It was then that she touched on the old rift with your mother. She did not speak of intimate details but confessed that over the years she had mellowed and often wanted to re-establish contact with your parents. Alas, her father forbade such a thing – I gather he was a tyrant."

"Mum certainly thought so," I interrupted. "There was definitely no love lost between them, even before the problems."

Adam continued, "Upon his death Catherine resolved to find your family and hired a private detective to trace your whereabouts. Sadly, his report arrived after the death of your father and rightly or wrongly she felt that your mother would be unable to take any additional emotional stress at that time. As you are aware, Catherine then had insufficient time to contact her sister in view of the sudden subsequent death of your mother. She was devastated at the news."

"I wonder why she didn't try to make contact with me after Mum's death?" I mused.

"I believe she intended to but then travelled extensively during the year 2000."

"Oh, where did she go?" At that moment a low flying jet appeared from nowhere. The noise was completely deafening and such a shock that my heart pounded wildly. I watched the silver streak of metal weave its way through the fells and disappear over the distant horizon. "I hate those things," I said turning towards Adam. "Do you get many around here?"

"I regret to say quite a few. I fear I shall never get used to them. The peace of this area is something which has always appealed to me." Resting his head against the wall he closed his eyes. A serene look came over his face and a mysterious smile played on his lips. I wondered what he was thinking and where he was: obviously far, far away.

We spent other days on the fells and, having learnt I was a proficient rider, on one occasion, Adam suggested we hire a couple of horses from a neighbouring stable and spend the day travelling further afield. It was a glorious day, despite the mixed weather and I wished it would last forever. It was good to feel the horse move beneath me: exhilarating as the biting wind stung my cheeks. It had been some time since I had ridden, in fact not since my split with Guy but I decided then and there that I must take it up once more – as soon as I returned to Cornwall. And that must be soon for the weeks had passed and I suddenly realised I had been at Overthwaite for almost a month. Where had the days gone? I was enjoying myself to such an extent that I wondered whether I wanted to return home. But no, for the sake of Jeremy and my job I had no choice, I had to go. Well, maybe in a few more days!

It was a particularly miserable day. The clouds were low and masked the fells completely: one wondered whether the hills were there at all. The rain had been relentless all morning and by late afternoon a wind had arisen, howling through the house with an eerie wail. I was restless. Wanting to get out but deciding against it in view of the weather, I wandered up to Catherine's studio to find a book with which to while away the hours.

Adam was hard at work and I apologised for disturbing him. Wandering quietly over to the bookshelves I had begun to scan the volumes when suddenly the silence was broken by a loud noise. I spun around.

"It will be one of the bedroom doors. It often happens when the wind blows in from the north," Adam reassured me.

The noise jogged a seed of remembrance in my mind. What was it? I frowned, deep in thought.

"Is something the matter?"

And then it came to me. "It's nothing really, just that door banging which reminded me of something a few weeks ago." I proceeded to relate the details of the night I had been awakened by the mysterious barking. "I could have accepted the dog, even though it sounded as though it was *inside* the house but a *baby* crying! That really was baffling."

Adam seemed oddly quiet, as though he was turning something over in his mind. "Do you remember when this actually occurred?"

"Let me see, it must have been … I'm not sure … perhaps a week, or maybe ten days after I arrived. Why?"

Adam was silent as he looked deeply into my eyes – coming to an important decision, perhaps? "Probably Thursday the 10th and I imagine the time to have been just after 10 o'clock in the evening." Then under his breath, as though talking to himself he added, "At least there is no need to double-check. It *is* still happening."

"As a matter of fact you're right about the time. I noticed the clock as I awoke," I was amazed. "How on earth did you know?"

He smiled and looked at me with that intense gaze which I had come to feel was so characteristic of him. "I think it is time for you to read Catherine's letter." He left the remark there, floating enigmatically in the air. Already seated at Catherine's desk he produced a bunch of keys from his pocket and proceeded to unlock the bottom left hand drawer. Withdrawing a large brown envelope his gaze again met mine before he added, "Perhaps you should retire to the lounge. It will take some time for you to digest the contents and I see no reason why comfort should not accompany your task."

I was intrigued and bewildered. What could Catherine possibly want to tell me that had any bearing on events of the other evening?

I followed Adam to the lounge and settled myself in a chair: my heart pounding as I wondered what I was about to learn.

Adam looked up. Once again that odd smile appeared on his face and with an intense gaze he said, "I have already mentioned Catherine's desire to re-establish contact with your mother. She also greatly wished to get to know you but alas, in view of her illness and early demise, had no opportunity to do so. Knowing that I would meet you, before she died she left this letter in my safe keeping with instructions that, once you had settled in and, she hoped, formed an attachment to the house, the letter should be given to you. I know that she also hoped you would turn out to be a person capable of relating to and appreciating its contents. I think she would not have been disappointed, although I fear the facts will take some digesting."

He walked towards me with the 'letter' and as I took hold of it I remember thinking how bulky it was. Tearing open the envelope I was surprised to see not only the letter but pages and pages of notes: I could think of nothing to say to Adam, so intrigued was I and eager to read what my aunt had written.

CHAPTER FOUR

"Dear Emma,

To be writing this to my niece, whom I know not at all, saddens me. Your mother was my dearest friend and companion in our youth and had I been able to spend my life in her company and thereby know and grow to love her daughter, surely that would have been my greatest joy. Where did it all go wrong? Where to begin?

Inevitably the starting-point was your parents' meeting but I am sure that over the years you will have heard most of the facts and I think it superfluous for me to repeat them here. Suffice it to say, the consequences of their love have necessitated the writing of this letter. To turn back the clock – an ironic phrase in view of what I am about to tell – to irrevocably alter the course of events if one could, would one choose to do so? I think not. I have led a happy, if solitary life and, as I trust Adam has now told you, one mellows with age. Upon the death of my father I did intend to make contact with your parents, to 'bury the hatchet' after all these years. Sadly my plans were overtaken by events; my heart truly goes out to you on the death of both of your parents in such quick succession. Not to have seen my sister one last time hurts more deeply than words can express but fate then takes a turn and I *find I shall soon be reunited with her as, despite the treatment, I feel my life is drawing to a close.*

I should dearly have loved getting to know you but, sadly, that was not to be. Instead I hope you come to know me a little through this very special house. Please enjoy Overthwaite as I have over the years – your mother adored the house when she was young. I hope you grow to love its nooks and crannies and take an interest in the people who once inhabited its walls. This leads me nicely into the following epistle. Please read it with an open mind. I can assure you it is not a work of fiction. I feel sure you will have many questions but, please, persevere until the end and all will become clear.

Lead a full and happy life and always follow your heart.

With fondest regards,

Catherine.
May 2001"

I looked up to see Adam watching me. "I will leave you alone." Making his way to the door he turned, "Until the morning. Be careful not to burn the candle too low tonight!"

I re-read the letter trying to get to know the character of my late aunt and then I turned to the many typewritten pages. Somehow I felt what I was about to read would be momentous and decided a glass of wine was called for. Settled, I began my task.

My story begins on 10th January 2000, or perhaps I should say the day before. It was a cold, dry day with some wintry sun early morning and I had decided to take advantage of the weather and spend time in the garden on some belated tidying of the beds. Returning indoors mid afternoon I turned to a backlog of paperwork and by early evening I felt *exhausted both physically and mentally by my labours of the day. I decided on a long, hot soak and an early night, falling asleep almost as soon as my head touched the pillow. I presume I had been in a deep sleep when suddenly the loud barking of a dog awakened me. The house was otherwise deathly quiet and as I wondered whether or not to investigate, the unmistakable wail of a baby drifted through the still night air. ......*

As I read those words my stomach clenched and the shock almost made me drop my wineglass. Surely it was too much of a coincidence – the same date, a dog barking, a baby crying. Eagerly I read on.

...... I looked at the clock to see the figures registering just after midnight. Almost immediately the stillness reverberated with the sound of the slamming of a heavy door. At this I felt I must ensure all was well. However after an extensive check, as all was fine, I returned to bed. Lying there I could not help wondering whether it had merely been a dream for, once again, the house was still.
My second experience was on 20th February. Earlier in the week there had been snow and rain but on the morning of the 19th, eager to leave the confines of the Hall, I was pleased to awake to a cold, sunny morning. I spent the day on the fells returning tired but mentally exhilarated. After my customary bath I retired to bed early, only for the same pattern of events to occur. At two minutes past midnight I was awakened by the dog, followed by the baby and finally the slamming of the door. My drowsiness vanished and instantly I connected the two incidents. What could have produced this strange combination of noises on two separate occasions? Could it be a coincidence? I thought not. As the days passed my mind frequently returned to those events and I re-lived the sounds over and over trying to make some sense of the whole thing. During my work on many occasions I found my mind wandering back and eventually tumbled to a possible solution, incredible though it seemed.

I have always been fascinated by figures. One day after arranging various appointments with a client, I was studying the calendar and after writing the dates down I doodled idly on the blotter, my mind once again far away. Suddenly the solution came to me. I wrote down the time I had been awakened followed by the full date to see the following: 00:02 20/02/2000. I knew that on the first occasion I had been awakened also around midnight and it occurred to me that had it been at two minutes past, the same principle could be applied i.e. 00:02 10/01/2000. Both figures were palindromic. My mind was in turmoil. What could it mean? Quickly I went through the calendar and found that it would occur again on 30th March, 1st October, 11th November and 21st December. I sat there for what seemed an endless period, going over the possibilities in my mind. What was I to do? I decided the only course of action would be to test out my theory in March. I looked at the calendar: only three days away! Those were three of the longest days in my life.

On the evening in question I had no need to fear falling asleep, I was fully alert. During the day I had realised that by putting the clocks forward for British Summer Time four days previously, my calculations would alter. It now meant that whatever was about to transpire would do so at 1:02 B.S.T., instead of 00:02 G.M.T. (Greenwich Mean Time). On the two previous occasions the noises had appeared to come from the other end of the landing and so I positioned myself there to await events.

A deathly silence settled over the house as the minutes ticked by and the hands of the clock approached two minutes past one. My tabby cat Czar had appeared by my side and I was idly talking to him when the old oak door at the end of the landing suddenly swung open. I could hardly believe my eyes. The door had been sealed since, well, certainly prior to my parents purchasing the Hall. Quickly hurrying towards it, once again I heard the unmistakable bark of a dog and the crying of a baby. I ventured inside the doorway with one hand on the jamb, the other on the door itself. Whether I was subconsciously bracing myself for what was within or attempting to stop the door from closing, I know not but what I saw through the aperture made my insides turn.

The sight that greeted my eyes could have been taken from the film set of a medieval castle. It looked to be the Great Hall of an old tower house. The room was in darkness but from the light behind me I could see the furnishings were sparse with sconces on the walls and rushes strewn across the floor. It had taken only seconds for my mind to absorb these facts but the clock was ticking and suddenly I felt an immense force surge through my arm, almost as though the door had a will of its own. I stepped back and with a resounding thud the thick oak swung into place, sending a shudder through the fabric of the house.

I stood as if rooted to the spot letting the images I had witnessed fix themselves firmly in my mind. I turned to see Czar at the far end of the landing, back arched and a chilling wail emanating from the depths of his throat. Yes, he knew something was wrong, but what? Tentatively I reached for the handle and turned the knob, knowing all the time that the door would remain firm. I hurried downstairs and made my way through the sitting room and studio to the library. Everything was as normal albeit a few minutes previously things had been very different. Although my mind was confused one thing was certain, I had not been hallucinating.

Next morning my first task was to look up the deeds of the hall. Attached to them were detailed plans, not only of the present house but also of the old hall together with the changes made over the years. I knew what I would find as I had studied them on several occasions but nevertheless I intended to double check. The door at the end of the landing had once been the main entrance to the early 15th century property, which at that time was merely a pele tower. The previous evening as I looked into that room I had noted that no opening existed into the studio and consequently I felt sure I was viewing the original tower house prior to any of the changes that had been made during the 17th century. Somehow at these palindromic times a doorway was opening into the past, a gateway back into history.

I could hardly believe it was true, and such an opportunity. With my knowledge of the mediaeval period and my love of all things past I decided there and then to cross the threshold and absorb any consequences that followed.

I had six months in which to make all the arrangements. Previously I had undertaken extensive researches into the Rutherford and associated families following discovery of the manuscript lodged with the deeds. I now learned as many of those names and relationships as I possibly could. I knew the 'window' in history into which I was stepping must be between the completion of the pele tower during the early 1400's and the date the new owners had made drastic changes to the property during the mid 1600's. I re-read my books on the period in question, soaking up as much background knowledge as my brain would take. I ransacked second hand clothes shops until I came up with an outfit for the period with which I was happy. I made certain that I un-picked any telltale labels, not wanting unnecessary questions or awkward situations to arise when I eventually 'went back'. My shoes, I felt sure, would fail to pass as 15th century specimens and so I had decided to go barefoot: my intended alibi would cover their absence. Living on my own I had no problems with being missed, I merely told people in the village I was going away for a few weeks: at that stage I had no idea how long I would be away, or indeed if I would be able to return. I ensured that my cat Czar would be fed by Claire at the Post Office – he was used to her, for she always looked after him whenever I was away from home – and covered as many eventualities as I could imagine. Then, feeling confident I had rehearsed my 'cover story' to perfection, I settled down to await the 1st October. ......

All had become clear. I had come full circle in my reading and, fantastic though it seemed, now knew how my aunt had succeeded in making her transition to the 15th century. But how on earth would she cope? I was intrigued to know what happened next.

...... *I found the following days fascinating as, gradually, I eased myself into mediaeval life. To a certain extent I was left to myself and so I was able to soak up as much detail as I possibly could.*

Inevitably the day started early. Around dawn we began the ongoing chores such as the bread making. Indeed my morning meal consisted of sampling some of the dark rye bread together with a bowl of pottage, a dish similar to gruel in consistency but made from barley and a mixture of vegetables. To my mind an odd dish with which to start the day. Not odd, however, to my colleagues who consumed large quantities with an eagerness which amazed me. Obviously the intention was to set the household up with full stomachs thereby sustaining them for the hard day's work ahead. Breakfasts were taken in the kitchen, one of the buildings separate from the Hall and abutting the barmkin wall.

In Sir Anthony's absence the running of the estate was in the hands of Stephen his 'steward' – a grand name for the Rutherford household – however, I was aware that knights and small landowners endeavoured to imitate the nobility whenever possible. He was a capable chap who could read and write and appeared to have a good relationship with Anselm. Stephen's wife Sarah, although a pleasant enough young woman, could at times be frivolous; I put this down to a marked difference in age between husband and wife. In addition to Margery, whose 'title' one supposes could be that of general maid, the household consisted of her younger sister Agnes who performed the menial tasks and Mary the cook. The Hall maintained a smithy, not only for its own use but also for the requirements of the whole village. Subsequently I learnt it was a substantial undertaking and necessitated five people to run it. Assisting Tom, the blacksmith, were John and Simon who worked as charcoal burners. Simon's assistant was Henry who tended the bellows and finally Tom's son William who was known as the portehache. His job involved fetching and carrying iron blocks for his father and in his spare time looking after the horses.

Overthwaite was a bustling place and a busy working farm and Sir Anthony employed a number of local men to carry out the general labour on the land itself. With the exception of Margery and Agnes who lodged at the hall, all others lived in the village.

From the family tree I noted Sir Anthony and Lady Margaret had a son, Matthew, born in 1477 and two daughters, Joan born in 1485 and Anne the following year. I wondered whether the son could have been one of the two boys whom I had seen from my window on that first day; however, I soon learned from Margery, thankfully always one to gossip, that Matthew was in fact accompanying his parents who were making a trip across to Yorkshire to visit Lady Margaret's parents.

"M'Lady's mother be ailing an' M'Lady be very close to her. Sir Anthony thinks as it be a good time fer Master Matthew to see his grandsires, them not gettin' over there much of late. An' it might be t' last chance M'Lady gets afore t' bairn comes. Oh, I forgot to tell 'e as she's with child. They've bin waitin' such a long time fer a second un so we all hopes as things'll go well fer t'Mistress." My mind visualised the family tree and I now knew the date must be October 1484. She continued, "Eh, I remember when M'Lady's sister came with her bairn, must have been ... let me see ... aye, 'twere just after Yuletide of this year. She'd had the babe over at her mother's and was journeyin' home. Decided to call and stay fer a few days." She paused, deep in thought, to wipe her hands down the front of her apron. "I felt so sorry fer t' mistress. I could see she was reet happy fer her sister but that *sad on t'other hand that she weren't wi' child hersel'."*

With my pretended sore throat I was obviously not expected to contribute much to the conversation and consequently I sat back and listened. She filled me in on Margaret's family and also provided some extra background details on Sir Anthony's immediate family. Margery had worked at the hall from an early age, as had her mother and grandmother through successive years, and she was a mine of Rutherford information. Sir Anthony, although a Knight and consequently bound in service to his liege lord, the nearby Lord Dacre, was a farmer at heart and loved nothing better than to remain at home managing the 'estate'. However, having to serve his customary 40 days service he had fought at the Battle of Tewkesbury when he was a young man and, Margery boasted, "Slain 15 men he did!"

I soon met the two young boys whom I had seen with the pony. They were both blonde and slight and Anselm introduced them to me by their Christian names only, saying they were the orphaned sons of his late sister. The younger one, Roland, was about 11 years old, a typical tomboy, full of energy and I could imagine would be a handful. Although his brother, Edwin, was around 3 years older he was no taller than his sibling and was a quiet, thoughtful boy obviously aware of his seniority. Both of them were extremely polite and well spoken and evidently had been appraised of my misfortunes.

"We do hope thou art quickly recovered and dismiss the events of late" Edwin addressed me in concerned tones.

"Mistress Phillips, how many outlaws didst thou see?" interjected Roland excitedly. "Had they daggers and cudgels?"

"Be quiet Roland. Know you not that the memory might be painful still to Mistress Phillips? Forsooth, though art such a child at times." I was soon to learn, Edwin seldom missed a chance to draw attention to his advanced years. Turning towards me he added seriously, "Pray, forgive him."

I shook my head to indicate I could withstand the memories and, winking at Anselm, held up five fingers whilst whispering the words "Five robbers, all with daggers and *cudgels!"*

Roland looked suitably impressed and with wide eyes attacked Edwin with an imaginary dagger. "Come Ned, let us find William and ambush him."

"Roland! How oft need I tell thee my name is Edwin?" Turning towards me he explained, "Ned was a name used when I was young and I fear I have now outgrown it." Again, I felt that his desire for adulthood was surfacing.

Edwin looked towards Anselm who, with an imperceptible nod of the head dismissed them. "Do not stray too far. Latin is on the agenda for today." Roland made a face as he and his brother rushed towards the staircase. "They miss their parents greatly and I fear I must allow them some leeway for they are good lads. Perchance thou could spend some time with them during thy stay. The Lady Margaret, though I ought not say so, is of tender years and at present her days are filled wholly with thoughts of her confinement. An older woman's guidance would greatly assist the boys in these early stages." I indicated my assent with a slight bow of the head and mouthed that I should be pleased to do so.

Those first few days began to fall into a pattern and I often helped with the harvesting, sorting, drying and storing of the late autumn fruit and vegetables. Everywhere was kept as clean as possible and at the end of a hard day the job of scouring out the dairy fell to Margery's sister Agnes. She appeared to be five or six years younger than Margery and bore little facial or physical resemblance to her sister being small and squat with fiery red hair and a sprinkling of freckles across her cheekbones. Although affection existed between the two girls I noticed Margery was aware of her 'superiority' and Agnes, in her 'position' as general skivvy around the Hall, spent the majority of her time scuttling from place to place at the bidding of virtually all other members of the household.

"An' don't yer be leaving t' door unlocked agin this even," Margery scolded her sister.

"I niver did," wailed her sister. *"I locked it every night thith week, jutht ath yer bid me do."* Her unfortunate lisp and stature were counterbalanced by a wilful disposition.

"I don't want none o' them lies here. Master Anselm told me it were open t' other morn." She turned to me and coloured, *"Really it be my task to lock t' door but I've been that tired these last few days I've bin asking Agnes to run down fer me. But t' other mornin' I got told off. Mind you, p'raps it's as well it were Master Anselm and not Sir Anthony. He be a good master but has a fierce bark to him when any of us does summat wrong."* I had to turn away to ensure Margery could read nothing in my face to say that it was actually *my fault the door was open the other morning.*

Margery was a good worker and with plenty of chores to fulfil she was thankful for any assistance I might provide.

"Course, half these jobs should be done by Sarah. But the steward's wife wouldn't stoop to do most of 'em. 'Twould be beneath her! She picks and chooses what takes her fancy does that one." I said nothing. Obviously no love was lost between the two. She laughed, "Still, if I hadn't got me work ter do, what would I do with meself all day? 'Tis a good place ter be and Lady Margaret be a kind mistress." She pointed to my outfit. "I shouldn't wonder if she don't urge yer to mek yersel' a new kirtle an' bodice, fer I think she 'as some homespun in the store."

Upon my arrival Margery had provided me with some old clothes of her mother's but they were not a good fit and I welcomed the thought of replacements. The same applied to footwear. Margery's mother had smaller feet than I and consequently my toes ached incessantly. However, I realised this latter problem would be more difficult to resolve. I must hope an opportunity would present itself for me to obtain a pair from either Penrith or Kendal in the not too distant future.

With Margery's outgoing personality and open manner it was easy to like her and we became firm friends. Mary was another matter. She must have been in her mid forties and had obviously worked at the hall for a number of years. I always had the feeling she viewed me with suspicion, perhaps because she felt I was 'above her' though why she should feel so I never knew as I always went out of my way to be pleasant to her.

Margery put it down to her marital status, or should I say, lack of it. "Shrivelled up old spinster she be. Tom reckons as she needs a good seein' to, an' p'raps he's right. Me ma said as how she were betrothed to a chap what went wi' t' Master to Tewkesbury. But he was slain an' no other man has ever wanted her." Only then did I realised what a parochial life these people led and felt a touch of pity for Mary whenever our paths crossed in the days that followed.

Finally came the day of the Rutherfords' return. I felt nervous of their arrival, as I was fearful of any awkward question that Sir Anthony might ask about the family. I would have to hope that, in view of the distances involved, there had been little contact between the branches of the family and consequently knowledge on his part was scant.

It was a crisp, clear October morning with a brilliant, blue sky when Roland first spotted figures in the distance and some little time later when the party came trundling into the barmkin. Eventually Sir Anthony made his way to the great hall where I had remained during the initial excitement of the group's arrival, awaiting introduction. I knew he was in his early thirties and the man who greeted me immediately came across as a warm and generous person. Of medium height and muscular build, his dark, wavy hair in pageboy style was fringed and hung to the neck. He was attired for the journey and wore a thick, warm cloak with a gypcière, or tasselled purse, attached to his waistband. As he strode forcefully towards me, arm outstretched, I made a small, deferential curtsey and, placing his arm around my shoulders, he guided me towards a seat against the wall.

"Mistress Phillips, Anselm has told me of thy misfortunes and I trust made thee welcome in our absence." His speech, whilst certainly a cut above the local dialect, had a distinct northern accent and was much more 'home spun' than that of Anselm. "Please be assured of our hospitality and feel not under any obligation to continue thy journey until such times as thou art fully recovered. Ah, here is my wife." I turned to see a slight young woman of, I had ascertained, twenty-three years who had wisps of blonde hair escaping from her 'Chimney pot' head-dress and was showing obvious signs of pregnancy. A further young woman of about the same age fussed around, trying to make her companion comfortable and assisted her as she seated herself opposite us. I presumed this to be Jane, a kinswoman and maid to the mistress of Overthwaite.

"My wife, Lady Margaret," boomed Sir Anthony, "and as is evident we are expecting a happy event."

"Yes my dearest. I doubt not that Mistress Phillips has eyes in her head but not cause for the enthusiasm which thou has my love." Turning towards me she continued, "Thou must forgive his excitement. It has been long since the birth of our dear son and we feared I was unable to get with another child.

However, the Lord has looked kindly upon us and we pray that all will go well. Now, if thou will excuse me. The journey has been long and tiring and I must rest. Come Jane." With that she struggled to her feet and leaning heavily on the other woman made her way towards the stairs and her chamber above.

I remained with Sir Anthony answering his questions: I had gradually become accustomed to the local way of speech over the past few days and was easing myself out of my 'sore throat'. As I had hoped, he was sketchy about the Fitzroberts as contact with them was virtually non-existent and with my knowledge of the family tree I probably taught him more than otherwise he might ever have known. Once again he insisted I had no need to make haste to Carlisle. This suited me entirely as I intended to spin out my 'recovery' until the time came for my return through the door.

Our discussions at an end he turned his attentions to Anselm, *"Come, let me show thee what I have acquired in York. Such a book hath come into my hands, which never before saw I the like."* From a chest carried in on his arrival he produced three books and showed two of them to Anselm. *"I promised Stephen to acquire one or two volumes on my travels and thought these might be suitable."*

Anselm studied the titles. *"Indeed, he should find them an enlightening read. I, myself, read them some years back – most enjoyable. I must discuss their merit with him."*

Sir Anthony fingered the third book tenderly. It was a beautifully bound leather volume. *"But this one ... here Anselm ... what thinkest thou of this one?"*

As Anselm leafed through the pages I could see vividly coloured illuminations. *"Ah yes, the 'Canterbury Tales',"* Anselm seemed genuinely interested.

"Know thou this work, Anselm?"

"Why yes. I came across a copy whilst at C..., whilst in London," he quickly checked what he had been about to say. *"With respect, Sir Anthony, I trust thou knowest the quality of this edition as there have been several inferior versions of late."*

"Indeed, what thou sayest is veritably true. But the man from whom I bought the book assured me of its excellent quality. This same bookseller is well known to my good Lady's sire and I wouldst trust him with my life."

I had already ascertained that Sir Anthony's 'library' was modest but he obviously had a passion for good books, an interest that I knew was growing during this period of history. However, I had been careful not to be seen to be too interested for it might be difficult to explain my reading skills should they be discovered. I decided to leave the two men to their discussions and stole away to my new bedchamber.

The Rutherfords' return necessitated a change in the sleeping arrangements. The pallet I had been occupying belonged to Jane who, during Lady Margaret's pregnancy, lodged in the same room as her mistress; the children had slept in the garret chamber at the top of the hall, together with Anselm. Now, I was to move into the garret and its former occupants would transfer to the small wooden hall on the far side of the barmkin. Although on the face of it they seemed to have 'drawn the short straw', their quarters were situated adjacent to the bakehouse and were, therefore, extremely cosy.

It had been my intention to seek solitude so that I might recover from Sir Anthony's interrogations and once upstairs I decided to explore the top of the building. Letting myself out I found that the pitched roof was surrounded by a wall-walk. This ran behind the battlements that were corbelled out from the wall face of the tower. Although the pitched roof had been removed in later years, the far-reaching view was familiar to me for I had stood in the same spot on many occasions. I remained outside, lost in thought, until the coldness of the day seeped into my bones. Over the course of the next few months I returned there many times. Times when I could hardly believe I was truly in an Overthwaite of yesteryear.

The following day, being a Sunday, the entire household made its weekly pilgrimage to the parish church.

"The master an' mistress be very devout," Margery informed me and I had further noticed that Anselm and his nephews observed devotions each morning in a corner of the hall prior to taking breakfast.

The good weather of the previous day had persisted and our party set off early in the morning, walking through the lanes to the church close by. Looking around me I realised I had never seen the autumn colours as vivid: the trees were clad in rich, russet tones, still reluctant to shed their leaves. Before entering the church Sir Anthony admonished the youngsters to "Be quiet, no fidgeting, pay attention and watch not the comings and goings of the congregation but think of our dear Lord!"

The church itself was a beautiful building. The architecture was Norman and although the stonework inside was plain the walls bore the heavily painted biblical scenes so typical of that time. I noticed several pieces of fine plate and Margery took pride in informing me that these had been provided at Sir Anthony's expense. A side 'box' adjacent to the Chancel was reserved for Sir Anthony, Lady Margaret, Anselm and the three boys but the remainder of our party together with the other members of the congregation either stood or knelt on the cold, stone floor. Through the delicately carved, wooden, open-work screens I could see the priest, a weasel of a man who, once the Mass had begun, droned on in Latin in a high pitched, nasal voice. Notwithstanding Sir Anthony's dictates the attentions of my fellow worshippers wandered and it was only at the consecration of the bread and wine that every gaze was transfixed on the altar. I was aware many viewed the Church's rites virtually as a magical ceremony and this was confirmed to me by the look on each and every face: a mystical hush permeated the building as the congregation received the communion wafer in a semblance of awe.

Once the Mass was over we walked out into the grey, cold morning and awaited the Master and Mistress who were talking to the priest and Anselm. Margery nudged me and pointed towards a young chap, probably in his thirties, who stood behind the priest patiently waiting for the conversation to end.

"See Jack there? Used to be a real wrong un. Then one Sunday when his Ma 'd dragged him to church, a marble statue of Our Lady comes crashing down an' misses him by that much," she indicated a centimetre between thumb and first finger. "All says as it's a sign. He were delivered by Our Lord." She crossed herself and carried on, "A miracle it be, an' he knows it. From then on he changed his ways, goes to church reg'lar now, without his Ma's biddin'. She be a widow an' he'd never help afore but he do now. Follows Father Mark round like a shadow, always askin' questions but not gittin' many answers. Not much time fer us ordinary folk hasn't Father Mark, only time fer the likes o' t' Master. If yer ask me, he don't know reet much anyhow." She paused for breath just as Sir Anthony, who had finished his discourse, waved us all to follow.

For once I found myself walking with Roland without the company of his brother and I sensed he had something on his mind. "Mistress Phillips, why do not more people from the village attend Mass?"

What a question! "Well ..." I stalled for time by readjusting my shoe. "I am sure they attend each of the important festivals. Why do you ask?"

"My father insisted that we all attend every morning. He said not to do so was unchristian and that God would punish us. Master Anselm also encourages us to pray to the Lord each day, even when the Priest does not attend."

"And so you should." I picked my way carefully. "But it is more difficult for the people of the village. They lead hard lives and although their chores are obviously not more important than their devotions, I am sure that provided they conduct themselves in a good, Christian manner God will look kindly on them when their time comes." He seemed satisfied with my reply and ran on ahead to join the other boys. I mulled over his words. Not many ordinary people attended church regularly during those times and for Roland to say his family had done so daily struck me as unusual. Once again I found myself thinking that the boys' background was intriguing.

I turned to see Margery dawdling behind and slowed my pace to keep her company: I was finding the more I befriended her the more I learned about the family and life in general. Making our way through the green lanes I gazed upwards. It was a breezy day and large, white clouds scudded across a deep azure sky. The sun was hot and I realised how cumbersome my clothing felt. Looking towards Margery I could see she was gazing ruefully at the back of Simon's head.

"He is a very good looking lad, isn't he?" She was obviously miles away and I had startled her with my remark. She quickly separated her hands and, fumbling in her pocket, I realised she had been rubbing something between her fingers. Her face was scarlet and she seemed stuck for words. Characteristically, once again she tucked a stray strand of hair behind her ear. "I am sorry I startled you Margery. I had not appreciated you had such a liking for Simon."

We walked on in silence and once she had regained her composure she turned to me with her cheeky smile. "I don't think as he knows I exist. So I be relying on this to do t' trick." She took her right hand from her pocket and there on her palm lay the communion wafer. Lowering her voice she continued, "Me grandma told me as it's a love charm so I didn't swallow it but brought it out in me hand. An' if I keep it wi' me at all times an' hold it an' think of him, p'raps he might start likin' me." Not knowing what to say I merely smiled and we continued on to the Hall in silence, Margery deep in her amorous thoughts and I ruminating on ancient superstitions.

The days were passing. Most afternoons I spent some time with the boys and gradually felt as though I was getting to know them better. As I had first surmised Roland was a lively lad, although I suspect he felt the loss of his parents the most. I watched them from my chamber window, fighting with wooden swords. Inevitably Edwin, being the older and more tactical of the two, won which often brought tears from his younger brother. Immediately Edwin would comfort him and at that stage I would wander down to provide a woman's touch and some moral support. Roland was always eager to talk about the past and at those times I noticed Edwin watching him like a hawk.

"Mistress Phillips, dost thou know what I miss the most? Tilting at the quintain. Father said I would make an excellent knight and he wouldst take me on campaign with him when I reached the height of his shoulder."

"Was your father a knight also?" I enquired innocently and was taken aback by the speed with which Edwin stepped in.

"To be sure, and a right good one too." He continued fiercely, "He was brave and fearless and we miss him greatly."

"When did he die, Edwin?"

"At Eastertide of last year, 'twas very sudden and was thought to be an apoplexy."

"You are both brave lads and your father will know so," I said, trying to give support as Roland's bottom lip began to quiver. "But you are being looked after very well by your uncle and Sir Anthony, I am sure. Was it he who gave you the pony?"

"Aye, her name is Lightning. Wouldst thou like me to show her to you Mistress Phillips?" Roland was soon getting over his moment of sorrow.

I agreed and we made our way to the stable where we stroked the muzzle of a pony as unlike lightning as any could be. She was slow and sedate with a thick, shaggy, dark coat and her large brown eyes were as deep as pools.

"I groom her every day," boasted Roland. "Sir Anthony said there was no need and that William would tend her but she is mine and I will care for her."

It was at that point I realised how lonely he must be and I decided to spend more time with the boys whenever I could.

By now we were nearing the end of October. After my initial 'recovery' I had been unsure how long I could expect to remain at Overthwaite before the family decided I must fulfil my obligations and continue on to the de Raisgill nursery. I determined that at all costs I must extend my stay until at least the 11th November if I was to have the chance of ever returning to the 21st century and if necessary would invent another illness in order to do so. However, as time went by Lady Margaret *and I had become firm friends: in fact I think in some ways she looked upon me as a mother.*

One evening after supper, when his wife had retired early to bed, Sir Anthony took me to one side. "Mistress Phillips, thou knows this babe means a good deal to both Lady Margaret and myself." I nodded and waited for him to continue. "It troubles me that when her time comes she will have little family around her. At the time of her confinement with Matthew she remained with her mother but thou knows that that good lady now ails?" He was obviously intent on conveying some message to me for his usual bonhomie had been replaced with an earnestness I had not seen in him before. He hurried on without awaiting my reply, "Childbirth is a time for friends and relations and so I have decided I should like thee to remain here with her ladyship and not continue north as was originally intended. 'Tis some time since I have seen my kinsfolk, but Sir Robert is a good sole. Thou shall not shoulder any blame for I shall right things with my cousin should he make enquiries as to thy whereabouts prior to the spring. I trust thou to be agreeable to this arrangement?"

Relief flooded over me and I assured him nothing would please me more. In the unlikelihood of his cousin arriving at Overthwaite I felt reasonably sure I could talk my way out of a tight corner: at all events, I would cross that bridge if I came to it. ......

Resting the sheets on my lap I considered Catherine's position. I could understand her relief at knowing she was now able to remain within reach of her 'escape route' but assisting with Lady Margaret's childbirth must have been a daunting thought. Bearing in mind the rudimentary aspects of medicine in the 15th century I should have dreaded the task. However would my aunt manage?

CHAPTER FIVE

…… *Next morning Lady Margaret asked if I would take a trip into Penrith the following Wednesday, it being market day.* ……

Now this should be most interesting, for having recently visited Penrith I was keen to savour its medieval atmosphere. I read on.

"…… "Were it not for the babe I should go myself but I fear I ought to take things steady at present for I have not been sleeping too well of late. No matter, what will be, will be," she waved the problem aside. "Now Catherine, I require some material and wonder whether thou would assist in acquiring it for me? Sir Anthony is insisting that I need a new outfit for the Yuletide festivities, mayhap thou hast heard we are to attend upon Lord and Lady Dacre this year?" She was a talkative person and once on a theme sailed ahead, with words tumbling out like water down a cascade. Not waiting for answers she hurried on, "In latter years we have spent the festivities with Sir William Parre and his good lady Elizabeth. Alas, by cause of his death early this year she is now a widow and to that end there will be no celebrations come Yuletide. Sir Anthony wishes that we look our best and acquired several new items for his own wardrobe whilst we were in York – including a pair of particularly long toed pomaine shoes! Ah well, they please

him and that is all that is of import!" The latter was uttered not unkindly and I could see she held great affection for her husband. "For my own requirements he has ordered a bolt of cloth which shouldst by now be ready for collection. Jane will accompany thee, she is aware of my likes and dislikes should there be a problem, though Heaven forfend the acquisition be unacceptable! However, I think it a good business that thou take charge of the boys for I fear Jane would be unable to handle them and I feel sure they would not wish to forego the opportunity of a trip into town on market day."

I assured her I should be pleased to go and later discussed the matter with Margery.

"'Tis a journey made each month or so. Sarah be in charge o' buying t' stores and alus says as how it be a grand day. And if t' Mistress needs some cloth ... ooh, it'll be lovely fer yer! Blue. That'll be what she's gone fer. Mark me words, she suits blue."

Eagerly I awaited the arrival of the following Tuesday.

The day dawned misty but mild and as soon as we had breakfasted we set off in the cart, in order to arrive at the market early and thereby obtain some good purchases. Tom's assistant John had been chosen to drive us the short distance into town and apart from Jane, Sarah and I the remainder of the party comprised Anselm, Edwin, Roland and Matthew. As we trundled along the rutted way I was fascinated to take in the surrounding scenery between Overthwaite and Penrith. In some ways the landscape brought a welcome familiarity in a time that was foreign and yet because of the absence of roads, railways, the majority of dwellings and many stone walls, the countryside I was viewing also presented an unfamiliar image. Our cart soon reached the track that would eventually become the turnpike road and latterly the A6: I could almost visualise Bonnie Prince Charlie and his men ahead of us, dropping their coins and personal effects for people to discover some 300 years later.

As we approached Penrith the castle came into view. How strange to see this building intact, a building I had visited on numerous occasions in its ruinous state, fingers of stone *reaching skywards. It was strange yes, but also exhilarating for how many times had I tried to visualise it in its former glory? Sir Ralph Neville, grandfather to Edward IV and Richard III, had built the castle as a refuge for both the inhabitants of the area and their livestock and it was used in times of border raids.*

We left the cart and made our way through the busy streets towards the market place. Here, the many stalls sold a variety of produce: vegetables, cheeses and various meats. People were jockeying for position and both Anselm and I had to keep a constant eye on the boys to ensure we did not lose them.

As we were passing one of the meat stalls Jane, agitated as always, pulled at Sarah's sleeve, "Sarah, do not forget Lady Margaret's request." She was of slight build with mousy coloured hair and a personality to match. Though a pleasant enough girl in her own way, she was extremely shy and had a small, timid voice that was difficult to hear.

"Aye Jane, I know – the pork for salting! 'Tis not my first year at the hall, thou knows. The Master alus hands some out to the households in the village ev'ry Yuletide." Adopting a self-important manner, Sarah continued, "Though whether or not the Mistress be right in her thinking, who can say? If you ask me, our pigs'll have enough meat on 'em to go round this year without buying any extra. But I just do as I'm told!"

Jane's head immediately went down: as to whether this was in view of the rebuke or Sarah's self-opinionated manner I was unaware, but little further conversation passed between the two women for the remainder of the day. With the little contretemps over, Sarah manhandled the pieces of pork until she had found the choicest cuts of meat. Following this she haggled with the stall holder in order to achieve the best price possible. Anselm and I stood watching, fascinated – Anselm's only job being to provide the means of payment once a deal had been struck. Sarah's manner could, at times, be considered arrogant but that afternoon she proved she was an asset to any household and was certainly worthy of her position as steward's wife.

After one or two other small purchases, including a well needed pair of shoes for myself, we made our way towards Sandgate where, Jane advised us, was situated the establishment from which we might purchase Lady Margaret's dress material. As we were approaching the parish church I noticed that a large group of people were beginning to congregate in the middle of the churchyard. Upon drawing nearer I could see a rotund, tonsured priest standing on a mound and our steps automatically slowed as his preaching drifted towards us through the general hubbub. His voice was compelling in its directness and he held the crowd enthralled as he railed against the clergy and an over-rich Church. Soon people were cheering in agreement as he accused the Church of levying extortionate tithes from good Christian worshippers. The boys seemed mesmerised by his commanding voice and I could sense that Anselm was eager for us to leave.

"Come, I think we have heard sufficient from this mendicant friar. Do not believe all that he preaches boys. The Church of Rome may have its faults but neither are the Dominicans without blame. They too have lost their ideals of poverty and are lavishing wealth on God's House and lining their own pockets where'er possible." With that Anselm ushered us away from the crowd and on towards our goal.

We meandered through narrow, crowded lanes where the general squalor and unsanitary conditions of the town were evident. Beggars crouched by every corner alternating with the aged or infirm. Sights and smells foreign to my senses overwhelmed me and in view of the dry day, I preferred not to imagine the cause of the wet and slippery cobbles beneath my feet. Turning the corner into Burrowgate I caught sight of the Moot Hall. This was a building about which I had read a great deal, never dreaming that one day I should actually view it; I stood transfixed, fascinated by the sight. We continued on to Sandgate and soon arrived at our destination.

The 'shop' was small and cheerless, unlike anything I was expecting and as we entered Anselm had cause to apply the weight of his shoulder to the creaking door as it caught on the stone slab flooring. I realised the dinginess was due, in part, to the contents of the shelves for the majority of the cloth was drab, homespun material and to my inexperienced eye of only average quality. I wondered why on earth we were there. The owner shuffled in from the back and in the half-light I strained to see an elderly, hunch-backed man with long, straggly, grey hair. He eyed us suspiciously and I thought I had better take charge, explaining the purpose of our visit. Immediately his attitude changed and he became almost obsequious, retreating into the rear of the building to fetch our required material. Upon his return, however, I had to admit he had redeemed himself. The bolt of cloth he displayed was of exquisitely fine wool and I allowed my fingers to linger on its soft texture, loath to end the pleasing sensation. I had no need to ask Jane whether or not her Mistress would find favour with it.

When he opened his mouth to speak hardly a tooth could be seen. "Lady Margaret will we pleased with the quality, I feel sure. But then, she will know I am a man of my word and would not let her Ladyship down, I feel sure. 'Twill not be the last time she requires me to obtain such a cloth, I feel sure. As long as the Good Lord grants me breath to breathe I will strive to please your Mistress."

We all waited for 'I feel sure' but this time the shop-keeper failed to deliver his line and the silence was at last broken by Matthew's excited voice. "Margery said 'twould be blue. 'Twill match Mamma's eyes a treat." With that Anselm paid the owner and we beat a hasty retreat from his establishment.

"A real Uriah Heep if ever there was one," I commented to Anselm as we lingered in the alleyway, breathing in the fresher air as if to cleanse ourselves after the mustiness of the shop. As soon as the words left my mouth I realised what I had said. "Oh, I had forgotten, you will not know him. He also is an unpleasant tradesman with whom the Fitzroberts deal." I glanced away, feeling sure I had managed to cover my mistake. "But whatever one thinks of these people they do appear to come up with the goods."

"Yes, and I am sure that Sir Anthony will feel he has obtained a bargain. Cloth of that quality sells for double the price in London." Anselm had made several references to

London during my time in Overthwaite and I took the opportunity to quiz him on his past as we made our way back to the cart.

"Both you and the boys have lived in London then, Master Knowles?"

"Lived, why no," he seemed flustered and I noticed he failed to look me in the eye. Instead he kept his gaze fixed to the ground and after seeming to gather his thoughts continued, "However, for a time I was tutor to the sons of a gentleman who resided in the City. My home was in the Marches – Ludlow – a beautiful place."

"Really, I have never been there." I thought I had better provide no opportunity for any detailed questioning.

"Yes indeed, although I have returned there little since I was a boy."

"Do you still have relatives in Ludlow?"

"Naught but one distant cousin – a mute by birth. My nephews were brought up in London and luckily I was there at the time of their father's sad demise."

"Of an apoplexy I understand?"

"He had lived life to the full and these excesses brought about his premature death." Anselm seemed resentful in his attitude.

"He was young then?" I asked.

"Merely his forty-first year."

I decided not to comment as I felt that forty would have been considered an average age and consequently was surprised that Anselm obviously thought otherwise.

At that moment we were pushed to one side brusquely by a young man who was running through the lanes shouting, "Make way, make way. The lads be comin'."

Anselm protectively shielded us in a doorway as a throng of youths headed down the middle of the street. Roland was straining to look over Anselm's arm to see what all the noise was about when Sarah informed us, "'Tis a game of football."

"Football!" I exclaimed.

"Aye, they have one every so often. 'Tis just a good excuse for a brawl, if you ask me, for like as not 'twill end in a *fight."* Thinking I was unaware of the game she went on to explain that as with modern day football two teams competed, their objective being to score goals. However, the 'goal mouths' were specific landmarks, usually one at either end of town and the ball, a leather covered pig's bladder, could be conveyed there by either foot or hand, or a combination of both.

During Sarah's narrative Roland had been watching the game open-mouthed and turning to Anselm excitedly, he pulled at his sleeve. *"Dost though think Sir Anthony would allow us a football, Anselm?"*

Not for the first time this address to his Uncle struck me as odd. I was unsure as to whether the word 'Uncle' was used by children when speaking to relatives, but I should certainly have expected him to call Anselm 'Sir'.

"I feel sure that if thou puts forward a good enough case to Sir Anthony, he may well accede to thy request." I noticed how affectionately his gaze lingered on the lads.

"Edwin, dost thou hear? Thou must accompany me when we return. What games we could have with William and the other lads."

By now the youths had passed by and we continued on our return to the cart, all the time Roland kicking stones both imaginary and real and giving vent to his energy by running to-and-fro as if taking part in the game he had just witnessed.

Upon our return from Penrith the following days were spent dealing with the cuts of pork obtained at the market: as usual the job falling to Margery. Her skills never failed to astound me and I was a willing helper as she set about the salting of the meat for the winter. She commented that she would have preferred to hot salt it in a mixture of salt and saltpetre. However, Sir Anthony had acquired a substantial amount of salt and consequently this was to be used to create a brine solution in which to soak the pork. Fine, white, table salt was an expensive commodity at that time, the alternative being the dark, impure variety, evaporated from sea water.

"Anyroads, it'll be cheaper fer t' master an' it'll still work fine if we does it reet," Margery informed me. She went on to explain, "Wi mun make sure as t' mixture's strong enough to float an egg on, that way the meat'll last through t' winter."

As with many of the other chores, by the time we had completed the task our hands were red and bitterly cold, and I felt sure Margery's cracked skin felt the effects of the salt to a much greater degree than my own.

The fine cloth had pleased Lady Margaret greatly and consequently she was in a receptive mood when Margery approached her with a plea for help.

Margery and Agnes's parents lived in the village and I had been aware over the past few days that Margery was worried about something. It transpired that her mother had an ulcerated leg, which was failing to respond to treatment. As with virtually all women those days medicine had been passed down from mother to daughter and recipes were often a guarded secret. Margery informed me her mother had tried several concoctions on the abscess but none had proved successful.

"But t' mistress has a way wi' cures," she told me quietly one morning. "Makes sure she collects plenty of herbs during t' year she does and then it be my job to dry 'em. She won't let mi help wi' t' making up o' t' salves though, keeps the receipts secret. Anyhow, she says a may take some this morning fer Ma's leg." And so we set off for the village.

It was a beautiful November morning as we headed down the lane heading towards the wooden buildings of the village. My gaze was drawn to the fell side where the bracken, in autumn colours, lay like a copper mantle around the shoulders of the hills. At that moment I felt my first pang of homesickness, longing to be lacing up my boots and climbing the slopes instead of wending my way to Margery's home.

In the crisp, clear air with the sun shining down on our faces we reached the outskirts of Overthwaite. Several long-snouted, ridge-backed pigs were scavenging for food on the common. I surmised each belonged to a different household and, as with those at the Hall, were being fattened up with a view to being slaughtered at Yuletide. As the day was fine, many women had stretched their laundry over bushes hoping the sun would dry the items before dusk and thereby ease the burden of finding alternative ways of drying clothes during the winter months. Although little was known about hygiene at that time and bacteria would only be discovered around four hundred years later, a connection was rightly thought to exist between dirt and disease. Consequently cleanliness in the home was high and considered to be a virtue.

We reached the far end of the village where I knew Margery's parents lived. The house we entered was constructed, as all the buildings were, of timber with a wattle and daub infill. Inside it was dim; nevertheless, my immediate thoughts were that the dwelling was thoroughly clean. The earthen floors had been meticulously swept and a pervasive smell of bleach filled the air. A small fire burnt in the centre of the room but the dwelling still retained its freshness, for the shutters had been flung open to allow air through the open framework. At one end stood a bed with a straw mattress and reclining under the woollen blankets was a figure which I took to be Margery's mother. Margery made a beeline towards the bed and by the way they embraced I could see genuine affection between the two.

"This be Mistress Phillips, as I've bin tellin' yer about, ma."

The woman who struggled up onto one elbow was obviously Margery's mother as the resemblance was uncanny. I judged she was in her early thirties but the lines on her forehead and careworn creases around her mouth advanced her looks by around twenty years.

"Pleased as to meet yer, Mistress Phillips. My Margery told me yer've been good to her and, no doubt yer be also keepin' an eye on Agnes. She have a headstrong way with her have that one, though not fer any lack o' trying on her father's part, I might add." Whilst she talked she had been slowly easing her way out of bed, exposing the large bandage covering the ulcerated leg.

"*Please, do not get up on my part. Margery has informed me of your leg. Is it still as painful?*"

Before she could answer Margery had unwound the bandage to reveal an extremely nasty looking leg. The calf had swollen to double its size and even in the dimness of the room the large, red, open wound was evident to see. As to whether the yellow substance oozing from the centre of the ulcer was ointment or infection I am unaware, but the smell which assailed my nostrils almost made me retch.

"*I must be getting' about ma chores, anyroad. It be not too painful today,*" she lied, as obviously the leg was giving her great discomfort.

"*Oh, Ma, it don't look to be getting' better at all!*" cried Margery. "*Let's hope Lady Margaret's new salve will do t' trick. An' don't yer go getting' yerself out o' bed. Our Annie can do what's needed.*" We had passed two young children playing outside and in the corner of the room sat a girl of about ten years of age nursing a young baby. I had already gathered that Margery had approximately eight other siblings, presumably Annie was nursing the youngest of them. "*T' Mistress 'as sent some cheese an' bread as well, so I'll put some out now an' we can tek father some unless he's teken his scrow wi' 'im. Get t' trenchers, Annie. And where's Tommy?*" A dirty face peered round the front door jamb. "*Run round to Ma Watson's fer a jug of ale an' be sharpish!*"

The table was laid with the wooden plates and we all sat to a light meal washed down with the ale Margery had carefully watered down to ensure sufficient for her father's return later in the day. As we ate I glanced around, taking in my surroundings. The family's few possessions were situated at the top end of the room close to the bed. Although they were meagre I noticed one or two items which I was aware had been provided by Margery's employers to try to ease the family's hardship. At the opposite end of the room was an area to house the animals: a goat now outside, tethered to a stake by the wall and perhaps one of the pigs we had seen on the common. Suddenly a cat rubbed up against my leg, his tail twitching vertically like smoke from a chimney, as silently he pleaded for some attention. I bent down to stroke him and as I did so my thoughts returned to Czar and his warm, cosy life at home. This one had to work for his living and was kept for the express purpose of controlling the numerous mice and rats constantly inhabiting the dwelling.

Having finished our meal, one of the children took the trenchers and tankards outside to scour them with sharp sand and rinse them in the large water butt by the door. After making sure her mother was as comfortable as possible we set off through the back of the house, our destination the nearby fulling mines where Margery's father worked.

Once outside I was interested to see the rear garden with its neat raised beds where Margery's family grew winter vegetables to supplement a meagre diet. Towards the far edge of the dwellings we passed "Ma Watson's", the village alehouse. Margery had previously mentioned this widow who was the local brewster: making ale was a simple affair and the water, barley, malt and yeast could virtually be brewed over the household fire. With the large demand that existed for the drink (beer was disliked as it was thought to be weaker than ale and a drink for foreigners) licences were often granted as a means of income for poorer women who otherwise found difficulty in supporting themselves.

The mile to the fulling mine proved to be a difficult trudge on a rough track over thick, tussocky grass. By now the landscape had lost all vestige of green; the moraines stretched out before us in yellowing mounds. Luckily the day was fine or our skirts and shoes would have been the worse for wear by the time we reached our destination. The wooden buildings of the mine were situated in a small ravine and as we approached, the sun glistened on the tumbling waters of the river, cascading over the craggy rocks to form a deep, dark pool below. The heavy clay of the fuller's earth abounded in this area and needed drying, crushing and grinding before it could be used as a bleach to clean the natural oils and grease from the wool of the many sheep that dotted the hillside.

Margery's father was a muscular chap with little to say and I kept my distance whilst she unsuccessfully tried to draw from him information about her mother's ailment. Margery was incensed by his seeming indifference and on our return *journey talked about her family: she visited her mother whenever she could for her parents' marriage was an unhappy one. I remember thinking that their situation must have mirrored thousands of other unhappy unions over the years: a loveless marriage, a hard life with little to look forward to and the prospect of an early death. For the second time that day I yearned for the 21st century and home.*

A few days later as we gathered for the evening meal I detected a sense of merriment about the place. All talk was of a professional troupe that was in the district and was to perform the "Castle of Perseverance" at the fair in Kendal (or Kirkby Kendal as it was then known) in two days time. Luckily that day Sir Anthony had been in the town on business with a friend and fellow knight, Sir Walter Strickland and had heard the two vexilatores 'reading the banns'. This was an announcement of the show and gave an outline of the plot. I had read about this play and knew it was popular and often performed but none of the household had seen it before and consequently a visit was planned for two days hence.

The day dawned crisp and clear and everyone had risen extremely early in order to be on their way at first light. Under normal circumstances (when no goods were to be purchased) horseback was used on such an occasion. However, this was to be a special treat and in addition to the three boys, the entire domestic household had been given leave to attend the fair. Consequently the cart was brought into use, with Anselm and Sir Anthony leading us on horseback; once again Lady Margaret stayed behind as the journey would prove far too tiring for her.

As on my journey to Penrith I eagerly drank in the surroundings whilst we travelled, comparing the 15th century landscape to the one I had grown to know well in 'my time'. What immediately struck me was the number of trees. Of the several valleys we passed en route, the majority were thickly wooded and although I had been aware this was the case, the visual effect was still striking. The rhythmic thud of the carthorse's hooves as the beast plodded along was somehow *mesmerising and had it not been for the beauty of the day and the constant chatter behind me I could have started to nod with ease. The 'mew' of a buzzard sounded overhead as the bird soared on the thermals in a brilliant blue sky. Looking up I followed its trail, drifting from right to left in the direction of the Pennines. They looked magnificent on such a day and appeared close enough to touch. Their familiarity brought me comfort: Cross Fell; High Cup Nick; and Great Dun Fell – minus its giant white golf ball of course!*

Kendal was bustling and in view of the crowds it was agreed that to try to stay in one party would be madness. Under the circumstances we decided to split into two groups. Due to his standing with the local community Sir Anthony had been appointed as one of the marshals for the occasion and had acquired a box from where we were to view the action. Consequently our party consisting of Anselm, Matthew, Edwin, Roland and myself were soon following Sir Anthony through the hordes of people after arranging to meet up with the others later in the day.

The play was to start at noon and so to while away the time we wandered through the many stalls which inevitably had sprung up to accompany the troupe. Anselm's nephews were thrilled. It was almost as though they had never visited such a spectacle before.

"Look lads, a juggler," I called as we passed a young man throwing brightly coloured balls into the air. Roland's eyes were like saucers and Edwin was almost as enthralled, all pretence of seniority forgotten on such a day. Having gathered a crowd the juggler turned his talents to the art of magic and proceeded to bewilder his onlookers with the age-old cup and ball routine. Then, focusing his attention on Matthew he both delighted and mystified the boy by producing a farthing from behind his ear.

"Didst thou see, Roland? His hands were empty!" Matthew cried in a high-pitched voice. "But how? Certes there was nothing there beforehand." Sir Anthony smiled in my direction as the three lads, heads together in earnest discussion, began to debate all possible solutions.

The sights and smells were fascinating and in addition to the pottery and food stalls I espied several selling more unusual wares including one sporting a sign "Spectacles with which to read", though how many could actually read the sign I do not know! Scribes, for a fee, composed letters and even drew up bonds and wills, providing the price was right. Street vendors shouting, "Hot sheep's feet", jostled to sell their produce. Blood curdling screams foretold the barber cum dentist whose only painkiller was oil of cloves. A cockpit overflowed with spectators gambling on its gory sport. And of course there were the obligatory beggars who obtained few donations from an audience solely interested in entertainment on such a day.

We were swept along by the crowd, making its way towards the afternoon's entertainment and on our journey took pains to avoid the slops and chamber pots being emptied from the overhanging windows: the offenders seemingly oblivious to passers-by and interested only in gossiping about the forthcoming performance.

Eventually we arrived at Goosemire, an area normally housing tenter frames for the buying and selling of sheep. Kendal was famous for its wool trade dating back to the late 12th century – attested to by the town motto "Wool is my bread" – but today the frames had been cleared away to make room for the erection of the stage.

The excitement of the crowd was almost tangible and was gradually building as mid-day approached. Sir Anthony ushered us through the seething mass and up to the relative quiet of our box where he left us to undertake his official duties. I looked over the balustrade, intrigued by the spectacle that greeted my eyes. I had read in depth about the show but nothing could have prepared me for the actual event.

A wooden tower had been erected on stilts in the acting arena and was encircled by a shallow ditch representing the moat. Four other structures had been built on scaffolding in a circle around the castle and as I lent over taking in these details I noticed Stephen's party milling around in the crowd below. Nudging Roland I pointed them out to him.

"William!" he shouted at full voice. "Prithee, up here." One by one they turned in our direction and waved but were soon swept on as the crowd continued to grow. Suddenly with a roll of drums the action commenced.

The play dealt with the attack of a man's soul by the Devil, the World and the Deadly Sins. Although the audience, in particular the children, must have found some of the moral themes difficult to grasp, the actors in their masks wove a spell which enthralled all. The action took place below the tower, on its battlements and within the scaffolding circle, with the crowd flowing like a giant wave as it followed the action from one acting area to another. We could see Sir Anthony and the other marshals struggling to control the audience and provide open passageways for the movement of the actors. Suddenly a character was launched onto the stage by, for its day, a piece of sophisticated stage machinery. He appeared to be flying through the air. Wearing a grotesque masque he was obviously portraying the Devil and I was surprised to hear Roland say to his brother, "Edwin, 'tis Satan. Dost though not recognise him from the walls of the Lady Chapel?"

"Aye and he will visit thee in person if thou dost not study thy Latin grammar with more diligence!" interposed Anselm, with a wink in my direction.

The performance continued, with the excitement building towards its climax in the early afternoon. By now we were all hungry, especially the boys and with Sir Anthony still officiating, Anselm took charge. Leading us unerringly through the winding alleys we soon arrived at an establishment proclaiming its status as an alehouse by its ale stake – a pole projecting from the first floor, bearing on its end a large hand. He assured me the establishment was clean and respectable, a place to which we could take the boys for good, wholesome sustenance.

We managed to find a table in one of the dark, smoky rooms towards the rear and whilst Anselm went in search of the landlord I took the opportunity to look around. Making things out in the gloom proved to be difficult. The low room was full of people and a strong body odour assailed the nostrils. To my right a rowdy game of dice was in progress and on the left two men were engaged in backgammon, the board merely being scratched out on the surface of the bench.

Anselm returned shortly with mugs of ale and platters of dried meat and black bread: not particularly appetising but a welcome filling to an empty stomach. We had soon finished and were rising to leave when suddenly, spinning around and gathering us in the circle of his cloak, Anselm ushered us into a small, dark passageway, his index finger pressed against his lips. We stayed thus for several minutes, all perfectly still and hardly daring to draw breath.

Slowly Anselm stepped back, cautiously looking around him. "Mistress Phillips, pray remain here with the boys whilst I ensure all is well." And with that he vanished back into the room where we had eaten. I whispered conspiratorially to the boys and hearing a whimper in Matthew's throat soothed him with a kiss on his forehead, an arm around his shoulders. Soon Anselm reappeared and indicated all was well and we should leave quickly. Once outside we made our way towards Soutergate where we had arranged to meet the remainder of our party. Anselm looked serious and his preoccupied manner caused us to press on in silence. Sir Anthony and the others had already assembled and the company was in buoyant mood but this was soon quelled by the look on Anselm's face. He and Sir Anthony walked on, heads together, leaving me to deal with the many questions flowing between the other members of our party.

Certainly a dampener had been placed on the afternoon and instead of animated discussions about the performance we journeyed home in the growing dusk in silence, not daring to enquire into Anselm's mysterious actions in the alehouse.

Once back at the hall, Anselm accompanied Sir Anthony to his chamber and the remainder of the group dispersed with suppressed queries and suggestions bubbling to the surface in the absence of any restraining hand. The boys, sensing tension in the air, decided on a visit to the stables where one of the cats had just given birth to five kittens.

In the course of making my way upstairs for a fresh handkerchief I heard Roland's excited voice behind me whispering, "Mistress Phillips, pray let me show thee a figure I have been whittling for Edwin. 'Twill be ready for Yuletide and me thinks he will find favour with it. Margery has it well hidden for me by her bed. Simon has been helping for several weeks and says I have a natural gift with a knife. I thought it a good business to fashion Lupus from the wood, for I know Ned is fair fond of him. But the head troubles me and is right difficult to do. Simon would do it should I ask him but 'twould not be right. Pray what dost thou think Mistress Phillips?"

As he paused for breath I informed him that, indeed, I should love to see his gift and sent him off to retrieve the carving whilst I continued up towards the garret. By now I had reached the upper floor and, passing Sir Anthony's chamber, I noticed the door was ajar. Some instinct made me delay, as the subdued voices of Sir Anthony and Anselm wafted through the narrow crack.

"Have no fear, Anselm. The lads will be safe under my guardianship until thy return."

"That is the least of my fears, Sir Anthony. His majesty knows full well where thy loyalties lie." I realised they were approaching the door and swiftly moved out of sight. Stepping into the stairwell Anselm continued, "Pray God that scoundrel Colyngbourne and his devious master hear not of their whereabouts or all will be lost. As time is of the essence I fear I must leave forthwith notwithstanding the late hour."

"Take good care, Anselm. The way will be in sore condition at this time of year, despite a surefooted steed."

"For certes thou speaks the truth but I must at least make Kirkby Kendal this e'en. The clear sky and moonlight will assist me and to speed my progress I shall endeavour to obtain a fresh mount whenever the opportunity presents itself," said Anselm. "I know not when I shall return, for the King may not be in the capital at present. However, we know that he is not resident in Penrith so let us hope I shall find him at Court."

Unbeknownst to the pair Roland had returned from the barmkin and, running upstairs, had picked up the tail end of the conversation. *"Art thou journeying to London, Anselm? Wilt thou be seeing our uncle the Ki...?"*

"Have done, lad!" Anselm quickly cut in before he had time to finish. Then softening he added, *"Wouldst thou have me convey any greeting from you, Roland?"*

"Tell him we are right pleased to be here, even Ned has come to like the place." And with that the three descended, Roland's mind now on Anselm's journey rather than the present for his brother.

I sank onto the stone steps and remained there for several minutes, my mind in turmoil. What did it all mean? Anselm had obviously witnessed something or somebody in Kendal of great import. And why this sudden need to visit the capital? It went without saying that I was bewildered at this revelation of his acquaintance with the King. What had he said to me previously – he had not lived in London but had worked there for a time – and what had Roland been about to say when he was abruptly interrupted? Something at the back of my mind had fleetingly stirred at mention of the name Colyngbourne, but had elusively drifted into the dark recesses of my memory. I hoped it would return when I had time to clear my thoughts but in the meantime I decided I should return to the household before my absence was noticed.

Once downstairs I was accosted by Roland: taking advantage of his brother's absence he proudly showed me the wooden figure of the dog. It was a good likeness and the workmanship excellent for a lad of his age. Obviously he had talent and I had no hesitation in praising his work. Around us the atmosphere was electric. All hands were busy preparing for Anselm's journey and he was soon ready to depart.

He took his leave of Sir Anthony and Lady Margaret and bade me ensure that in his absence the boys were diligent in their studies. *"Although I am aware that thou cannot school them, perhaps thou could encourage them to take up their books."* I felt quite elated and took his request as an acknowledgement of my level-headedness.

His farewell to Edwin and Roland was a tender affair and once again I realised the affection he must have for the lads despite his usual lack of any outward sign of emotion *towards them. They followed him out into the courtyard and watched him ride from the barmkin but his figure was instantly enveloped in the darkness, despite a clear sky and a full moon. An air of melancholy settled on the household and I was relieved when I could retire to my room, alone with my thoughts and musings........*

My aunt's knowledge of history was considerably more detailed than my own: the name Colyngbourne meant nothing to me. What was the mystery surrounding these people? Resuming the narrative I turned the page.

CHAPTER SIX

…… *Anselm returned around three weeks later, but before he did so another visitor arrived at Overthwaite Hall. I had previously heard tales of Hugo, Sir Anthony's younger brother, primarily from Margery through her uncomplimentary chit-chat but nothing could have prepared me for him in the flesh.*

Since the day of the Kendal fair the temperatures had dropped dramatically. The pond in the centre of the village had developed a thin covering of ice, which thickened with each day that dawned. The birds were busy hunting for any remaining berries and I remember thinking of my bird table at 'home' and musing idly on how a suggestion of putting out scraps might be greeted!

For the past few days Lady Margaret had stationed herself in front of the roaring fire in the hall accompanied by Jane, the two of them busy with their needlework. Lady Margaret had decided that in addition to her own new outfit, dresses for Jane, Margery and I were to be made in readiness for the Yuletide celebrations. Not, of course, from her expensive fine wool but a generous gesture nevertheless. Margery's chores continued as usual and I regret to say that I had failed to offer my assistance to the same extent as of late in view of the worsening weather. The bitter cold was eating into my bones and no doubt appeared obvious to Lady Margaret who, appreciating my advanced years, on several occasions invited me to help with the gowns. It was during one such interlude that Hugo arrived.

The skies that morning had been heavy with snow since daybreak: a dull, pink glow permeated the heavy atmosphere and a deathly hush settled all around. By mid morning large, feathery flakes began to fall and a thin covering of snow was soon in evidence as far as the eye could see. The sky promised more to follow and soon the boys had sufficient to wage war, with snowballs as their weapons.

During the previous week my mind had been going over and over the conversation I had heard between Anselm and Sir Anthony, trying to remember the exact words that had been used. An unbelievable, almost fantastic, idea was slowly forming and I decided to use the times I spent with Lady Margaret to try to gain information to confirm my thoughts.

The logs were crackling in the grate and the sounds of boyish squeals drifted through the window as we sat in companionable silence over our sewing. I decided to break the silence.

"Matthew seems to get on right well with the boys, m'Lady."

"Tis true Catherine. Ere their arrival he was verily a withdrawn child but now 'twould appear he has become quite talkative and even boisterous – 'tis only normal for the boy – 'twas unhealthy afore, having no siblings. Tom's lad is a good child but a little slow if thou take my meaning. Methinks he caused Matthew not to extend his brain overly. Whereas Edwin and Roland, well, such bright lads they be. And by cause of Anselm's teachings, Matthew benefits twofold. Aye, 'twas a good business the day they set foot across our threshold, although I must admit, I thought not at the time."

"They were not known to you then?"

"Why no, 'twas a direct request from Humphrey, Lord Dacre – Sir Anthony's liege-lord – fulfilling some obligation he had previously made. Sir Anthony was a little vague." She brushed the matter off, not questioning her husband's explanations. "Aye, the lads have been here now nigh on a twelve month."

"Anselm informed me his birth town was Ludlow. Was that also from where the boys came?"

"Er, let me see," she thought for a moment, "I fear they lived in ... could it be London? To be honest I cannot say for sure." I had decided further questioning would seem suspicious. Thankfully I was spared any awkwardness by the sound of Lupus's loud, persistent barking and a breathless Roland who burst into the hall.

"Prithee ... a rider ... over the fields ... dost thou think it could be Anselm?" I made a move towards the window whilst Lady Margaret struggled to her feet and slowly followed me across the room.

She frowned, "Methinks Anselm hath made exceptional time should this be him, though saying so we do not expect any other visitors." Throughout these exchanges Jane, never a talkative young woman at the best of times, had stayed silent. Lady Margaret now turned to her, "Jane, run down to Margery and ensure we have bread and ale ready, also hot water. 'Twill be needed by any traveller on such a day."

After Jane had departed Lady Margaret remained with me by the window. Her manner was unusually agitated and her fingers busily worked the folds of her skirt. As the rider approached I could see him regularly whip his horse's flank and by the time he pulled up in the barmkin the beast's coat was lathered with foam; ears pricked; eyes wide; nostrils firing plumes of steamy breath into the chill November air.

"Heaven preserve us, I feared we were well overdue a visit," Lady Margaret mumbled underneath her breath. She crossed herself and turning towards me continued in a louder voice, "Sir Anthony is engaged in the inspection of the new bridge, down by the river. Perchance thou couldst ask Tom to get one of the stable lads to ride and fetch him? Inform him 'tis his younger brother Hugo come to pay a call."

As I emerged outside my gaze took in a man in his late twenties, around the same height as his brother but slimmer and with a much more athletic build. He too was clean-shaven and although his dark curly hair made the family resemblance more evident, where Sir Anthony's face was open and friendly the one I now looked into was cold and hard. His close-set eyes were of such a dark brown as to appear almost black and his nose was long and aquiline: altogether, he had a most sinister appearance. As I crossed the courtyard he swung out of his saddle and began issuing orders.

"Thee, lad!" he shouted across to William. "Take my horse and have him seen to. Have a care 'tis done thoroughly, mind. I'll stand for no slipshod work." He clipped William around the ears and as the boy led the horse away Hugo spotted me, "I cannot remember seeing thee afore. What be thy name?"

I turned and, looking him straight in the eye, unflinchingly informed him, "Mistress Phillips. Mistress Catherine Phillips."

"Ah, Mistress Phillips is it? Well Mistress Phillips, perchance thou wouldst kindly fetch me some victuals ... at thy leisure!" His voice was hard and menacing and his insolence set the scene for our future encounters. I should dearly have loved to slap him across the face.

"Certainly, Sir. The mistress has asked that I send a rider to fetch Sir Anthony. He is out inspecting the bridge building at present. I understand Lady Margaret has already organised food for you and hot water to warm and refresh you after your journey." Although I refused to let him intimidate me, I determined he should find no cause for any disrespect in my manner.

"God's wounds, my brother is after earning indulgencies by his pious acts, is he? 'Twould appear he values providing bridges for travellers greater than giving support to his own kith and kin! By Christ, does nothing change?"

Feeling any comment would inflame him further I continued on my errand. Suddenly, Sarah appeared from the small hall. She sauntered across the barmkin in a provocative manner and, as though seeing Sir Anthony's brother for the first time, turned to face him. "Why, Master Hugo," she fluttered her eyelids, "'tis right good to see thee." Moving closer and looking up coyly into his eyes she added, "Is there aught thou desires?"

"Sarah! As welcoming as ever, I see. Do I desire aught? Well ..." drawing the back of his index finger across her exposed bosom he let his gaze linger lasciviously on her décolletage, "... I think not, for I have had a long, hard ride and am about to eat." He turned abruptly and made for the hall.

Sarah blushed and flung her head back: the spurn had obviously angered her. Across the barmkin I noticed Stephen who had entered through the gate and witnessed the encounter. In his placid, reserved manner he quietly turned away, a resigned look upon his sad face. I felt there would surely be trouble ahead.

By the time I returned to the hall Hugo, greedily devouring bread and cheese washed down with copious amounts of ale, was nevertheless complaining about the quality of the fare provided. "I warrant thou wilt serve some decent victuals tonight Margaret? This pig swill will do to initially quench a traveller's appetite but have a care – I shall not stomach it again!"

I noticed that Lady Margaret failed to rise to the bait and said little to her brother-in-law, her contempt for him being evident in her eyes. Sir Anthony appeared shortly and greeted his brother with guarded reserve. It was clear little love was lost between the two of them and just as obvious that the younger brother bore a deep resentment towards his older sibling.

Over supper Edwin and Roland were introduced to Hugo who eyed them suspiciously.

Sir Anthony explained about the death of the boys' parents and Lord Dacre's request to house the lads. "I thought it a good business for, if nothing else, Matthew will benefit from the teachings of Anselm."

"This Anselm, the lads' uncle thou says, where dost thou have him hiding?"

"'Twas necessary he journey to London on urgent business."

"What business?"

"Hugo, why dost thou have this bee in thy bonnet? Thou hast not even met the man." Sir Anthony was losing patience, "On business of his own making. Be done with it!"

"Pray, do not come the heavy hand with me brother! I'll trow there is more to this than meets the eye – something in it for thee no doubt. I cannot imagine thou dipping thy hand in thy pocket for strangers when thou wilt not assist even thine own brother!" Hugo was struggling to keep his temper under control. Contemptuously he turned his back on his brother, supping his wine in silence.

"Prithee, let us not argue yet again over money. Thou knows how much thou art allowed each quarter. If thou choose to spend it all during the first month, that be thine own choice." I felt sure that Sir Anthony's patronising tone would only inflame matters: it did.

"Goddam it, Sir, do not lecture me!"

"Then do not act like a child!" Sir Anthony's voice was rising in line with Hugo's.

"If I act like a child 'tis because thou treats me like one! But we are in the nursery no longer! The time is well overdue for an increase to my portion! A man cannot live on the meagre pittance allotted to me!"

"Increase, increase thou says? Thy portion should have been decreased these nine years past to compensate for monies I have laid out in payment for thy son!"

"Canst thou not find something new to say? I am well nigh bored with thy repetitions!" He stifled a mock yawn. "This conversation tires me. I am for bed."

Having drunk far too much wine during the evening Hugo staggered to his feet with difficulty. In the process he knocked over his chair, caught his leg in the spindles, collapsed in a heap and further made a fool of himself by refusing to accept assistance in recovering his posture. We were all relieved by the time he had managed to transport himself upstairs.

Upon his arrival he had refused to sleep with the boys in the small hall, demanding a chamber of his own. Consequently, for the duration of his stay he was to have the garret whilst I slept with Margery in the bakehouse. That night as I snuggled down on my pallet next to her, appreciative of the residual warmth from the ovens, I felt sure that in the darkness I would be privy to many tales about Sir Anthony's younger brother. She fulfilled my expectations.

Margery was sketchy about the details but reading between the lines, I pieced together a story of a petulant and wayward younger brother who was desperately jealous and resentful of the fact that he was the second-born. Being landless and consequently lacking any income he was therefore unable to meet the financial obligations required of a Knight. Sir Anthony, feeling responsible for his sibling, was constantly being called upon to settle his debts. In order to give Hugo a good start in life he had found him employment in Lord Dacre's household. However, the wilful brother had failed to last long there and (here Margery was unsure of her facts) soon moved to a different branch of the Dacre family. Once again he had failed to stay the course and word eventually filtered back to Sir Anthony that, true to his character, he was fighting as a mercenary soldier abroad. This had all happened some ten years previously and since that time Hugo had been paying infrequent calls to Overthwaite, on each occasion leaving a trail of mayhem and chaos behind him. I remember falling asleep thinking the more distance I could place between Hugo and myself the better.

Life revolved around Hugo over the following days and although Sir Anthony's patience was not inexhaustible, to a certain extent he was tolerant of his brother, presumably on the basis or in the hope that his stay would be short-lived. However, I became aware that Sir Anthony appeared to be keeping Edwin and Roland out of Hugo's way. He took them out with him during the day – an action previously not undertaken – and at night tried to ensure they had retired to their chamber before Hugo's return. When this was impossible Sir Anthony was extremely attentive to any question Hugo might ask about the boys' origins or past, on several occasions stepping in to answer before they could reply. Whether or not this made his brother more suspicious of the lads I am not sure but certainly he seemed determined to quiz them at every opportunity.

Hugo's days were spent idly lounging around the hall or out riding when the weather permitted but on several occasions he set off for Penrith. There he spent the day drinking and the evening in his favourite whorehouse. If he returned early he would be totally inebriated, but more often than not he stayed out all night and it was mid-day before his horse could be heard galloping into the barmkin.

On one such morning I had cause to enter the stable on some errand or other, only to hear a commotion towards the back of the building. Investigating further I found, within an empty stall, two bodies writhing in the straw. Even from behind it was evident one was Hugo but the other was shielded from my view. I ran over and yanked him off by the shoulder; the stench of stale wine assailed my nostrils. I must have caught him unawares for he toppled onto his back in a most ungainly fashion.

Thinking his conquest to be Sarah, I was surprised to find his prey was Jane, unusually separated from her mistress. His right hand had been fumbling beneath her skirts and his left, the one by which I had pulled him away, had been clamped over her mouth. She lay there dishevelled and bewildered, a quiet succession of sobs beginning to emanate from her now unfettered mouth. She resembled a startled, injured fawn and my heart went out to her. Kneeling down I straightened her skirts and pulled her towards me, holding her close and gently rocking her to-and-fro. Meanwhile, Hugo had regained his composure and, brushing the straw from his doublet, glanced contemptuously at the pair of us.

Without giving him a chance to gloat I hissed, "You animal. Is it a measure of your character that you have to force your unwanted attentions on the girl? You're nothing better than a ..., a cur! But no, for surely that would be disrespectful to the dog!"

Pulling himself up to his full height he towered over us and I felt sure I was about to feel the back of his hand across my face. I stared into his eyes defiantly, willing him to strike me, but for some reason he hesitated. Turning on his heel he stalked angrily out of the stable, totally unmoved by Jane's plight and, finding his horse still saddled and waiting in the courtyard, was soon heading at full speed away from Overthwaite and the hall.

"'Twas only the k...k...kittens that I c...c...came to l...l...look for," Jane stammered between sobs.

"Yes ... yes. Sh now, do not fret." Holding her to me I tried to comfort the thin, trembling body, finally convincing her he had departed and so coaxing her out of the stable. Taking her straight to the pallet she occupied in her mistress's chamber I put her to bed and after asking Margery to take a warm drink up to her went in search of Lady Margaret.

I related the scene I had witnessed and assured her I had intervened in good time. Naturally she was horrified, though I might add not surprised, and told me she would inform Sir Anthony.

I retired to the bakehouse where a sympathetic Margery informed me Hugo had forced his attentions on virtually all the young women in Overthwaite during his previous visits. "Th' only one not to 'ave bin pestered by 'im is Sarah – an' I think that's only 'cause she throws herself at him." It was said with no malice, merely stated as a fact. "Good job she's not around at present or she might be jealous!" She raised her gaze to heaven.

I dearly hoped Sir Anthony's disruptive brother would soon be gone.

That evening, Hugo had failed to return by the time supper was served and the hour was late when his horse galloped into the courtyard. Lady Margaret had retired and as Jane was still traumatised by her morning's ordeal I had offered to help her mistress undress. The door of the chamber was ajar and snippets of the conversation drifted up the stairs to our ears: Sir Anthony's voice angry; Hugo's slurred with drink.

"... thou hast gone too far this time, Hugo. Thou knows Jane be from a good family ... 'twould be too much to hope that in view of your connection with her brother thou wouldst *spare her your attentions. Though perhaps you and he are from the same nest and have no respect ..."*

"... aye, aye, thou hast said it all before. Have done with thy lectures."

"Then take heed ...... a good business that thou be gone ..."

"Have no fear, brother, for I shall leave the morrow ... and right glad shall I be to leave this hell hole ..."

The argument and raised voices continued for some time before silence descended on the hall. Hugo's footsteps could be heard striding noisily to his chamber and shortly afterwards I descended to the bakehouse, passing Sir Anthony who was staring despondently into the dying embers of the fire.

Next day dawned crisp and clear and by mid morning a vociferous Hugo was slowly making ready to take his leave. Margery and I were in the dairy from where we could hear the last angry interchange between the brothers. This done Hugo had obviously decided to seek me out before leaving, as suddenly the door was flung open and his menacing figure crossed the short distance between us.

"Prithee, Mistress Phillips," he hissed between clenched teeth, "fear not that I shall forget thy part in this or that thou art too old to find thyself being manhandled one quiet, lonely night. Have a care when thou art crossing the barmkin after dark, for thou might not be fortunate enough to find any to protect thee!" Suddenly he plunged his hand down the front of my bodice, ripping the material in the process. Cupping my right breast in his hand he roughly squeezed the nipple between his thumb and forefinger, whilst insolently letting his gaze linger on my cleavage. The pain was almost unbearable and I grabbed his wrist with the intention of removing his hand. However, he was much stronger than I had imagined and we remained in the same position for what seemed like an age.

Slowly he brought his gaze up to my face and said with a leer, "Let us see if thou art worth pursuing." Roughly removing his hand he pulled the ripped material down, exposing my breast as he did so. Once again he let his gaze drop and linger there whilst hastily I tried to cover myself. "Nay do not worry. Thou art too old for my liking!" With a sardonic laugh he turned on his heel and was gone. I can only presume he was unused to servants gainsaying him and decided to re-establish his authority by humiliating me.

Margery hurried across the dairy to comfort me but I was determined not to let him think I was cowed by his actions and threats. I moved to the doorway in time to see him mount his horse and prepare to depart. Again Sarah was dallying in the barmkin, her gaze never leaving Hugo's face.

At that moment a shrill voice from above, which I recognised as belonging to Roland, cried excitedly, "A rider approaches. Methinks it is Anselm!"

A few moments later amidst excited roars from Lupus, Anselm rode into the courtyard looking cold, tired and muddy. On seeing Hugo a look of suspicion crept into his eyes and I could almost read his mind as he weighed up this stranger, wondering what business had brought him to Overthwaite.

Before Anselm could speak Hugo nudged his steed towards the other's and the two horses pranced around each other as though engaging in some bizarre dance. "So this is the mysterious Anselm!" Hugo commented sardonically. "'Tis pity we shall not have the opportunity of becoming acquainted. I was hoping to learn of thy hold over my brother, for 'tis not charity moves him to provide shelter for thee and thy nephews, I'll be bound. Were it so then 'twould be new to me, for I have yet to benefit from his charity, financial or otherwise, let alone strangers. Nay, I'll trow there is more to this than meets the eye. Farewell, Sir, 'till we meet again." Digging his heels into the flanks of his horse he tightened the reins and without more ado galloped at full speed from the barmkin......

I shook myself: what a blackguard this younger brother had turned out to be. I shuddered at the thought of Catherine's ordeal.

...... After supper, Lady Margaret having retired early with Jane once again shadowing her closely, I settled in front of the fire for a short spell, intending to warm myself before making my own way up to bed. Overcome by the heat and exhausted by the trauma of Hugo's visit I must have dozed for I awoke with a start as my head fell forward onto my chest. Sir Anthony and Anselm failed to notice me, as they were deep in conversation, the strains of which drifted across from the table where the pair had remained drinking wine. Would I learn anything of Anselm's journey to London? I listened carefully but they discussed only Hugo.

"Nay, I should not think he means anything by his remarks. I feel he has no inkling where the lads are concerned. He always did consider fortune to have been sore against him. I'll trow his idle bantering was once more aimed at me."

"He has always been a burden on thee?" Anselm enquired.

"Aye, both financial and otherwise, even afore our father died. As a young lad he would oft be found in Penrith or Kirkby Kendal, blind drunk and a fair tally due to the landlord. Plus, of course, his gaming debts." Sir Anthony sounded tired as he continued, "Our father did attempt to keep a tight rein on him and on his deathbed extracted a promise from me that I would look after Hugo. He always was right fond of the lad." Anselm seemed to sense Sir Anthony's need to talk and made no comment. "I thought that, should he become a 'bachelor' in Lord Humphrey's household 'twould be best for us all. It troubled me that he always seemed resentful, so I hoped it might be the making of him." A long pause ensued, Sir Anthony seeming in another world.

"I take it 'twas not the making of him?" prompted Anselm.

"Nay!" Sir Anthony laughed wryly. "Knowing Lord Humphrey was our liege lord – for by then he had been awarded back his lands by the King – Hugo thought 'twould be fair game to muddy the waters for me. His thinking was that, should he offend Humphrey, I might be the one to suffer the consequences. I know not whether thou art aware, but there have been problems with the Dacre title and lands since Towton in '61. Humphrey's brother fought for Henry and so was named by Edward under an act of attainder thereby losing all. The northern lands were seized by Joane, Humphrey's niece, and her husband Sir Richard Fiennes – though not in a hostile way, I might add, but more as a safeguard for Humphrey pending restitution. However, some thought there might be more to their actions and were not aware of the good feeling all round. Hugo was such a one. He thereby thinks to have found a way to harm my cause, so to that end leaves Lord Humphrey's manor at Lazonby, notwithstanding he had already sworn fealty to him, and obtains a similar position in Sir Richard's household at Herstmonceux! 'Twas a good business Humphrey was on fair terms with his niece and her husband and knew of Hugo's ways. He hast never held my brother's actions against me." Momentarily he paused, "As for Hugo's position at Sir Richard's, well, that lasted scant longer. He soon had need for change. To shorten the tale, he ended up abroad, fighting as a mercenary – always one to side with the highest bidder!"

"From what I have heard of him, a soldier's life would suit him to the ground."

"Aye, Anselm. Perchance thou art right." Once again a resigned note was creeping in.

"And since then thou hast seen him on infrequent occasions?"

"When the money has run out, or when the fighting tires him and he prefers to make sport with us. Thou heard of his pleasure-seeking with Jane and the incident with Catherine I take it?" Anselm nodded and Sir Anthony continued, "Aye, and Jane's brother is a companion of Hugo's! One might have thought by cause of their association he would leave her be. But no, he cannot resist. Mind you, I fear her brother is of the same ilk as Hugo and would no doubt look upon it as sport! A sorry state of affairs, indeed." Pausing, he shook his head slowly before continuing, "Inevitably Hugo has fathered his fair share of by-blows around the county, or country for all I know. He has a wife and child over in York who ne'er see him from one Yuletide to the next!"

"He is married, then?" Anselm sounded surprised.

Sir Anthony laughed wryly, "'Twas as much a surprise to us as it is to you. Thank God it was after our father's death for 'twould have caused him much grief. We knew naught of the matter 'til well after the event – 'til the girl's father came knocking on our door to be precise. It seems Hugo had 'charmed' the lass and his way into her bed. She was from a good family in York – her father a merchant in the same city. Anyways, the father catches them in the act and, being a forthright and forceful citizen, insists Hugo marries the wench. 'Twas no surprise when in less than nine months she gave birth to a son! Needless to say, Hugo has ne'er set eyes on the lad nor his wife since the marriage ceremony and to provide any financial assistance would not have crossed his mind. Her father came here in a right temper but, when I had sat him down and talked things through, he was a reasonable chap. Once again it was necessary to account for my brother's vices but in all conscience, Anselm, I could have done no less. I settled an annual portion on the lad, 'twas all his grandsire was after." Again he sat in silence, mulling over things past. "It may be several weeks or months or longer afore we see him next. Let's hope 'twill be the latter. There is only one sure thing about Hugo – he will always be steadfast in his unpredictability. I thank God I have sired Matthew, for the estate would not last long in my brother's hands!" His bitterness was almost tangible. Overthwaite was obviously dear to him. He roused himself, "Come, Anselm. I fear my tale was long and rambling. Enough of this, it depresses me. Another cup of wine afore bed, what says thou?"

 I thought it was time I made my presence known but in case Sir Anthony wished his brother's indiscretions not to be widely recognised, I stifled a yawn as though I had been sleeping all along. Bidding the pair goodnight I made my way upstairs towards the chamber recently vacated by Hugo. I could almost smell his scent as I entered the room and thoughts of our last encounter in the dairy came flooding unbidden to my mind. I sincerely hoped I would forego the 'pleasure' of Hugo's company again during my stay in the 15th century.

 The weather had taken a turn for the worse: milder, but certainly worse. Persistent rain had turned the snow initially to slush. Gradually this was washed away until not a trace remained. Day after day we awoke to grey skies heavy with unshed rain and inevitably by early morning a torrential downpour swept through the valley from the distant hills. The river swelled, the village pond doubled in size and the fields around the hall became a sodden quagmire, in places forming vast sheets of water stretching as far as the eye could see.

Throughout the days between Anselm's return and Christmas we had spent the time in preparation for our Yuletide stay at Dacre Castle. All were to attend with the exception of Stephen and his wife who were to remain behind to handle the day-to-day running of the Hall in Sir Anthony's absence. Sarah, piqued by their exclusion, made it evident any assistance given was done so without good grace. This apart, tasks were completed in a light-hearted spirit and we were all thankful when, shortly before we were due to set out, a window of good weather ensued which enabled the final arrangements to be made more easily. Jane busied herself with her mistress's wardrobe; Margery was in charge of Sir Anthony, Edwin and Roland's attire; Anselm as usual ensured the boys' educational needs would be catered for; and Tom's job was to create a safe mode of transport for Lady Margaret, now in her sixth month of pregnancy.

Generally, travel in the 15th century was undertaken on horseback. Our previous outings had been on the cart but, as I have stated, the reasons were for the procurement of provisions on the first occasion and logistics on the second. Consequently for this trip the majority of the party was to ride – our belongings accompanying Lady Margaret who would be secured safely in the cart on a contraption resembling a litter, rigged up by Tom for the journey. Being one of the eldest I would also be allowed on the wheeled transport, a concession for which I was heartily thankful. Although I was a proficient horsewoman the thought of managing my skirts whilst riding side-saddle filled me with some trepidation.

Sir Anthony's last task was to deliver the salted pork to the villagers. Margery informed me this had become somewhat of a tradition with him: his final act before the Yuletide celebrations began. This done, we were ready to leave by mid *morning and the party was soon making its slow progress north towards Dacre.*

The journey was uneventful and not overly long; nevertheless I am sure Lady Margaret was thankful when the crenelations of the castle came into view. This too was a pele tower but a far more substantial one than Overthwaite and as we traversed the lanes towards its grey-pink sandstone walls the solidity of this imposing edifice dominated the landscape as far as the eye could see. It's dour façade and narrow windows were anything but welcoming and although I had visited modern day Dacre on numerous occasions, seeing virtually the same view, I felt a shiver run down my spine as gradually we approached the gate in the south east corner of the curtain wall.

We were not the only visitors to be invited to the Yuletide celebrations and consequently the courtyard was alive with the comings and goings of household servants, baggage, horses and of course the guests themselves. The entrance to the castle was in the south west tower and upon passing through the arched doorway with its thick, studded door I looked back to see a heavily bolted and barred yett or iron grid, which I felt sure would effectively repel all unwanted intruders to the stronghold. We climbed the newel staircase to the great hall where Lord Humphrey and Lady Mabel greeted us with a warm welcome. Although I had hardly any contact with them during my stay, they appeared to be an hospitable couple and our party surely lacked for nothing whilst under Dacre's roof.

We were hungry after our journey and pleased to see the array of refreshments laid out on trestle tables. After partaking, we went about the business of settling ourselves into the accommodation provided. Sir Anthony and Lady Margaret had been allocated a well-appointed, large room on the second floor of the newly built north east tower; Anselm joined the other male members of the gathering in the old hall across the courtyard; and the women and children slept communally in the gallery situated above the solar or private apartments of Lord and Lady Dacre.

It had been an extremely long day and I was exhausted by the time we were ready to retire. Lying on my pallet I could hear the wind whistling round the castle walls, any draught being lessened by the heat from many bodies. I pulled the coverings under my chin but can remember little else: I was asleep in an instant.

Dacre Castle was a well-oiled machine running like clockwork due to the knowledge and expertise of its staff, many of whom had been there since the previous occupant, Lady Eleanor, the widow of Ranulph Lord Dacre.
For the clerk controller the day began at four a.m., his first task being to arrange the day's menus with the cooks. The remainder of the household then swung into action with several jobs being accomplished by each member prior to the family and guests rising soon after dawn. After the usual breakfast of bread, ale and meat Sir Anthony accompanied Lord Humphrey to the solar to assist with the business of the estate. On those times when I had cause to pass through, I could hear Lord Dacre's deep, authoritative voice dictating letters to his secretary. Some conveyed instructions to his agents; others relayed directives to the bailiffs at his more remote manors; and on one occasion he dictated a reply relating to repair work he was financing at Lanercost Priory.

Throughout the next few days the party settled in to their new routine. The lads were in high jinx, totally revelling in their new surroundings and temporary release from lessons. Into everything, they amused themselves by the river; played with the many hounds which inhabited the castle; spent time in the stables and blacksmith's, both of which were considerably larger than their counterparts at Overthwaite; and as a special treat, on one occasion, joined the men for an afternoon's hawking.
I kept myself busy, alternating between helping Margery and keeping company with Lady Margaret and Jane. Every afternoon the ladies gathered round the fireplace in the solar, conversing and amusing themselves with their embroidery. On occasion Lady Mabel would be present but

with the Yuletide preparations looming large on the horizon more often than not she was absent. Some of the ladies' names meant nothing to me, although I had chatted to several of their maids during our stay. However, I learnt one of the guests, a lady clad in black mourning garb was Sir Thomas Parre's widow Lady Elizabeth, herself a sister-in-law to Lady Mabel. Although quite young and pleasant, she was a matronly woman who loved to chat about all and sundry.

"'Twas fair provident Humphrey had a mind to celebrate Yuletide at Dacre this year," she intoned in her unusually deep voice, "for I fear the boy and I would not have ventured far, so shortly after my dear husband's sad demise." Her son, also Thomas, was a lad of around Roland's age. He was a shy boy but had his mother's pleasant disposition and followed Edwin, whom he seemed to hero worship, like a shadow.

"I should have thought Irthington might be a more favoured venue with Lord Humphrey," suggested Lady Margaret.

"Had not the new tower been completed then perchance 'twould have been Irthington." Lady Elizabeth went on to explain, "My brother-in-law is right pleased with his new building works and 'twould appear he wished to show them to all his friends this Yuletide."

"And well he has cause to be pleased. Our chamber is excellent situated – would that we could afford such an addition at Overthwaite!"

"Aye, our Kirkby Kendal residence could do with some refinements but 'tis best things remain as they are 'til such times as Thomas comes of age. I think not that Humphrey would have embarked on such a major build had not the old tower been vulnerable."

"How didst come about, Elizabeth?" enquired Lady Margaret.

"By all accounts 'twas some trouble with the foundations. Whether or no it first began with some reiving raid years past, who is to say? Lady Eleanor was in residence for many a year and, being an old lady, only requisite repairs were carried out. Perchance she felt there was insufficient plunder available to warrant additional attack. Whatever the reason, the tower was left to decay and 'twas in a sorry state when Humphrey and Mabel took possession. It hath cost him sore to put right but hath given him pleasure also. I fear after all the years he suffered under the act of attainder he is now right pleased to be able to care for his rightful manors. Aye, the late King, God rest his soul, came good eventually with my brother-in-law. 'Twould not necessarily have been so had our present ruler been on the throne at the time!"

"Come, come, Elizabeth! I fear you base that statement on scant evidence. King Richard is our good and true monarch. He has long been an honest deputy for his brother over the northern counties and I feel sure his kingship will prove just as virtuous," Lady Margaret was prompt and sharp with her retort. "But then, thou knows where Sir Anthony's and my loyalties lie."

"Dear Margaret, pray excuse me. In defence I would say my recent bereavement hath affected me more than I can tell. I knowest not what I say at times."

"Think naught of it. But pray have a care, for thou art aware walls have ears and the consequences can oft be dire!"

An uneasy silence descended on the party and the remainder of the afternoon was spent with little or no conversation accompanying the ladies' concentrated efforts at their needlework.

In no time at all Christmas Day was upon us. Although no snow had fallen, the good weather remained. After a bitterly cold night, hoarfrost made the barren branches sparkle in the sunshine and the air was crisp.

A special early morning Mass was celebrated in the chapel situated on the top floor of the new tower. Thereafter the household erupted as bodies scurried hither and thither in busy preparation for the mid-day feast, taken earlier than usual in view of the previous day's fast. Late morning I wandered across to the outbuildings abutting the curtain wall in the courtyard, seeking to give my assistance to Margery and paused to take in the brilliant blue of the sky. It hung like a huge backdrop to the castle walls and I wondered whether I was the only person to notice such beauty. I hurried on; for I was aware time was of the essence.

Margery was diligently ensuring everything was ready for her mistress's toilet. Castille soap (made with olive oil instead of the usual animal fat) had been made available for all the guests and Margery had also procured some herbs with which to perfume Lady Margaret's washing water. Jane was there too, making sure we had everything we needed and the three of us then made our way up to the bedchamber to lay out the clothes for the feast. Sir Anthony's outfit was already arranged on the bed: not having a valet of his own Lord Humphrey's man-servant was to perform the duties during our stay. We carefully unpacked Lady Margaret's new blue gown: it smelled exquisitely of the lavender and wormwood that had been used not only to perfume it but also to keep moths at bay. Next to this we placed her kirtle, hose and pattens – flat shoes with short pointed toes and straps which crossed over the instep. When everything was ready Margery and I left Jane to await her mistress's arrival, as we too wished to don our best outfits for the festivities and make ourselves look as presentable as possible.

At last the celebrations were ready to begin and we made our way down to the great hall where the usher, who was master of the seating arrangements, had the task of ensuring all the guests were placed strictly according to their rank. He was also responsible for the decorations and hangings and I must say when we entered, the hall looked a festive picture. Holly, mistletoe and a profusion of greenery decked the tables and walls and perfectly complemented the two rich tapestries Lord Humphrey had had commissioned expressly for the Yuletide celebrations. On this special occasion expensive wax candles had been brought out for use on the high table. Here Sir Anthony, Lady Margaret and the other guests of honour would join the family for the occasion on the raised dais that was situated in the large window bay. Trestle tables were ranged around the walls and although we were seated towards the 'new' tower doorway, we were pleased not to be too far from the large fireplace and range where the food was being cooked: enticing aromas constantly wafted across the hall, tickling our nostrils and making our mouths water.

The guests were slowly making their way to the dais and I felt a surge of pride as Sir Anthony escorted his wife towards their seats; she looked radiant. The blue gown suited her perfectly and cleverly mirrored the colour of her eyes. In view of her pregnancy the bodice, which would normally have hugged her figure to the waist, ended below the bust with the sleeves fitting tight to the wrist. The full skirt hung in elegant, rippling folds ending above the ankles to reveal her kirtle, which almost brushed the floor. The gown's neckline was low, usually so low as to reveal a great deal of cleavage. However, as a result of her enceinte state the top edge had been designed to rise to a point in the centre in an attempt to cover, at least in part, her full, heavy breasts. Bordering this was a flat collar, which passed below the centre point and broadened out over the shoulders: made of ermine, with co-ordinating cuffs the whole effect was utterly charming. On her head she wore a Butterfly headdress of delicate, blue gauze. Worn at the back with the hair enclosed in a small, decorated, fez shaped cap, the wire-framed veil fanned out to resemble a pair of translucent wings and completed the outfit to perfection.

Sir Anthony's costume also was new for the occasion and complemented that of his wife's. He wore a front-laced doublet over his shirt, stomacher and hose, and his dark blue velvet jacket was also ermine trimmed. Covering his head was a small, round cap with turned-up brim sporting a feather attached by a brilliant jewelled brooch. And to round off his outfit he was wearing proudly the long toed pomaine shoes.

The usher soon had things in full swing aided by his company of tipstaffs who ensured all the gangways were clear in order to facilitate easy service of the food to the tables. At that stage I was unaware of the extent of the meal that was to follow: there were three courses, each one comprising numerous different dishes. These were placed down the middle of the table and, although I found the combinations interesting, by picking and choosing, the meal I consumed was surprisingly *delicious and certainly a welcome change from the limited diet at Overthwaite. Haunches of venison, poultry and pike in a thick sauce were succeeded by dishes of bream, tench and rabbit, and between each course were produced displays of 'sotelties' – pastry and sugar confections, cleverly formed into symbolic designs.*

Throughout the meal a group of minstrels had been providing music by way of harps and lutes but suddenly a loud flourish of trumpets was heard. Every gaze turned to the doorway where one of the tipstaffs, a good looking young chap, ceremoniously carried a tray, preceded by one of the trumpeters. The pièce de résistance had arrived – a soteltie in the shape of the newly built tower! Everybody cheered and clapped and a solemn faced Lord Humphrey slowly rose from his seat to accept the tray from its bearer.

The whole meal was rounded off with sweetmeats and spices and, of course, copious amounts of ale for the masses and wine for the top table.

The evening's experience had been totally exhilarating: speed and deftness of serving was a joy to behold; the cacophony of strange dialects and voices was intriguing to the ear; belches, farts and bawdy remarks emanated from all around; and the sheer difference between life in the 15th and 21st centuries could not have been more evident. Knowing these procedures were modelled largely on those at court, I wondered what it would have been like to attend such a royal function.

Once the meal had ended the tables on the opposite side of the hall by the newel entrance were cleared away, obviously making way for the evening's entertainment. What would it be, I wondered? A commotion could be heard outside. Word quickly went round: "'Tis the Interluders – come to perform a morality play! ... ...

CHAPTER SEVEN

…… A buzz of excitement filled the air as the strolling players made their way into the hall and very soon there was a great deal of activity. Temporary screens were erected by the doorway in order to form an entrance for the actors, and the diners who had vacated their benches huddled around these partitions causing the players to force their way through the congestion. A majestic figure having done so, we were aware the play had begun. A second player quickly followed and these two solemnly made their way down the hall, with one settling in a chair by the hearth of the great fireplace and the other seating himself directly below the dais: at this stage their identities remained a secret.

The guests on the high table strained towards the screens, eager to see what would follow. They were not to be disappointed, for soon 'Prologue' entered and saluted the assemblage informing them that a performance of 'Mankind' had commenced. Three villains 'Newguise', 'Nowadays' and 'Nought' now stumbled into the hall and, rolling around in a confused and excited manner, planned their scheme to allure 'Mankind' who was shortly to wander into the proceedings in an unsuspecting and nonchalant manner.

Tension mounted, as all were aware the devil, 'Titivillus', was soon to arrive on the scene. However, before this could happen it became obvious a collection was to be taken: the audience must pay to see Satan. After much cajoling and diligent searching of purses, finally sufficient income was amassed to enable the demon to arrive.

Notwithstanding that on the whole he was a jocular fiend, his mask was terrifying and as he circled the tables his evil demeanour caused many of the ladies to shy away in fright. Having joined the action his first pronouncement was a sinister caution to those guests who had tethered their horses in the courtyard, for dire consequences were to follow. Adding nothing further to this enigmatic presage he turned his attentions to intensifying the assault on 'Mankind' using all his hellish powers to endeavour to get the ingénue out of the way whilst he purloined his rosary. To do this 'Titivillus' forced 'Mankind' to loosen his bowels, "Arise and avaunt thee, nature compels" he commanded. Abruptly finding himself in urgent need of a toilet 'Mankind' hurried outside to relieve himself. Inevitably the audience found the whole episode extremely comical and raucous laughter emanated from all parts of the hall: including the high table.

'Mankind' soon returned and his persecution continued. Falling into a deep sleep, brought about by the devil, his dreams were haunted by images of 'Mercy' – the character seated by the screens – being arrested for purloining horses. A sharp intake of breath could be heard around the hall as people harboured doubts as to whether their steeds remained safely secured. This elicited a demonic laugh from 'Titivillus' which hung in the air like a question mark whilst once again he slowly toured the hall in diabolic fashion, terrorising the audience at every step.

It was now the turn of 'Newguise', 'Nowadays' and 'Nought' to inflict further torment on 'Mankind' whose belief in humanity was quickly eroding. They had managed to obtain his gown, which was of decorous length, and proceeded to instigate alterations. Inviting audience participation at every opportunity they made numerous exits and entrances each time producing a robe shorter than the last. With off stage taunts and derisory comments to 'Mankind' they eventually brought forth a garment that had been transformed into a doublet of indecent length which even failed to cover the buttocks. Things *were rapidly building to a climax: the consigning of 'Mankind' to perdition. However, in true fairy-tale style a happy ending was achieved by the intercession of the first character to appear in the evening's performance – the majestic figure seated by the fire who turned out to be 'Heaven'.*

The morality play held several messages, some of which no doubt, were lost on a great number in the hall but I was sure none failed to grasp the meaning of the 'tailoring' scene. As in every age, fashions constantly changed and I was aware young trendsetters had influenced dress by sporting the immodest doublets depicted in the play. This behaviour had attracted criticism not only from the church but also from some self-righteous dignitaries; however, I presume the audience still formed its own conclusions.

After the interluders had departed, the high table guests adjourned to the solar for a quieter interval before retiring. The remaining occupants of the hall continued with their carousing for several hours, accompanied by varying degrees of sexual intimacy. This was obviously not a time when romantic relationships were conducted in privacy: some couples kissed shyly; furtive fumbling could be detected amongst other pairs; and a few indulged in intercourse with gay abandon, seemingly oblivious to all else around them. Margery certainly enjoyed herself and spent the majority of the evening flirting with a young chap seated next to her. It was a pleasure to watch her innocent coquettish behaviour.

St. Stephen's morn dawned crisp and clear and I felt sure several heads would be pounding after the previous day's excesses.

Having some free time, later that morning I decided to take advantage of the fine weather and wander out for a stroll around the castle environs. As I came down from the gallery I encountered Jane who informed me Lady Margaret was feeling tired and had decided to return to her chamber to rest. Although a walk on my own seemed eminently appealing I decided it would be churlish not to invite her to join me and I was delighted to see her face light up in a transforming smile at the prospect. She returned for her cloak and re-appeared wearing the newly acquired hand-me-down Lady Margaret had given her for the Yuletide trip. Although the garment was hardly new Jane was proud of the gift and I must say it bore no evidence of wear or tear. Its sable edging had grown hard from damp at Overthwaite Hall but Margery had worked miracles during the short time the cape had been in Jane's possession. She had carefully removed the edging and then, to my astonishment, had filled her mouth with wine and squirted this over the fur working the liquid in fully with her fingertips. Once totally dry, the sable had been repeatedly rubbed until the fur was virtually back to its original pristine condition. The cape looked charming and Jane had every right to feel delighted with her new acquisition.

We arrived in the courtyard and turning right took the doorway through to the garth, or outer bailey, passing more of the castle's outbuildings on our way. Crossing the cobbles we soon attained the gate that would take us from the environs of the castle and I suggested we follow the path down towards the river. We skirted the moat that bordered the stronghold on two of its sides and as we walked I looked back over its murky waters to see the palisade rising high on its inner side – a tough defence to breach.

Jane was her usual quiet self and I knew that any conversation must needs come from me. I was aware she was a distant relative of Lady Margaret's and had been lady's maid to her for several years but she was such an introvert that my knowledge ended there. "Do your family reside in the vicinity of Lady Margaret's?"

"I have no family – or none to speak of – but my home was nearer York, at Thoresby," she whispered in her distinctively shy manner. "Do you know of it?"

"Not that I recall."

"'Tis a most beautiful place. The dales are peaceful and though some think them a place of solitude, I have always found comfort there. I knew naught else 'til my arrival at Overthwaite and ne'er did I wish to leave the confines of our valley. Oft times I wandered down to Wharram Percy," I sensed she was there in spirit, "to worship alone at our church

of St. Martin, where my parents were married." Stirring from her reverie she continued, *"But then my father and mother passed away and Lady Margaret's parents were kind enough to take me in. For when my father died I had nought else and nowhere to go – our lands were once again lost in '71 by virtue of Alan's treachery."* The last was added in a particularly sharp manner for Jane.

"Alan?" I enquired, for never had I heard her speak of her family before.

"My brother, though I am ashamed to call him such." She proceeded to outline her family's history and by the time she ended her sad tale my heart had warmed to this frail, timid, young woman.

The family name was Vescy and a forebear had been a knight, holding a small manor at Sledthorpe. The village was one of many to be hit by the plague and with the population decimated the village was abandoned. Fortunately Jane's family had survived and moved to the nearby township of Thoresby but with no inheritance it took some time to regain the family's wealth. Alan was Jane's only sibling and the age gap between the two was considerable, some twelve years. He bitterly resented the hardship his family had suffered.

"Though why he should do so, I know not. The Lord saw fit to test our faith and the family was not found wanting. Alan, on the other hand, is forever sorely lacking when tribulations are aplenty," her voice was scathing. She added, *"His bitterness was his undoing."*

Turning his aggression to fighting he became a soldier. The family had always been staunchly Yorkist but Alan, twelve months after attaining his knighthood, fought at Tewkesbury on the side of Henry VI and was taken captive by a Yorkist knight.

"My father received Alan's right gauntlet," Jane explained. *"We were assured my brother had given his pledge and shaken on it and so had no option but to agree to pay the ransom."*

Luckily I knew of this procedure and so understood the meaning of her statement. The process she had outlined was common in warfare. Any knight implementing this sequence of events was assured of protection but also bound to his captor *by his word until such time as the ransom was paid. It had taken Jane's father a great deal of effort and time to raise the money and six months after doing so he had died a broken man. Alan's freedom had been secured but because he had remained steadfast to the Lancastrian cause the family's lands were confiscated by Edward IV under an act of attainder. Landless and penurious, Jane's brother had followed the same career as Hugo and the two soldiers of fortune had met up whilst fighting abroad as mercenaries.*

"I have seen nought of Alan for many a year, nor do I wish to. My father was the sweetest of men and it fair broke his heart to learn his son had turned traitor. I can only thank the dear Lord that I possess such generous relations." *Lady Margaret and Jane were much of an age and it occurred to me that, as they had known each other for 13 years, they had grown together from childhood, hence Jane's closeness to her mistress. We continued in silence and I sensed Jane's unease.* "Where my future lies I know not – I refer to my marriage prospects. It troubles me that I am not yet betrothed for I am no longer young."

The last was said in earnest: I struggled to hide my amusement. "I feel sure many a chap would eagerly seek your hand in marriage."

Virtually ignoring my comment, seemingly lost in her own thoughts, she resumed, "I should hate to leave Overthwaite for I have come to love the place and I couldst not bear to forsake Lady Margaret even though I would dearly love to be wed. Besides, who is there for me?" *Not knowing what to say and feeling the last question had been rhetorical I remained silent.*

By now we had reached the shores of the beck and ahead of us could be heard the excited laughter and chatter of the boys. We rounded a bend to see Roland and Matthew busy building dams in an attempt to divert rivulets away from the general flow of the river, whilst Edwin was demonstrating to Thomas the technique needed to skim pebbles across the surface of the water. We called across to them and seated ourselves on two large boulders not far from the bank's edge. Tilting back my head I closed my eyes, pleased to feel a little warmth from the sun's rays. Soon Roland came running up to us and, seating himself between Jane and myself, took his knife out of its sheath and began to whittle a piece of wood washed up as debris against the improvised dam.

"Did you enjoy last night's performance, Roland?" I enquired.

"'Twas fair entertaining, though Edwin and I have seen the like before – two years ago ere our father died." I noticed that, although Edwin continued with his pastime, he seemed tense and alert as though straining to pick up every word of our conversation.

"Was that in London?"

"Aye, we were staying there over the Yuletide festivities. Course, 'twas a much grander affair than that of last even, and the celebrations lasted much longer."

I wondered whether this was childish exaggeration or whether in truth the boys had attended a much more formal affair. "London does everything more splendidly," I ventured.

"Indeed. I do miss the excitement of living there."

"I should hate it. All the noise and bustle," Jane shuddered at the imagined thought.

"Nay, Jane, thou wouldst enjoy it. For every day there is somewhere to go or else something to do. Didst not Anselm tell thee of his visit to the Abbey of Westminster whilst there on St. Andrew's Eve?" Without waiting for a reply he rushed on, "Hundreds of candles are burnt ..."

"One hundred candles, in fact," interrupted Edwin, "which are burnt from the eve to High Mass the following day."

"Have done, Edwin! Wilt thou always gainsay me?" exclaimed Roland, his feathers ruffled by his elder brother. Turning his back on Edwin he continued, "In addition all the bells of the Abbey are tolled throughout the day and holy services, which every noble must attend, are recited by the hour. 'Twas endowed by our ..."

"'Twas a chantry endowment by King Edward in honour of Queen Eleanor," stepped in Edwin cutting his brother short. A knowing look passed between the two and a pale shade of pink suffused Roland's cheeks. Lowering his head he began whittling ferociously, all conversation stilled for the time being.

"That really must have been a spectacle," I interjected, breaking the tense atmosphere. "I shall certainly ask Master Anselm to relate the whole experience to me." Winking at Jane I added, "Come Jane, my bones are becoming chilled. I feel it is time we returned."

Certainly the temperature had dropped, prompting a swift retreat to the castle. As we strode out I mused over what I had heard which supported my earlier suspicions. Something else intrigued me. During our earlier talks Lady Margaret had indicated Anselm and the boys were at Overthwaite due to a specific request from Lord Dacre but I had not seen any recognition between them during our stay at the castle. What was the truth of the matter, I wondered?

The rest of our visit was uneventful but abruptly cut short. We were due to remain until Epiphany; however, the celebrations had been taking their toll on Lady Margaret. Her husband, ever solicitous, had begun to worry and by New Year's Eve decided the best course of action would be to return to Overthwaite.

Although she was apprehensive at the thought of the return journey Lady Margaret certainly wished to be at home and so by mid morning our baggage was safely stowed and the party assembled in the courtyard ready for the off. After bidding farewell to our hosts and ensuring Lady Margaret was secure and comfortable in the litter (enhanced by more blankets from Lady Mabel) we left Dacre for our slow progress home. I was sad to leave for our stay had been both pleasant and educational. However, I was also relieved we had departed before Twelfth Night, as this would have been perilously close to 10th January – the date I had set in my mind to make my re-entry into the 21st century.

The travelling had taken even more out of Lady Margaret than had the Yuletide celebrations and upon our return she retired directly to bed. Consequently all festivities for the evening were low key and amounted to nothing more *than the usual communal meal hastily improvised by Mary in view of our premature return.*

The next day, being New Year's Day, the children giggled with excited anticipation, knowing presents were soon to be exchanged. Lady Margaret, although still weak, made an effort and allowed the boys into her chamber in order to receive their gifts. From the money I had received in payment from Sir Anthony I had managed to put together some small items to give to the family and to my surprise I received a beautiful comb from Lady Margaret which I knew I would treasure for the rest of my life. Whilst at Dacre, Anselm had promised he would furnish Matthew with two books which he had in his possession at Overthwaite. Upon the lads' return to the hall he produced both of the volumes.

"Here, Matthew, as I promised thee." He held out the books which Matthew eagerly accepted, wide eyed in anticipation. "They will serve thee well during thy time of education as squire at Dacre."

"Well lad, where are thy manners?" boomed Sir Anthony.

"Th...thank you, Master Anselm."

"Firstly we have the 'Book of Nurture' by Master John Russell. It will give thee invaluable instruction on seating arrangements – from the highest in the land to the lowest woman marrying above herself!" Matthew's eyes grew even wider as he thumbed through the pages. "The second is the 'Book of Carving' – another tome worth its weight in gold!" Taking the book from the boy Anselm quoted from its pages. "Here – instructions on how to splat a pike, fin a chub and unbrace a mallard!"

"Confound it, lad! We shall have to mind our words once thou art well versed in the language of carving. Thou wilt put us all to shame with thy new found knowledge!" Sir Anthony gave a knowing wink to Anselm.

Although Edwin and Roland had also received books from Anselm, Matthew's volumes were the ones which provided entertainment for the three boys for several days to come.

Things reverted to normal relatively quickly, with one exception. Over Christmas Simon had become betrothed to a young maid in the village. The couple had undergone a handfasting ceremony at which betrothal promises would have been performed before witnesses, accompanied by the clasping of hands. Margery was heartbroken. Although she was aware a matchmaker had been employed who had paired the couple some time previously, nevertheless she had still harboured hopes that the union would come to nothing. She went about her chores with an uncharacteristic muteness and no matter how hard I tried to comfort her with assurances that time healed, she was inconsolable. I felt, in the short term, I could do no more.

During those first few days of the New Year, one evening after we had retired, Jane came bursting into my room in an hysterical panic.

"Catherine, come quickly, Lady Margaret is bleeding."

I was out of bed and had pulled a shawl around my shoulders in a trice. In their chamber Sir Anthony was comforting his wife in an effort to keep her calm but the rush lights did indeed reveal blood on the blankets.

"Pray send Agnes to fetch the wise woman from the village. Bid her make haste, Catherine." His gaze held mine and I could read his thoughts. Not wanting to alarm his wife he was attempting to minimise the urgency in his voice. I ran from the room, bumping into Anselm on the threshold and after explaining the situation to him he volunteered to go on horseback for the wise woman in order to save valuable time.

"Dost thou know where she lives?" he enquired.

"No but Margery will."

We hurried to the bakehouse, I for hot water and Anselm for directions. Pushing open the door I stopped in my tracks, for kneeling on the stone floor was Margery; a strange monotonous chant was emanating from her lips. In her hands she held a straw effigy and as she waved it to-and-fro before the cresset lamp, a grotesque shadow danced on the whitewashed walls behind.

Anselm brushed past me and knocking the effigy to the floor shouted, "Hast thou taken leave of thy senses? What pagan act art thou practising girl?"

Margery seemed not to notice our presence and continued with her mutterings as though in a trance, "As the fire consumes the figure, Simon Jackson thou shalt wither. As the fire consumes the figure, Simon Jackson thou shalt wither." Over and over she intoned her macabre rhyme accompanied by a steady swaying motion; the atmosphere was magnetic.

Taking her by the shoulders Anselm shook her vigorously. Slowly, as the glazed look left her eyes, Margery emerged from her hypnotic state.

Anselm repeated his question, "What pagan act is this? Whatever possessed thee girl? Dost thou not know thou could be tried for witchcraft?" Seeing her start he continued, "Aye, and burnt for thy practices!"

Overcome by emotion Margery's shoulders dropped and as her sobs echoed around the walls, I could only pity the huddled creature slumped before us on the cold flagged floor.

I knelt down to comfort her and turning towards Anselm informed him quietly, "The knowledge of Simon's impending marriage has made her sick at heart, for she was greatly smitten with the lad." Anselm shook his head. Suspecting that matters of the heart were beyond him I added, "Time will heal, although she thinks not at the present."

"Had but the girl known what I know, then she would mind her ways. Why, eminent doctors have been charged with magic and necromancy, let alone young serving wenches!" I could see he was ill at ease as, turning towards Margery, he lectured, "One John Stacey was hanged at Tyburn not many a year past. The charges against him included assisting a lady to procure the death of her husband by the melting of a leaden image. Mark my words well, Margery – 'twas lucky thy spell casting was discovered by Mistress Phillips and myself and none other. Let this be an end to thy dabbling!"

I was impressed by his grave tone and from the look on Margery's face Anselm's words had struck terror into her. However, two things occurred to me. Firstly, I was amused at the example he had used: to compare Dr. John Stacey's crime to that of Margery was risible. He had conspired to effectuate the deaths of King Edward IV and the Prince of Wales – hardly on a par with Margery's straw effigy! Nevertheless, I felt sure Anselm had overplayed things in order to emphasise his point and dissuade Margery from repeating the exercise. Secondly, Anselm's knowledge of the case once again made me think that the vague statements he had made regarding his profession as a tutor were suspicious. The doubts I had experienced earlier came rushing back to my mind.

"Should Lady Margaret lose the babe by cause of thy actions 'twould be a sorry affair. Thou hast delayed matters, now I must make haste. The wise woman, where can she be found?" Anselm's words only served to make matters worse but between renewed sobs Margery did manage to provide the required directions to Aggie Bowman's.

After he had left I set the water to boil and chatted to Margery about her mistress's state in order to help her calm down.

"As soon as this is ready bring it straight to Lady Margaret's chamber. By then Master Anselm should have returned with Mistress Bowman and we can only pray she will be able to aid her ladyship." I turned to leave, hoping that by the time Margery arrived in the bedchamber she would be fully composed.

"She's brought all t' b...babes in t' village into t' w...world, so if Old Aggie can't do it then n...none can. I'll be up shortly but you g...go an' look after t' m...mistress." Some of her old self was returning; she would be fine.

Back in the bedchamber things were largely as I had left them and in no time at all Old Aggie came shuffling in. To a great extent she was as I had imagined her – a stereotyped wise woman or, dare I say it, a 'witch'. Although probably around my age, her leathery skin and wrinkled brow made her appear ten years older. In profile she resembled 'Punch', with a large hooked nose and prominent chin. Her long, grey hair was tucked under her tight fitting hood and gathered together in a knot at the nape of her neck. Divesting herself of her cloak she revealed a loose fitting kirtle over her homespun smock and the bibless apron that covered her other garments was spotlessly clean. Her dark brown eyes sparkled in the light and almost mirrored her manner which exuded hope and optimism.

"Get you gone! 'Tis no place for t' men-folk and tha good lady'll fret all t' less knowing th' art out of t' way with a good cup o' wine to cheer thee."

Notwithstanding their differing ranks, Sir Anthony acknowledged that for the time being Aggie was in charge and so took no offence at her peremptory manner. He left the chamber, pausing fleetingly in the doorway to cast a tender look in the direction of his wife.

With our help the old woman set to work vigorously and in a short space of time all was organised. Her patient had been cleaned thoroughly; the soiled blankets were removed and additional furs obtained for warmth; a small chest was placed at the end of the bed against which Lady Margaret rested her ankles in order to keep her legs raised; and Aggie had administered a dose of belladonna to try to prevent a miscarriage.

"Where be thy eagle stone, Lady M?" enquired Aggie.

"By cause of the Yuletide festivities I had forgot about it," she sounded tired and weak. "It troubled Sir Anthony that I wore one ere Matthew's birth – he fears the old ways are not always best – but in view of the bleeding I think it a good business. Thou thinks so too, Aggie?"

"Aye, I surely do! Men know nowt about these things. I'll trow that with t' stone an t' belladonna tha shalt come to full term and produce another healthy son, a brother for tha first born." She paused momentarily, furrowing her brow, "'As tha bin eatin' fish at Dacre? Tha knows it's not good for thee in thy condition."

"An' that Titiv... Tituvi..., whatever his name be, that Devil surely caused yer fright, m'lady," Margery ventured in a grave tone.

Ignoring these suggested causes of her present state, Lady Margaret addressed Jane, "Pray fetch the stone. 'Tis wrapped in blue velvet, in the casket inside yonder chest."

Jane hurried across the room and after rummaging for a few minutes, returned with a beautifully smooth, oval shaped *stone resembling an egg both in size and shape.* As she handed it to Aggie I heard a rattle and could only imagine it contained a pebble or similar object capable of producing such a sound. The old woman took the talisman over to the rush light and after warming its surface gently in the flame, rubbed the good luck piece between her palms whilst murmuring a strange invocation quietly to herself. Placing the stone into the hands of Lady Margaret and closing her own fingers around those of her ladyship she continued with her soft incantations for several minutes more. I glanced across at Margery, who was watching the proceedings with wide, staring eyes and could only think it provident that Anselm was absent.

Finally, taking hold of a strip of cloth Aggie bound the object securely to the upper arm of her patient. "Tek care that this remains 'til tha time is due and tha pains commence. Wi shall then place it below thy belly or else t' babe'll not come."

"Aye, I remember such from Matthew's birth," Lady Margaret was growing wearier by the minute and sensing this, Aggie made to leave.

"'Tis best tha sleeps. I'll return the morrow t' see thee."

Jane remained with her mistress whilst quietly the three of us withdrew from the chamber. Needless to say Sir Anthony was eager for a report on his wife and having assured him that, she hoped, all was well Aggie departed for the village.

Totally exhausted we dispersed to our chambers to salvage what was left of the night. As I collapsed into bed I felt not only physically but also mentally drained after the events of the evening. In the quiet of my room I should have loved to consider my misgivings about Anselm but my eyelids were leaden and sleep had overcome me almost before I had extinguished the light.

By Twelfth Night Lady Margaret had fully recovered and ventured downstairs for the first time. This pleased me particularly, in view of my imminent departure. Although she was still extremely careful, the bleeding had ceased on the day following Aggie's visit and her bed rest had been purely precautionary. She had felt the baby kicking and once again a proud smile was evident on Sir Anthony's face.

Upon our return to Overthwaite he had informed Simon and his bride to be that their exchange of wedding vows could take place at the hall, additionally offering to host the traditional feast normally held at the home of the bride. Now wishing to give thanks for Lady Margaret's safe recovery, Sir Anthony decided to expand on the celebrations and consequently all spare hands were directed to the kitchen to assist Mary with the food preparations for the evening. As luck would have it, mid afternoon a group of wandering minstrels arrived in the barmkin offering its services and the players were promptly hired to entertain at the conclusion of the meal. All was set.

The bride, groom and their families – attired in best clothes for the special occasion – arrived before dusk. The ceremony was straightforward and consisted of the boy and girl plighting their troth with a simple avowal. Although they had decided against exchanging their vows in church, as it was Epiphany and the village priest had been invited to the hall, once the exchange had taken place he gave his blessing and the feast commenced.

Although hardly on the scale of the food served at Dacre, Mary had excelled herself and with the limited provisions available had prepared a repast befitting the event. Throughout the meal and the remainder of the evening the minstrels played their lilting music to the delight of all present: even Margery failed to let the sight of Simon and his bride spoil the atmosphere for her.

Later it was time for the bedding ceremony: consummation of a marriage was considered extremely important and needed witnessing in order to be believed. The bride and groom set off for the village and their marriage bed followed by a group of adherents no doubt intent on providing a boisterous accompaniment to the marital initiation. I too decided to retire for the evening – with less than four days to go the anticipation had caused my stress levels to increase and a good night's rest should help to calm my nerves.

I lay in the darkness with sleep evading my fertile brain. Yet again I went over events past, trying to piece together the fragments of a puzzle I felt sure existed. Anselm's curious behaviour in Kendal; the snippets of his conversation with Sir Anthony before his urgent departure that same evening; slips of the tongue from Roland, and Edwin's immediate camouflage; details of the boys' past, always vague; the names Stacey and Colyngbourne ... suddenly it came to me.

Like the last piece of a jigsaw slotting into place the picture finally became clear. I was sure I was right and going through each part of the mystery I found my solution fitted perfectly. The names Edwin and Roland; their father dying of an apoplexy at Easter in 1483; their knowledge of ceremonial events in London; the many references to the safe keeping of the boys; and Roland's request to Anselm to convey a message to their uncle the Ki.... Their uncle the King – King Richard – Richard III!

My mind was reeling, could I be right? If so, history must be re-written, for here were Princes Edward and Richard still alive in January 1485 – some eighteen months after they were supposedly murdered by their wicked uncle, Richard. I could not sleep: my imagination knew no bounds. Time and again I searched my memory for more fragments of confirmation and each time they fitted to perfection. I was convinced I was right, but what could I do? And what was to happen to the two Princes? I would never know, for in three day's time I would be over five hundred years away........

I could hardly take in what I was reading. Could she possibly be right? Wondering what further revelations there might be, I hurried on.

...... My conclusions about the boys caused me to regard them in a totally new light. On one such occasion Richard – for I could now think of him with no other name – caught me looking at him in an unguarded moment.

"Art thou troubled, Mistress Phillips?"

"No R...Roland. My thoughts were far away. You are a good lad." Instantly he blushed and once again I reflected

how much I should miss him and all the residents of Overthwaite Hall whom I had come to regard with an abundance of affection – never before experienced in my solitary life. But miss them I must, for were I to stay there would always be the possibility of being forced to move on to the de Raisgills and my opening to the future would be lost forever. I dare not take the chance.

In November I had checked to ensure the route was still available. Consulting my watch I arrived by the old oak door before midnight and settled myself to wait with baited breath. The minutes ticked by for what seemed an eternity but at last two minutes past the hour arrived. I waited. Slowly the door opened and hastening towards it I viewed, to my delight, the familiar setting of Overthwaite Hall in the 21st century. Relief flooded through me and I slumped onto a nearby bench by the wall to enable my thundering heart to return to normal. A sound I remembered from six weeks earlier came unbidden to my ears as the door slid back into place with a powerful thud, echoing throughout the hall in an otherwise silent building. All was well.

In December I had been unable to check for we were at Dacre on the twenty first but now I felt confident nothing would bar my return and as the 10th January approached I knew I was ready for my journey.

At last the day dawned. With the exception of Anselm, I managed to bid my farewells to every member of the household in a covert, methodical fashion.

After much soul searching I had decided that, had I seen Anselm, I would confront him with my suspicions: what had I to lose? However, Margery had informed me he was out on business for Sir Anthony and because of this I had resigned myself to the fact that my theory would remain unproven.

I gathered together my meagre possessions, checked my watch to ensure I had my timings right and decided to take one last look in the boys' chamber before descending to the hall. The room, although empty, was redolent with their personalities. They were not the tidiest of lads and here and there lay a hairbrush, a piece of clothing. Idly I bent to pick up a discarded shirt of Edwin's. Although initially he had been the more reserved of the two, latterly there had grown an understanding between us. He was a boy, like any other, on the threshold of early manhood and if I was right in my assumptions he had recently undergone an enormous upheaval in his life. I hugged the shirt to me and could smell his scent – I would dearly, dearly miss him. On an impulse I hastily folded the item, pushing it into the sack with my other belongings and hurried from the room lest I should be discovered.

It was around 9.45 a.m. when I settled myself in the hall to await the appointed hour. Although I felt sure that, at that time of day, the hall would be deserted, I was still extremely tense. Suddenly the sound of a horse galloping into the barmkin drifted up to my ears. Looking through the window I found Anselm had returned and within a few minutes he had mounted the stairs and entered the hall by the door through which I should shortly be passing. I had much on my mind and presumably my distraction was evident.

"Prithee Mistress Phillips, is ought the matter? Thou looketh extremely pale." Walking towards the fire he placed a bundle of official looking papers on the table.

"No, no ... my thoughts were far, far away, but there is nothing wrong. I was just startled by your entrance. Margery informed me you were on business for Sir Anthony. I thought I might not see you."

"I should not have returned this early but the business was soon concluded."

My heart was pounding. I was aware time was slipping away. I decided it was now or never. "Master Anselm, I have something to say to you which I hope you will not take amiss."

His expression was one of ironic amusement as he knit his brows fleetingly in a look of concentration. "I cannot imagine thou saying ought that would be offensive. Pray continue."

By the main entrance, in a niche behind the arras, I had placed my scant possessions. Walking towards the door I now retrieved them, too preoccupied to consider whether or not my actions would appear unusual to Anselm. Placing the small bundle on the bench by the door I turned to face him and taking a deep breath I began. "Very shortly I shall be leaving here and you will not see me again." He made to interrupt but I raised my hand and continued, "Please, let me finish before you speak. During my time at Overthwaite I could not help but notice you have always been protective of the boys. As their uncle that is perfectly normal but there have been one or two instances when, how should I put it, things did not seem quite right." I proceeded to mention the details I had found odd. Now I had started I was finding it easier than I had feared. "I have spent much time contemplating these facts and have come to the conclusion that the boys are in fact Princes Edward and Richard, sons of the late King and that they are here under assumed identities, presumably for their own protection. I can only surmise events in November and your subsequent hurried departure for London were somehow connected to the safety of the lads."

 I paused in anticipation of a response from Anselm but he remained silent. His shoulders were tense and as he sat, clenched fist to his mouth, elbow supported by his other hand, I knew his mind was in turmoil wondering what actions he should now take to safeguard the boys in his care. Time was getting on. Surreptitiously I palmed my watch (safely in the pocket of my skirt) to see the fingers pointing to 10 o'clock exactly – only two minutes to go. I pressed on.

 "I am not aware from whom they are at risk but I can assure you I would never betray them to a soul – never let them come to any harm. During my stay here I have become extremely attached to them, for they are both dear, dear boys. And although you will not understand what I am about to say, where I am going nobody is capable of doing them harm. Were I able to explain, well, I fear you would think me mad. Suffice it to say, I assure you the boys' identities are safe in my hands."

 As to whether Anselm was about to comment I am unaware, for at that moment I heard a noise behind me and an icy blast of air gusted into the room wafting his papers to the floor. He bent to retrieve them. Turning, I could see the opening gradually widen as, with creaking hinges, the thick piece of oak swung slowly into the interior of the hall.

Moving swiftly towards the door I retrieved my possessions and turned to make a brief farewell. "Goodbye Master Anselm. Our paths shall not cross again."

I stepped through.

From behind I heard Anselm's voice and with dread in my heart turned to see him rushing towards me. "Mistress Phillips, wait. Pray let us talk on the matter."

I was horrified: already he was through the entrance and I knew time was of the essence. Placing my hands on his shoulders I tried frantically to push him back ... back through the doorjamb ... back to his own time. But he was surprisingly strong and remained firm, as though rooted to the spot. Taking hold of my upper arms he propelled me backwards ... further from the doorway ... further from his only means of return ... further into the unknown.

Distraught I shouted, "Please, Anselm, please go back ... now, or it will be too late!"

But as the words left my lips I knew that already it was too late and with a sinking feeling in the pit of my stomach I heard the all too familiar thud as the door slotted firmly into place. ... ...

CHAPTER EIGHT

My mind in a whirl, I paused to gather my thoughts. Catherine's tale had knocked me for six and a multitude of questions exploded like fireworks in my brain. Absentmindedly I picked up the remaining sheet of paper: I should finish her account before giving the matter any further attention. Her postscript extended to less than half a page.

...... Here I end my narrative. Anselm – or Adam (we thought it wiser to change his name to one that would attract less attention in such a small village community) will supply any missing details. His friendship and help during the final stages of my life have been invaluable: he is a kind and thoughtful person as I am sure by now you have appreciated. What he intends to do with his life I do not know: it had been his intention to return but my illness prevented him from so doing. Whatever his decision, he knows I wish him well.

All that is left for me to say is this: my time in the 1400s, through which I gained the friendship of Adam, has enriched an otherwise lonely life. Had I the chance to return, I should do so without a moment's hesitation.

I looked at the clock: 7.30 p.m. Tomorrow morning seemed a long way off and I decided my curiosity could wait no longer. I wanted answers to the many questions thrown up by my aunt's story. Adam must be quizzed tonight.

The squalls of the day had given way to a bitterly cold evening and donning warm outdoor clothing I set off for Adam's nearby cottage. As I approached I sensed a fluttering in my stomach. Was this from a physical attraction or due to the facts I had just learned about him? I paused at the knocker to compose myself. Suddenly the door swung open and Adam stood in front of me, an all-knowing look on his face.

"I heard the gate and was not surprised to see you in the porch light. Come in." He moved to one side and with an amused look added, "Perhaps my suggestion of tomorrow morning was a little optimistic!"

"Please, if it's not convenient … it's just that … well yes, you're right. After what I've just learned I couldn't have slept without at least seeing you in the flesh … just to make sure that it's all true. Not that I disbelieve Catherine but it's so much to take in …" My words were coming out in a jumble but he seemed to understand.

"Come. Let us sit and talk." He led the way into his tiny lounge where roughly hewn oak beams supported the low ceiling. The heat from the open fire provided welcome relief from the piercing cold outside and as I moved to warm myself I noticed, by the settee, a coffee table. On it lay cheese, bread, fruit, a bottle of red wine and two wineglasses.

"Was it that obvious I would call?"

"Human nature changes little over the centuries. Besides, it is not every day that you get the opportunity to converse with a man over 500 years old!" As I slumped into an old leather armchair I could see he was trying to make light of the matter. "Having gained such momentous knowledge I felt sure you would need some sustenance. Let me minister unto you before the questions begin. Wine? I surmise I shall certainly be in need of a glass to lubricate my vocal chords!"

I knew hardly where to begin but gradually over the next few hours the missing pieces of the puzzle slotted into place.

"Catherine was correct in her assumption. The boys were indeed the sons of Edward of York and Elizabeth Woodville and were not murdered by their uncle. I have been fascinated to read present day speculation on the motives and deeds of Richard of Gloucester. Allow me to present the truth and relate events as they actually unfolded. But first, perhaps I should begin by outlining my background and explaining my connection with the House of York." He took a deep breath, "I was born on 28th of October 1441 at Ludlow Castle. My father, Roger, was Master of the Horse to Richard, Duke of York …"

"As in Edward IV and Richard III's father?"

"Yes. Please do interrupt should I go too fast or should anything be unclear." I nodded. "My mother Elizabeth, had for many a year been Maid of Honour to the Duke's wife Cecily Neville ……" So Adam began and I listened with fascinated interest as his tale unfolded.

His childhood had been a happy one at the castle where he experienced a close relationship with his father; sadly he never knew his mother for she had died giving birth to him. Destined for the church, it was decided Adam should join the Brothers at Worcester Cathedral, then a Benedictine monastery, with his education being financed by a generous Duke of York. At the tender age of seven he entered the cloister school as a novice where his studies included Latin, logic and philosophy.

"Our master, Brother Adam, was an elderly monk who became my mentor – hence my 'pseudonym'." I smiled at this touch of sentimentality. "I had always been a bright, intelligent boy," it was stated as fact without any hint of boastfulness, "and I think initially he warmed to me because of my aptitude for learning. In retrospect, I realise he was a father figure to me. Never more so than when my own father died, fighting bravely for the Yorkist cause at the Battle of St. Albans." After all the years his voice still held a note of pride. "The cathedral possessed an excellent library and my nose was never out of a book. Consequently by the time I reached fourteen years of age I was considerably more learned than any of my fellow students. At that time it was the practice for each house to send a fixed quota of its members to university to study theology and canon law. So it was that I entered Gloucester College, Oxford with the intention of completing my education before taking holy orders. But it was not to be. Times were violent and for safety's sake Duke Richard had moved his two younger sons from Fotheringhay to Ludlow. As a boy I had always held a special place in the Duchess's heart – as had my mother – and she now requested that I leave Oxford and become tutor to their sons George and Richard. I was seventeen at the time and my life was to change from one of peaceful study to one of intense activity." Adam paused, deep in thought, and his face suffused with a tender smile, "Richard was a pleasure to teach. Such a serious lad but nonetheless he had an impish sense of humour and an engaging smile. Unlike his brother, who never mastered the art of laughing at himself – a self-centred boy always with an eye to feathering his own nest." Again he lapsed into silence, remembering times past. "Forgive me, but having learned of his tragic end, sometimes I find thoughts of Richard hard to bear."

"It seems odd listening to you talk about a King of whom I've read countless times over the years – a much maligned one at that!"

"Yes, he has certainly received an abundance of vilification. Not that Richard was an angel by any means but he was a product of his time and naturally acted in a way wholly foreign to the comprehension of modern man, but more of that later." Placing the tips of his fingers together he continued, "Now, where was I? Ah yes, the York household. It was at that time that I re-established contact with the eldest son, later to become Edward, the fourth of that name. We had known one another as lads, indeed we were close in age and as historians have portrayed correctly, he was a charming person and certainly had a way with him – especially with the ladies! Yes, although life was uncertain, those few months at Ludlow were good. Then Duke Richard fled to Ireland and we were left to fend for ourselves." A frown creased his brow as he strove to relive those unpredictable days. "Initially we were placed in the charge of the Duchess of Buckingham and the following year moved to the household of Thomas Bourchier, the Archbishop of Canterbury." I pinched myself, hardly able to take in all I was hearing. "But by December Duke Richard had been slain at the Battle of Wakefield and we knew we had cause to flee. Duchess Cecily, the two boys and I took ship bound for the Low Countries where we remained as guests of the Court of Burgundy until news of Edward's victory reached our ears in the April. By then we were at Utrecht and soon set sail for England." He paused to lubricate his throat with some wine.

"How alarming life must have been. Why, you were hardly much more than a boy yourself but the things you must have gone through ......" I shook my head in wonder.

"Life was precarious in those days, especially in royal circles. Cecily Neville, however, was a redoubtable lady and not one to be taken lightly. We were as safe in her hands as we would have been, should Edward himself have been protecting us. But I fear I provide too much detail ..."

"Not at all, I'm finding it absolutely fascinating."

"Nevertheless I must press on or we shall still be here at first light!" Gathering his thoughts he continued, "Following Edward's coronation it was decided that Richard's further education and training should be conducted in the Warwick household at Middleham. Knowing that we had an affinity towards one another, his mother suggested I accompany him and so it was that I assisted the Master of the Henchmen with the language side of Richard's learning."

"Master of the Henchmen, is that something to do with the sons of the aristocracy being boarded out?" I had a vague recollection at the back of my mind.

"Yes. They were known as henchmen and the Master was in charge of indoctrinating them into the arts of knightly conduct – jousting, hawking and the like. Additionally they learned to dance and play music and, of course, it was essential their studies should not fall behind. It was in this respect that I continued as tutor to Richard and indeed to some of his contemporaries – Francis Lovell and Robert Percy to name but two. By the spring of '65 Richard rejoined his brother at Court and it was at that time Edward decided my services as tutor were no longer required. He was in need of a scribe and, although I had little say in the matter, the change of position suited me well enough."

Over the next five years his meetings with Richard, Duke of Gloucester were minimal as the latter spread his time between Middleham, York, Sudeley and London. Adam spent this time in the Edward's employ but during 1470 his life was to take a distinct change of course.

"Warwick had been disaffected for one or two years, transferring his loyalties to George, Duke of Clarence in an attempt to become 'Kingmaker' for a second time. By the end of the year things were coming to a head. Edward had journeyed to Doncaster at the time and it was only by happenstance that he was not taken prisoner. We managed to flee and our small party took ship – no, not ship, Edward commandeered a small fleet of fishing boats – and we sailed from Lynn to Burgundy. His sister Margaret was wed to the Duke. Indeed it was through her efforts that Clarence spurned Warwick and as a result returned to Edward's favour. By April we were back in London, to the delight of its inhabitants, and within two months Warwick had been slain at Barnet dealing a body blow to the aspirations of the House of Lancaster. The end of their challenge came when – through Richard's shrewd leadership – Margaret, Henry VI's Queen, was defeated at Tewkesbury."

"Did Edward have Henry VI murdered?"

"Heartless though it may sound to have had such a saintly man killed, the answer is yes. Edward took no pleasure in the decision, but he had no choice. Such a pious man would always attract support and Edward was keen to bring peace to the country after many years of warring. Besides, as I mentioned earlier, one cannot apply present day standards to events of yore. Edward was a strong King and well liked by the populace."

"And the suggestion that Richard carried out the deed is just Tudor spin?"

"Spin?"

"Sorry! Er, a fabrication, a Tudor invention?"

"Undoubtedly! Why, to suggest that Henry was put to death by the hand of any member of the royal family is absurd," he tossed his head in contemptible anger. "Edward had many a lackey employed for such an enterprise!"

I sat in silence, twisting the stem of my wineglass between thumb and forefinger.

"Forgive me." Breathing deeply, Adam took time in subduing his momentary anger. "There is little to say of the following years. I continued my secretarial duties to Edward, Richard married Anne ..."

"Did they love each other?"

"Why do women always set such store by romance?" He smiled lopsidedly, "I cannot say for sure. Richard's time was taken here in the north, at Middleham, Sheriff Hutton and Penrith, and I saw little of him. They certainly had affection for one another but I would surmise Anne's feelings were stronger than those of Richard – he brought some steadfastness into her hitherto unsettled life." He paused. "So to the events of 1483, following the death of Edward in the April." Taking a sliver of cheese he continued, "I could speak at length on affairs during those years preceding his death– the furtherance of the Woodville fortunes, Edward's inability to refuse his wife's entreaties, the death of Clarence – but it would add little to the various theories propounded, the majority of which come perilously close to the truth. Suffice it to say Richard had naught to do with the murder of his brother. On the contrary, when Clarence was confined to the Tower Richard was again on business in the north and upon his return he remonstrated with Edward, pleading on Clarence's behalf – I was present at the meeting and know it to be so. Richard held the Woodvilles responsible for manipulating Edward into killing his brother, hence his subsequent withdrawal to the north and minimal visits to Court. However, unbeknownst to Richard a further consideration drove Edward to sentence Clarence to death, but I shall touch on that later." I reached for my wine, feeling we were now about to get down to the real nitty-gritty of the tale and, curling my legs beneath me, settled back in the corner of the sofa to listen.

"Let me say at the outset I found Edward's queen a difficult woman with whom to communicate. She was a dispassionate, artful woman and her Woodville relations certainly benefited from her position and the influence she held over her husband. Having said such, I assure you I will not allow these prejudices to colour my judgement in relating the incidents that followed." Closing his eyes he marshalled his thoughts before continuing, "Edward had ever been a shrewd leader and even on his deathbed anticipated the rancour that would follow. To this end he charged not his queen but Richard with the welfare of his son, naming his brother Protector during Prince Edward's minority."

"Were you there when he died?"

"Yes. As scribe I was entrusted with the recording of his last wishes and it was evident he feared repercussions from the nobility with regard to the powers he had invested in his wife's kin. At the time Richard was again on business in the north and the Woodvilles were of the opinion time was of the essence. Knowing that Richard held them answerable for the death of Clarence they were in mortal dread of the consequences should he be allowed to govern alone. To have Edward crowned was their uppermost intent and without reference to Richard the Queen's brother, Earl Rivers, set out with an army of two thousand men intent on escorting the boy to London from Ludlow. Edward had been created Prince of Wales at the age of six months in 1471 and had, with his council, lived in Ludlow permanently since 1472 representing the King. On a previous occasion I had had cause to travel to Ludlow and consequently had become acquainted with Edward. The Queen decided an additional familiar face would help to ease any tensions her son might be feeling at the time – hardly surprising in view of the size of Rivers's retinue – and decreed that I should accompany the party."

"So you were actually present when all this took place?" I shook my head in amazement at all I was hearing.

Aware that my question was rhetorical Adam continued, "Unbeknownst to the Queen, however, Lord Hastings had been corresponding regularly with Richard to keep him informed of developments."

"Am I right in saying the Queen had no time for Hastings?" Although quite well read on these events I obviously wished to hear a first hand account.

"None whatsoever. She had always viewed him as a lecherous individual and thought him a bad influence on her husband – the two were ever comrades on their bouts of drinking and sexual philandering. Likewise Hastings had no love of the Woodvilles. He urged Richard to arm himself and return to the capital ahead of Rivers. But that was not Richard's style – he did not wish such an early head to head clash. Arranging to meet Edward and Rivers at Northampton on 29th April he arrived with an escort of a mere six hundred men. Rivers, duty bound to agree to the meeting, still hoped to out-manoeuvre Richard. He lodged Edward at Stony Stratford, twelve miles nearer to London, with the intention of making a pre-dawn start the next morning. Not only would this enable their party to arrive at the capital prior to Richard and his men but it would also guarantee the furtherance of Woodville control over Edward."

"Didn't he conjure up an excuse, saying Northampton was too small?" I queried.

"Indeed, although he knew it to be a feeble one and that Richard would not be deceived. Nevertheless he felt obliged to maintain the bluff and in order to allay Richard's suspicions he decided to journey back to Northampton and extend to him his Edward's salutations. Rivers, though, had grave misgivings where Richard was concerned, as he knew him to be a cunning adversary. He was of the opinion that he may be detained and to that end I was to accompany him. Should his suspicions prove correct, I was charged with returning to Stony Stratford to ensure Edward's immediate safe conduct to London."

Suddenly the atmosphere was shattered by a loud crack. This heralded a flying spark which traced a perfect arc from the open fire to the worn, rectangular hearthrug.

Rising from his seat Adam rubbed the glowing spot absentmindedly with the tip of his shoe. I could see he was still at the hostelry in Northampton. "Rivers was right to be wary. Richard had the measure of the man and requested his company for the evening in order that they might sup together.

To refuse would have aroused suspicion and so, having no option, Rivers assumed a brave face and accepted." Reaching for the poker, he manoeuvred the offending log to one side, making room for a second: I presumed we were in for a long night! "It was good to see Richard again – there had been scant opportunity over the preceding five years – but I noticed immediately that his new found authority as Lieutenant of the North had hardened him. Inevitably so, one might say." He sighed. "Later the Duke of Buckingham joined the party – another royal personage to detest Elizabeth Woodville by cause of his forced marriage to the Queen's younger sister." Almost to himself he added, "Somehow I could not find it in my heart to trust Buckingham. He professed to be Richard's man but was a slippery character. Charming on the face of it but I suspect his real motives were always with an eye to accepting the Crown should it be offered to him and I believe Richard came to the same conclusion in time. But I digress, where was I?"

"Buckingham had arrived in Northampton."

He went on to explain that the evening had passed in a tense atmosphere at the end of which Richard had invited Rivers to stay the night in order that they might jointly accompany Edward in the morning. Once again Rivers was aware he dare not refuse and upon retiring had reminded Adam of his mission. "Had I intended to carry out his wishes I should not have been able to do so, for Richard had ordered none should be allowed to leave the town. Needless to say, I had ever been of a mind to apprise Richard of the situation and did so at the first opportunity." Again he added almost as an aside, "I have often mused on Elizabeth Woodville's choice of myself as escort to Edward for she knew of my previous connection to Richard. I can only assume exaggerated self importance blinded her to another's loyalties." After a slight pause his eyes focused once more on mine. "There followed a long night of discussion between Richard and his counsellors during which all manner of Woodville skulduggery was advanced by an extremely convincing Buckingham." His dislike of the man was plain. "Richard's suspicions of Rivers were strengthened by Buckingham's case and at dawn he had the Earl arrested.

He was accused of attempting to establish the Woodvilles as true rulers of the land, as Edward would be a mere pawn in their hands. Richard declared that the country had no wish to be governed by Elizabeth and her kin, telling Rivers that Edward would now be supported by an independent council, as his father had intended." Reaching for the grapes he returned to his tale. "Richard was anxious that Edward should not be too distressed upon learning the fate of his uncle Rivers. He decided that I should accompany Edward and Buckingham to Stony Stratford, feeling my presence would be a measure of reassurance to Edward who knew that I was in his mother's confidence. The meeting was a difficult one. Richard was somewhat a stranger to Edward whereas Rivers had been his governor and on close terms with him all his life. I must say Richard's handling of the situation was not particularly diplomatic. In his usual forthright style he proceeded to denigrate the Woodvilles, blaming them for the death of Edward's father by their abetment of his vices. The young lad was naturally confused. His changing circumstances were hard enough to come to terms with at the age of twelve let alone this character assassination of his mother's family!" Moved by the memory he shook his head slowly as he spoke. "Why, his household was made up of his mother's relations. Lord Lyle, her brother-in-law was master of horse, two of her brothers were Edward's councillors, yet another her chaplain and Edward's half brother, Richard Grey, was Comptroller of the Prince's household. I am glad I was there for I feel the lad took some comfort from my presence. Whatever his thoughts it changed naught, for Richard had Grey and Sir Thomas Vaughan swiftly arrested and removed to Middleham and Pontefract."

"Who was Vaughan?" I queried.

"Forgive me – he was the lad's chamberlain."

I nodded, peeling off my cardigan as the heat from the fire was becoming intense. There was another distinct crack, this time from the movement of the beams but Adam, intent on his narrative, appeared not to notice. "We were soon on our way to London where things were in a state of chaos, despite Hastings's attempt to assuage the nobles who were unsure of

Richard's motives. Queen Elizabeth and her six children had taken sanctuary in the Abbey at Westminster and were joined later by her son Dorset who had unsuccessfully tried to raise a force to capture Edward. Nevertheless much outward support existed still for Richard – he had not lied when he told Rivers that the country had no love of the Woodvilles – and this was strengthened upon our arrival at the capital by his request to the nobility to swear allegiance to Edward." Adam turned to face me, intent on conveying his next words. "Richard was no scheming villain. At that time he had every intention of seeing Edward crowned and the date was set for 24th June."

"Was Edward in the Tower throughout this time?"

"Initially he resided at the Bishop of London's Palace but was later moved to the more capacious royal apartments in the White tower on Buckingham's recommendation. But he was no prisoner. Indeed he was visited by the likes of Hastings and his mistress Jane Shore, both of whom Edward found amusing. Hastings, however, was growing bitter and increasingly resentful of Buckingham's closeness to Richard. You must remember that with many, loyalty was merely a means of obtaining favour and lining one's pockets. Hastings felt Buckingham had been excessively rewarded for his support whereas *he* had received all but nothing. So it was that he changed allegiance and Richard was duly informed of Hastings's treachery by their mutual acquaintance William Catesby." Adam paused for another drink. "Jane Shore was mistress not only to Hastings but also Dorset, who by now had escaped from sanctuary and was again attempting to raise an army. She had become a regular caller on the Queen and was acting as go-between. Richard had allowed this, thinking it no threat but when Hastings himself visited Elizabeth Woodville in the Abbey and gave promise of his support to Dorset's cause, Richard knew he must act before events got out of hand and developed into war. I was present on the morning of 13th June and can attest to his state of mind. He was devastated to think such a close friend could be duplicitous."

I had read that Richard was disposed to be too credulous of his friends; after all, his motto was 'Loyalty binds me'.

Adam continued, "In my presence he worked himself up into an angry frame of mind, despite my urgent pleas for moderation and reflection. This anger resulted in him confronting Hastings at a meeting, having him arrested and taken away to be beheaded immediately. It was all over in a trice."

"Without even a trial?" I was amazed.

"You must remember that justice was an entirely different concept then, to present day standards. Rightly or wrongly, Richard was certain of his facts and dared not risk the vagaries of a court of law where many were too easily bribed. Nevertheless he was sick at heart over his actions and gave vent to his feelings of betrayal by having Morton, Stanley and Rotherham arrested at the same time. Later, however, he realised that Stanley and Rotherham were no threat and released them, but retained Morton who had ever been a shrewd, devious opponent." He rose from the chair and stretching his legs paced the short distance between front and back wall. "Three days after the death of Hastings a Council meeting was called to discuss, amongst other items, details of Edward's coronation. His younger brother still resided in the Abbey and Richard wished him to attend the ceremony in order to give a public display of unanimity. Initially Elizabeth refused. This, I feel, arose from her distrust of Richard but it was finally Archbishop Bourchier who convinced her that she had no need for concern. Prince Richard became a companion for Edward although at that time they were hardly acquainted with one another. It was a mere two days later that Richard received a note from Robert Stillington, the Bishop of Bath and Wells, saying he had urgent news to impart." He paused to take another drink of his wine.

"Wasn't that supposedly when Richard was told about Edward IV's previous marriage?"

"Oh, there is no question about it. I can testify to its authenticity, for I was present at the meeting."

CHAPTER NINE

A frisson of excitement ran through my body as his words took my breath away. I was well aware of the argument existing between the supporters of Richard III and the historians who viewed him as a vile usurper: had the meeting ever taken place? Yet here I was, learning of the events from a person who had actually been present at the interview. The ensuing silence was broken only by the haunting hoot of an owl and an echo-like response from its mate.

"Stillington's words were a complete surprise to Richard, although I must say he found them easily believable in view of Edward's reputation with the fair sex. The Bishop advised him that, as a youth, Edward had formed an attachment to Lady Eleanor Butler. She was a widow, several years older than Edward and, presumably, reluctant to share his bed without some form of commitment from her suitor. Stillington had acted as go-between and was indeed witness to their troth-plighting."

"Oh yes, '… and thereto I plight thee my troth …'" I dredged the phrase from the back of my mind. "I presume it was binding?"

"Totally and also legally. Provided the vows were exchanged in front of a witness no need existed for a formal ceremony in church. And so it became immediately evident that this contract nullified Edward's subsequent marriage to Elizabeth Woodville, ergo their children were bastards."

"Why on earth had Stillington kept quiet about it for so long?" I queried.

"The very question put to him by Richard once his initial anger at his brother's folly had cooled. The Bishop explained that some years earlier, in an unguarded moment, he had mentioned the betrothal to Clarence. Richard realised immediately the implication of the comment." Leaning towards me he explained, "Let me go back to the time immediately preceding the death of Clarence. His wife had recently died in childbirth and he was on the lookout for a rich heiress to provide funds to swell his coffers. Mary of Burgundy was one such lady and her mother, being sister to both Edward and Clarence, had petitioned the King on behalf of her younger brother. Edward, however, was not inclined towards the match for the house of Burgundy had a legitimate claim to the throne of England and with increased riches once again Clarence might feel disposed to challenge Edward for the Crown. The King, however, proceeded to inflame Clarence's anger all the more by promoting Anthony Rivers as a contender for the hand of Mary. Clarence had already begun spreading the old rumours of Edward's illegitimacy and knowing Clarence as he did, Richard could well imagine that his brother had further taunted Edward with his knowledge of his marriage contract to Eleanor Butler. To suffer gossip of his own bastardy was one thing, besides none believed his mother to be guilty of such an act. But the latter accusation was entirely different, particularly when a witness could be produced. Richard now suspected this knowledge was the real reason for the haste with which Clarence had been executed and his suspicions were strengthened by the knowledge of Stillington's imprisonment by Edward immediately after Clarence's death. The Bishop informed us of his dread, how he had feared he would be the next to die. But Edward had a capricious nature – he had oft forgiven Clarence in the past – and when the waters had settled he released Stillington on the strict understanding that his lips must remain sealed at all costs. Sadly Clarence had not received the same stay of execution, for he had overstepped the mark once too often. So, to answer your question as to why Stillington had remained silent for so long – once again it was fear. Having escaped death once he was loath to tempt providence a second time and Richard did have a reputation for being quick to anger. However, being a man of God he had battled with his conscience and decided he could not let the coronation go ahead without first revealing the secret of Edward's past. Thereafter it would be Richard's decision."

"How *did* he react to the Bishop's revelation?"

"With his usual level-headedness he took three days to mull things over during which time he was constantly in discussion with his chief advisers Ratcliffe, Lovell, Catesby and of course, Buckingham. The latter, in his usual impetuous manner, urged Richard to take the crown quickly and disregard any consequences. Thankfully he received more balanced counselling from the others but when all was said and done he had no choice other than the one he made."

"And Clarence's children, presumably they weren't eligible because of their father's crimes?"

"Precisely, under Clarence's attainder his progeny forfeited all rights to succeed to the Crown. Richard was a pious man with a strong sense of virtue and morality – indeed he had always abhorred the late King's lascivious nature. Difficult though the decision was, he knew his duty. I think he truly believed that once the truth was out, people would accept the facts, acknowledge him as the rightful heir to the throne and welcome a stable reign under him in contrast to a volatile one which Edward's minority would inevitably bring. I fear he was a little naïve. His adversaries were merely 'holding their horses'. The news was made known by Dr. Shaa, the Lord Mayor's brother, in his Sunday sermon from St. Paul's Cross and reiterated by Buckingham two days later at the Guildhall. Thereafter the die was cast and within a few days Richard had agreed to Parliament's petition to accept the Crown. It was on that day that Earl Rivers, Lord Grey and Sir Thomas Vaughan were executed and by these actions Richard hoped to effect an end to any further threat from the Woodvilles." Adam paused and I could see something was troubling him. "He had always had a genuine belief that the Queen and her family posed a real threat to his life and, on balance, I must say I would not have been surprised if it were so. Nevertheless, on occasion I had cause to wonder whether he was developing a taste for his new found power." He was silent for a moment. "I am now aware that Tudor historians accuse him of many crimes and although for the most part they are totally unfounded, in this instance I fear there was more than a grain of truth."

Placing his palms together he interlocked his fingers, still deep in thought. I looked across at him, once again taking in his features and noticed two deep furrows forming between his eyebrows as he strove to rationalise these perplexing thoughts.

Attempting to lighten matters I asked, "Did you attend his coronation?"

"Yes, I did." The moment had passed and a smile transformed his face as he resumed his tale. "It was a lavish affair held at the Abbey on the 6th July, ironically, utilising many of the arrangements already in place for the coronation of young Edward. Two weeks later, eager to be seen by the populace, Richard embarked on a tour of his kingdom. By the end of August we had reached Pontefract and …"

"You accompanied him?"

He nodded, "Richard had decided that I should assist with the education of his son and as the boy was to be invested as Prince of Wales in the September at York, I joined the King on his progress north. I met Ned for the first time at Pontefract. He was a frail, shy boy with a touch of his father's gravity in spite of his tender years. But he had endearing qualities and I warmed to him instantly. Indeed, I should have enjoyed instructing him but it was not to be. Cautious as ever, Richard deemed it essential to be kept abreast of events in the capital and achieved this by means of regular couriers from the south. By the time Anne and Ned departed for Middleham, news had begun to filter through that Buckingham was becoming disenchanted with his lot and feeling that I might be needed for more urgent duties, I remained with Richard instead of accompanying them. By 11th October we had reached Lincoln and it was there that he received unequivocal reports of Buckingham's defection for he had joined forces with the Woodvilles and the supporters of Henry Tudor." Replenishing our wineglasses he continued, "After his coronation Richard had had his nephews moved to the Garden Tower where the constable, Sir Robert Brackenbury, could better keep an eye on them. His motive was twofold. He feared that in his absence the Woodvilles may attempt to abduct the boys and additionally he was anxious for their safety. Abduction would be unhealthy for the harmony of the kingdom and, despite all that has been said, Richard did not wish any harm to befall his nephews."

"Whom did he suspect might harm them?" I queried.

"An interesting question, for several possibilities exist. Buckingham himself had a legitimate claim to the throne but lacked supporters and at that time Richard had no cause to suspect his betrayal. Henry Tudor laid a tenuous claim being of bastard stock through both lines of his family but inevitably there would always be supporters of the House of Lancaster to rally to his cause. Lastly there were the Woodvilles who, although no direct threat to the boys, might inadvertently bring about their downfall through an alliance with either of the former. To take them one by one, for Buckingham's claim to succeed Richard must be a usurper but this then made the boys legitimate and a stumbling block to Buckingham's own claim – ergo they must be eliminated. Likewise with Henry Tudor, who further strengthened his Yorkist support by proposing a marriage to one of the daughters of Elizabeth Woodville. Indeed it was even more so in his interest to deny the existence of the troth-plighting in view of this suggested union, or else an annulment of the decree would be necessary. In either event, the boys' demise would be requisite. Now to the Woodvilles and here you must remember that, with Richard's insistence on keeping the boys in the Tower, they had not been seen for several months. Coupled with this was the rumour regarding their murder."

"Was there any way of knowing where the rumour came from?"

"No definitive way but it was suspected that the supporters of Henry Tudor were behind it. Consequently Elizabeth Woodville, thinking her sons dead, decided to pledge her support by placing her remaining power and influence behind Henry Tudor but only on the proviso that he marry her daughter Elizabeth. She was such a loving mother that, if our report was correct, she stipulated should any mishap befall her eldest daughter the marriage must still take place but to her second daughter, Cecily!" his tone was scathing as he uttered the last sentence. "As I have said, by giving either Buckingham or Tudor their allegiance, the Woodvilles were signing the lads' death warrants. Upon hearing of the conspiracy between all three parties, Richard knew he must act fast and ensure the boys' total safety by removing them from London where they may have been seen by prying eyes. Ironically, because the boys were not seen, this was to fuel the fire where rumours of their deaths were concerned but Richard decided it was of no consequence compared to their safety. So it was that I was despatched from Lincoln with the express purpose of collecting Edward and Richard and transporting them north."

"And that's where the Rutherfords came in?"

"Precisely. Did Catherine explain the connection between Richard and Sir Anthony?"

I shook my head, "No. She merely referred to Sir Anthony as being a supporter of King Richard but gave no further details."

"Richard saved his life at the Battle of Tewkesbury so it is not surprising that henceforth Sir Anthony should give Richard his undying loyalty. Knowing this, Richard decided it was an ideal place for the boys to remain until a long-term solution could be found – at that time he had more urgent business pressing. Sir Anthony was the only person to know of their true identities, even his wife believed they were staying at the behest of the Rutherford liege Lord, Humphrey Dacre, a totally fabricated tale. It was an ideal solution. You can imagine that this spot was certainly remote five hundred years ago," he gave a wry chortle. "The only problem remaining was the acquiescence of the boys to the venture. Although I must say Richard was of the opinion that they would go, irrespective of their feelings! Perhaps I was a little more tactful in the way I explained things to them. Young Richard was not the problem. He was a happy, carefree lad who, although he little knew his brother, quickly struck up a friendship with Edward and viewed their journey to the north as a favourable turn of events – particularly after his confinement in sanctuary and at the Tower. To persuade Edward, on the other hand, was another matter."

The dying embers shifted in the grate making me aware a chill was enveloping the room. I pulled my cardigan around my shoulders.

"Forgive me. I am far from the perfect host!" Rising effortlessly from his seat, Adam moved to the fireplace and reaching into the basket removed a log and placed it on the glowing remains. "Let us hope we are not too late for the fire to rekindle." Obviously he had still some way to go in his tale! "In the meantime, have some more wine to warm you. Now … ah yes, Edward. Some viewed him as a precocious child. Not surprisingly, in view of the upbringing he had received at the hands of the Woodvilles! His days revolved around his devotions, lessons and food. Why, none was allowed to sit at table with him unless Rivers had given his specific approval of worthiness so to do! He grew up expecting to take the throne, so it is hardly surprising that when an uncle whom he hardly knew plucked him from familiar surroundings, executed his intimate relations and took the crown for himself, he harboured feelings of hostility. Richard had many faults, insensitivity being one of them. When I broached the subject he would have none of it, saying it was a hard world and the lad must learn to live with it. I spent many an hour with Edward, explaining matters – the pre-contract of his father to Eleanor Butler being but one – reasoning with him and attempting to make him see there really was no course other than the one upon which he was about to embark."

"Did he accept it?" I enquired.

"Gradually – eventually – over the course of the next twelve months, yes. I convinced him that Stillington's revelations were true and consequently Edward could never hope to attain the throne. But although he accepted that the concealment was solely to safeguard their existence, he had no time for his uncle." He paused. "It was of no import, for when last I saw Edward he had not set eyes on Richard for eighteen months and from what I have now learnt, well, I know not what to think of the lads' fates." He was downcast as he mulled over the various unsavoury possibilities.

"You had no contact then with King Richard prior to Catherine's arrival?"

"None whatsoever. News eventually filtered through of Buckingham's abortive challenge and subsequent execution. We also learnt of Henry Tudor's unsuccessful attempt to launch an attack, and of the release by Elizabeth Woodville of her daughters from sanctuary."

"Why did she allow them to leave if she believed Richard guilty of the murder of her sons?" I was intrigued to hear his views on the matter.

"Elizabeth was a wily creature. It suited her cause well to act the wronged woman and although she had no love for Richard she knew him to be a pious individual. Likewise she had little regard for Buckingham for she was aware of his treatment of her sister. Whether she believed Richard guilty of the crime or whether she suspected the followers of Henry Tudor or his mother Margaret Beaufort of duplicity, I know not."

"But surely she wouldn't have let her daughter marry Henry Tudor if she thought he was responsible for her sons' deaths?" I was amazed.

"As I have said, she was a shrewd individual. To bemoan the fate of the Princes was necessary for outward appearances but I imagine her future as mother of the Queen was of greater import to her. Believe me Emma, she was not an honourable woman!" Once again his loathing was evident but bringing himself back to the task he continued, "The next news to reach our ears was of the tragic death of Richard's son, Ned. It occurred a mere twelve months after the demise of King Edward – to the day. From the accounts we heard, Richard and Anne were devastated, near mad with grief. The Queen took to her bed and the King refused to see a sole for nigh on a week. Although tales have a habit of growing with the telling, my knowledge of the love and devotion bestowed on Ned by his parents made me fear the reports were true." He was silent for a moment, head bowed, reliving the imagined heartache of the royal couple. "During the summer Richard appointed his nephew John de la Pole as his successor and ..."

"Clarence's son?"

"No. Clarence's son Edward, Earl of Warwick, was ... how should I say ... slow to learn, simple-witted? He could not have been made heir apparent. John de la Pole, Earl of Lincoln, was the son of Richard's sister Elizabeth. Of course the possibility did exist that Anne would conceive again but in view of her barren state for the previous eight years I do not imagine Richard held out much hope in that quarter. This brings us to the episode on the day of the fair in Kendal. The person I espied was a man named William Colyngbourne, a scoundrel if ever I knew one, whose master was Lord Thomas Stanley, husband to Margaret Beaufort," he raised his eyebrows, querying whether my knowledge covered the association to Henry Tudor. I nodded in confirmation. "Stanley was a shrewd individual and although his support of Richard appeared steadfast on the surface, on occasion I found myself wondering. I am convinced that his primary concern was in looking after his own interests, and I assure you I do not make that remark with the knowledge of hindsight. Although he and his wife were, hardly close, Lady Margaret was an indomitable woman and Stanley found her difficult to control. She was under attainder and thereby forbidden to communicate with her son but Richard surmised that she was using both her own and, presumably without his knowledge, her husband's servants to convey messages to-and-fro England and France."

"So it *was* Richard you visited when you left Overthwaite after the fair?"

"Correct. Stanley held estates in the north and it would have provided a convenient cover for Colyngbourne to be travelling under that pretext. Whether or not he was on genuine business for his master I do not know but I decided to take no chances. Should knowledge of the boys' whereabouts reach the wrong ears, well, I am sure you can guess the consequences. Colyngbourne knew me well for he had previously been a member of Cecily Neville's household and although I hoped he had noticed neither the lads nor myself in Kendal, I was not totally sure. It was a long and hard journey to Court at that time of year but I was driven on by my sense of urgency to inform Richard. Upon my arrival I found that Colyngbourne *had* been one of the servants passing information to Henry Tudor and Richard desired his apprehension. He was also unaware as to whether any knowledge of the boys' removal from the Tower had leaked out, for rumours of their death were still rife at that time, but the swift arrest of Colyngbourne was necessary on both counts. Richard viewed his treason all the more personally because of the prior connection with his mother's household. In addition, the man was the author of a most insolent rhyme about the King and his chief advisers."

"Oh ... was that the one about a rat, or a dog or something?"

"'The Cat, the Rat and Lovell our dog, Rulen all England under an Hog'. The words were nailed to the door of St. Paul's during the summer of that year. Richard was incensed and redoubled his efforts to apprehend Colyngbourne. Before I departed for Overthwaite he had been arrested and was soon to suffer a traitor's death. As to whether the man knew of, or was able to pass on, details of the lads' location, well, we shall never know. But this I do know, if they have been killed their deaths can be laid at the door of only one man and he is Henry Tudor."

Rising from his seat Adam moved to the window where he paused to gaze into the black abyss beyond and, obviously tense, massaged the knotted muscles at the base of his neck. From Catherine's account it was evident he had formed a deep attachment to Edward and Richard and I suspected he was struggling to control his emotions. I remained silent fearing any intended words of comfort simply might appear empty or trite.

The silence lengthened until, sighing, he resumed his tale. "Catherine correctly guessed the identities of the boys' and had it not been for her revelation of that fact I should not have made to follow her and would have remained in my own time where I could protect them. But I do not blame her," he added quickly and turning to face me continued, "for she urged me not to follow, to remain in the hall. Had I done so ... who knows? Perchance I could have saved them."

"Perhaps they remained at Overthwaite and just lived out their lives there," I suggested.

"Perhaps – I shall soon know for certain."

I had dreaded the possibility and now my fears were confirmed. I strove to keep the emotion from my voice, "You intend to return?"

"But of course. I had determined to return the month following my 'arrival' but with the immediate onset of your aunt's illness I decided to postpone my departure. I could not have deserted her, left her alone during those last few months once I realised she had no close family or friends. In her selfless manner she implored me to go but I would hear none of it. After all, I had still several opportunities to go back. I decided to remain until she recovered or alternatively provide support should her health deteriorate."

"That was considerate of you. I'm sure your friendship and assistance was invaluable to Catherine," I responded.

"I had grown to like her during our time together with the Rutherfords. Her account, I imagine, says little of the appreciation and wealth of feeling which she received from the people with whom she came into contact during her stay at Overthwaite. I shall always be indebted to her for the love and understanding she gave to the lads – something they had failed to receive from their own mother!" Again his hatred of Elizabeth Woodville was patently clear. "Once she had accepted my intention to remain, Catherine insisted that I stay here. Although I would be within call to provide assistance she was determined that I should have some time to myself."

"This house belonged to her then?"

"Yes. It had been attached to the estate many years ago and retained by your grandfather when others were sold off. During the intervening years it had been leased on various occasions but fortunately was unoccupied at the time of my arrival."

"Did Catherine suffer a great deal during her illness?" I feared the worse.

"Inevitably she had days when the pain was intense and her periods of chemotherapy" he pronounced the word carefully, obviously foreign to his vocabulary "were particularly distressing. But your aunt's strain of leukaemia," again he enunciated the word with care, "was a particularly virulent one and towards the end the disease accelerated making any suffering swift. She was an extremely brave woman and I shall ever admire her fortitude."

"I *do* wish I had known her."

"I feel the two of you would have been at one with each other for I can see certain similarities of character." My curiosity was aroused but I refrained from quizzing him further. "Indeed, she had strength of personality which often precluded the acceptance of advice." What a tactful way of describing pig-headedness. Did he see that in me, I wondered? "Her work was of paramount importance to her. I frequently suggested that she allow me to assist in relieving her burden. Eventually, as time passed and she became over-weary she agreed, and gradually I assumed greater responsibility thereby enabling me to alleviate her workload." Suddenly he smiled, "But there were also many good days. Days when her humour shone through and we laughed together, days when we would sit in the sunshine discussing our time together at Overthwaite." Again he paused, deep in thought remembering times past.

"And when you return, what then?" I had spoken my innermost thoughts involuntarily. The question was as much about my future as it was about his but Adam took it literally.

"Who is to know? Much depends on the timing of my arrival. I intend to return on 30th March, almost fifteen months after my departure. If time has remained still I shall do my utmost to prevent the death of Richard at Bosworth, some seven months hence. Though at this stage I cannot begin to imagine how I could achieve such a thing. If times in the 15th and 21st centuries have kept apace then I shall arrive in 1486 and the boys' welfare will be my only concern. I pray to God they are still alive."

I was confused. Adam's reasoning sounded plausible but I *knew* Richard had been killed at Bosworth so how could he prevent it from happening? As to the boys, even though no proof existed that they had been murdered, no trace of them survived. What had become of them? Could Adam change history? Was it possible? No! I tried to sound casual. "So if you arrive during 1486 and the boys are no longer at Overthwaite …?" I left the question unfinished, unable to voice the terrible possibilities.

"Should that be the case then I reiterate my previous convictions. The burden of guilt lies with Henry Tudor. During my time here you will not be surprised to learn that I have read extensively on the subject. As you know, opinion regarding the perpetrator of the crimes against Edward and Richard is split, and speculation still rife. Over the years Richard has been unjustly cast as the murderous blackguard responsible *but* – and this I find extremely significant – the devious, mean spirited nature of the Tudor is still evident." I thought him perhaps biased but refrained from comment. "For *that* to be apparent, notwithstanding that the majority of accounts are based on Tudor historians, well …" he turned up his hands and shrugged his shoulders, obviously feeling there was no need to say more. "It was certainly in Henry Tudor's interest to blacken the character of his predecessor. His claim to the throne was an extremely tenuous one consequently he would have needed all the support he could muster. What better way than to feed propaganda to the masses? If any one individual is to be condemned for his treatment of a royal prince then it is Henry Tudor himself. You remember I mentioned Clarence's son, Edward of Warwick?" The question, presumably, was rhetorical for without awaiting confirmation Adam continued, "From the age of five the poor lad had been imprisoned in the Tower. Richard righted the situation by installing him at Sheriff Hutton and providing him with a household of his own. I now find that upon taking the crown the Tudor returned the lad to the Tower, where he was eventually put to death on a concocted charge of treason. Utter hypocrisy!" He shook his head in disbelief. "The next rumour to circulate was that Richard was responsible for the murder of his wife! And all to enable him to marry his niece Elizabeth – how utterly preposterous! Had Henry Tudor known how seriously Richard took his motto he would have realised how ridiculous the suggestion was." I decided to remain silent for he was obviously incensed and I thought it wise to let him air his grievances. "As I have already mentioned, he cared for his wife. They had grown together at Middleham and he was always of a mind to marry her. Elizabeth was a young girl and the daughter of his brother – he viewed her in a totally different light. In addition it served Richard's cause naught to marry his niece for he knew she was a bastard. The accounts of Richard's grief for Anne are the ones which ring true for I *know* he would have been distraught at her passing. Why, it was still within a twelve month of him losing his son! No, I would imagine Henry Tudor was fearful of Richard genuinely taking a fancy to Elizabeth, for that would have ruined his own chances. To counterbalance any possibility the rumour was started, thereby forcing Richard into the denial of an act he had never intended in the first place, simple but effective. There is nothing more damning or suspicious than a genuine disavowal!" Once again he moved to the window, attempting to regain control of his emotions – the white knuckles contrasting sharply with the raised blue veins visible on his tightly clenched fists. His anger subsided as quickly as it had arisen. "Forgive me – there are times when my emotions run raw."

"Please don't apologise, you obviously thought a lot of Richard and the boys. It's perfectly understandable you should find it difficult going over all the events again. Perhaps I'm the one who should be apologising."

"No, not at all. I made a promise to Catherine that I should explain everything to you, for she worried that you might disbelieve her tale and think her mad."

I laughed, "It's funny but never for one moment did I doubt her. And I'm sure it had nothing to do with my hearing the door open. It's just that, whilst I was reading her account I warmed to her, felt as though I knew her, and she certainly came across as a very down to earth person."

Adam too gave a wry smile. "Yes, your assessment is an astute one. Catherine was an extremely matter of fact person." He stifled a yawn with the back of his hand and, glancing towards the clock, made to stand, "Well, unless you have any burning questions, may I suggest we retire for the night? Should you require any further clarification, I shall be pleased to resume in the morning."

Over the course of the next few days one or two things did cross my mind but Adam was always patient in his explanations. I was intrigued to know how he had managed to cope with life in the 21st century.

"Initially I found it extremely difficult. To try to impart the full impact of the changes would be, well, I do not think I should truly be able to convey my feelings of amazement, utter bewilderment and a million other emotions. Apart from such obvious day to day things as electricity, water at the turn of the tap and the numerous modern labour-saving devices, the whole ethos of today's 'mind-set' I think you call it, left me in a state of confusion in view of my 500 year old outlook! Catherine, of course, helped to ease my transition and shielded me from the consequences whenever she could. It was for that self-same reason she thought it prudent to change my name to Adam, in order to minimise questions and not arouse suspicion at such an unusual name as my given one!" Despite these difficulties he did go on to say there were a number of things he would miss, "… including listening to music whenever the mood takes me – certainly a change for the better!"

However, more to the forefront of my thoughts was the knowledge that soon I would be bidding him farewell: an altogether disheartening prospect. It was apparent he was striving to tie up any loose ends prior to his departure for he worked late into the night on several occasions, trying to complete the few remaining cases from Catherine's genealogical business.

I was restless. Arriving at Overthwaite and viewing my inheritance had been an enormous adventure. Meeting Adam and experiencing the stirrings of long forgotten feelings had been an exciting experience. Reading Catherine's narrative and hearing of Adam's past had been an unbelievable revelation. And all within the short space of four weeks! What now? What did life hold in store for me? Owning Overthwaite Hall was a thrilling prospect but, long term, did I want to live in the north? Should I return to my life in Cornwall? What of my feelings for Adam? I was almost sure it was not merely infatuation but what did he feel for me, anything? Should I confront him and bring matters to a head? It had all happened too quickly and my brain was nearly on overload. What to do?

I found it difficult to settle to anything. Days alone on the fells, when I hoped the biting wind might clear the dense fog from my mind, did nothing. Riding on the common in torrential rain and returning home bone-weary and chilled failed to help resolve my indecision. After many hours of soul-searching I decided to return to Cornwall. I would spend time away from Overthwaite, away from Adam and review my emotions.

Before leaving I extracted a promise from him that he would still be at Overthwaite upon my return: that he intended to remain until 30th March. I drove away with minimal possessions: certainly I had less in the car than upon my arrival, merely my overnight bag and Tenzing. Perhaps I shouldn't have been driving for my mind did wander and I think I drove more by instinct than observation of road conditions. However, we arrived safe and sound and it was good to be home. I stayed away for five weeks and during that time my thoughts crystallised. It was no bolt from the blue, no earth-shattering moment when everything became clear but a slow realisation of how I wanted to spend the rest of my life – or should I say, with whom. I had never believed in love at first sight and, if I am totally honest with myself, had not experienced that with Adam. What I had felt was a definite initial attraction, which had grown to an all-consuming certainty that he was the one for me. Of course, I was still unaware of Adam's feelings. I would have to work my womanly wiles and hope I succeeded!

I had decided to return and play things casually, make sure I still felt the same about him (hardly an uncertainty) but say nothing for the time being. My second decision was to accompany Adam back to the past. Although I knew of the risks I would be taking they seemed nothing in comparison to life without him. And besides, what an exciting journey it would be! However, I felt sure Adam would disagree, would forbid me to return with him ... if he knew. And so I had resolved to say nothing. I would tell him I had returned to make my farewells, had still not decided upon my long-term plans for Overthwaite but in the interim would shut up the Hall and resume my former life in Cornwall. Then, when the 30th March arrived, I would just follow him through the door.

Easy ... or so I hoped!

Once again I crested the hill and as in the New Year marvelled at the raw beauty of Sleadale. On this occasion my sense of anticipation was heightened at the prospect of seeing Adam and I pressed on, eager to reach the Hall.

He was not aware of the exact time of my arrival but, as usual, was working in the studio and upon catching the first glimpse of his smiling face my heart was in my mouth. Nothing had changed. In addition to the familiar butterflies in my stomach I felt a warm glow which extended through my whole being. I was out of the car in a jiffy and, without thinking, ran across the cobbles to embrace Adam in a warm hug. Even his smell was familiar to me, clean and aromatic but definitely masculine. Was our embrace too long for just friends or was that wishful thinking? I hoped not the latter.

"Emma, it is good to see you again. I trust your journey was uneventful?"

We were soon enjoying a warm drink in the lounge and, as is my wont when nervous, I chattered away scarcely pausing in my recital of events whilst in Cornwall.

"The absence of Tenzing surprises me. Did he refuse to accompany you on your travels to the north?" He was teasing, for I felt sure that already Adam had appreciated the strength of affection I had for my cherished pet.

I replied in like fashion. "You bet! He told me that he had travelled enough recently and wanted a holiday in the local cattery instead!" I saw Adam frown and hastened to explain. "A cattery – let me see. It's a bit like a hotel for cats. They're looked after, boarded in cages while their owners are away. And of course you pay for the service."

"Mm ... and you say Tenzing wanted to go there!"

"Well," I replied, "put like that it doesn't sound too appealing does it? But in my defence I would say that he's been there on several occasions and does seem to enjoy himself. I think it's probably because he's surrounded by lots of other cats and Jan, the woman who runs it, makes such a fuss of him that I don't think he misses me at all!"

Of course, I would miss him enormously. Thinking I may not return I would never have left Tenzing to spend the rest of his days in a cattery. My next door neighbour was looking after him and, a cat person herself, I felt sure that she would 'adopt' him should I remain with Adam in his time. This tale was a fabrication purely for Adam's benefit.

"I gather, therefore, that you have decided on your future and the fate of Overthwaite Hall?"

Averting my eyes from Adam's gaze lest he detect my lies I replied, "Yes, I intend to remain only until the end of the month," well strictly speaking that wasn't a lie. "After your departure," I raised my eyebrows in enquiry and Adam nodded in assent, "I shall shut up the hall until later in the year. I may or may not return. I'm not sure at this stage –it all depends on a number of things." I brushed some imaginary crumbs from my lap and inspected my nails, hoping he was no expert on body language.

"So you intend to return to Cornwall?" He sounded surprised.

"Probably, er ... possibly," I was becoming flustered. I told myself to calm down.

"Forgive me, for I am too inquisitive." Once again he frowned, forming the two familiar grooves between his brows. His concern made my heart melt and I realised how much he meant to me.

"No, not at all. It's just that, at this stage, with the acquisition of this," I turned up my palms to indicate the building around us, "my life seems to be at sixes and sevens. I *really* don't know where I want to be." Mentally I crossed my fingers.

"Well, I can assure you it is a beautiful part of the country in which to live. Nevertheless, I can understand your dilemma for, as you know, I too have had unexpected responsibilities heaped on my shoulders in times past." He smiled and I knew instantly to whom he referred – Edward and Richard. "Consequently, I *must* go back." I caught my breath. Was he saying he didn't actually want to? Or was I deluding myself? "My duty has not yet been fulfilled. The boys were left in my care and I must resolve their future." He crossed himself, "Dear God let them be alive!"

The intervening days were spent in preparation: by Adam and also by me.

With the intention of retrieving Catherine's clothing, on one occasion I visited the attic, only to find that Adam had previously taken his own items: fortuitous, for that meant the removal of my garments would go unnoticed. I found two dresses. One was of good quality, presumably the Christmas outfit and a second was made of coarser material: the word homespun sprang to mind. I tried them on and as I suspected they were roomy. Not to worry, with some simple alterations I felt sure the dresses would do nicely. The shoes were also suitable, albeit a touch on the large side but with a small amount of packing in the toes they would serve the purpose.

I contacted Jeremy, for although I had intended to confront him during my time in Cornwall, at the last moment I had cold feet and decided to discuss the matter by phone. Not knowing my fate, ideally I hoped he would keep my position open to cover the eventuality of my return, but I knew that was a lot to ask, for I might never reappear. Much depended on Adam and his response at the time. I had decided that, should he have no feelings for me, I would return at the first opportunity: October. However, if he loved me or could grow to love me, I would have no hesitation in remaining with him for the rest of my life. At all events, Jeremy made things easy for he readily accepted my offer of unpaid leave until the end of the year. If I failed to return, well ... I would simply be another missing person: I *had* endeavoured to tie things up neatly in my will.

Lastly, I had spent every free moment reading up on the late 15th to early 16th centuries in the hope that with basic knowledge of that time I might not give myself away too easily. It was then simply a case of awaiting March 30th."

Thankfully the day was a beautiful one. I spent my last morning in the garden, drinking in the views, sounds and smells of the time. Buds were sprouting in the hedgerows heralding the onset of spring and a recent spell of warm weather had even encouraged the grass to grow. I would miss Overthwaite for although I would still be here, inevitably it would be different. Catherine's wish that I grow to love the place had come true for even though I had only spent a short time here it was beginning to feel like home: would it feel the same without Adam? I hoped I would have no chance of finding out.

The hours passed slowly and I felt as though I was treading water. I avoided Adam, convinced that somehow I would give the game away by my nervous attitude but I need not have worried for he appeared to be avoiding me also – the atmosphere tense whenever our paths happened to cross. Early evening, by arrangement, we met in the lounge.

"Everything ready?" I tried to sound casual and chatty.

"Yes. I have endeavoured to tie up all the loose ends."

A long pause – this wasn't going to be easy.

I looked at my watch, "Two hours to go – I take it the door will open at two minutes past nine?" I assumed he had taken into account B.S.T., even though it had not been mentioned, but decided to make sure.

"Yes, or perhaps I should say I hope so!" He managed a weak smile.

Another awkward pause.

"So if you're right about the timing, Sir Anthony will be dead and Lady Margaret will be in charge of the boys?"

"Er, precisely," I could see Adam was surprised and I wondered whether my show of knowledge was perhaps a give-away. Obviously it was for he continued, "Emma, reassure me, tell me you are not contemplating anything."

"Contemplating anything?" My mind was working overtime, wondering how to play things.

"To consider 'crossing over' would be an act of absolute folly, it would be highly dangerous for you!" He held my wrist tightly and his gaze was intent. "Please tell me I am wrong."

I pulled my wrist away, rubbing the impression his fingers had made. I was playing for time. Tucking my hands under my thighs I crossed my fingers – childish I know, but something I had always done – and told the lie. "If you mean do I intend following you then you're certainly wrong! Good heavens, how could I hope to pass myself off in the 15th Century?" Did he believe me? I had tried to sound convincing. He said nothing but continued to look me straight in the eye and somehow I managed to hold his gaze. After what seemed an age he appeared to relax. I decided to make no further denials. "You won't have any problems arriving during the evening will you? With the barmkin, I mean."

"I hope not, but that is the least of my worries. Once I am there I shall fabricate some tale or other. Do not fret for me." He reached forward and gently squeezed my hand. "Emma …" he looked straight into my eyes and I held my breath, hoping against hope to hear the words I longed for – but they did not come. Suddenly he stood and walked away from me. "I must make my final preparations."

The moment had passed and I felt a dull ache in the pit of my stomach, still unsure of Adam's feelings. I rallied and decided to put my plan into action. "Well, I shall say goodbye now. I hate farewells and intend to have a long, hot soak and an early night."

I could see he was taken aback by my cavalier attitude but managed to control his surprise. "I shall strive not to disturb you when I leave. Goodbye, Emma …"

What he was about to say I will never know for I could bear it no longer and, standing, I kissed him lightly on the cheek. "Goodbye, Adam. I hope you attain all you desire in the future."

I moved to the door and without a backward glance left him alone.

Once inside my room I stood, back to the door and heart pounding as I tried to control my emotions. What did he feel? How could he exhibit such self-restraint? I hoped *I* attained all *I* desired in the future, never mind him!

Later, after my long hot bath, I laid out Catherine's clothes on the bed. Quietly I slipped into them, feeling as I did so my aunt's watch which once again had been secreted in the hem of the skirt: as a safeguard I had had the old fob serviced. I retrieved a bag from the wardrobe. It had occurred to me that I could hardly rely on Catherine's tale of 'robbers' and therefore needed some item in which to carry my belongings. I had obtained a thick piece of woollen material and had fashioned a bag that I felt would pass muster where I was going. I had also taken the precaution of dying both of the dresses to ensure neither would be recognised. Carefully folding the Christmas outfit I laid it in the bag and turned to look at Catherine's comb. Dare I take it with me? Dearly I would have loved to, but I thought not. It was folly to risk the chance of somebody remembering it had once belonged to my aunt. Lastly I placed in the bag the drawstring purse of coins: I hoped there would be no need for them but one never knew.

I prayed Adam would keep his promise and not try to disturb me, then seating myself in the chair I went through my last minute preparations. I was sure I had covered everything, even down to the security of the house: Mrs. Holmes would look after the place in my absence and I had told one or two of the locals I was going away indefinitely. I had already decided on my strategy. Close to the 'door' was a small recess in which I intended to hide myself whilst awaiting the appointed hour. In order to ensure Adam did not notice me, I had removed all the light bulbs on the landing.

Quarter to nine. I opened my bedroom door carefully: all was quiet. Quickly I slipped onto the landing. Silence. I moved into the niche and, tucking the bag behind me, paused in the darkness. My senses were heightened: I heard the blood pounded in my ears. The minutes passed.

At last I heard a noise; a footfall on the stair; a quiet oath as Adam fumbled for the light switch; again silence. My eyes were accustomed to the darkness and I could see his form as he moved along the landing. I held my breath, afraid he would hear me. The minutes ticked by, seeming like an age: then the familiar sound. Slowly, the old door creaked its way open. Even from where I was standing I could sense a change in the atmosphere, could see an eerie light moving along the landing carpet. Suddenly Adam had gone.

It was now or never, I knew time was of the essence. I left the safety of my niche and swiftly moved towards the door.

CHAPTER TEN

Lifting my skirts I took a deep breath and before the door began its swift, inevitable, return journey I had left the 21st century and entered into a new and strange world.

    The draught from the door was intense but I stood my ground and with heart pounding loudly, paused to let my eyes become accustomed to the dim light of the wall sconces. Adam was standing before me: he seemed to sense my presence and slowly turned towards me. Realising my uncertainty related as much to Adam's reaction as to my new surroundings I searched his face eagerly for clues. What I saw gave me cause for hope, as in addition to the anticipated concern and annoyance I detected a hint of relief.

    He swept me towards the wall, pressing his body against mine and spoke in hushed, intensive tones. "I thought we had agreed thou wouldst not follow me. I told thee that 'twould be too dangerous." I noticed he had quickly lapsed back into his 'native' tongue and although I genuinely believe he was bothered by my actions I cherished that glimpsed look and clung onto it like a lifeline. Before I had chance to response he rushed on, "Well, 'tis too late for such talk now. Let me think for a moment as to our best course of action." With fingers to his forehead he quietly paced up and down urgently trying to formulate a plan. "I have it. Thy tongue would surely give thee away and we must needs have reason for thy silence. I have a cousin, a mute who lives Ludlow way and will endeavour to pass thee off as her. I shall spin the tale as and when required – mayhap it could provide a reason for my extended absence – no matter, I shall see how things progress and tailor our responses to the needs of the moment. Let us hope all goes well and none suspect. Once we are alone I shall provide thee with any details but I implore thee Emma, thou must not speak at all costs."

My head was reeling with the speed of events and I concentrated on his words, trying to take in my new identity. Nevertheless, I felt I must say something to him – after all, it might be the last chance I had in view of my imminent loss of speech. I whispered, "Please don't be too angry with me. I know I should have stayed behind but ..." swallowing hard I gathered my courage. Finally I told him, "I couldn't just let you walk out of my life, let you go without telling you how I feel, how I've felt for almost three months. Adam, I think I have fallen ..."

"Hush," he placed his finger across my lips "now is neither the time nor place for such talk. Later." His gentleness warmed me and the look in his eyes helped to allay any fears I might have had. "Firstly we must sort out our present predicament. 'Twould have been bad enough lying for one, now I must think for two!" His quick smile told me the words were partly in jest and meant kindly.

For the first time since entering the room I took the opportunity to look around. The hall bore little resemblance to the one I had left. Nevertheless my surroundings were familiar due to Catherine's excellent description. I was mesmerised and could hardly believe that I was standing in the 15th century. A figure was dozing by the fire. From her profile I recognised her instantly as Aggie, the wise woman and touching Adam's arm pointed in her direction. We made our way towards the hearth where Adam shook her gently by the shoulder. She awoke with a start.

"Mistress Bowman, 'tis Master Anselm, dost thou not remember me?"

What a good job I was to be mute for I feel sure I would never become accustomed to calling him Anselm.

Slowly coming out of her sleep induced stupor Aggie peered at us suspiciously. Recognition took some little time but eventually she ventured, "Aye. Thou wast here some time gone – when Lady Margaret had her bleeding afore the bairn's birth." By her feet rested a small cradle containing a young baby. Our voices must have disturbed the child and Aggie bent to offer some comfort. "Hush, hush, little un. None will harm thee with Aggie by tha side." She turned to Adam. "Tha probably won't know but things are bad here – what with Sir Anthony dyin' and the Mistress about to give birth," this then confirmed the date was March 1486, "then on top o' that we've got that scoundrel Hugo causing trouble." I shivered involuntarily at the mention of his name. "Ay, her ladyship be having a rough time of things that's for sure."

"Dost thou think Lady Margaret is well enough to see us? Is she in her chamber?"

"Aye, she be upstairs an' should she be awake I feel sure she'd want to see thee. Come." Picking up the baby she moved towards the spiral staircase and we made to follow. Suddenly a figure emerged before us, having climbed from the floor below.

"Ay, Stephen, look who's turned up!" Aggie motioned towards Adam.

"Stephen! 'Tis good to see thee again!" Adam moved towards the man, arms outstretched in a warm greeting. This, then, was the man with whom he had been on such friendly terms.

"Is't Master Anselm? Well, I'll be! I ne'er thought to be seein' thee the neet." Stephen too seemed genuinely pleased to see Adam. Turning to Aggie he added in a quiet but assertive voice, "I've just bin down to see if there's any signs of him but can see none. The gate'll have to be left open … yet agin!"

"On another drunken bout, nay doubt!" I took it they were referring to Hugo. Aggie continued, "I was just about to tek them up to see Lady M," she paused, "afore it gets too late." The meaning of this broad hint was apparent and so, before the men lapsed into further conversation, Adam and I turned to follow her.

"We will talk later, Stephen," Adam called quietly over his shoulder as we climbed the stairs to the floor above.

On the way he whispered in my ear, "'Twould appear we were correct in our assumptions about the date." Nodding, I followed him up two flights of stairs where we emerged into the garret storey of the building. Four pairs of haunted, suspicious eyes turned in our direction.

"Fear not Lady M, 'tis not thy brother-in-law," Aggie spoke directly to the figure lying on the bed. "'Tis Master Anselm, just arrived!"

The scene in the room caused me to recall Catherine's description of the night of Lady Margaret's near miscarriage and I felt sure the three young women hovering in the background were Jane, Sarah and Margery. Adam approached the bed and its occupant managed a welcoming smile on her pale, drawn face.

Raising herself from the pillow she murmured, in a voice bearing a distinct Yorkshire accent, "Anselm, it *is* good to see thee." However, even those few words drained her and she slumped back, seemingly exhausted. The young woman I took to be Jane was quickly by her side, with Aggie a close second.

"Here Margery, take care of tha bairn whilst I tend the mistress," and thrusting the baby into her arms, Aggie proceeded to refresh the cloth which lay across Lady Margaret's forehead. Margery had eyes only for the child and as she rocked gently to-and-fro, whispering endearments into its tiny face, I wondered whether her circumstances had changed and the baby was hers. Over by the far wall Sarah was bending over a second bed on which a young boy was sleeping: no doubt this was Matthew. Between the two beds stood a cot containing an infant whom I assumed to be his sister Joan and on the far side of the room a pair of pallets abutted the wall. Presumably, in view of Lady Margaret's condition, she had vacated the lower floor. This room which had been Catherine's sleeping quarters during her stay now provided a safe haven for the women and children out of Hugo's way. But in that case, where was Edward and where was Richard?

Lady Margaret had rallied and bade us sit by the bed. "Where are my manners? Come, seat thyselves. And pray tell us Anselm, who is the lady?"

Adam introduced me as his cousin, saying I had contracted an illness as a child, which had left me without speech. "Whilst in London I was made aware that Emma's mother had died and, being her only remaining relative, I decided that in view of her affliction it behove me to take care of her. Besides, I had always promised my aunt so to do. I returned by way of Ludlow to rendezvous with my cousin and felt sure her presence at Overthwaite would not prove an imposition."

"Indeed not. Thou art welcome, Emma, though I fear you arrive at a dire time." Turning to Adam she added, "Did Aggie tell thee that Sir Anthony is dead?"

"Aye, she did." Although we were aware he had died the previous month Adam enquired, "How didst come about?"

"'Twas after Bosworth. My husband fought bravely for King Richard and I shall e'er be proud of him but his wounds never healed. He suffered greatly and 'twas a blessing when he passed away last month." The words brought back sad memories and she paused to compose herself.

"'Twere not long afore t' master's brother landed at our door – seein' what rich pickings were about, I'll be sure!" It was the first time Margery had spoken and had I possessed any doubts about her identity they would now have been resolved: idly she tucked a stray strand of auburn hair behind her ear and into her hood.

"Why art thou always so harsh on Master Hugo, Margery? Could he not have just wanted to visit his family?" Sarah seemed almost wistful.

"Pah, what kind of slip-slop talk's that? *Master* Hugo wants only one thing!" Margery's tone was full of contempt.

Lady Margaret looked askance at Sarah. "What Margery says is so. Once word of his 'dear' brother's death reached Hugo's ears he arrived post-haste and we have been suffering him since. Needless to say his speed owed naught to the memory of Sir Anthony. No, he took the line that his concerns were for Matthew and that he wished guardianship over the boy during his minority. His only real desire, of course, is to possess Overthwaite. But until Matthew comes of age things will be uncertain and what with the babe arriving at any time, I know not what to do."

"What of thy liege lord at Dacre? Couldst thou not appeal to him for assistance?" Adam suggested.

"Alas, Lord Humphrey died last year and his son Thomas, as thou knows, has sworn his allegiance to the new King. As Hugo fought for the Tudors at Bosworth and in view of Sir Anthony's loyalty to King Richard, I fear Lord Thomas would have scant time for my son. Besides, the time approaches when Matthew must further his education as squire and, what with all that has passed of late, I cannot begin to think where we might place him." Looking directly at Adam and with a catch in her voice Lady Margaret continued, "I have been at my wits' end, Anselm and I am right glad to see thee. This month past I have sorely needed someone I could trust and rely on." Realising the implication of her words, she turned towards Sarah, "Not that Stephen has not been worth his weight in gold – I really do not know what I should have done without him." Before Adam could comment she rushed on, "Which reminds me, 'twas such a shock when thou left so unexpectedly, we were all troubled some mishap had befallen thee. Neither have we seen aught of Catherine since that day, dost thou remember Mistress Phillips?"

"Forgive me for my sudden disappearance." I knew Adam had rehearsed the reason for his absence but had he thought about Catherine? "If I remember aright, I was out on business for Sir Anthony that morning and upon my return I encountered a messenger from my Lord, summoning me to London with all speed. The nature of the command was so urgent I had not even time to return and inform thee. As to Mistress Phillips I know naught. Mayhap she decided to return to Oxford and the Fitzroberts." He was obviously playing safe by being non-committal. "Once my Lord's business had been attended to it was my intention to return for my nephews but as I said afore, news had reached me of my aunt's sudden demise. Sorting out her affairs and taking charge of my cousin took much longer than I had expected. I felt sure thou wouldst continue to look after the lads in my absence." Trying not to sound too concerned he added, "Speaking of my nephews, where are the boys?"

A strange look appeared on the young women's faces and turning to their mistress they waited expectantly. Taking a deep breath she informed us in a sad voice, "I have sorry news, Anselm. Young Roland passed away last year."

Adam dropped his head into his hands and let his shoulders fall. He was on the verge of tears, having grown close to the lads, and this show of emotion was the greatest I had seen in him. Although I longed to take him in my arms and nurse him in his grief, I merely placed a comforting hand on his forearm.

Lady Margaret continued, "'Twas during the autumn. Sir Anthony returned from the battle with a fever and soon the lad was suffering in the same way. My husband lingered long with his, though whether 'twas *that* or his thigh wound which killed him I know not. But thou can take some comfort, Anselm, for Roland's ordeal was soon over."

"Aye, the lad's fever burnt hard and bright and the poor mite had such ravings," Aggie had obviously nursed him. Thankfully his delirium, possibly revealing his true identity, had been heard only by one who was none the wiser. "But he had gone within a twelve day."

"Master Edwin never left his side." Until then Jane had been silent. She continued in hushed tones, almost a whisper, "He was so distraught when his brother died, he shut himself away and would talk to none."

At the mention of Edward's name Adam's head shot up. "Where *is* Edwin?"

"Have no fear, he is safe and well." Turning to Sarah, Lady Margaret instructed, "Make sure Hugo has not yet returned and then you may see to thy husband's needs."

Sarah flounced out of the room, aware that her mistress's words were not for her ears. As I watched her go, the thought crossed my mind that Adam's fears about the barmkin had been unnecessary. Not only had the gate been left open in view of Hugo's imminent return but also, due to the present circumstances at the Hall nobody had showed the slightest interest in hearing how we had arrived at Overthwaite.

Lady Margaret was tiring but with one last effort she continued, "Sarah is a good girl and, generally, a good wife to Stephen. But she can be a little, how can I put it, fickle. She finds Hugo's attentions flattering and has a tendency to play the tease." Adam made a grunting sound and I wondered whether at some time he too had been prey to her advances. "I have warned her but she pays no heed. Not that I think she would betray any confidence but all the same, I do not intend to take that risk." She paused for breath and with a deep sigh continued, "As luck would have it, Edwin was in town with Tom on the day Hugo arrived and by the time they returned Hugo had already taken himself off on one of his drunken sprees." The contempt in her voice was tangible. "My fears for Matthew are, naturally, those of any mother and even though I hope Hugo would do naught to harm him, I intend to keep my son close by me at all times. But with Edwin, I thought 'twould be best if he were away from here, away from Hugo's influence and provocation. Edwin was still suffering from the loss of his brother and I felt he would provide too ready a target for Hugo – to taunt and sport with weakness was ever one of Hugo's favourite diversions. I was convinced he would find a youth such as Edwin fair game and would make his life a misery, so to that end I made arrangements for him to lodge at the Abbey of St. Mary Magdalene. Sir Anthony was oft generous with his gifts to the Brothers and I felt sure they would not refuse my request."

"And 'tis there the lad abides at present?" I could see a mixture of hope and relief in Adam's eyes.

"Aye. Forgive me, Anselm, I fear I must rest now. The morrow I shall talk to thee more about Edwin." Was I imagining it or did I see a knowing look in her eye as she stared intently into Adam's face? "But fear not, Hugo knows naught of his whereabouts."

It was arranged I should sleep with the others in the garret and a truckle bed was wheeled out from beneath Matthew's bed. Adam, meanwhile, would join Stephen and Hugo (should he return) on the floor below.

I followed Adam down to the hall to retrieve my bag and finding the room empty he spoke in hushed tones. "Our arrival appears to have been accepted without query. I fear Hugo will not prove so amenable but providing he does not ask too many awkward questions we should not arouse his suspicions. I must visit the Abbey the morrow and pay a call on Edward for the lad will be sore distressed." His last words were spoken half under his breath and I knew his thoughts were of Richard.

Again taking hold of his arm I whispered, "I'm truly sorry about Richard and, as you say, Edward must be beside himself with the uncertainty of his future. But you'll be able to give him some crumb of comfort tomorrow and I'm sure he will be extremely pleased to see a familiar face."

"Now that we know he lives I must decide what is to be done with him, for he cannot stay here. And what will befall the remainder of the family under Hugo's influence? One thing is certain - I shall not leave thee in his company. We will journey to the Abbey together."

Before I returned he filled me in on some relevant details regarding my new identity: presumably so I would know when to shake and when to nod my head!

As I turned to leave he caught me by the shoulders and spinning me round, gently took hold of my chin. "Although 'twas a shock when I found thou had followed me this evening, in all honesty I cannot say some part of me was not overjoyed. I know what thy true feelings are for me Emma. I have seen it in thy face these months past." He moved a stray lock of hair that had fallen across my left eye and caressed my cheek with his finger. "I too have grown to love thee but would not admit it to myself in view of my imminent departure. It is madness, for God alone knows what the future holds in store, but try as I may I cannot alter my feelings."

"Oh, Adam!"

"Hush, we must be careful. Remember, thou art mute and, after all, we are cousins!" His eye glinted in the firelight and his lips were warm as they brushed lightly against my own. "I shall see thee in the morning." Turning me round he gave my shoulders a gentle push towards the stairs.

My heart pounding, I lay on the bed remembering each and every word he had spoken. My mind was alert and sleep eluded me. I thought of what had passed that evening; of the people around me whom I had met for the first time yet felt I knew intimately from Catherine's narrative; of Catherine herself and how alone she must have felt during her stay; but most of all I thought of Adam. With his features etched vividly in my mind's eye, sleep eventually came. That night my dreams were numerous and each one was of Adam.

The grey, March daylight and early morning household noises awakened me to a new, exciting world. I looked around. Lady Margaret and the children were sleeping soundly with Jane nodding in a chair by her mistress's bed. My movements must have roused her and as she looked across towards me I raised my finger to my lips to show I would be careful not to waken her patient. Having slept in my clothes, I merely splashed my face with water from the pitcher, straightened my skirts and made my way quickly to the hall below. Adam was already there and guided me across the barmkin to the kitchen. As we opened the door we were greeted by a roar, which seemed to be coming from somewhere beneath the table. A large, grey wolfhound emerged and although I had an affinity towards most dogs I felt apprehensive in view of his size and the ferocity of his bark.

"Down, Lupus, down!" Margery turned towards the table, hands on hips. "Tom, I told yer not to bring him over, t' Mistress bein' due any time an' all. He'd 'ave bin fine left at home."

"Now now, lass. Don't get yerself in a bother, eh? Dog'll be fine here, he's just a bit wary o' t' newcomers, that's all, eh? All know his bark's worse than his bite, eh?" Tom's easy-going manner appeared to calm Margery for she turned back to her task by the hearth.

"Hello, boy. Dost thou remember me?" Adam bent towards the dog, fingers outstretched tentatively. Lupus obviously recognised Adam's scent for, ears down and tail wagging, the dog ran towards Adam, and began a comprehensive licking of his hand with a tongue as pink as candy-floss. Confidence bolstered by this show of affection I too made a move towards the wolfhound. Immediately he backed off, teeth bared, hackles raised and a deep growl rumbling in his throat. I withdrew my hand in surprise.

"Have done, Lupus, or yer *will* go home!" Margery glowered at the animal as Tom struggled to push the dog back beneath the table. Usually dogs took to me but not this one. Could it be he sensed I was from another time? I remembered Tenzing's similar reaction towards Adam although Catherine seemed to have had no problem with the animals she encountered. I would never know for sure one way or the other but common sense told me to give the dog a wide berth during my stay at Overthwaite.

This little incident over, I was introduced to the occupants of the kitchen, all of whom I felt I knew thanks to Catherine. The food was as I had expected; I realised the taste of the bread and pottage would take some getting used to and I was certainly not accustomed to drinking watered down ale first thing in the morning! I was fascinated, listening to the general chat, to find it all sounded completely normal – though what I had expected I don't know – and I had cause to bite my tongue once or twice to stop myself from joining in.

I soon learned Margery was married to Tom, the blacksmith and they lived in his old dwelling near to the Hall. She later informed me he had asked her to marry him when his first wife died, not long after Catherine's return. Had she married Tom on the rebound from her infatuation with Simon? Whatever the answer, they always seemed close and certainly happy. She was devoted to her new baby daughter but was an equally good mother to Tom's son William.

"What that ne'er-do-well would 'ave done to t' mistress or young Master Matthew had Stephen and my Tom not bin here, I shudder to think." Margery gazed at her husband proudly.

Stephen and Sarah had moved to the Hall during Sir Anthony's illness, since whose death and Hugo's return, Stephen's presence had helped to provide a small measure of security to Lady Margaret, who inevitably was feeling vulnerable.

"Now now, Margery. I did nowt, eh?" He was a large man with even larger hands and as he downed his ale he winked at her over the rim of his cup. No doubt his years as a blacksmith had helped to develop his muscles: the breadth of his shoulders' was immense. Had he had cause to use his strength yet and was just being modest? I imagine his physical appearance had helped curb any rash intentions Hugo might have had.

Stephen and Sarah were seated at the far end of the table. Perhaps due to the events of the previous evening Sarah seemed out of sorts and was silent. Last night, in the gloom, it had been difficult to see her features fully and so I was unprepared for such stunning looks. No other word can describe her. Her pale, flawless features and eyes of deepest blue were framed by thick, lustrous tresses of jet-black hair. She was beautiful. Her husband smiled at Margery's comment but said nothing, stolidly consuming the contents of his bowl of pottage. He was a complete contrast to his wife. Catherine had described him as a gentle, laconic man and this, coupled with his slight build, made me think he would have little influence over a person such as Hugo.

Although I had yet to meet him I felt sure the experience would prove to be an unpleasant one. He had, we were informed, returned home during the early hours of the morning and was now sleeping off his night's exploits in the barn on the hay: on the very spot where, in a drunken stupor, he had fallen from his horse upon arriving back at the Hall.

Jane sought us out after we had eaten and informed Adam that Lady Margaret wished to see him alone in the garret chamber. He motioned me to follow. Talk at breakfast had intimated that the loss of Lady Margaret's husband had greatly affected her and that, coupled with the stress of Hugo's return and her forthcoming pregnancy, had caused her to weaken considerably. Aggie had recommended Lady Margaret should take to her bed in order to minimise any risk of losing the baby and as this also enabled her to avoid her brother in law, it seemed an extremely sensible course of action. We seated ourselves by the bed and in answer to Lady Margaret's query Adam assured her she could talk freely in front of me.

"'Twas of Edwin that I wished to talk to thee, or perhaps I should call him by his given name of Edward," she spoke urgently, in hushed tones. Her comment made him start but before he could respond she continued, "Nay, Anselm, pray let me explain afore Hugo rouses himself. I knew naught of Edward's true identity until after the death of his brother. At the time of thy arrival with the lads, my husband told me only that 'twas at the behest of Lord Dacre. I thought little on't especially as I knew Matthew would benefit from thy tutelage. Besides, the boys were such a joy to have under our roof. But as thou heard last night, once Richard died his brother was a changed lad. All joy and spirit left him. He would shut himself away for days on end, letting no food pass his lips throughout." She paused momentarily; saddened by the memories her words had reawakened. "When Sir Anthony died Edward and I found comfort in each other and he talked to me about Richard, talked about his loneliness as a child and how he had only found real joy since coming to Overthwaite. But still he gave no inkling as to who he was. Then one day his pent up emotions became too much for him and his defences crumbled. He cried for Richard for the first time – aye and cried for himself if truth be told – sobbed with all his heart until I thought it might break. 'Twas then that he told me. It might be that my comforting provided a mother's love he had missed for so long. I know not. Suffice it to say, he was at peace when he had unburdened himself and slept in my arms that night like a babe."

She too was spent and lay there, gazing down at her hands, reliving those tragic events. Adam made to speak but before he had managed a word she roused herself and rushed on, "But thou needst not worry, Anselm. None other knows. All still believe he is thy nephew and of course I need not say Hugo knows naught about the lad. As I explained last night, Edward's safe-conduct to the Abbey was achieved during Hugo's absence and as none have regard for my brother-in-law he will not find out aught from any here." She saw my expression and, as if reading my thoughts, added, "Not even

Sarah. For all her faults her loyalties lie with me ... and her husband of course. I feel sure she views this dalliance with Hugo as a mere game, little does she know how dangerous the game might be. But even were she to know, she would say naught to him. Besides, she and Edward got on well together. I fear he had a soft spot for her. Perhaps she was the first to stir feelings of manhood in him. When all is said and done, she *is* an extremely striking young woman."

Adam was seemingly oblivious to such talk and wanted to get on. "Lady Margaret, thy quick-wittedness may have saved the lad's life. Should knowledge of his whereabouts get into the wrong hands 'twould surely sign his death warrant. With Richard on the throne his nephew's life was safe but I do not imagine King Henry would allow the existence of a contender for the throne to whom a new Yorkist cause could rally." He then repeated the thoughts he had previously outlined to me. "Hints of illegitimacy would hardly serve Henry's cause in view of his marriage to King Edward's daughter." I could see Lady Margaret was too exhausted to follow his line of thinking but she refrained from questioning him. "Nay, 'twould be much easier to arrange for young Edward to be eliminated." Rising he paced the length of the room, his strides long, deep in thought as he pondered over Edward's situation. "We must continue to take great care. I shall make haste to the Abbey in order to see the lad and try to put his mind at ease, though what I can promise him I know not."

We left Lady Margaret to rest and once below Adam informed me he would apply himself to the question of Edward's plight. "Wilt thou be well enough without me, whilst I take some time alone in thought?" I assured him I would be O.K. I felt happy enough in the company of Margery and the others and I further promised that, should Hugo surface and cause any problems, I would seek out Adam instantly.

Making my way across to the barmkin I tried to envisage my aunt treading these same steps, undergoing these same emotions and once again I was amazed, as I had been upon reading the narrative, at her temerity in embarking on such an adventure alone. Had I not possessed these feelings for Adam I should surely not have taken such a momentous step.

Seeking out Margery I indicating my willingness to help – surprising how one can communicate sufficiently even without words – hoping she would want me only to fulfil an easy task and not one beyond my 21st century capabilities. However, I need not have worried for, to a great extent, my 'disability' caused her to treat me as though I were infirm.

"You be seated by t' fire and rest. Yer mun be right tired after yer journeying yesterday." And there I stayed for the remainder of the morning, convincing her to allow me at least to beat the salted stockfish prior to its soaking, in readiness for supper. She busied herself with numerous chores whilst caring tenderly for her baby and I listened to her ceaseless chatter about all and sundry at the Hall. It appeared that, with the exception of her sister Agnes who had gone off to London and Mary the cook, who had at last found a husband and moved to the next village, Overthwaite's inhabitants remained unaltered. However, she was obviously troubled by her sister's absence and proceeded to outline the circumstances of her departure.

"'Twas just after t'master had left last summer. She'd bin talkin' about London fer weeks. Seemed she'd bin chattin' to some lad in town whose sister got this *ap-ren-tis-ship*," she stumbled over the unfamiliar word. "Leastways I think that's what it were. Wi' some woman down in London and was going to make her fortune! I told her. I said if yer believes that, yer believes anything!" As she related her tale I was fascinated by her actions in attempting to remove a stain from a velvet doublet: from the quality of the garment I thought it probably belonged to Hugo. Beating a quantity of soapwort until soft she rubbed the juice onto the fabric, setting it to one side to take effect. "But it made no difference what I said to her, what Tom said to her or what Ma said to her. She'd made up her mind that she was good at sewin' and as far as we know that's what she's done. One day she was here and t' next she'd gone. Nobody's seen hide nor hair of her since." She paused for a moment, staring straight ahead of her. With tears in her eyes she continued, "I know I used to shout at her an' she right angered mi at times but I fear fer her … on her own … in that big city … wi' all them folk. That's if she iver got there!"

Hastily she wiped away her tears on her apron and once again applied herself to the task in hand. I felt impotent through my lack of speech and frustrated that, having met her only the previous evening, I could offer no comfort even though I felt I had known her for years.

Late morning Adam and I set off for the Abbey: I had thought Lady Margaret was referring to Shap Abbey and my assumption had been right.

The day was crisp and the horses, smelling freshness in the air, were eager for a gallop. Lady Margaret's palfrey was a spirited little mount and I was glad of my riding experience to keep her in check. Nevertheless, mastering the side-saddle took some doing. As we journeyed across the fields and along the lanes it was exhilarating to feel the wind on my face and although the conditions underfoot were firm I surmised there had been recent heavy rain. All around, the swollen rivers and streams coursed with a mighty force. Rounding a rocky outcrop I guided my horse towards the edge of a deep gully where down below the cascade terminated in a seething cauldron of foaming liquid. Quickly moving my mount away from the brink I paused to watch the sheer force of the waters churning below, brown in colour from the peaty beds through which they flowed. It was good to be out and I longed for a decent ride, but glancing towards Adam I could see he was eager to reach our goal and we pushed on.

I followed in his wake for I had no idea of the way but knew Adam was familiar with the route having visited the Abbey on several occasions during his prior stay at Overthwaite. We were soon there and cresting a rise I espied the graceful features of the abbey's limestone buildings, nestled in the valley below. Although the general surroundings were austere, this quiet, remote spot must have provided a haven to its unworldly inhabitants.

Arriving at the precinct wall we were presently admitted to the Abbey confines and ushered towards the warming house by one of the younger Brothers. Depositing us by the fire he excused himself to inform the senior canon of our arrival.

Adam turned towards me. "Unless Abbot Redman is in residence 'twill be Brother Norbert in charge. He is a good, kind man whom we can trust implicitly." Before he could say more, the door opened to admit a tall, spare man in an off-white habit whose dark hair sported the expected tonsure. My first impression was of a serious cleric but upon recognising Adam the monk's features dissolved into a smile and with arms outstretched he greeted Adam as a long, lost friend.

"Anselm, 'tis good to see thee! Such a time since thou visited us," his voice was deep and low and the short clipped sentences were spoken in measured tones.

"Pray forgive the hour – I am aware 'tis thy time for silence," said Adam.

"I feel sure He will allow a short transgression," Brother Norbert smiled.

"Indeed. And I see thou hast been making alterations since I was last here." They began to discuss the new tower we had seen upon our approach and which Adam had informed me was only in the planning two years previously. During the pair's embrace Brother Norbert noticed me for the first time and Adam was quick to explain, "Pray forgive the intrusion of a lady to your brotherhood. 'Tis a cousin of mine, new to the area, who sadly does not possess the power of speech and being responsible for her, I feared to leave her at Overthwaite in view of Hugo Rutherford's presence."

Brother Norbert inclined his head and I could see he was aware of Hugo's reputation. Adam continued, "Which brings me to the purpose of this visit – my nephew. Lady Margaret informs me thou hast kindly been lodging the boy of late pending my return from London."

"Indeed. We shall be sorry to lose him. A willing lad who has adapted well to our routines. Nonetheless, I am sure he will be overjoyed to see thee. Gladdened in spirit also. For there is great sadness in him. No doubt due to the loss of his brother. I will send for the boy." Speaking to the young Brother who had showed us in, he returned to the fireside.

"Thou must stay for dinner. Sext and mass have been completed and we are about to eat."

Having had nothing since breakfast his words were like music to my ears and I felt sure my stomach rumbled in thankful response.

Whilst Brother Norbert was arranging our meal Edward arrived. I had wondered what to expect in him: after all, he was the son of a King. But the person who entered the warming house that March morning was simply a sad and lonely fifteen year old and my heart went out to him. He was obviously pleased to see Adam but adolescence and a stately upbringing caused him to temper his feelings with an outward show of reserve. However, his quick nervous eye movements belied that cool exterior and I am sure that beneath, his emotions were in turmoil. Adam clasped him by the shoulders and although not normally one to openly show his emotions, held the boy in a tight embrace for several seconds. Edward responded with a joyful smile and the tension was soon broken.

"Anselm, 'tis right pleasing to see thee. I had not thought we would encounter one another again. A good deal has passed since last we met." He averted his gaze, "Dickon …"

"I know, I know. Lady Margaret informed me of the sad news. But let us not blight our first moments of reunion with sadness. We shall talk more of those things later, but for now let me look at you. Thou hast grown tall in my absence."

"Not nearly as tall as my father." He was still only of medium height and would possibly never reach the stature of Edward IV who by all accounts was a giant of a man. But inevitably he had inherited some traits: with his father's good looks, mother's delicate bone structure and his shoulder length locks of fair hair, he would surely break a few hearts.

"Fear not. Thou hast many years to catch up with him, Edwin." Adam introduced me to the boy and whilst awaiting the arrival of our meal, I listened with interest to their gentle banter which evidenced the closeness of their relationship.

In view of Adam's desire to speak to Edward, Brother Norbert had arranged for our meal to be taken in the warming house during this period of enforced silence. Although a frugal affair consisting of cereals, beans, bread and a smattering of meat, the food went some way towards gratifying my hunger. Ale was abundant and, watered down though it was, I decided against drinking too much in case I was unable to control my horse on the return journey. Having finished our meal and with the afternoon remaining fine, Adam suggested continuing discussions in the open air: a neat way of keeping Brother Norbert out of earshot should he return after lunch.

Upon leaving the warming house I was curious to catch sight of several of the Brothers walking around the cloister: some had books, some were presumably meditating. Over the years I had visited several ruined abbeys and priories, on each occasion trying to envisage what life was like at that time. And now here I was, actually witnessing it! It was unbelievable.

We wandered through the Abbey precincts, heading down towards the river. A watery, spring sun filtered through the high cloud adding brightness to the late afternoon. I sauntered along behind the men, watching a solitary dipper perched on a rock in the fast flowing stream search for food, whilst further down the bank a grey wagtail sought out material with which to reinforce its nest, no doubt in some nearby crevice. Here too, encouraged by the warm sunshine, buds were appearing on the trees, heralding the onset of spring. This truly was an idyllic spot the canons had chosen to build their monastery albeit some might consider the surrounding area bleak. I emerged from my reverie to hear Adam and Edward discussing the future and hastened to catch up with them.

"... Lady Margaret informed us this morning. I do not blame thee for telling her, Edward, for I know things must have been difficult when thy brother died." Adam had already informed Edward I was aware of his true identity and could be trusted implicitly. "But she did right in secreting thee here. We should continue to be vigilant and thou must be diligent in maintaining your assumed name. Should Hugo get to know the truth ... well, I must be blunt ... I shudder to imagine the consequences. He is an opportunist and knows his future lies with the Tudor." Clasping his hands together in front of him as he walked, intent on his narrative, Adam continued, "Thou knowest we have oft discussed your Uncle Richard's motives in taking the crown but I shall repeat again, thou hast no legitimate claim to the throne. Whate'er thou might think I was present at Bishop Stillington's revelations about thy father's prior trothplight and can ..."

"Anselm, forgive my interruption but thou must not worry. I have no designs on the crown." Sounding weary and dejected Edward continued, "Events of these three years past have changed me. I may once have been a spoilt child, intent on my, *rightful*," he spat the word out with sarcasm, "position, but I desire it no longer. My time at Overthwaite has changed me. The short time I had with my dear brother has changed me. I have come to realise there is more in life than to covet a troubled throne. I no longer blame my uncle, events gave him no option but to take the actions he did. Time has helped me see that, helped me appreciate the realities of life. Nay, if I blame any 'tis my father, for though I loved him dearly, 'twas his actions which damned us. That and his deceit and the lies told to my mother all those years."

Gosh, what a speech! I looked at the young boy whose staring eyes were lifeless and far away and I viewed him differently than I had five minutes previously. What a mature head rested on those slight shoulders. In his short life he had undergone events such as most young people could never contemplate. To have been raised in the expectation of ruling the country and now to relinquish all thoughts of that claim with such good grace and a mere shrug of the shoulders took some doing. I admired him enormously. I could see Adam, too, was proud of him.

Gripping Edward's shoulder Adam turned to face him, "It warms my heart to hear thee speak thus for I have been agonising this entire morn on what is to become of thee. Thou cannot stay here, indeed it was never intended that thou should remain at Overthwaite indefinitely, merely until your uncle had dealt with the Tudor and felt the country was settled. Thou knowest that thy sister Elizabeth is now wed to the King?" Edward nodded. "By marrying her, Henry Tudor cannot acknowledge the illegality of thy parents' union. 'Twould serve naught to his cause. But 'tis a double-edged sword. For by discrediting thy bastardy he provides thee with a legitimate claim to the throne, thereby placing thy life in jeopardy."

Adam paused momentarily, then continued in earnest, "What I am about to suggest may be parlous but thy prior words afford a glimmer of hope. Mindful of the affection existing between thyself and Elizabeth it occurred to me that we could do worse than throw ourselves on her mercy and advise her of thy whereabouts." With an ironic glance in my direction he continued, "Rumour has it that your Uncle Richard brought about the sad demise of both thyself and thy brother. Consequently Elizabeth will be overjoyed when she discovers that thou, at least, are still alive. The risk, of course, is that we are unaware of any feelings and loyalties she may possess towards her husband. Had thy sentiments been aught different to those expressed a few moments ago then I should not have suggested this course of action. But whatever be thy sister's standpoint, thou wilt pose no threat to the Tudor and this should ease any guilt she may experience by cause of split loyalties. What thinkest thou, Edward? Should we rely on fortune?"

With head bowed Edward absentmindedly kicked a small stone with the toe of his shoe, deep in thought on the proposition Adam had put to him. He raised his face towards us, "Aye, Anselm, let us trust to chance. Elizabeth will not fail me." With a gleam in his eye he continued, "I was ever her favourite!" We all laughed.

"Thou art truly thy father's son! Now, thou must remain here whilst I journey to London. Brother Norbert, I feel sure, will extend hospitalities to thee a while longer – thou hast made a fair impression on him by all accounts!"

Edward looked embarrassed but managed a sheepish smile, "I have been practising illuminations. Brother Eustace says I have a talent – 'tis most absorbing. But a favourite place is the fishery near Hawes Water. I help the Brothers there on every occasion."

"Good. I am pleased thou art filling thy time gainfully – idleness prospers naught. But it is also requisite for thee to continue with thy lessons whensoe'er possible. I trust thou hast thy books here with thee?"

"Assuredly, Anselm. Lady Margaret was most solicitous to ensure that I brought them. And I study daily, whene'er the time permits."

"Thou wast always a model pupil!" Adam teased. "Now we must away. I shall talk to Brother Norbert ere we depart and thou may be assured I shall approach thy sister at the earliest opportunity. Fear not, Edward. I *shall* return for thee."

CHAPTER ELEVEN

We were in no rush to return to Overthwaite, allowing the horses to amble along at their own pace. On the way we discussed the turn of events at the Abbey. Adam was relieved at Edward's stance and hopeful of a positive response from his sister.

"The lad has verily matured both in disposition and stature this past twelve month. Edward was never overly tall. Indeed Richard was ever a match in height despite his lesser years. But Edward has grown a little and looks in some small measure less childlike since his golden tresses have darkened." Thoughtful for a moment as the horses jogged along he added, "Elizabeth ever was an agreeable girl – always one to please. And Edward spoke truly, saying she favoured him. But I shall not give him up merely to be imprisoned by the Tudor. I would not have mentioned it to the lad, would not have wanted to sow the seeds when he has undergone so much, but it must remain a possibility should knowledge of his whereabouts get into the wrong hands. I do hope we shall be able to get Elizabeth to see sense."

"Did you say we?" I couldn't help but keep the surprise from my voice. "Shall I be accompanying you?"

"Thou surely dost not think that I would leave thee in Hugo's presence? 'Twill be bad enough leaving the others. What the future holds for them I cannot imagine."

Throughout the remainder of the journey my mind was in a whirl: the thought of visiting mediaeval London with the possibility of meeting the Queen was beyond my grasp. It was fortunate my mount knew her own way home as my concentration lapsed on several occasions and had the mare not been sure footed we may well have stumbled before reaching the Hall.

My euphoria was short-lived as the place was in turmoil when we arrived. It transpired Hugo was up to his old tricks and had been causing trouble. Emerging from the barn early afternoon and intent on creating mischief, once again he had gone in search of Jane. Tracing her to the garret chamber he had entered uninvited and attempted to force her from the room. Lady Margaret, struggling from her bed, had tried to assist Jane but in doing so the strain and shock had caused her waters to break prematurely.

Luckily Aggie Bowman was nearby and had taken charge of matters, seemingly the only person capable of bringing Hugo to heel. Sarah, in petulant mood because Hugo's attentions had been directed elsewhere, had been placed in charge of the children: Tom had been instructed to intervene should Hugo consider giving vent to his high spirits at their expense. I was swept up into Lady Margaret's chamber to join the remaining ladies and in between assisting with the usual trappings of childbirth – the constant provision of boiling water – I viewed the medieval proceedings with curiosity.

Aggie began by removing the eagle stone from where it was bound to Lady Margaret's arm and placed the talisman on her lower abdomen. "There. Now the child may come. We mun have summat reet." Although the wise-woman was a matter of fact person, Lady Margaret appeared to find her presence comforting. "Had tha' gone thy full time then we could ha' shut up thy chamber against th' harmful fresh air, but there's no point cryin' o'er spilt milk now – we shall just have to put our faith in t' powers that be. Margery, go prepare a caudle for Lady M. She needs t' keep her strength up. An'

Jane, tie them strips to th' head o' the bed. Your mistress'll be needin' them later."

So the evening wore on. A fierce fire burned in the grate and the rush lights cast distorted shadows onto the stone walls. The chamber was becoming hot and stuffy and we were all aware Lady Margaret's labour pains were increasing by the hour. They had been gentle at first but were now coming at regular intervals and sharpening in intensity. With only ergot to aid Lady Margaret's distress, Aggie ensured a constant supply of spiced wine caudle was available and I imagine a combination of the two helped to alleviate the pain.

It was the early hours of the morning before her contractions started.

"Now, breathe deeply, breathe deeply ... that's reet ... we're getting there," Aggie knew Lady Margaret was already exhausted even though, more than likely, she had still a long way to go.

As the pain of each contraction deepened, Lady Margaret grasped the cloths above her head; pushing down she strained to give birth to the babe inside her. But time was passing and the only advancement was the new day: slowly daylight lit up the chamber. Aggie sensed that things were wrong though she tried her hardest not to convey this to the prostrate figure on the bed.

"There we be, there we be. Things'll soon be a' reet," she crooned at regular intervals.

But things were not all right and by mid day, after almost twenty-four hours of labour and the loss of a great deal of blood, I feared Lady Margaret had little more to give. Covered in sweat, she writhed in agony on the bed and screamed with an intensity that made the hairs on the back of my neck stand on end. Knowing as I did that she was shortly to die, the whole episode seemed unreal, as though I was merely an onlooker and I wondered whether she would live long enough to hold the child in her arms.

At last the baby's head appeared.

"That's reet, bear down now, bear down. I can see the babe's head. Come on lass. Bear down now, one last time."

Aggie, positioned at the bottom of the bed, urged Lady Margaret with her encouraging words.

The effort the mother expended in those final throes left her torn and barely breathing but she had been delivered of a girl, a healthy one at that and when the child uttered its first cry, drained though she was, Lady Margaret rallied. With a look of euphoria on her face she craved to nurse the baby she had struggled to bring into the world.

"All in good time, m' Lady, all in good time. Now Margery, see to t' bairn as I've shown thee," and with Aggie's help Margery set to, working the little girl's limbs. "That's reet, chase them evil humours away, mek the child healthy and bonny … good girl, good girl. Now, rub this o'er her … all o'er, that's reet."

Margery had already prepared a mixture of honey and salt and this she now massaged over the howling babe. Honey was then rubbed gently onto her gums followed by a few drops of warm wine, which were trickled into her mouth. Finally, she was swaddled in silk and only then placed at her mother's heavy breast for some essential, nourishing milk. Having given birth twice before, Lady Margaret knew instinctively what needed to be done and, gently squeezing her nipple between thumb and forefinger, she encouraged her milk to flow. Aggie, meanwhile, had been ensuring the afterbirth was entire whilst I tidied away the soiled cloths and bedding and prepared to go below. Margery's last task before following me was to cleanse the room with wormwood and rue: a safeguard against infection. Jane, ever solicitous to her mistress's needs, remained behind to provide support and to nurse the patient.

Adam was in the hall, reading, but as we entered he looked up eagerly, "How goes it?" I had to bite my tongue not to reply.

"Lady M's had a reet rough time. But I don't need to be telling thee that. Tha mun heard her cries. She's quiet now, so let's hope all will be well," Aggie's unspoken words were telling, "but the babe be thriving and looks healthy enough."

"A boy?" Although Adam knew, he asked the question.

"Nay, not a boy but a sister for Matthew and Joan." Then she voiced what was hanging in the air, what nobody else would say, "And if Lady M don't live to see her grow, 'twill be that devil what brought about her going!"

What a fickle mistress fate is. Had Adam and I not been at the Abbey we may have been able to avert Hugo's actions and thereby perhaps prevent the premature death of Lady Margaret. Once again I wondered whether one could change history. I thought not.

Hugo returned the following morning, by which time Lady Margaret's condition had worsened. He showed a total disregard for her state of health and presumably took an interest in the birth of his niece only for reassurance that the baby was in fact a girl and therefore of no further threat to his inheritance. Seeing me for the first time he made a beeline across the hall.

"Well, well. So this is the mute I heard tell of." Looking into his brown eyes I remembered Catherine describing him as cold and hard. I was alone in the hall and I could feel my neck begin to suffuse with blood. I cast down my gaze, not wishing to aggravate him in any way. Lifting my chin roughly with his hand he continued, "Pray look at me, woman, when I speak to thee! Mmm ... quite pretty. And there is one thing canst be said for thy lack of speech – thou cannot report aught back to thy dear cousin."

So saying, he made a grab between my legs through the folds of my skirt and as I was wearing no under garments the action brought tears to my eyes. I gasped and pushing him away was about to run out when Adam entered the room.

Hugo let out a deep, evil laugh and brushing past me whispered in my ear, "There will surely be a future time when we shall not be disturbed." Continuing towards the outside stair he addressed Adam. "Good day, *Master* Anselm. I trust thou art well?"

"I know not what passed between thee and my cousin but I warn thee, Hugo, leave Emma alone!" The malevolence in his voice surprised me: could this be a measure of his feelings for me? I felt sure it was.

"Dear dear, I fear the lady can look after herself," his insolent tone mocked Adam. "And she may have to, for thou cannot shadow her indefinitely, Anselm."

Adam grabbed the front of Hugo's shirt.. "Mark my words. Should any harm befall Emma, shouldst thou lay a finger on her … I *swear* I shall kill thee!"

I held my breath. The ever present dagger at Hugo's waist looked all too handy and I feared for Adam's life: Hugo was a trained mercenary and could easily get the better of him.

Thankfully this time Hugo was not to be drawn and with exaggerated aplomb he removed Adam's hand and, eying him suspiciously, hissed between clenched teeth, "And *I* swear I shall unearth the true reason for thou being here!" With one last backward glance in my direction he was gone and I was in Adam's arms.

"I fear that man will cause trouble in more ways than one. The sooner we are out of here and about our business the better," he spoke the words quietly under his breath so only I should hear.

Eight days later Lady Margaret was dead – what a sorry end to her short life.

After the rigours of childbearing she had remained in her darkened chamber – childbirth weakened the eyesight I was told by Margery – during which time she had contracted what I imagine was puerperal fever. A form of blood poisoning caused by infection, this illness claimed the lives of many women during that period – Jane Seymour for one. Having read an account of her symptoms I felt sure Lady Margaret died of the same complaint.

During one of her lucid moments she imparted a desire for the baby to be christened Anne, after her mother. In view of her worsening state and lest anything should happen to the child, this had been effected swiftly by the parish priest at a time when Hugo was safely out of the way. Lady Margaret had been adamant he should have nothing to do with the ceremony and before the baptism, which was conducted in her chamber, she requested that Adam and Jane should stand as godparents. Once the formalities had been completed her delirium increased. This was perhaps as well, for her shaking limbs and the prolonged bouts of pain that accompanied the illness would have been almost impossible to bear by one who was fully conscious. Since the day Lady Margaret had given birth Jane was never far from her chamber but throughout those last few days she became her constant companion: sitting by the bed to mop her mistress's brow, hold her hand or murmur words of endearment, the latter as much for her own comfort as for that of the writhing figure who lay before her. I often took a bowl of broth in and longed to urge Jane to take some sustenance herself – she was painfully thin and I hoped she too would not fall ill – but her primary concern was always for her patient. Her painstaking devotion was heart-warming but at the same time heartbreaking to see.

It was as though Lady Margaret had been determined to survive until the christening had been accomplished and having done so, she lost the will to live. Jane was loath to leave the chamber even though she knew her mistress had breathed her last. I went up to the garret once again and placing my hands on Jane's narrow shoulders applied pressure to indicate she should come away. The body of her mistress lay on the bed: the peace she had lacked during the previous week had now come to her. She looked as she had on the evening of my arrival; as though she still lived, merely sleeping. But all life had sapped from her, her spirit had flown and there remained only an empty shell.

Jane's torment reminded me of my own agony on the death of my mother. I shall never forget the moment I heard the news. A wail emerged from deep within me, as of a dying animal. The pain was intense. For a time all reason to continue living left me: we had been so close. Eventually Jane's pain would ease but never truly disappear.

Lady Margaret was buried on a cold, wet, April morning, in the Rutherford family grave next to her husband. The whole village was in attendance and from comments I overheard, the inhabitants held Lady Margaret in high esteem.

Needless to say, Hugo was absent: once again on a drunken spree in Penrith. But his non-attendance was welcomed by all, allowing each of us to pay our last respects and grieve in our own way. Lady Margaret's death was no surprise: we had all been expecting it since the day she gave birth. Nevertheless, we were inevitably sad and Jane, who had wept silently since the day of her mistress's passing, was inconsolable.

The funeral over, we returned to the Hall trudging silently along in the constant rain: a solemn procession on a solemn day. Upon our return we gathered in the hall to drink hot, spiced wine in an attempt to warm both inside and out. Looking around, one thing was patently clear: with the exception of Jane, the sadness felt at Lady Margaret's passing was now at an end. Death was no stranger to the inhabitants of Overthwaite; they took it in their stride and got on with things. More important now was safeguarding the lives of Matthew and his sisters'. Hugo's absence made matters easier for Adam who addressed us whilst we drank.

"Your mistress's passing changes things greatly. Whilst she lived, and in view of her enceinte condition, I surmise Hugo would have made no move to snatch his unlawful inheritance." Turning to Matthew he told him, "The title and estate are yours by rights, lad. However, in view of thy minority he will surely take over thy guardianship and who knows what will befall thee then." I was surprised at his direct approach but he had already informed me he intended to be open with Matthew.

The boy responded well, especially when one considered he had recently lost his mother, "Have no fear, Master Anselm. I have my father's sword in my bedchamber!" We all smiled, trying to hide our amusement at this plucky young lad.

"Let us hope 'twill not come to that," he ruffled Matthew's hair fondly. "Over these days past I have been giving much thought to the matter and have concluded that thy swift departure is our only course of action." His gaze moved to the others, "With Lord Dacre no option, I think it a good business that the children be taken to their relations in the north." Again he looked towards Matthew, "Thy apprenticeship as squire must be delayed lad. For now we must lodge thee with thy kith and kin."

"I understand, Master Anselm, but fear not. The books thou gave me are safe and sound and I shall take them with me to the north. I shall study them diligently until such times as my training can be arranged." Such an old head rested on those young shoulders. My heart went out to him.

"Good lad, Matthew. I feel sure in time they will serve thee well." He turned to the others, "Now, although I heard mention of the de Raisgills from Sir Anthony I know little about the family, nor even their whereabouts." Adam looked about him hoping for some guidance from the others.

"Happen I could be helping thee there, eh?" Tom responded in his deliberate manner. "Some years back I had cause to tek Master up there ... on some sort o' business it were ... an' I think as how I could remember me way back there, eh?" I had already noticed how he had an odd habit of turning his statements into questions.

"Is it far, Tom?"

"Not too far, Master Anselm, though it be north of Carlisle. Sir Anthony alus reckoned it were eight or nine leagues, eh?"

"Manageable in a day?"

"In t' cart? Aye, so long as we mek an early start, eh?"

"That then shall be our aim. I cannot imagine the de Raisgills refusing their kinfolk succour ..."

"Thou can rest assured of receiving a warm welcome." Jane's small, timid voice surprised us all. Since the death of her mistress she had spoken little and her usual shyness now seemed tinged with a pitiable emptiness. "Lady Margaret says that ..." she paused and spent some moments composing herself before continuing, "Lady Margaret was always of the opinion that they are a kindly, generous family although to my knowledge she only visited on one occasion." What a pity, I thought, that I must remain mute: for Jane to talk about her late mistress would certainly have been good therapy.

"Excellent, I am pleased to hear so." Again addressing them all Adam continued, "Speed must be of the essence but we should all take care to avoid arousing Hugo's suspicions. I would suggest that the party consists of the children, Jane, Margery as wet nurse and therefore Tom and William also." Raising a questioning eyebrow in Tom's direction he received an imperceptive nod in agreement. "Stephen." Adam looked towards the steward. "Wilt thou stay behind and address thy usual duties?" He too nodded.

Still addressing Stephen, Adam continued, "All are aware that thy position over the past few months has not been an enviable one – not only with the increased workload on the death of Sir Anthony but also in the handling of his brother. Not an easy task I am sure. But I know that Lady Margaret held thee in high esteem and although the future is unpredictable, the estate is in need of a pair of reliable hands."

"Master Matthew can rest easy in t' knowledge that I shall do my best." Matthew beamed at this note of deference from Stephen and even Sarah looked momentarily proud of her husband.

"Can all be made ready by the end of the week?" Adam looked around for confirmation. "Good!"

Thankfully Hugo's absence enabled us to make preparations without his knowledge: although as Adam instructed those who were to remain behind, none should put themselves at risk by withholding information of our whereabouts. Adam felt confident that Hugo would refrain from following and would welcome trouble free possession of the Hall.

Four days later all was prepared; our departure luckily coinciding with one of Hugo's drinking sprees. The day was mild and dry and we left at first light. In view of our anticipated onward journey to London, Adam and I were on horseback – a fact of which I was thankful as I watched the faces of those in the cart on the bumpy, rutted track. The day's travel was uneventful but interesting for me and I remembered Catherine's description of her own journey to Dacre. If *I* found my surroundings changed, knowing little of the area, what must *she* have felt?

We passed through several villages on the way, though some were hardly large enough to warrant the name: perhaps township would be a better description. Each bore a strong resemblance to Overthwaite and our presence provided a welcome diversion for the younger members of the community in contrast to the cautious note of interest displayed by the adults. The children would follow our small procession well out of the village, exchanging childish banter with Matthew and William.

As predicted, it was dusk when Tom announced the crenelated building visible on the skyline was Raisgill Hall: a statement that helped lift the spirits of our weary party. In view of our hasty departure we had been unable to advise the de Raisgills of our arrival. Consequently we were met by hostile looks and kept on the far side of the moat with only Tom, the one person who might be recognised from his earlier visit, being allowed to cross once the barmkin gate had been lowered.

We waited – the horses as impatient as ourselves to have rest and sustenance for the night. In the failing light I had been unable to see much of the Hall on our approach but on closer inspection it became obvious this was a much more substantial affair than Overthwaite Hall. In addition to the moat, its barmkin walls were constructed of stone rather than the clay covered timber we had left behind us that morning – presumably to withstand the inevitable border raids that occurred in this more northerly position. At last, our credentials established, we were allowed admittance to the interior where, as at Overthwaite, buildings were ranged around the barmkin walls but on a much grander scale. We made our way towards the huge pele tower beside which were footings and several piles of stones, although whether this was new building work or an old ruin I found difficult to tell for nightfall was now almost upon us. We were ushered up to the first floor there to find a roaring fire that, although making little impact on the cold fabric of the building nevertheless enabled a thawing of our chilled bodies.

Sir Robert and Lady Alice gave us a friendly welcome and we were soon being warmed by spiced and honeyed ale. A swiftly assembled but satisfactory meal was served and Sir Robert apologised for the display of caution on our arrival.

"We had grown comfy under King Richard for he always maintained a tight rein in the north, having resided here so many years. So comfy, in fact, I had embarked upon a new building project to improve our living quarters. Sadly things are now reverting to the old ways and once again reiving is on the increase so the building works are in abeyance. We find it serves us better to remain permanently here as opposed to the old hall o'er yonder," he pointed in the direction of the large wooden structure I had noticed situated on the opposite side of the barmkin. "All the more easy to make ourselves secure at short notice, you understand."

Sir Robert was a small, precise man, rotund in build and I estimated he was around Adam's age. His thick, auburn hair was streaked with grey and, perhaps unusually for the time, he sported a trim moustache and small, goatee beard. He had a pronounced limp and walked with the aid of a stick: I noticed his left leg was shorter than the right and withered around the calf.

His wife was a jolly person who smiled profusely and during our short stay at Raisgill I gleaned her main purpose in life was to produce babies – the nursery numbered seven (including two sets of twins) and was still growing as, evidently, she was pregnant again! The pair reminded me of Tweedledum and Tweedledee for Lady Alice, though considerably younger than her husband, resembled him in both height and girth – hardly surprising in view of the amount of food they both consumed. Although they informed us they had already eaten, the pair tucked in heartily to the repast set out for our party and soon only crumbs remained on the trestle table.

"So Anselm … 'tis alright for me to address thee informally?" A nod from Adam and Sir Robert continued, "We were aware of Sir Anthony's death but I take it things have moved on apace since then?" His deliberate manner of speech held the slightest trace of a Scottish lilt.

Adam recounted recent events at Overthwaite Hall, outlining the reason for our visit. The de Raisgills, however, were obviously aware of Hugo's nature.

"I have said more than once to Sir Robert that I cannot believe those brothers were sired by the same father!" Appreciating the implications of her last remark Lady Alice hurried on, "Not that I mean to cast any aspersions on Sir Anthony's mother, heaven forbid that my remark should be taken so! But that brother of his, he is the spawn of the Devil, you mark my words, the spawn of the Devil!"

Sir Robert seemed to ignore most of his wife's vociferous comments, a trait I was to notice several times over our short stay there. "Your decision to remove the children was a wise one, Anselm, for I would put nothing past Hugo."

"I hope you will think it no imposition to arrive unannounced but I was of the opinion time was of the essence and Hugo's temporary absence was fortuitous."

Sir Robert anticipated his wife's lengthy assurances and pre-empted her. "Not at all, not at all. When all is said and done what are family for? Another three in our large nursery will make no difference, will it Alice?" he winked at his wife and in an unguarded moment gave her an intimate smile. Obviously much affection existed between the two.

"The more the merrier, that's what I say!" and with a throaty chuckle she patted her growing stomach.

Adam continued, "I am aware that it was intended Matthew serve as squire to Lord Humphrey but with his demise and the allegiance of the new Lord Dacre being to King Henry, I thought it wiser not to follow that course."

"*King* Henry! If more men had fought as bravely for King Richard as did Sir Anthony, we would not be in this predicament. But for this leg of mine ..." with a clenched fist Sir Robert thumped his leg in frustration.

"Now then, Robert, 'tis no use to talk such for thou knowest it only makes thee angry. The Good Lord saw fit to give thee other fine attributes – as can be witnessed by our nursery!" Lady Alice gave another deep chortle and her husband, obviously embarrassed in front of strangers, coloured at the meaning of her comment.

Adam continued as though nothing had been said, "Hugo – true to form I understand – came down on the side of the victorious. Consequently should any petitions be made to

Lord Dacre he would surely not find in favour of Matthew, besides who is to say that the King might not bestow the Overthwaite lands on Hugo in recognition of his welcome support?"

"What thou sayest is true, Anselm. Lord Thomas is more unpredictable than was his father. He appears a just man but at times I find his decisions strange. Perhaps for the time being 'twould be better for the lad to keep his head down, until we see how the land lies. He may regard Raisgill as his home for the foreseeable future."

Throughout these discussions I had been watching the comings and goings in the hall. Because of its much larger scale, Raisgill possessed many more inhabitants than Overthwaite and to my untutored eye it appeared the majority of those people had passed through, on one errand or another, since our arrival!

We remained by the fire and as the evening wore on I struggled to keep my lids from closing as the familiar prickle of tiredness stung my eyes. Tom, Margery and the children had already departed for their quarters, leaving only Jane, Adam and myself with the de Raisgills. But thankfully the conversation soon drew to a close and we said our goodnights and vacated the hall.

Collapsing onto my pallet in the communal sleeping area for the women and children I hoped sleep would come easily. My prayers were answered, for although it had been another interesting day, limbs that were weary after a day in the saddle soon forced my active brain into slumber.

Adam and I remained at Raisgill for only thirty-six hours whilst we made arrangements for our trip to London.

Our party settled in quickly. Margery took up duties assisting in the kitchens, Tom slotted in at the forge, William helped with the horses and Jane, surprisingly, found her niche in the nursery where her shyness vanished and she became an instant hit with the young children.

"With a little more meat on her bones, that lass shall make a grand wife to some lucky chap," chucked Lady Alice. "Aye *and* a grand mother."

It was mid-day and she had suggested I keep her company in the hall whilst she completed some needlework she had underway. I wondered why she wanted as a companion someone who was unable to speak. As the hours wore on I realised Lady Alice was a person who had no need for reciprocal conversation: she would always be the one to do the talking and I doubted she would make a good listener. Nevertheless, her views on Jane matched my own and it had only taken her a few short hours to assess the young woman's character.

I was amused that Lady Alice talked of Jane as though she was a young girl when, more than likely, the two were similar in age: obviously Lady Alice had an old head on young shoulders. She chattered on about the de Raisgills and all that was required of me was the occasional nod of the head or a raised eyebrow. By the end of the afternoon I felt sure I had known the family all my life. She was Sir Robert's second wife and they were married shortly after his first wife had died, several years ago. Consequently, as was common in those days, in effect Sir Robert had two families. From his previous marriage he had two children, Lucy, married and living nearer Carlisle and Jonathan.

"But they are grand children and we all get on well together. Though I must admit to holding a soft spot for Jonathan, Sir Robert's firstborn – he has a quick mind, like his father. But that is where the similarity ends for Jon is as tall as his sire is broad!" She rocked back and forth in mirth at her quip. "He is a kindly lad, gentle in nature and by virtue of his scholarly ways Sir Robert trusts him with the day to day running of the Hall. Besides, 'tis easier what with poor Robert's leg," I noticed she had dropped the formal title in her moment of tenderness. "Likewise Lord Thomas has recognised his value – Jon is away on his lordship's business at present, collecting taxes throughout the shire." She struggled to her feet, intent on refreshing the fire, for it was another bitterly cold day. I touched her arm to show I would perform the chore, as in view of her build and pregnant state, it was a laborious task for her to rise from the chair. "Aye, he has his head screwed on a'right does Jon – would doubtless break a few hearts besides, were he to shed some of his bashfulness, for his looks are right fair."

I mused that Sir Robert's first wife must have been a far cry from Lady Alice to have produced a shy, retiring offspring and wondered how Jonathan related to this jolly, talkative stepmother.

That evening, over our meal, Adam advised Sir Robert of our plans – or should I say our supposed plans. He had already informed me of the excuse he was to use, so that should I be asked any awkward questions, I knew how to react. It was as well we were prepared, for our paths had failed to cross throughout the day and during the afternoon, one or two of Lady Alice's comments had required a silent response.

"We would thank you for your hospitality Sir Robert," ever the gentleman Adam turned towards our hostess, "and of course, Lady Alice. However, urgent family business necessitates the presence of my cousin and myself in London."

"I am right sorry to hear that, Anselm. Thou must surely know that thou art both welcome under our roof for as long as thou wish," responded Sir Robert seriously. "When must thou leave?"

"Now that the horses are rested we shall make an early start on the morrow."

"'Tis a pity for I was hoping thou might prove a challenging adversary at chess during thy stay here. 'Twould seem I must await Jonathan's return before honing my skills once more."

"I would welcome the chance of a game, Sir Robert. Perhaps we could return once our affairs are settled in the capital?"

"Indeed, for thou wilt always receive a warm reception at Raisgill. Is't not so Lady Alice?" His eyes brightened and I suspected that in the absence of his son, he found life with his wife rather tiring on the ears.

"But of course!" Lady Alice turned towards me. "Another chance to chat with Emma would be grand. We got on a treat, did we not?"

I nodded and smiled, trying not to look Adam in the eye for I fancy he could guess the way the 'conversation' had gone during the afternoon.

"'Tis agreed then. For, in fact, I should have cause to visit York in the not too distant future and Raisgill will make an agreeable diversion." Adam rose and gripped Sir Robert's shoulder. "But until our contest may I suggest that thou challenge Matthew to a game or two? I believe thou might find the lad a more than competent opponent."

"In truth? Then I am pleased that my kinsman shall make his home here. I have always been of the opinion that the game of chess is a true character builder and therefore essential for a lad such as Matthew – with all he has undergone recently, you understand?"

"Aye, and some love and affection would not go amiss either," his wife shook her head, "the poor lamb! His mother lost and his father less than two months buried – 'tis such a pity!" Unconsciously her hand went to her extended stomach and I felt she was thinking of her own forthcoming childbearing. "Let us hope this child is as eager to enter the world as were all the others. Which brings something to my mind ... a wet nurse."

Whatever we had been anticipating, I think I can say on behalf of all present that it was anything but her last words. We sat expectantly, waiting for her to continue.

"Margery is doing a grand job in that capacity with the new babe and for the time being we should not change things." Again her hands gently rubbed her growing bulge, "Nonetheless, my own wet nurse from the village is ready to be called upon when my time comes and there are one or two other reliable women whom I know. Margery and her family may then, should they so wish, return to Overthwaite – though should Hugo still be in residence they are more than welcome to remain at Raisgill!"

"And Jane?" Adam voiced my thoughts.

"If memory serves me right she is related to Lady Margaret," Sir Robert's brow creased in thought.

"Aye, and she was telling me that her only kith and kin be a ne'er do well brother. And an ally of Hugo's into the bargain!" Before her husband could comment Lady Alice continued, "If thou were to ask me, I would say she should remain here indefinitely, for what else has life in store for her other than a nunnery? Nay, although she is as quiet as a mouse a life of seclusion is not for her. Why, the babes adore her and she would make an excellent mother. Besides, there may be a chance of fattening her up should she remain here!" Once again Lady Alice chortled with glee. "But that is only my opinion dear, your word holds sway."

Sir Robert gave a rueful smile and raised one eyebrow to Adam. "How could any man gainsay such reasoning from his wife? Of course Jane must stay, if only for the sake of peace and harmony in the household!"

Everyone laughed and although I was looking forward to the forthcoming trip to London, as our last evening at Raisgill drew to a contented close, I felt I would miss these people whom I hardly knew but who had readily opened their home and hearts to us.

CHAPTER TWELVE

The anticipation of our trip to London induced a restless night. Tossing and turning I sought sleep but it evaded me. Conscious of varying degrees of snoring from other occupants of the chamber, on more than one occasion I rose quietly to gaze from the embrasure, my mind alert to recent experiences. Whatever the day might hold in store I could hardly begin to imagine.

    I must have slept for I awoke with the dawn and was out of bed in a trice taking care not to waken Jane who was still asleep beside me. I was eager for the day to begin and dressing quickly went below. Adam was already up and out in the stables, checking on our horses and asking William to make sure they were ready for our departure. At Lady Alice's insistence we had a hearty breakfast, packed our meagre possessions and were soon bidding fond farewells to all at Raisgill.

    "Lady Alice says as how yer must tek this for t' way. She says t' food in some '*hos-tel-ries*'" Margery said the word deliberately, presumably pronouncing it in the same way as had Lady Alice, "is worse than slops!"

    Taking the bundle I smiled to myself and looking up towards the Hall spotted Lady Alice's figure, arm raised in a vigorous wave to speed us on our travels. I waved back and held up the parcel of food to show my appreciation for her thoughtfulness.

We were then on our way, moving out of the barmkin with rolling, green fields and hummocks stretching out before us. The day was raw and I pulled my woollen cloak tightly around me feeling sure that soon I would be chilled by the cold. Thankfully it was dry and despite the bitter wind good to be out in the fresh air again, good to be alone with Adam.

"I don't think I'm a particularly talkative person but it is good to use my vocal chords again."

"Yes, I should compliment you on your restraint. Although I must say that on more than one occasion … am I correct in surmising thou hast had cause to 'bite thy tongue' perhaps?" He had a twinkle in his eye and although I assumed the question to be a rhetorical one I decided to reply in like manner.

"Hmm, perhaps I possess more of that feminine trait than I thought I did. But you try sitting with Lady Alice all afternoon without being able to respond to her constant flow! It's not easy I can assure you."

"Forgive me. Thy conduct was impeccable!" his tone was still tongue in cheek and he made a mock bow with his head. "But all jesting apart, the de Raisgills are a most hospitable family, are they not? And even though the children are not my responsibility I feel safe in the knowledge that they will be well cared for."

Although Adam wished to settle Edward's future as soon as possible, he was cautious of not tiring the horses in view of the uncertainty of obtaining fresh mounts and so we had decided to travel at no great speed. He estimated that, at a leisurely pace, it would take around ten days to reach London. Accommodation was an unknown factor, for his last trip had been a totally different affair – pushing his horse to the limit and obtaining a fresh mount wherever possible, with overnight stops being few and far between.

"Wayside taverns should be our last resort, more oft than not they are lice-ridden and may be dangerous besides. Where'er possible we shall take refuge with the Brothers –

good, plain food and a clean, if somewhat austere chamber is all that we require."

By now I had been 'back' for almost three weeks and during that time one of the main topics of conversation between Adam and me – on the odd occasion when I could actually speak, of course – was my future. Adam was determined I should return to my own time as soon as possible; I, on the other hand, was unconvinced. My decision depended on Adam's feelings towards me when the 'crunch' time came – but at the moment I was keeping that snippet of information to myself. I knew that should Adam detect the slightest chance of my remaining he would brook no argument and if necessary, manhandle me through the door at the given time. My only hope was that by October he would love me as much as I loved him … or at least love me! To that end I had decided to wear my heart on my sleeve and miss no opportunity to let him know my feelings. Whether this was the right way to go about things I don't know but having made the decision I would stick to it: after all, I had nothing to lose.

So began our journey. Adam informed me the tracks in the west were less used and therefore more likely to harbour thieves and cut-throats. Consequently we made our way across country towards the east following the higher, less wooded ground whenever the opportunity presented itself. The major road network from north to south ran from Berwick to London but we aimed to cut across country through Appleby and Brough, joining the route above York at Boroughbridge. Had we the time, Adam informed me, he would dearly have loved to visit the abbey at Hexham for there his old friend Rowland Leschman was Prior. However, not knowing whether he was in residence and considering this would add appreciable time to our journey, Adam decided against the detour.

The countryside was bleak and at several remote crossroads we came upon chantry chapels, set up to act as a shelter for travellers where no other existed. We pressed on and in due course joined the London road, following its course down through Pontefract, Nottingham and on to Leicester. There, not a million miles from Bosworth, Adam became silent and I guessed in which direction his thoughts were running. Initially I too remained quiet, not wishing to intrude on his sadness but the miles passed and still no words were spoken.

"You could have done nothing, even had you returned in time." Adam still said nothing. I continued, "How could you have convinced him of what was about to happen? How could you explain how you knew? Why, you'd have been burned at the stake for witchcraft – if there is such a thing as a male witch!"

"Thou art right of course," he sighed deeply. "But it does not help to lessen the feeling of grief."

At Northampton we had a choice of routes: to the left a direct approach to London on Watling Street through St. Albans, to the right a longer journey via Towcester and Oxford.

"The right hand course is ours," Adam advised, consciously averting his gaze. "Albeit many a year past, I cannot bring myself to ride through St. Albans."

His words were no surprise for I had remembered his father had died there in battle. Our horses were close enough for me to reach out and gently squeeze his arm.

"I still miss him, Emma. Dost thou find that strange?"

I looked across at him, this gentle man who meant the world to me, and my heart skipped a beat. "No Adam. When the bond between parent and child is a close one, the ache never truly goes away. I understand entirely. It is one of the reasons why I love you so."

Thankfully our journey to London had been an uneventful one – no accidents and no acts of aggression. But the elements conspired against us: things could not have been worse.

We had awakened at the start of our second day to atrocious weather. The skies were dark and heavy with rain. It fell continuously: swept across the landscape by savage winds that buffeted the newly forming buds and leaves around us. By nightfall I was chilled to the bone and believe I have never been as wet before. To attempt to dry our clothes that evening was merely a token gesture but it was of no account, for conditions had worsened when we set off next day and by noon once again I was sodden. As the days wore on the winds became gale force and as heavy bouts of hailstone assaulted our bodies I became weary.

Not only the weather, however, was depressing my spirits – the sights I had seen would remain etched in my memory for all time. In the towns where we rested I glimpsed poverty and squalor on a scale I could never have imagined. In the villages we passed through I witnessed hopelessness and deprivation the likes of which I had never seen before. I saw numerous beggars; lepers heavily bandaged in an attempt to hide their gangrenous and ulcerated bodies; dead and dying by the roadside; and on the odd occasion a rotting corpse high on a gibbet, viewing the world through empty sockets, a deterrent for all who passed by.

The awful weather conditions had slowed our progress and the journey had taken longer than Adam had envisaged. By now we were nearing the end of April and for the first time in days my spirits were lifted when at last he announced we had reached our goal: London lay ahead. Approaching from the north we had arrived at Highgate Hill and I looked to where he pointed. A large cloud of dense smog hovered over the rooftops of the city and through the haze was visible a skyline littered with the towers and spires of churches and monastic buildings. One in particular stood out above the rest.

"Thank God we're here!" As usual my blasphemy brought a look of disappointment from Adam. I put my hand to my mouth, "Sorry! What's that very tall spire straight ahead?"

"It is the steeple of St. Paul's," replied Adam, "built in soaring tribute to God. As fine a building as one could imagine."

"Steeple? Oh, of course, Christopher Wren hasn't been born yet!" By now Adam was used to such remarks.

Soon the City walls were visible; stretching out in front of us for what I estimated must have been around two miles. We entered via the Aldersgate but sadly I was to appreciate little of my first steps into London as dusk was already falling. Our night's rest would be spent in the hospitality of the Dominican Blackfriars and as we made our way down towards the river we passed below the looming steeple I had espied earlier.

I had always thought Wren's St. Paul's to be a beautiful construction but this earlier version was truly impressive with its numerous Gothic bays and imposing central tower topped by the spire which Adam informed me was five hundred feet high. We turned in the direction of the Fleet River and were soon entering the Blackfriars domain. We had stayed at several smaller Houses on our journey south, all totally adequate, but we were obviously now in a different league. These buildings were grand and it came as no surprise when Adam informed me Parliament had met here during the early part of the 14th century. His knowledge of London was a boon and I avidly soaked up all he imparted.

Next morning Adam advised me that on the previous evening he had made discreet enquiries regarding the whereabouts of Edward's sister. He had learned that during early spring the King had left the capital on a progress of his eastern counties but had left his Queen behind.

"Providence appears to have played into our hands! Elizabeth is with child, the first, and hoped for heir. Such being the case her husband would wish no chance of losing the infant, hence his solitary procession. Elizabeth abides in the manor at Greenwich."

"At Placentia?" I ventured.

Adam frowned, "Placentia? The manor is known as Plesaunce, named so by Margaret d' Anjou, old King Henry's Queen."

"Of course," I realised my mistake. "The new manor isn't built yet. Henry Tudor virtually demolished the old one soon into his reign and renamed the new building Placentia."

"I had not appreciated thou wast so knowledgeable on the subject!" Adam seemed taken aback.

"History has always been my favourite subject." Remembering Catherine I added, "I think it must run in the family. But before we came back I decided to do some reading about this period and the early years of Henry's reign – on the off chance we would actually return in 1486."

During our conversation we had been making our way along the waterfront and I was absorbed by all that surrounded me. From the friary precinct stretching ahead for what must have been over a mile towards the Tower, was an area of quays, piers and warehouses extending out into the Thames by, in some places, as much as 350 feet. This had been done in a piecemeal manner for in places there were indentations where individual property owners must have lacked the funds to extend a particular section of waterfront in line with a neighbour's. In order to protect these wharves from the tide and the current of the river, defences of both timber and stone had been erected. The whole area was one great hotchpotch.

The quayside was a hive of industry and as we neared Queenhithe, an ancient Saxon harbour, activity suddenly intensified. A ship had docked and as the crew casually unloaded the cargo, an anxious merchant fussed around like a mother hen, complaining to the captain and warning him that if the goods were damaged payment would be withheld. People were everywhere, noise was in abundance and my avid senses struggled to embrace the unfamiliar sights and smells.

We threaded our way through the hustle and bustle and soon arrived at a jetty from where Adam hailed a ferry to Greenwich. Sailing down river the wind stung my cheeks and brought tears to my eyes but with at least a temporary abatement to the recent spell of bad weather I basked in the warmth of the watery spring sunshine. My mind was alive with the history of the area and as we passed the great, whitewashed keep of the Tower my thoughts inevitable turned to the Princes, even though I now knew they had survived. Further downstream I gazed towards Blackheath and remembered that here Wat Tyler had assembled his followers just over one hundred years ago for the Peasants' Revolt – totally mind blowing!

Greenwich soon appeared on the right bank of the river and I gasped in delight at my first glimpse of the palace. Plesaunce was a picture of contrasting pink brick, white stone and copious ornate masonry whilst Duke Humphrey's Tower, rising from the grassy hill behind, was prominent for miles around.

We disembarked at the landing stage and made our way through the gardens, passing a delightful arbour shaded by a copse of hawthorn trees. I remarked on the beauty of it all.

"It is my understanding that Queen Margaret had the gardens planted with daisies and hawthorn – the devices of herself and her husband – or wast thou already cognisant of that fact?" Adam teased with a twinkle in his eye.

"I can't be expected to know everything about the place!" I laughed. "No, actually there wasn't much detail about the old building and I didn't delve too deeply because I never dreamed we would be coming here."

"In which case, allow me to enlighten thee!" Adam was still in jocular mood. "The lady in question made extensive alterations to both the fabric and decoration of Bella Court, as it was then named. Her palace was structured around two courts, one set of apartments for herself and one for the King. In addition she commissioned an abundance of glass, numerous bay windows, a Treasure House, pavilions, courts," he pointed back towards the river, "the landing stage … and a multitude of other features." By now we were approaching what appeared to be a chapel and Adam slowed his steps as we drew level with one of its windows. "The manor had previously belonged to Duke Humphrey – uncle to Henry VI. Queen Margaret attained the manor upon his death. Indeed, some would say the lady's followers had a part to play in the demise of the Duke." He gestured towards a brightly coloured shield in the glasswork. "Hence an unexpected act to include her victim's escutcheon in the chapel – a pious gesture or, perhaps, an act of absolution?"

I was intrigued. "How do you know so much about the place?"

"Upon Edward's accession to the throne he granted the lordship and manor to his queen, Elizabeth Woodville. The family was oft in residence here during my time as scribe." This, then, explained how it was Adam had been expertly guiding us through the labyrinthine gardens with such ease. "'Twill not be possible for thee to see much of the interior on thy visit today but be assured, the manor is grand. Queen

Margaret was lavish in her decoration and spared naught in the name of luxury."

On our journey south we had discussed my identity during our stay in London and had eventually decided I should continue to be Adam's mute cousin. The reason for this was twofold. Firstly, Edward knew me in this role and should he and his sister be reunited at some stage in the future it would tie in nicely. Secondly, would Adam take any person other than his mute cousin to a meeting such as the one into which we were about to enter where such vital information was about to be divulged? We thought not. This arrangement suited me fine for, although by now my ears were attuned to the 15th century tongue, I must admit I found it a trifle daunting to contemplate actually opening my mouth.

Adam was also feeling uneasy, as he feared recognition by prominent members of the Court who had once given their allegiance to Edward but subsequently transferred their support to Henry Tudor. The life of any person identified as a possible Yorkist supporter would no doubt be in danger and to that end he had borrowed a set of robes from our previous evening's hosts – their assistance secured by the provision of a small donation to the friary funds. These garments, coupled with a few days growth of beard, altered his appearance considerably and I was still undecided as to whether I liked the new look Adam. We had now arrived at the gatehouse and I considered it time to recede into the background and allow Adam space to negotiate our entry into the manor of Plesaunce.

Pulling forward the hood of his cloak and tucking his hands inside the wide cuffs of his robe he advanced towards one of the guards. "I understand the Queen is in residence," his words were delivered in an even, confident tone, "and would request that thou convey this note to her, with regard to a private audience at her Majesty's pleasure." Like a magician he produced the sealed note from his sleeve.

He seemed to have struck the right vein, somewhere between self-assurance and deference, for although the guard seemed reluctant to comply with Adam's wishes, after a sideways glance at his companion he accepted the note and slowly made his way through the courtyard beyond.

"By signing the note 'Brother Anselm' our entry into the Queen's presence should be assured – 'twas a familiar name she had for me as a young girl, a play-on-words in view of my prior intentions for a spiritual life. However, I did not wish Elizabeth to show too much emotion nor disclose my true identity upon our meeting and warned her of the same, further advising her to refrain from hastening our progress lest she arouse suspicion. Needs must grant us patience for no doubt 'twill be some time afore we progress further."

We waited. As the minutes ticked by I turned to face the river watching with interest as a steady stream of traffic ploughed the waters, supplying the capital with essential wares and sweetmeats. It was as though I looked upon a tableau; a painting by one of the Old Masters; a scene from a film.

Adam was right: it was a long time before the guard returned. He had been instructed to escort us, with the aid of a fellow sentry, to the main buildings of the palace. Silently we were ushered along and deposited within, where our custody was transferred to two fresh sentinels; and so the process continued. The Queen's protection was of paramount importance. With her husband away and in view of her expectant state, stringent security measures were in place. Over the course of the morning we gradually progressed through a series of rooms towards the Queen's apartments. Adam was right to describe Queen Margaret's decoration as luxurious. The rooms were magnificent to behold with their rich wall tapestries, ornate woodcarvings and elegant, if sparse, furniture.

Finally we encountered a serious looking, elderly gentleman whom I presumed to be the steward. It was his duty to vet any petitioner who wished to see the Queen.

"I am informed that thou dost seek an audience with Her Majesty." His tone was patronising and waving Adam's letter in front of us he continued, "This manner of communication flouts protocol. Pray inform me of thy requirements and *I* shall deal with the matter."

"Master Steward, no doubt thou art full versed in shielding the Queen from unnecessary trivialities and, presumably, perform thy undertaking in a meritorious fashion."

Adam's voice was low and even; somehow he managed to hide his contempt for this bumptious official. "However, with all due respect, the purpose of my visit is a delicate one and 'tis imperative that the Queen should read my communication. I can assure thee that having done so she will agree to see me."

Still the steward was loath to comply. "Her Majesty hath given specific instruction …"

"Master Steward, forgive my interruption, but I must repeat that the Queen *will* grant my request. I *can* assure thee. If thou wouldst only do the honour of humouring me I promise that, should there be any censure laid at thy door, I shall take full responsibility."

With exaggerated unwillingness the steward turned to go, instructing us to wait outside the Queen's Chamber until bidden to enter the inner sanctum. His receding back disappeared through a large oak door studded with curious dice-headed nails and, still sandwiched between our escorts, we settled down on a bench to wait. My heart was pounding with anticipation as I gazed about the hall enthralled by the amount of activity around us. People were rushing hither and thither and I felt this scene must mirror the one viewed by Catherine upon her visit to Dacre Castle: mine, however, must surely have been a much grander affair.

At length the door opened and the steward reappeared: with a sour look on his face he motioned us to follow. We moved into the Queen's Chamber and although I had been impressed by the grandeur of the palace since my first steps on the landing stage, nothing could have prepared me for the sight that now met my eyes. This room was indeed magnificent and more splendid than anything I had witnessed so far with its terracotta monogrammed floor tiles and huge bay window. The oriel must have measured all of fourteen feet and once again I noticed the delicate coloured daisies and intricate hawthorn buds replicated to perfection in the glass. The view across the river was spectacular: even the murky waters of the Thames appeared breathtaking as the sun's reflected rays caught the uneven surfaces of the panes.

So absorbed was I in my surroundings that at first I failed to notice the tall young woman seated on a dais at the far end of the room. The hurriedly concealed look of pleasure that flashed across her face on seeing Adam confirmed what her sumptuous garments and hovering attendants had inferred: this was Elizabeth of York, Henry Tudor's queen. Her maids were engaged in various tasks; several were intent upon needlework; one was rummaging through a coffer by the window; and another fed titbits to a lap dog perched on a red velvet cushion. But upon our entry every gaze was turned in our direction and varying degrees of interest could be seen upon the ladies' faces. As to what had passed between the Queen and her steward I am unaware but it had certainly aroused curiosity.

"Leave us." She lifted her hand towards her attendants and immediately the ladies-in-waiting melted away towards a door behind the raised platform. The steward and our escort, however, remained in the chamber.

"Thou too, Thomas," her mellifluous tones nevertheless held a note of authority, "together with the guards. The friar has a private matter he wishes to discuss." Seeing the mixed look of concern and annoyance on the steward's face she continued, "Come, come, Thomas. Surely thou dost not fear this man of God or his companion? Besides, his credentials," she held out Adam's note, "are assured by Brother Dominic." Still piqued, the Steward reluctantly retired motioning the guards to follow.

As soon as we were alone Elizabeth arose from her seat and, arms outstretched, approached Adam with a warm smile. "Anselm, 'tis really thou? It hath been so long!" Adam made to kneel before her but taking his elbow she raised him. "Nay, there is no need for such formalities. Surely we are still friends?"

She had inherited her father's height but I imagine her good looks came from a combination of both parents: her skin was flawless and with her small full mouth, rounded cheeks and soft brown eyes she truly was a beauty. Wisps of thick golden hair peeped from beneath the high-crowned bonnet head-dress. This was trimmed with the same elaborate gold braid as the neckline and cuffs of her maroon velvet gown and from the gilt girdle hung a simple bead rosary.

"My lady …"

"Please Anselm, call me by my given name as thou always hast. I may be a Queen by title but I am little changed inside!" With a twinkle in her eye she gave a girlish laugh and at that moment she appeared no older than her twenty years.

Adam paused and a contemplative note entered his voice. "Elizabeth, thou dost so remind me of thy father at times." He was obviously at ease with her and I fancied the two had once had a good relationship.

"'Twas not long after his death when last I saw thee," a fleeting look of sadness crossed her face. "But tell me, where hast thou been during the intervening years? And thy beard – if 'twere not for thy note I warrant I should not have known thee!"

Adam stroked the ten days' growth on his chin. "A recent acquisition – fear of recognition made me cautious. I hear thy husband dealt harshly with adherents to Richard's cause." I surmised he was referring to the fact that Henry Tudor had proclaimed himself King from the day before Bosworth, thereby deeming all surviving Yorkists traitors.

Elizabeth obviously understood the reference for she coloured but holding her head high she said with some conviction "Henry may not be perfect but I feel sure he had good cause for his actions. Uncle Richard's deeds forced his hand. He was petitioned by several disenchanted Yorkist supporters." I felt sure she was merely repeating her husband's words. "Nonetheless, I take thy point. Caution never did go amiss. Indeed, 'tis the reason for my vigilance with Thomas. By mentioning the name of Brother Dominic from the friary yonder," she pointed to the neighbouring monastic buildings visible through the window, "his mind should rest easy." As if seeking Adam's blessing on her marriage, she looked him directly in the eye and added earnestly, "But I have a good husband, Anselm. Whatever his other faults, Henry is a good husband." Her hands moved instinctively to her stomach where they rested in protection of the unborn child.

"For that I am truly thankful. I would not wish thee to spend thy life in a union without affection." Adam squeezed her arm gently. "As to my whereabouts since last we met, I fear the answer will take some time in the telling. Firstly, may

I introduce my cousin, Mistress Emma Harvey?" We had decided upon a slight modification to my character: I was to be feeble-minded. To this end Adam's words to me were spoken slowly. "Show thy respect for the Queen, Emma." I curtseyed and kissed the Queen's outstretched hand, my eye coming into close contact with the massive ruby ring – the colour of blood – adorning her middle finger. Adam continued with his explanations, informing the Queen of my lack of speech, simple-mindedness and his obligation to take care of me. "Emma's future has yet to be resolved but that is of no real import ...."

Before he could continue Elizabeth cut in, "Really, Anselm! Surely thy cousin's infirmity gives thee not the right to speak in such condescending tones. Thou sayest she is a little slow but she can surely hear!" Turning to me she added gently, "'Tis a pleasure to meet thee, Emma." She placed her hand on my arm and smiled sweetly. Returning the smile I gazed around the room trying to achieve a vacant air.

Adam was duly contrite, "Forgive me, 'twas never my intention to sound offhand, merely to inform thee of the true reason for my visit. I am here on much more urgent business."

Over wine and sweetmeats Adam began his story. Commencing with his journey to Ludlow for her brother he related succinctly to Elizabeth the sequence of events from the time of the death of her father. Adam pulled no punches when conveying his thoughts on her husband and made no attempt to hide his feelings for Richard. As he neared the part disclosing Bishop Stillington's revelations I held my breath. How would she react? It was as though a firework's touchpaper had been lit.

"But all said 'twas a lie, a mere fabrication on Uncle Richard's part! That he had invented the tale as a means of seizing the throne for himself!" she paced up and down, clearly agitated by the news. I had often read of the Plantagenet rage and felt Elizabeth was struggling to keep her emotions under control. "How could my father do such a thing? If my mother new the rumour was true ..." Although she had her back to us her outrage was evident for her tightly clenched fists were taut and white. Suddenly she turned. "Then I am a bastard!" Adam said nothing, letting the impact of his news sink in.

Eventually he spoke. "Elizabeth, it matters not. Apart from those present there is only one other person privy to this knowledge and I shall come to him shortly. Besides, 'twould serve thy husband's cause naught for such a revelation to be made known. Thou art the Queen of England, all else is of little import."

Slowly, Elizabeth appeared to be coming to terms with Adam's words. She returned to her seat and, eyes glassy, gazed ahead deep in thought. The minutes ticked by.

Two deep furrows formed on her brow. "But if that be so, then why have my brothers killed?" Shaking her head she continued, "What need would my uncle have?" I glanced at Adam out of the corner of my eye.

Leaning forward and taking her hands tenderly in his own he faced her squarely and said gently, "Elizabeth, thy brothers were *not* murdered." She opened her mouth but no words were uttered. "Richard would never have harmed them, despite all that has been said. I knew him well and he had many faults but the death of his nephews cannot be laid at his door. That is where I have been these two years past – with thy brothers." I excused him his white lie: after all, he could hardly tell her the truth. Puzzlement, disbelief, hope: all three emotions crossed Elizabeth's face within a matter of seconds. Adam hurried on, "Sadly, thy brother Richard is dead but Edward still lives."

"*Deo gratias!*" quickly crossing herself with the right hand, her left sought to locate the rosary at her waist. "I was always of the belief that my uncle would not have had them killed, no matter what Henr..., no matter what hath been reported. But then where is he, where *is* Edward?" Whilst Adam related the remainder of his tale Elizabeth listened enthralled, sometimes hugging herself with joy, at other times striving to control her sadness.

Adam was nearing the end of his narrative. "Upon Sir Anthony's death his ne'er-do-well brother was soon to arrive for the rich pickings – on the pretext of wardship of his nephew of course. In truth I feared for the lad's safety for Hugo was sure to stake his claim on the inheritance. 'Twas at that time we thought it best for Edward to remove to the nearby Abbey – I had become acquainted with the Brothers during my time in the north and felt assured of his safety in their care."

"And Edward resides there still?"

Adam nodded.

Elizabeth frowned in consternation and again her fingers were drawn to the rosary like a magnet. "But what is to become of him?"

"What indeed? Thy brother is aware of our meeting and sends his warmest greetings. I advised him that, once I had safely settled the Rutherford children with their kinfolk further north, I would journey to the capital and inform thee of his whereabouts."

Elizabeth soon appreciated the danger her brother was in. "Who else knows that he is still alive? For although I wish to be loyal to my husband, methinks 'twould not be in Edward's best interests should Henry learn of his existence. 'Tis early in his reign and my husband is still 'finding his feet' as it were. I fear the existence of a Yorkist claimant, legitimate or otherwise, would not sit easily on his shoulders. Having found that my brother lives, I have no wish to lose him again!"

"When your Uncle charged me with the Princes' care, only one other was privy to their true identities. That person was Sir Anthony and his silence was assured for he was a true and loyal subject to Richard – the King had saved his life in battle. To all others, even Sir Anthony's wife, the boys were introduced as my nephews. After the death of Sir Anthony and the subsequent demise of thy younger brother, Edward was in such an emotional turmoil that he revealed to Lady Margaret his real name. That Lady, being no supporter of the Tudor cause and having formed such an attachment to Edward during his stay at Overthwaite, informed none prior to her untimely death. The secret is safe with those present in this room."

Elizabeth glanced towards me, a look of concern on her face, and then turned to Adam, "Forgive me for what I am about to say but my brother's safety is uppermost in my mind. Thy cousin is truly unaware of the significance of our conversation, I trust?"

"I can assure thee that 'tis so. Besides, apart from her lack of speech and in view of her infirmity she hath never been schooled in the way of handwriting, so is incapable of divulging details of thy brother." Throughout the whole conversation I had tried to appear absent-minded, interested only in the trappings of the room. I hoped I had been convincing.

Elizabeth seemed reassured and smiled at me through her distraction. We sat in silence, the stillness broken only by the crackling of logs in the fireplace. After what seemed an eternity she spoke. "Evidently Edward must be moved. Perhaps abroad? I do not know. Pray, Anselm, let me mull over the matter. As yet my mind is too full of all thou hast imparted to me this day. Perhaps I shall think more clearly once my emotions have calmed."

Arrangements were made for Elizabeth to send word to the Blackfriars a few days hence when we would return to discuss the matter further. We took our leave and, once more on the ferry, were both in quiet mood: each preoccupied by our own particular train of thought.

CHAPTER THIRTEEN

It was seven days before Elizabeth's message reached the Brothers of Blackfriars. By then we were no longer availing ourselves of their hospitality.

A distant cousin of Adam's, a merchant by trade, lived in the capital and on the day following our visit to Greenwich we set out for his address in Bishopsgate. Adam's intention was for us to arrive by a circuitous route, thereby avoiding the seamier parts of the city but I persuaded him to change his mind.

Informing him of my desire to soak up the sights and smells of 15th century London I assured him the experience would certainly not harm me. "And the walk will do us good."

"'Twould be far easier to journey by horse," replied Adam.

"After all our recent travels I think I would prefer a change!" A rue smile on my face, I pretended to rub my backside.

"Very well, I shall accede to thy request but I fear thy sensibilities may well be offended!" Adam shook his head in mock exasperation. "I had intended that we make our way via Moorgate, perchance viewing the gardens and moors to the north since 'twould have been a much pleasanter way to reach our destination. But the choice is yours."

We made our way towards Newgate where market stalls abounded; foods of all description surrounded us; people jostled for wares; filthy urchins lurked in dark recesses, an eye to rich pickings should the opportunity arise. The narrow street, less than fifteen feet wide, was dark and stuffy, in pressing need of light and fresh air. Waste and sewage littered the ground and a channel running down the centre of the street formed an open sewer. The stench was unbearable and I shuddered to imagine its impact during a humid summer. Shielding my nose and mouth with my cloak we pressed on, along Newgate Street and into the Shambles, the heart of the butchery trade. Again the going was slow, our progress being hampered by milling townsfolk.

Adam had informed me that the population of London was around sixty thousand and I felt sure the majority of them were out on the streets that day! Suddenly I felt my foot slip and grabbing Adam's arm glanced down to see the bloated entrails of some slaughtered animal lying at the side of the road. I turned away, only to find myself staring into one of the establishments. A burly chap in a dirty, stained apron was in the process of skinning a sheep. The floor ran red with its blood and steam rising from the carcass heralded its recent departure from this life. Meat hung on hooks from beams in the ceiling; the smell of death permeated the air; and a sudden cry from a terrified animal informed me of its imminent demise. I felt sure I was about to faint. Adam, who had been watching me intently, was by my side in an instant.

"Come. Let us hasten from this place. I fear thy curiosity was stronger than thy stomach!"

"Well, you did warn me. Perhaps a little water ..." and I made for a nearby fountain at the end of the street.

Adam caught my hand. "Nay Emma, do not drink. 'Tis fed from the city's streams – recipient of waste and slops. Let us press on. After the air of the north country I find this fetid locale plays havoc with mine own insides!"

We moved on and immediately I was grateful Adam had prevented me from drinking from the fountain: there, in front of me, were public latrines situated over the running water. "Surely that's not the same stream that feeds the water fountain?" I asked Adam incredulously. He nodded and a shiver ran down my spine.

Once out of the Newgate area I could feel my queasiness beginning to lift and made no objection to Adam's insistence that we take a more northerly route. Soon we were arriving at his cousin's house in Bishopsgate, rather a grand affair with the entrance from the street leading into a wide courtyard. Buildings to the right of this forecourt housed, amongst others, a large kitchen, buttery and coal-house, whilst on the left stood a warehouse and a hen-house with a small run for poultry. A short flight of steps led to the front door through which a young servant girl soon admitted us to the house. We found ourselves in a large, well-proportioned hall that had a warm, welcoming air to it.

A mountain of a man emerged from rooms behind the hall and Adam introduced me to his cousin, James Pearce. Again he went through the rigmarole of explaining my lack of speech but this time my identity was to vary. Following our host we made our way through to a small parlour where his diminutive wife, Hannah, was busy with her embroidery.

"Look, Madam," boomed James, "'tis cousin Anselm come to pay call. And this young woman be Mistress Harvey, kinswoman to the wife of Anselm's employer." Turning to us he added, "Pray sit thee down, sit thee down." His shock of white hair made a sharp contrast to bushy eyebrows that had retained their dark colour. He must have been in his late 50's and with his large, bulbous nose and ruddy face dotted with warts he put me in mind of Oliver Cromwell.

"'Tis a pleasure to welcome thee to our humble abode." His wife addressed her remarks directly to me and turning towards Adam continued, "And 'tis always right good to see thee, Anselm. But 'tis so long since thy last visit. Why, it must be ... I'll trow 'tis over three years! 'Tis assuredly before King Edward's death." She was the complete opposite to her husband and with her chirpy voice, sharp features and quick, nervous movements she resembled a tiny songbird. Behind her deep, hooded head-dress and voluminous gown I found it hard to pinpoint her age but she seemed much younger than her husband, perhaps similar in years to me. "First to refreshments, then thou must tell us thy news."

Over some heady, spiced wine Anselm related the tale we had concocted on our journey to London. "Upon Edward's death I had no heart to remain with his Queen, never having had much affinity towards the lady. I determined to return to Ludlow and trust to fortune in my home town."

"Certes, thy position at Court would stand thee in good stead, Anselm." Adam's cousin leant forward, eager to hear the tale.

"As luck would have it I soon gained employment as a tutor to the sons of a country gentleman not far from the centre of the town. They are good lads and eager to learn and I find the position most agreeable." Adam paused for a sip of wine and I wondered whether he was thinking of Edward and Richard.

"So what brings thee to London?" chirped Hannah, her gaze never leaving her needlework.

"Mistress Harvey," Adam nodded in my direction, "has a younger sister, a foolish, wilful girl by all accounts. Hearing of the possibility of an apprenticeship with a member of the Guild of Silkwomen she determined to seek her fortune in the capital. Confiding her intentions only to a servant girl she set forth and hast now disappeared." I tried to look duly saddened. "Mistress Harvey's mother is a widow and, needless to say, fearful for the girl. She turned to her brother-in-law, my employer and in view of my knowledge of London I proffered my assistance."

Hannah had been shaking her head throughout Adam's account. "She is not the first nor shall she be the last to think these streets are paved with gold." I should have loved to ask her whether she was thinking of events earlier that century upon Dick Whittington's arrival in London! Turning towards me she added, "Right sorry I am to say this for I know 'twill be hard to take but many a youth has landed in debt and many a lass has ended as lackey, or worse. Some manage only to scrape a living by turning to the whorehouses!"

Our tale, based on the disappearance of Margery's sister Agnes, obviously reflected the fate of many. Raising a hand to my mouth I lowered my gaze. Adam patted my shoulder.

"My wife speaks the truth, Anselm." James was a successful wine merchant and his abrupt, no-nonsense manner must have assisted in this accomplishment. "'Tis obvious that youngsters from the country should be tempted – who would not find the prospect of becoming a freeman through apprenticeship alluring? But some of these employers take advantage of their naivety. Why, some are not freemen themselves, nor even skilled – 'tis unscrupulous practice!" He banged his fist on the table. "Would that I could help thee, Anselm, but I sail for Italy on the morrow."

"Business continues to prosper?"

"Indeed, and could not be better. I have customers far and wide." Raising a finger he leant forward conspiratorially, "One such, a Knight from Hertford way, is in the habit of purchasing wine to the value of around £50 each time he is in the capital. He then transports it back, storing it until he can sell it on at a profit! How be that for initiative? Aye, 'tis certainly the right business to be in, for wine hath become almost a form of currency." He paused absentmindedly trace one of the bushy eyebrows with his forefinger. "But 'tis hard work, Anselm, and no easy task."

His wife, clucking like a hen, shook her head from side to side and muttered under her breath, "Works all the hours God sends." Clearly she was disapproving.

James continued, "Recently I have been dissatisfied with one of my suppliers – the quality hath fallen short, thou understands? But I have learnt of a man in Florence and have high hopes of a profitable outcome."

"Wilt thou be away long?" Adam enquired.

"Aye, more than likely, for after verifying the calibre of the wine in Italy, I must continue on to Cyprus." Once again Hannah shook her head in disapproval of her husband's workload. "In addition to the problems in Italy I suspect my supplier of sweet Malmsey is trying to foist inferior quality wine on me and as 'tis a much more expensive brew I intend paying him an unexpected visit. 'Tis twice the price of claret, Anselm!"

The conversation trickled on with James eagerly apprising Adam of all aspects of his business. I sat quietly and, with the warmth of the room and the intoxicating wine, found I was having difficulty in staying awake. Eventually Adam made to leave.

"Thou must stay here, Anselm!" James was insistent. "No cousin of mine shall visit London and be denied our hospitality." He turned to his wife. "What says thou, Madam?"

"But of course. Besides," she looked askance at James, "they will provide good company for me whilst thou tarries abroad!"

And so it was. We retrieved our horses and meagre belongings from the Blackfriars and for the remainder of our stay lodged in immaculate bedrooms situated behind the parlour. In order to keep up the charade of finding my 'sister' Adam made daily excursions into the city whilst I stayed behind assisting Hannah with her needlework. Upon his return we would settle ourselves in the larger parlour towards the rear of the house where the late afternoon sunshine streaming through the large oriel window in the west wall enhanced the rich colours of the expensive glazed floor tiles. I busied myself with even more embroidery – I was becoming an expert at the art – and Adam read. At first he contented himself with his cousin's collection of books but one morning informed me he could stand James's tastes no longer and we set off for Westminster. Hannah insisted that "in view of the great distance" we take our horses and on this occasion Adam made sure our route kept well away from the disturbing scenes I had witnessed previously.

Leaving the city walls behind us we crossed the Fleet River and set off down the street of the same name. Along there and down The Strand the dwellings were much more up-market and Adam informed me they were the property of bishops, abbots and the like. We were soon arriving at the Abbey precincts: the Benedictine buildings looking comfortingly familiar, being little changed from those I knew.

Passing through the gateway leading to the Almonry, I noticed an unusual sign inside.

"'Tis the sign of the Red Pale," Adam explained, "William Caxton's printing establishment. Thou hast heard of him?"

Sadly I was denied the opportunity of meeting the gentleman as Caxton was away on business but standing in his establishment, surrounded by books and leaflets, I felt totally overawed. The first book in England to be printed in the English language came from these premises – incredible. The shop was small and, in view of the large, cumbersome printing press dominating the central area of the room, noisy and cluttered. Notwithstanding Caxton's absence his assistant was knowledgeable and enthusiastic, proffering several choices. Adam selected two volumes with which he was delighted: for once exhibiting uncharacteristic extravagance by using some of the money Elizabeth had given us in case we needed funds. On leaving the shop I persuaded Adam to show me the ancient buildings of Westminster and we were soon making our way through streets leading to William Rufus's Great Hall and the Parliament House at St. Stephen's Chapel. I could have remained all day, soaking up the atmosphere but at length I allowed Adam to drag me away, back to our lodgings in Bishopsgate.

It was upon our return that same afternoon that we received the Queen's note. Hannah informed us that the message had been delivered by a novice from Blackfriars: thankfully Elizabeth had been cautious and the letter bore no evidence of its originator. We had previously decided that Adam should go unaccompanied to the palace, for now that we were lodged with relations my safety would be assured by remaining under their roof. Although I was disappointed to miss the opportunity to meet the Queen again, I fully understood the wisdom of the decision. At length Adam retired to his room and later informed me of the note's contents. They were short and sweet – Elizabeth had requested his return to Greenwich the following day.

On this occasion Anselm's entry into the palace was achieved smoothly and with great speed.

Once in Elizabeth's presence he sensed an underlying excitement in her manner and immediately the two were alone together she leant forward, gently squeezing his forearm. "Methinks I have the solution ... 'tis not entirely straightforward but achievable nonetheless ... of course we must await his return, for his agreement is obviously paramount ..." she may have been a Queen but she was girlish in her exuberance. Suddenly noticing the perplexed look on Anselm's face Elizabeth paused. "I am rambling. I must marshal my thoughts and explain. But firstly, where is thy cousin, safe I trust?"

"Indeed. We are now lodged with a distant cousin and there she abides. I had left words with the Brothers to forward any communication to Bishopsgate and received thy missive without hindrance." Anselm paused, allowing Elizabeth to gather her thoughts.

"Good, now, where to begin?" With a sigh she paused. "There is at Court a loyal supporter of my husband, Sir Richard Guildford ..."

"His father was Sir John, controller of the household to thy father, was he not?" Anselm interrupted.

"Aye, I had forgot. Thou wouldst have known them both, Anselm, from thy time with my father." She paused to gather her thoughts, "Sir Richard joined Henry in Brittany, fought with him at Bosworth and in recognition of his service was knighted by my husband and made a Chamberlain of the Exchequer and Master of the Ordnance. He is a good and kindly person and in all of my dealings with the gentleman I have never found him wanting." Although intent on her tale absentmindedly she reached for a sweetmeat from a bowl near her elbow. "He has a son – coincidentally Edward by name – gravely ill with the pox. Indeed, 'twould be a miracle were he to pull through. Sir Richard knows naught of his son's plight for at present he is abroad, on business for my husband ... the lowlands of the Duchy of Burgundy ... land drainage or some such business," she dismissed the purpose with a flick of the hand, "but he is due home within the month. I know 'twill be a blow to him – for he is right fond of the lad. Indeed, if 'twere not for my present condition I should have visited the lad's mother, Anne, for I know the lady well."

"And thou says the lad is not likely to survive?" Anselm queried.

"Sadly, no. The illness came with much speed and as his fever burns ever brighter, he deteriorates by the day." Elizabeth looked directly into Anselm's eyes and again he could sense her excitement. "Although Sir Richard's son is two or three years younger than Edward there is a marked likeness about their appearance and the lad has always looked older than his years. Besides, my brother was ever short in stature – pray tell me Anselm he hath not suddenly become a longshanks!"

Anselm leant forward, catching the drift of Elizabeth's thoughts. "No ... no he hath not gained much in height o'er the past three years. But thy thoughts are ... what?" He added in an incredulous tone, "That perhaps Edward could take the lad's place?" The Queen nodded. Anselm, his head reeling, continued in a dumbfounded manner, "Surely that could not be. With respect, Elizabeth, the idea sounds quite fantastical!"

She was affronted, "I know not why thou should think so! There are one or two obstacles, I grant thee, but with some small care I am sure they can be overcome!"

Anselm was undeterred. "Given that Sir Richard could be persuaded to the idea – a difficult enough task I'll trow in view of his allegiance to Henry – what of the lad's miraculous recovery? If, as thou reports, he is at death's door then surely 'twould not be feasible. On the other hand he might in truth pull through the illness. And what of any witnesses to the swap? 'Twould surely not be possible to achieve such a feat without at least one pair of prying eyes. Not to mention Edward's thoughts on the matter!" His doubts came tumbling out, one after the other.

"I know, I know ... for I have turned those self same misgivings over in my mind tenfold times and more. But list," she bent forward earnestly, "Sir Richard's reasons for turning to Henry do but strengthen my argument. He was outraged and appalled at the thought of Edward and Richard being put to death by my uncle. Certes he feels thus, I know for we have talked on the matter at length. He would be protective of Edward for that selfsame reason and would let none other harm him." With a knowing look to Anselm she had no need to name her husband for they both knew to whom she was referring. "I know not where his innermost loyalties lie but his prospects are good under Henry and I cannot think he would welcome another battle for a change of monarch. And there, I feel, is the double-edged sword – whilst safeguarding Edward's life he can also monitor his actions and dissuade him from any rash desires."

"As to that, Edward's feelings are for peace and tranquillity. His time in the north hath tempered his outlook on life. He is a changed lad." Anselm slowly shook his head, "But I am still unsure. And as to the swap itself ..."

"Sir Richard's son is ensconced at his grandfather's manor of Rolvenden in Kent with his mother. The substitution would needs be made elsewhere ... I cannot think where for the moment ... but once made perchance Edward could go to Iham. 'Tis a new acquisition of Sir Richard's in Sussex, recently granted him by my husband and although the papers have not yet been finalised I feel sure he has taken possession of the place." She looked beseechingly at Anselm, in need of reassurance. "Albeit besetments are inevitable I feel sure there must be a satisfactory outcome if only we put our minds to it, Anselm."

"Mayhap, thou art right. Thou hast given much thought to the matter and thy plan hath some merit – provided, of course, Sir Richard is in agreement. I fear 'twill not be an easy task to put the matter delicately to him."

Elizabeth frowned, "Nay, I cannot say I look forward to the meeting, but he is a pragmatist so we must hope for a successful resolution. I shall send word to Rolvenden requesting his attendance immediately he returns. Pray to God his son doth not die 'ere to Sir Richard setting foot once more on these shores." In different circumstances her last comment may have seemed unfeeling.

"I shall await thy further contact. And in the meantime, shall certainly give some thought to the matter." Trying to sound positive, Anselm struggled with his misgivings.

I was as sceptical as Adam when he relayed to me the gist of his meeting with Elizabeth: surely the plan was fraught with pitfalls. However, he was determined to apply himself to the problem and do his utmost to come up with a solution, if at all possible. For two days he sat in his cousin's parlour, one of the new books open on his knee, his thoughts elsewhere. It was a difficult time and Hannah must surely have noticed a change in the atmosphere. Adam became more and more introverted. He had informed me that, in all probability, it would be several weeks before Sir Richard returned and I decided something must be done. One morning when Hannah was out I broached the subject.

"Adam, we really must begin our search for Agnes. I know you have other things on your mind but Hannah may become suspicious, especially as we are supposed to be looking for my 'sister'."

He roused himself. "Thou art right. This contemplation leaves me addle-brained – the change will clear my head. We shall begin this very afternoon."

Hannah provided us with the names of one or two contacts in the Guild of Silkwomen who might be able to throw some light on the whereabouts of my 'sister' – we held out little hope but had to begin somewhere. As the weather was continuing to improve I prepared myself for the worse: the warmth and humidity would make conditions unbearable in those narrow, crowded streets. We made our way to Cheapside, London's principal retail centre. Shops and open-air stalls nestled cheek-by-jowl and were interspersed with tall five storied houses, gable end on to the street.

I turned to Adam, "Gosh, they're like sky-scrapers!" He looked puzzled, though whether due to the hubbub or my vocabulary I was unsure. Shouting to make myself heard above the noise I pointed upwards, "The height of the buildings – they're so tall."

He brought his mouth close to my ear to enable me to hear his words. His warm breath sent a shiver down my spine. "'Tis due to the value of land in this part of the city." What a pity the subject was so impersonal. I tried to concentrate. "Three storeys would be more normal but here, land shortage has occasioned the need to build ever higher. And in some places," he pointed upwards to where the brick, timber framed extensions overhung on either side of the street, "ever deeper to provide additional lodging space."

This was certainly a more up-market area than the one I had viewed on my first foray into the city, as could be evidenced by the numerous glazed windows. However, the projections Adam had pointed out to me, which almost met down the centre of the street, blocked out the light so effectively that it was as dark and claustrophobic as Newgate had been. Weaving our way through this busy thoroughfare we arrived at one of the addresses Hannah had given us and were directed through the small shop into an alleyway behind. The narrow passage was lined with cabinets and crates in which the merchants stored their goods and from where they were arrayed to tempt passers-by. Adam found the proprietor, mentioned Hannah's name and outlined the nature of our quest. Although the lady was sympathetic and gave us the name of another possible contact, she could provide no immediate help. We moved on to the next and the next, all with the same result: our search would be a long one.

Two weeks later we were beginning to give up hope: our enquiries had proved fruitless and we decided we should have a break from our search. That evening, after our meal, we retired to the great parlour soaking up the remains of the evening sunshine; Hannah was feeling unwell and had gone to bed immediately after eating.

As we sat in companionable silence Adam suddenly asked, "What is the date today? With all this toing and froing I have quite lost track." I shook my head and watched him mentally reckon up. "I thought as much, 'tis May 24th and Corpus Christi on the morrow. Hast thou witnessed the spectacle of this feast day, Emma?" Again I shook my head and Adam continued, "Thou hast a treat in store. Let us hope the day is set fair."

It was a beautiful day with the sun shining brightly and a gentle breeze lessened the humidity of the city. Harsh though it sounds I was thankful Hannah was still unwell thereby leaving us unaccompanied, for not only would I have Adam to myself on this holiday, but also I should be able to speak freely. He had informed me he wished us to attend mass, terce to be exact, around 9 a.m. before the festivities began and so it was not too early as we made our way to the nunnery of St. Helen not far from our lodgings in Bishopsgate.

Once inside the church its beauty struck me: the rich stained glass of the windows; the brightly painted walls with their religious depictions; the sacred carvings and tall votive candles. Each in its own way helped to effect a sense of awe and wonder. As I had expected, a screen separated the monastic and parochial sections and I was suddenly reminded of Catherine's narrative by the large empty space created by the lack of pews. Some of the congregation stood, others kneeled, all listening but most failing to understanding the Divine Liturgy spoken in Latin as they awaited the Communion wafer on this its feast day.

The service over, we made our way down into the heart of the city where already the celebrations were beginning. Horses and carts were used to manoeuvre the stages into position at strategic street corners whilst performers could be glimpsed in the shadows making last minute adjustments to their costumes. The streets were crowded as onlookers jostled for good viewing spots, deciding which of the numerous mystery plays to watch first: each guild acted out a different allegorical scene from the Bible beginning with the Creation and ending with the Last Judgement.

We drifted from one corner to the next, from one play to another, although I have to admit I was as much intrigued by the audience as much as by the performance. With intent faces the crowd were obviously able to relate to these characters – the moral of each story being much more understandable when portrayed in such a fashion. At last it was time for the solemn procession in honour of the Blessed Sacrament; the representation of the body of Christ – Corpus Christi. The sacrament was preceded by a number of decorated waxen torches, their flames flickering in the breeze; then followed a congregation of singing clergy, robes the colours of the rainbow; next came the dignitaries of the city in their cloaks of scarlet and blue; and finally members of the skinners' guild whose dedication was to Corpus Christi. The enthusiastic crowd pushed ever forward determined not to miss a thing – I even saw one child standing precariously on the rump of his father's horse!

"What a spectacle!" I shouted to Adam.

"Indeed. Had the King been in London thou wouldst have seen him for 'tis customary for the monarch to take part."

The day had been a treat and by the end of the afternoon, as we wended our way home, I felt tired but exhilarated. Many others, however, were still well into the swing of things, overindulging in food and drink from the abundant stalls and vendors attracted to such a festival. Gorging, supping and general carousing would, no doubt, continue well into the night.

I said as such to Adam and, nodding, he replied, "Certes they should focus their attentions on the miracle plays and absorb the intrinsic veracity of Christianity rather than yield to such improper behaviour! The clergy have long advocated thus, though few will heed their exhortations." Although I loved him dearly, on occasion he did sound pompous and straight-laced. I told myself I must strive to keep the nature of his upbringing in mind and be grateful he had not taken holy orders!

It was only a matter of days before Adam received a second message from Elizabeth, informing him of the return of Sir Richard to the shores of England. The Queen had summoned him to Greenwich and requested Adam's presence at a meeting arranged for June 3rd. Again I was to remain behind and as I watched him leave early that morning I was as nervous as I would have been had I actually accompanied him.

CHAPTER FOURTEEN

Sir Richard's audience with the Queen, in her private apartments, was under way by the time Anselm arrived and pleasantries had been exchanged regarding Sir Richard's recent voyage.

"I believe there is no need for introductions, my good friend Master Anselm reminded me that you and he are acquainted, Sir Richard." With a steely look Elizabeth defied him to exhibit hostilities towards Anselm although she knew he must harbour some.

Sir Richard ignored the warnings. "Indeed, though 'tis several years since last we met and thy appearance has altered somewhat. Pray, where hast thou been, Sir? Rumour had it that thy master had not only his kith and kin done away with but his lackey also!"

He was a pleasant-looking man in his thirties with a thatch of tow-coloured hair falling in waves to his shoulders, a small up-turned nose and eyes of the palest blue-green. Although his gentle features were somewhat feminine, he was imposing yet not dogmatic, eloquent yet not verbose. Well-groomed and with a taste for good-quality ornate clothes, he displayed not a trace of vanity. Anselm kept in mind the man's principles: how could he fault him for despising a man whom he thought to have murdered his own nephews? This alone stopped Anselm from taking offence at Sir Richard's remark.

"I can assure thee that rumour has it decidedly wrong! I have been in the north on my late master's business and if I may be allowed to explain that business then I hope thou may think anew on the man whom I still hold dear to my heart." Adam managed to keep his voice calm and controlled.

"Bah!" Sir Richard turned away in disgust.

"Sir Richard, please," Elizabeth interceded. "'Tis understandable that thou shouldst think so. In truth I myself had misgivings where my uncle was concerned. But, pray defer judgement until thou hast heard Master Anselm's tale." She paused and rising from her seat took hold of Sir Richard's hand. "Come sit beside me for I have a request to make of thee." Staring him intently in the eye she continued, "Thou wouldst say that we have become good friends, wouldst thou not?"

"Your Majesty, thou knowest that I am a loyal servant to both thyself and the King." Sir Richard spoke with utter sincerity.

"But of course, for thy loyalty to my husband was made manifest by thy support at Bosworth. Nonetheless, what thou art about to hear is a sensitive matter of great import, a matter so close to my heart that 'tis for thy ears only and I beseech thee to tell none save those whom I give thee leave to inform." She spoke gravely, her gaze never leaving his face, "I am aware that thou sets great store by family values and loyalties, that these principles matter to thee above all other. I cannot in all conscience ask thee to swear secrecy ere knowing what the promise entails but I dearly hope when thou hast heard our news thou wilt find it in thy heart to keep thine own counsel."

"Your Majesty, I would not betray a confidence told to me by a stranger, let alone my Queen." Her words had touched his heart.

Relieved, Elizabeth closed her eyes, a smile playing on her lips. "Then, pray listen to Master Anselm with an open mind. That is all I ask."

Anselm related his tale succinctly, beginning with the meeting at Stony Stratford where he had 'changed sides' and ending with Edward's removal to Shap Abbey and his own journey to London.

Sir Richard was dumbfounded, shaking his head from side to side in amazement. At last he found his tongue, "This is no fiction?" but before Anselm could reply he continued, "Nay, forgive me. Whate'er my opinion of thee in the past, thou wouldst not be so cruel as to raise false hope with our good Lady. But this tale is wondrous strange. For if 'twas not Richard's intention to dispatch the princes, why then did he not show his hand and prove his innocence when rumour was rife?"

"Pray let us take some wine, all this talk will make thee hoarse, Anselm." Turning to Sir Richard, Elizabeth added, "If truth were told, the actions of my uncle are not paramount. However, in view of my subsequent entreaty I feel thou hast the right to know all the facts – Richard has been branded monstrous far too long."

Anselm endeavoured to clarify the late King's motives to Sir Richard, explaining Richard III's own fear and distrust of the Woodvilles and his worry that other hands might harm the princes. Anselm confirmed the authenticity of Bishop Stillington's revelation and told of Richard's consequent belief that no course of action was left open to him other than the one he subsequently took.

Gradually Anselm sensed a change in Sir Richard, a slight softening in his manner when Richard III's name was mentioned. "'Twould seem that he has been misjudged somewhat. But what were his intentions? What to the lads' future?"

Elizabeth stepped in, "That we shall never know. More to the point, what of Edward's future now?" She rose and moving towards the bay window paused to watch the dark, uneven waters of the Thames. The two men behind her were silent – Sir Richard not knowing how to answer and Anselm wishing to leave this delicate matter to the Queen. Gathering her resolve she returned to her seat and faced Sir Richard. "We spoke earlier of thy son, Edward. I know thou art close to the lad and sorely troubled by his affliction." Sir Richard's head dropped. "Dost thou hold out much hope for him?"

With a catch in his voice he replied, "I should love to say yes but in all honesty I fear the worst. My good lady *informs me that his health is worsening by the week, as the fever continues to weaken him. I'll trow we cannot hope for a recovery."* Slumping forward in his seat, his appearance utterly dejected, he continued, *"He was ever a good lad, lively, full of fun and quick-witted to boot. I shall miss him dearly."*

Placing her hand on his shoulder Elizabeth attempted to comfort the despondent father. After a seemly interval she ventured, *"Indeed, Anselm tells me 'twas thus when my brother died. Praise be to God that Edward was spared,"* quickly she crossed herself. Mention of her brother's name jolted Sir Richard out of his reverie. Sensing an opportunity Elizabeth continued, *"I have given much thought to his future for 'tis a perilous issue. Should Henry learn of his existence, would he feel threatened? I could well understand his fear that Edward might consider himself the rightful holder of the crown. Or might even become a rallying point for the Yorkist cause and disaffected Nobles."* Turning to Anselm she added quickly, *"Neither of which would apply for Anselm tells me my brother has softened throughout his stay in the north. Is that not so?"* Before Anselm could reply she continued, *"In truth, Edward gave his assurance that he no longer has designs on the crown. 'Tis almost three years since he left London and during that time he has seen life through different eyes, lived in the midst of a loving family and formed ties to people who value him as a person rather than a means to furthering their advancement."*

"Besides which," Anselm added, *"he accepts his bastardy and fully understands his uncle's actions. He will be no threat to King Henry."* True though his words were, Anselm hoped they were convincing.

"Nonetheless, I would not wish to give my husband cause for concern," Elizabeth's pretext was understood by both men. *"The more I think on't the more I am assured that Edward must take on a new persona, must change his name and forever put his past life behind him."*

Sir Richard had been listening intently to these last exchanges and now nodded in agreement. *"For the sake of all concerned 'twould perhaps be the best course. Thy husband would be none the wiser and Edward,"* he turned to Anselm, *"if what thou says is indeed so, could live his life in peace."*

He frowned, "But how to achieve such a state ...? Perchance he may fare better o'erseas?"

Elizabeth, heartened by his words, was nevertheless swift to press any possible advantage, "As to that, I had hoped for a remedy nearer to home. Although I may be unable to see Edward often 'twould grieve me to think that, having found him, he would now be totally inaccessible to me." She turned to Sir Richard, "I am glad to find we are in one accord with regards to my brother's future, however, I fear that what I am about to say may cause thee some alarm." Taking a deep breath she pressed on, "Since thou sayest thine own son Edward is unlikely to survive, I wonder whether – should that sorry state come to pass – thou wouldst be agreeable to my brother taking his place." She waited a few moments allowing the initial impact of her suggestion to register. "I know thou art a good and trustworthy friend whose life has at all times been ruled by integrity and honour. Although the loss of thy son would be right hard to bear, perchance the furtherance of another's life might help ease thy heartache?"

Sir Richard was still, his eyes glazed and far away as though in a dream. Silence engulfed the room. Anselm was tense, uncertain as to the outcome but Elizabeth was optimistic that the response would be positive. At length Sir Richard rose from his seat, moving to the bay window to stand in the position occupied by his Queen only minutes before: time passed.

Slowly he turned and in a grave voice began, "Your Majesty, when I received thy summons I knew not what to expect but never in my wildest dreams could I have anticipated the nature of what has passed between us this morn," he paused. "Certes thy request is an onerous one and not to be undertaken lightly. I fear that I am unable to give thee an answer at present – within the space of two days, I have learnt that not only is my son at death's door but I am now entreated to take a new one! I find my emotions in shreds and besides, I must discuss the matter with my wife for 'twould not be right to agree to such a course without first informing her."

"Verily, Sir Richard, if I gave the impression that I awaited your immediate reply then forgive me. I am fully *aware that, with a request of such import, the decision will take time in the making."* Elizabeth had joined him by the window and taking his hand in both of hers she continued, *"Please give my warmest regards to thy wife and assure her that, had it not been for my present condition, I should have called at Rolvenden to comfort her in her distress."* Smiling tenderly she paused and having concluded the difficult and sensitive part of the meeting became more business-like in manner. *"In view of my husband's imminent return I think it a good business that the three of us should not meet again – these comings and goings may already have aroused suspicions in Thomas. Anselm must be the recipient of thy answer, the finer details being arranged at that meeting, Sir Richard, and conveyed to me by thy good self when next we meet,"* obviously she was convinced the outcome would be positive. *"Master Anselm lodges with his cousin in Bishopsgate but may I suggest the nearby church of St. Alfege as a suitable meeting-place?"* The two men nodded.

"Anselm, I have something for Edward which I wish thee to give to him – one moment whilst I retrieve it." She crossed to the door opposite, giving entry to her private chapel. From the adjoining vestry she returned with a small casket which when unlocked revealed a myriad of brightly coloured, shining jewels. Solemnly she took out an ornate brooch; a large, gleaming sapphire surrounded by intricate silver metalwork, almost Celtic in design. *"'Twas our father's and I should dearly love Edward to have it as a keepsake – lest I be unable to see him again."* The business-like manner had gone, replaced by the tender tones of a loving sister. *"Tell him ... I miss him dearly."* Neither man uttered a word, both aware this young Queen had undergone much in her short life.

Composing herself once more she reached for a second item from the casket, a sheet of paper which she handed to Anselm. *"This may be of use to thee,"* she said. *"'Tis an unbound decree, commanding whomsoever is presented with it to comply with the directives of the bearer. Should it prove unneeded or once its purpose has been served, I trust thou wilt destroy it?"* Anselm gave a brief nod.

Turning to Sir Richard the Queen softened her tone. "Please think hard on the matter, Sir Richard. We shall await thy communication." To achieve maximum effect she paused before adding earnestly, *"But I beseech thee, for the sake of thy son, let not his death be in vain."*

What a masterly stroke thought Adam: the final coup de grâce.

The sapphire glistened in the sunlight and with difficulty I tore my gaze away, trying to pay attention to Adam's words. He described the meeting in detail and I found myself wishing I could have been present. Would Sir Richard agree? I dearly hoped so for the sake of the young boy I had met only briefly but who, in some small way, had touched my heart. As to how long it would take Sir Richard to come to a decision we were unaware but mindful that our time in London was coming to an end we felt it prudent to resume our search for Agnes.

Taking up our enquiries in the East Cheap area we had an immediate breakthrough. In one of the establishments the proprietress informed us that only a few days ago a young girl, answering to the description of Agnes, had approached her. She had been looking for work but had been turned away as none was available. The woman added that she had advised the girl to give up all hope of ever becoming an apprentice as there were lots of young girls seeking that type of work. We were about to leave when a young apprentice, overhearing our discussion, advanced towards us nervously. She explained that as the girl had looked dejected she had felt sorry for her and, even though she had nothing concrete to suggest, had followed her onto the street merely to offer some comfort. The girl had broken down saying she had been taken on by a certain Dame Martha, a ruthless, unprincipled woman who had induced a number of young girls to sign articles for an apprenticeship which ultimately failed to materialise. The conditions were atrocious and the girls had been used almost as slave labour until most of them, being able to stand it no longer, had moved on. The apprentice told us the girl had said that she would now look for work in a tavern, having given up all hope of ever becoming an apprentice in any trade. Although we thanked her for the information, our hoped-for breakthrough had been short-lived: hundreds and hundreds of taverns littered the city both inside and out. The question was, should we start on the inside and work out, or vice-versa. Adam decided we should opt for the latter on the basis that a greater number of drinking establishments was situated beyond the city walls. This would be our objective.

Two major areas of exploration beckoned – Westminster with its seat of royal power, hierarchy and consequent higher-class traders or Southwark with its immigrant population, many prisons and general lawlessness. Both had their fair share of inns, prostitutes and brothels but on the whole Adam thought Southwark was more likely to yield fruit.

We set off in the direction of London Bridge and as we paralleled the river I suddenly noticed on my right 'Pudding Lane'. Stopping my horse in its tracks I turned to Adam, "Pudding Lane. May we just take a look?"

"Take a look at what?"

"Now it's my turn to give you a history lesson. In 180 years time there will be a Great Fire which will start in this lane and rage for two or three days."

"Ah yes, I do now recall reading the account of the tragedy. If I remember a'right thousands of houses were destroyed were they not and even St. Paul's burnt to the ground?"

"Yes although miraculously only half a dozen people were killed. And here we are, in the very street. Amazing!" I looked about me, at the timber shacks with their roofs of thatch, hearing telltale noises of forge work and baking from within. It was no surprise that these buildings, standing shoulder to shoulder without a break, would one day be reduced to ashes.

Retracing our steps to the waterfront we were soon at that great thoroughfare, London Bridge. This was my first outing to the south side of the river and as we wended our way over the water, through the many, crowded lodgings and stalls I wondered how Southwark would compare to the city. The first difference immediately became apparent for soon after crossing the bridge my senses were accosted by a disgusting stench. The nearer we drew to the heart of the district, the stronger the smell became.

"What on earth *is* that?" I asked Adam, my hand to my nose.

"'Tis the urine and such agents used in the tanning process – a much more prevalent trade here than in the city itself," he explained. Pulling my cloak up over my nose I urged the horse forward, eager to be through these evil-smelling passages.

The majority of the taverns were situated on the main street and consequently over the course of the next few days not only did our journey across the river become a familiar pattern but also the repetitive trudge into one hostelry after another. Adam wondered whether Agnes might have been lucky enough to obtain work here with a lesser craftsman – Southwark was outside the walls of the capital and so free from all trammels of the Guild and City. Questions were asked, leads followed up but inevitably the result was the same: not a trace of Agnes could be found.

One morning, arriving on the south bank of the Thames we came upon a party of travellers. They were a varied bunch; some were without limbs and others on crutches – the most badly afflicted being supported by companions.

Adam witnessed my interest in them. "This shoreline is a well-used by pilgrims. Indeed, Southwark and Greenwich are important anchorages for foreign wayfarers particularly ascetics or palmers bound for Canterbury and the shrine of Thomas à Becket, hopeful of a miraculous cure." He stopped his horse in its tracks. "But of course … St. Thomas's shrine … the ideal place." Adam's look was far away as he concentrated on whatever had occurred to him. I frowned and he explained, "As yet I have not organised my thoughts fully but suffice it to say that Canterbury would be an ideal rendezvous for Edward's substitution." For the remainder of our journey Adam was deep in thought, running through the implications of his new idea.

Having exhausted the central area of Southwark that afternoon we had decided to spread our search to Bermondsey Street but again our efforts were in vain. It had been a hot day and as we were making our way wearily towards London Bridge, Adam suggested we stop and quench our thirst.

On the main street I espied Chaucer's Tabard and asked if we could go in. We had previously bypassed this tavern as it was a good establishment, providing food and drink, stabling and carting and Adam thought the place too respectable to employ the likes of Agnes. He was right in his assessment: the inn was far superior to those we had recently visited, the standard perhaps contributing to the number of people inside. Slowly we made our way through a crowded room of hot, sweating travellers and I was reminded of Catherine's description of the tavern in Kendal. Managing to find a table at the rear, Adam soon returned with some palatable wine which, after the rigours of the day, tasted like nectar. A serving girl brought fish pie to the table on our right and from the left the aroma of spicy pasties wafted across my nostrils. I hadn't realised until then I was hungry and began daydreaming about our evening meal but was jolted out of my reverie when suddenly Adam grabbed my arm.

"A girl passed me at the counter and whilst I failed to see her features I feel sure she had a lisp."

"Surely there are dozens of people who lisp?"

"Aye, perchance I am imagining things." He was silent for several seconds before continuing, "But the more I dwell on the matter, the more I convince myself 'twas her. Come!"

He rose from his seat and was half way to the door before I had managed to squeeze past a man who was intent on gazing down the front of my bodice. Outside it took some time for my eyes to adjust to the light but once they had I noticed Adam was already several yards ahead, beckoning me to follow. He disappeared through a small doorway and I pursued him quickly.

The room we entered was cramped and dingy and I felt sure it was one of the seedier alehouses we had visited several days previously. I could see no sign of Agnes.

"So thou knows not the girl?" Adam was deep in conversation with a man whom I took to be the landlord.

"Ah told 'e last time the answer's nay," the man was fat and dirty and spoke in an insolent manner.

"And nonesuch person entered but a moment ago?" Adam persisted. The publican wiped his nose on the back of his sleeve before shaking his head in a desultory manner: I felt sure Adam was struggling to be civil. "Certes I am troubled for I fear my eyes are failing me."

The man shrugged his shoulders and turning his back on Adam poured a flagon of ale for a waiting customer. At that moment a woman entered through a curtain in the back wall. She sidled up to the landlord and whispered something in his ear.

Adam addressed his next remark to her, "Perchance the girl slipped through the back. Hast thou seen a young girl pass through here, Madam? Around twelve or thirteen years of age and small of stature with bright, red hair and a smattering of freckles?"

She shook her head and answered too quickly in a high pitched voice, "Nay, mister, there's none here like that!" She gave the landlord a furtive, sideways glance and backed slowly towards the curtain.

As to what our next steps would have been I am unaware but at that moment we heard a piercing scream and without further ado, pushing the woman to one side Adam rushed through the curtain towards the rear. I was in close pursuit and hearing a noise from above we climbed the stairs in haste, following the trail of frightened sobs. The door was partially open and with one fluid movement Adam burst into a squalid room hardly larger in size than a dog kennel. The sight that greeted my eyes made my heart turn cold. The room was a hellhole. It was unfurnished with holes in the roof and cavities in the wattle and daub walls; the floor was filthy and covered with straw which resembled sweepings from a stable; the air was rife with the foetid smell of decay; and from one corner I caught a glimpse of black fur and heard the unmistakable squeak of a rat. Agnes was lying on the straw, her skirts thrown up over her waist to expose plump, white thighs glowing luminously in the gloom. A large, kneeling figure loomed over her and as he turned to face us I caught sight of an ugly looking cutlass in one hand. His other had been fumbling between her legs but as Adam approached the man made to stand. Hampered by his hose, which were down below his knees, he stumbled and in that one moment Adam took advantage of his immobility. Scooping up a tankard from the floor he gave the scoundrel a mighty crack on the back of the head: large though he was he went down like a log.

I rushed over to Agnes and kneeling by her side held her tightly in my arms. Her tears came in deep, racking sobs and her body shook uncontrollably. I rocked her to-and-fro and without thinking uttered words of comfort, "There, there. Hush, hush now. You're quite safe … we're here for you … he's gone … the danger's passed."

Agnes struggled to speak through her weeping, "I c…couldn't underthtand him … he wath f…foreign an' angry th…that I d…didn't know what to d…do. He had a kn…knife an' I wath *thow* th…thcared…"

"There, there. Don't fret." I carried on rocking her as the crying subsided. "You're coming away with us, away from here."

The landlord had followed us up the stairs and witnessed events but seeing the look on Adam's face, he backed along the landing without a word, leaving the way clear for our departure.

We were soon out of that foul place and into the street, into air that now smelled surprisingly sweet. We took Agnes to a seamstress on Bermondsey Street, a woman we had met earlier that same afternoon and who had agreed to employ her should she be found. Her establishment was small but clean and we had learned of her through a friend, of a friend, of a friend of Hannah's – far enough removed, we thought, to prevent any awkward questions about my 'sister'. She shared Adam's horse on the journey and later he recounted to me the gist of his conversation with her. She had informed him she had been at the alehouse for only one day and, thankfully, the foreign sailor was her first 'customer'. The encounter, therefore, should leave her not too deeply scarred and Margery could be assured that her sister had been, virtually, unharmed.

That evening back at Bishopsgate we were unable to show too much elation in view of our need for secrecy in front of Hannah: had we found my 'sister' she would, inevitably, have accompanied us back to our lodgings. In addition, once our quest had been successfully completed there was no reason for our further stay in London. Despite this concealment we both had a feeling of contentment and were satisfied we had sorted out at least one problem.

By the end of the week Adam received a note from Sir Richard Guildford requesting a meeting in Greenwich the following day. Would our second problem be resolved as satisfactorily?

The church was dimly lit and the heady scent of incense permeated the air. It was quiet and still and as Anselm's eyes became accustomed to the gloom he perceived a shape in the corner: a figure silently kneeling in prayer. Quietly approaching he realised the supplicant was indeed Sir Richard and so, retreating to the shadows, he awaited the conclusion of the other's devotions. Finally the bowed figure rose and as he approached the rear of the building Anselm stepped from the darkness.

"Master Anselm, 'tis good to see thee again," his greeting was friendly and immediately Anselm sensed much more warmth in the man than at their previous meeting.

"And thee, Sir Richard. How is thy son?"

"Sadly he worsens by the day – how long he can last I know not – but thank ye for thy concern." He paused, but shaking off his moment of vulnerability continued, "Now, I have instructed the priest to make himself scarce and not return within the hour, so we may speak freely." Anselm waited, although eager to learn Sir Richard's decision, not wishing to rush matters. "I have thought long and hard on the matter we last discussed and am come to the conclusion that,

as it would take a miracle to save my son, should he die, by agreeing to the Queen's request some good would come from this tragedy." He added quickly, "But 'twould be on the understanding – and mark my words, only on the understanding – that after meeting the lad I am convinced of his true intentions. I'll have no hothead or disaffected claimant in my household! Should things turn sour and King Henry find out I had been harbouring a Yorkist, well, I need not tell thee where my future would lie."

"Assuredly, Sir Richard. I know the Queen well enough to say that she herself would not wish the matter to progress further, should the person in question hold such desires as those of which thou speaketh. But, again, let me attest to the lad's innermost desires – I have been his companion these three years past and know him well. Thy fears will be unfounded."

"Pray to God thou art right for I cannot imagine what other course his future might take."

"And what of thy lady wife, what are her feelings on the matter?" Anselm enquired.

"'Twas a shock I'll grant thee but over time she will warm to the idea. After all, 'twill give her another 'son' to mother and that she does right well." His tone was tender for he and the Lady Anne had great affection for one another.

"And none other knows of the plan?"

"Not a soul. Nor shall any henceforth for my wife is aware of the import of the situation and is sworn to secrecy." Sir Richard's words were spoken sincerely. Gravely shaking his head he continued, "But how we shall achieve the switch I cannot imagine."

"Well, as to the modus operandi ..." Anselm proceeded to explain to Sir Richard the Queen's thoughts on his new manor in Sussex.

"Iham ... 'tis a good thought. As Her Majesty rightly says 'tis not long since 'twas granted me by King Henry and although the letters patent have yet to be issued 'tis mine to do with as I please. Aye, 'twould be ideal, for the steward and his wife are local by birth and know naught of the family. But in truth that matters not for although I have visited the place to put in hand some very necessary improvements, neither my wife nor Edward have been there." He pondered a moment or two. "But what to the swap itself? My father is still sharp and would smell a rat if I suggested taking my son to Iham, even though the place is now a goodly residence."

Anselm nodded thoughtfully, meticulously turning things over in his mind. "As to that, I have been giving the matter much thought. Supposing thou were to announce thine intention of taking thy son to Canterbury, to the shrine of St. Thomas, hopeful of a miracle. There is a church o'erlooking the town, St. Martin's, whose priest is known to me from my time in that City ... " suddenly struck by a thought Anselm added, "I trust he abides there still. 'Tis some twenty years since his installation and many since we last conversed ... let us hope that is the case. He is a good man, the soul of discretion and in view of the Queen's billet he will ask no questions – he would not be privy to the switch, of course. 'Twould be the ideal meeting place and ... when thy son departs this life," both men crossed themselves, "his mortal remains may be interred in the consecrated grounds of the church." Sir Richard silently contemplated Anselm's words. "The lad shall then accompany thee back to Iham where, given time, he may be thought to have regained his strength, divine intervention having rewarded his pilgrimage to Canterbury. Should thy father have any misgivings thou canst explain the move to Iham as being a goodly place for thy son to convalesce."

"Aye, 'tis an ideal spot on the coast and away from the city. But 'twould be necessary for him to recover slowly – remain in confinement away from the likes of my father." Sir Richard was warming to the idea, "And he should remain scarce for some time, perchance accompanying me o'erseas when next I sail. The sea air would be the making of him!" He laughed wryly, the first humour to pass his lips in over a week.

"Should mention be made of change in thy son's appearance then 'twould be a good business to blame it on the pox – it does oft mark the skin and if truth were told, the lad suffers thus at present in view of his adolescence. Moreover, 'twill not be long ere he may alter his guise by the addition of a *few whiskers such as these."* Anselm rubbed his hand over the short, stubbly beard still present on his chin.

"Aye and lads of his age are prone to shoot up in fits and starts. I'll trow none will know him by the time he has course to attend Court." Wagging his forefinger Sir Richard added thoughtfully, "'Twould be a good business to ensure he stays well away from my father for some time to come, although 'twill have been many a year since he set eyes on the Queen's brother."

Anselm was beginning to admire this man who, despite great adversity, conducted himself with such aplomb. He thought it only right to proffer a lifeline. "But when all is said and done, should thy son recover his health we must think anew on the other's future."

"Aye, mayhap the journey to the shrine will prove rewarding," adopting a brave tone Sir Richard attempted to sound positive but both men expected little hope.

"So, 'twould appear our business is at an end. Thou wilt convey the content of our discussions to the Queen?"

"Indeed. With the King's return I must report on my recent travels and will find an opportunity to speak with Her Majesty. Once done I shall leave, with Edward, for Canterbury."

"Thou wilt, undoubtedly, arrive ere myself and my charge. Perchance thou couldst leave note of thy whereabouts at St. Martin's." Anselm was struck by a new thought, "I think it requisite that, for the sake of all concerned, Elizabeth Woodville hears naught of this business."

"Verily, thou speaks the truth! I cannot begin to imagine the consequences should that woman get the slightest hint of her chick's existence. She would certainly take pains to feather her own nest! At all costs she must hear naught of this affair!"

Anselm nodded ruefully, faced his fellow collaborator and smiled, "And so – to Canterbury."

"To Canterbury!" Sir Richard grasped Anselm's hand in a firm shake, a common goal uniting the two in purpose.

CHAPTER FIFTEEN

The incense almost lingered in the air, so vivid was Adam's description of his tryst in the church. As he related the tale and confirmed Sir Richard's agreement, a wave of relief flooded through my body: although Edward was little known to me I felt deeply involved in these crucial events. All that was necessary now was to obtain his acceptance of the plan. That, Adam told me confidently, would be straightforward and from my recollection of our last meeting at the Abbey, I felt sure he was right: after all, what other option was left to Edward?

Soon we were bidding farewell to Hannah as we set off on our return to the north. All was well with the world: the skies were clear; the sun shone; our spirits were high; and it was good to be leaving the hustle and bustle of London behind.

With fairer weather than on our outward journey we made good progress and by the last weekend in June we were approaching Shap. Feeling Edward had been on tenterhooks for long enough, Adam decided we should call and inform him of the proposition on our way to Raisgill. He was pleased to see us.

"I assured thee we would return. Didst thou think that I would not keep my word?" Adam quizzed. We were in the abbey precincts, once again meandering down towards the river.

"Nay, not that ... just ... mayhap something might have prevented thee from returning." Both joy and relief were evident on Edward's face. "It is not that I am not grateful to the Brothers but ... it seems as though I have been here *forever*." Excitedly, he hurried on, "Now, what of Elizabeth? How fares she? Is she distant and withdrawn in her new role of Queen?" A boyish giggle escaped from his lips and I realised how sad and alone he must have felt over the past few months. Confirming this he continued, "I had not realised how much I have missed her."

"Likewise she has missed thee, Edward and sends her fondest love." We had reached the river and seating ourselves on a large boulder Adam reached into his pocket. "She bade me give thee this." The summer sun glinted on the precious metal as he placed the sapphire brooch on Edward's palm. "Thou may recognise it as belonging to thy father. Elizabeth wished thee to have it, not only as a keepsake of him but also as a pledge of her affection for thee."

As Edward turned the trinket over in his hands, obviously touched by the gesture, Adam recounted what had passed between Elizabeth, Sir Richard and himself. Edward listened intently, occasionally frowning, sometimes asking a pertinent question but generally appearing to accept the plan.

Adam was approaching the end of his account. "However, thou must be aware that 'twill be requisite to remain hidden, certes initially. Once thou hast 'recovered' 'twould certainly be a good business to journey abroad a-time. The details have not yet been resolved with Sir Richard but he is well versed in artillery and shipbuilding and I feel sure would take pleasure in schooling thee. In addition he hath acquired certain knowledge in the art of land drainage." Edward frowned and Adam, intent on throwing him a lifeline, continued by outlining the possibilities for his future, "'Tis a method new to this country – a system of draining the low-lying marsh lands, reclaiming them from the sea and thereby increasing the acreage of the land. Thou art a quick-witted lad. Perchance thou might make a name for thyself in that field."

"'Twould certainly be different, unlike all that hath gone before." Clearly Edward was intrigued. "And I shall be nearer Elizabeth – although I'll trow I shall not be able to see her?"

"Nay, 'twould be folly to risk all, for the sake of a brief encounter with thy sister. In time 'twill be possible to attend Court, when thou hast filled out a mite and none can recognise thee. But on no account must thou disclose thy true identity – ever." Edward opened his mouth to speak but before he could do so Adam hurried on, "I am aware that thou didst divulge the same to Lady Margaret ... I know ... 'twas a trying time after the death of thy brother. But be aware, Edward. Should the faintest whisper emerge, 'twould put not only thine own life at risk, but that of thy sister, Sir Richard, myself and my cousin." He gestured towards me.

Edward looked defiant. "I can assure thee, Anselm, thou hast naught to fear. I shall let slip not a trace which could connect me to my previous life." He shook his head slowly and a glazed, far away look came into his eye. "Those days of preparation, away from kith and kin are long gone ... another life. I have no desire to live with intrigue or conspiracy. I crave a settled, family life – something I have only recently tasted. Besides, I could not knowingly bring harm to thee or this gentleman who has so bravely offered me a new life. And certes I would not endanger Elizabeth's existence."

As Adam looked at Edward tenderly I reflected on the diverse emotions the two must be experiencing: Edward was unsure as to what the future held; Adam knew their time together was coming to an end. At least I hoped those were the thoughts going through Adam's mind for that would signify we had a future together. Although Adam had expressed words of love to me on the night of our arrival at Overthwaite, during our trip to London he had been reserved: this I had put down to his preoccupation with the task in hand. With difficulty I had refrained from pursuing the subject but hoped with all my might that once Edward was settled, Adam would turn his attentions towards me. That was when I would make my move – in slow, insidious stages!

Adam was nearing the end of his explanation. "Thy words give me heart for Sir Richard's one condition was thy acquiescence to a life free from contention. A life in which all claim to the throne has been renounced. A life as his son, in which thou would needs accept Henry Tudor as the true and rightful King. Sir Richard is a fine, honourable man – was a staunch supporter of thy father. Thou wilt do well with him."

We overnighted at the Abbey during which time Adam advised Edward of the way in which the swap would take place. Early next morning we set off, promising to return immediately after checking all was well with Matthew and his sisters at Raisgill. In truth, Adam was unsure as to my immediate future. That I should return – with or without him – through the door in October went without saying, as far as he was concerned. Where I should stay in the meantime was the uncertainty. I knew he preferred me to remain in the north in case, for whatever reason, his journey from Canterbury was delayed. However, to leave me at Raisgill was impossible for it might be that I would be unable to return to Overthwaite on my own. Ideally, the Hall itself was the best place but the presence of Hugo made that precarious: Adam was determined that I should not be left alone with him. Consequently he had decided to await events; see the lie of the land at Raisgill and make his decision accordingly.

The one factor Adam had failed to take into account was my opinion. He was used to compliant 15th century women who agreed to his bidding without the slightest demur. I doubted whether, during his short stay in the 21st century, he had experienced the emancipated female – although Catherine must have made him suspect that, over the years, women had changed. I intended not to remain in the north; how I was to achieve my goal remained to be seen.

We rode at a pleasant canter with the beauty of the Lakeland fells on our left and the Pennines to our right. I could see Adam was more at ease, feeling positive about Edward's future. The only obstacle remaining was the fate of Sir Richard's son: sadly the outcome was virtually a foregone conclusion. I sensed Adam needed a break and kept the conversation well away from Edward. We chatted about many things as we travelled and gradually I felt a return of the warmth in our relationship that we had enjoyed several weeks ago. Still I shied from broaching the subject of our future: that could wait until Edward was firmly housed with the Guildfords.

By mid afternoon the village of Raisgill came into view on the horizon and below, nestling in the folds of the valley, a cluster of outlying dwellings appeared as black dots against the green of the summer grassland. Initially I failed to notice anything amiss for I was still pleasantly light-headed from the day's stolen moments alone with Adam. Only when we rounded a small copse of oak trees in the valley bottom did the acrid smell of burning reach my nostrils. All was peaceful ahead: almost too peaceful. Adam urged his horse forward and by the time I reached the first cottages he had dismounted. The scene was one of devastation and pitiful to behold. The houses had been torched and as the embers continued to smoulder, the wispy columns of smoke rising from blackened roof beams bore witness to earlier events. No evidence of life existed. Half a dozen victims had fallen foul of the raid: all were men and their throats had been slit.

"Reivers," Adam had been kneeling by one of the bodies. "'Twould appear to have happened some time ago for they are long dead." Nodding towards a burly figure he continued grimly, "At least one received his just deserts!"

The man was dressed in a coat of quilted leather that had been reinforced with horn to aid protection. His boots and breeches were also of leather and beside his head lay the so-called steel bonnet: a home-made, peaked, metal bowl – trade mark of the border reivers'. He lay on his back but at a strange angle. The pitchfork protruding from his chest proclaimed the manner of death and had been driven with such force that the lifeless body was pinioned to the ground by the weapon's prongs. A small trickle of blood from the corner of his mouth had congealed into a black scar and the startled look on his face spoke of an unexpected attack: a violent death for a violent marauder.

The attackers had ransacked the dwellings before setting them alight and the ground was littered with household effects, carelessly left behind by the raiders in their eagerness to depart. I shivered despite the warmth of the day. What had become of the women and children, I wondered.

"We must thank God that these men died a swift death. Come, we have no time to tarry here. Let us make haste to Raisgill." Adam left unspoken the question that dominated our thoughts: had the reivers moved on to the Hall?

"'Twas last night when we saw the beacon signalling another raid," Sir Robert was tired and resigned. "Not knowing if 'twas a solitary affair or a full-blown attack we had no option but to gather all in."

We were seated in the great hall, surrounded by the inhabitants of Raisgill village who would remain until all chance of incursion had passed. On our arrival the gates of the barmkin had been heavily barred but a lookout posted on the tower's battlements had relayed our approach to Sir Robert and we were soon admitted, relieved to find the residents unscathed.

"Thankfully they passed us by. Had they not we would have lost much livestock for by then 'twas too dark to gather in the animals. But we managed a goodly number at first light, for their return journey may be by way of Raisgill." In addition to a hall filled with tenants Sir Robert's barmkin was overflowing with cattle.

"They were close by for we observed the result of their plunder at the dwellings in the valley below," Adam pointed in their direction.

"Easy pickings – 'tis much easier to make isolated raids than attempt an attack on a stronger hold such as ours." Our host nodded towards a group of women in the far corner. Some tended children; others cared for the old and infirm; but all went about their business with a sense of resolve and determination. "They made off with the widow Graham's cattle, several women lost husbands, Maude Carruther's son-in-law was burned alive trying to defend their home and many of the younger women were violated." Angrily he added, "'Tis always the same when Black-Lock Willie and his Carleton men go a-reiving. Pray to God the Warden apprehends the villain. 'Twould be a welcome sight to behold his body swinging from the gallows on Harraby Hill!"

Life at Raisgill bore little or no resemblance to that which we had left some two months earlier. The place was awash with people who busied themselves with the mundane tasks of existence as though lodging at the hall was second nature to them. Death, illness and misfortune were accepted as a matter of course: life continued. An air of hustle and bustle pervaded and I helped where I could. By nightfall I was weary, instantly falling asleep on my cramped pallet despite the ever-present smell of body odour and the underlying murmur of voices.

The following morning Adam was absent and I decided to seek out Margery. She was pleased to see me and began her usual ceaseless chatter – snippets of gossip, things I had missed and general tittle-tattle on life at Raisgill.

"It's grand bein' here – oh, not just now o'course – but what wi' Lady Margaret dyin' I'm really not lookin' forward to goin' back. *And* I'm not on me own!" She nodded enigmatically and looking round to ensure she was not overheard mouthed the word "Jane". Again she nodded knowingly and lowering her voice continued, "She's right sweet on Master Jonathan and if yer ask me, he feels t' same!" This time the nod was accompanied by raised eyebrows. I mirrored her expression, trying hard not to laugh. She veered onto a different tack. "Master Anselm came by at first light, told mi about Agnes an' how yer'd found her in London. Right glad I am that she's aright and when I tell Ma I know it'll stop her from worryin'." Putting her hand on my shoulder she gave a gentle squeeze. "I cannot thank yer enough fer rememberin' what I'd said and gettin' Master Anselm to look fer her."

I wondered how much Adam had told her but suspected he had imparted only edited details of our discoveries in Southwark. Suddenly I was struck by a thought: had it occurred to Margery that I had passed on the information to Adam even though I was unable to speak? Of course, I could have written it down for him but would she expect me to be able to read and write? Perhaps she would consider that my upbringing provided such learning. At all costs, whatever her thought processes she was satisfied and showed no signs of harbouring any suspicion.

I wandered up to the great hall. The previous day had been hectic and I had had little chance of 'talking' to Lady Alice but now decided it was a matter of good manners to renew my acquaintance with her. Now well into her pregnancy she was seated at the far end of the hall, propped up on cushions, directing proceedings in her friendly, jocular fashion.

Seeing me approach she gestured and called across the room. "Emma, come sit with me," she patted the empty place beside her on the settle, "and tell me all about London." By now things were organised in the hall and I felt it a welcome distraction for her from the worries of the past thirty-six hours. "My father took me once, as a girl and I have always yearned to return. Say, was't as busy as ever? And what sights thou must have seen ... for 'twas Corpus Christi! What dids't thou think of the Mystery Plays? I saw them once only, in York ..." and so she continued. I nodded and shrugged, made my face as expressive as I could and became the perfect foil for her nattering.

Soon Adam returned. He had accompanied Sir Robert on a reconnaissance to ensure all was well with his outlying tenants. Thankfully the pair had caught no sight of the raiders nor had they found any further evidence of assault.

Adam turned his attention to matters closer to home. "I trust the children fare well?"

"Indeed they do. Why, I fear young Matthew has grown in height since last thou saw him! And right settled he is. I'll not say he has forgotten all that has passed but a little affection and some battles on the chess board with Sir Robert have helped to ease his mind." Lady Alice chuckled, "Aye, and he's not the only one to be blossoming from a show of tenderness! 'Twould not surprise me if a reading of banns were to be made in the not too distant future!" I smiled to myself: Margery was not alone in noticing the growing relationship between Jane and Sir Robert's son. Adam frowned and Lady Alice explained, "My step-son Jonathan and young Jane are developing a likeness for one another."

"Ah." Adam's lack of interest was evident. I hoped he had more enthusiasm for his own romantic attachment! He wandered off and Lady Alice proceeded to explain in detail the growing signs she had spotted in the happy couple. It helped to while away the afternoon.

The following morning I was restless and arose early, finding Adam already up and taking some air in the courtyard. I hurried out to meet him, eager to be able to have a word or two beyond the earshot of others: still I had no knowledge of his plans for my future.

"It's good to have a few moments alone" I whispered.

"Indeed. I had intended to seek thee out today and advise thee of my findings." He glanced around but we were not overheard. My heart pounded, wondering what he would say. "Although it is imperative for Edward to reach Canterbury I thought it prudent to remain here a little longer, in view of the reivers you understand?" I nodded and waited for Adam to continue. He remained silent for what seemed like an age and I could stand the suspense no longer.

"Well? What did you find out?" I fought hard to keep my voice in check but it was still higher than I would have wished.

"Sir Robert is of the opinion that Hugo may reside still at Overthwaite. Most recent news indicated that he had appeared at the Pie-Powdre court following the annual fair at Penrith – some drunken brawl or the like. Under the circumstances I have decided that thou must accompany Edward and myself to Canterbury." In an unguarded moment he sought my hand, "Besides, I cannot now imagine being without thee." I realised I had been holding my breath and as the import of his words hit me I was both elated and startled. Did he mean he could not imagine *ever* being without me? It was fortunate my role was one of mute for at that moment I was lost for words. "Should all be well we shall leave on the morrow."

But events were to take a frightening change, for during the early hours of the following morning the border reivers struck.

Shouting awakened me. The sun's first rays had scarcely pierced the horizon and in the dim light of the upstairs chamber all appeared to be in chaos. Gradually, as my eyes adjusted, it became clear that what I had taken for alarm was in fact a dogged resoluteness to prepare for the attack. Yes, people were scurrying around but evidently the occupants of Raisgill Hall had undergone this terror before. A sense of foreboding hung in the air. Nevertheless, in the main, the women and children were composed and the men knew which tasks had to be performed.

I made my way downstairs but Adam was nowhere to be seen and crossing to the window I looked out, eagerly searching for his face. In the grey light of dawn I had difficulty discerning one person from another: what I could see made my blood run cold. The determined resolve inside the tower was far from mirrored out in the courtyard. High on the inside of the barmkin wall ran a stone walkway and a number of Sir Robert's men had stationed themselves along this ledge. The majority was armed with longbows, caught up in a frantic attempt to prevent the raiders from scaling the barmkin walls. With the moat to negotiate and the smooth wall to content with, most found the exercise well nigh impossible. Nonetheless, here and there a reiver had succeeded and the ensuing fight, inevitably to the death, yielded sickening scenes of carnage. Some fought with halberds others with spears and the horseback riders wielded fearsome looking lances. The fighting was fierce with casualties on both sides: several men were wounded but only two killed outright; and on one occasion I witnessed the horrific cleaving of a man's skull with a formidable weapon which I later learned to be called a Jedburgh axe.

The walkway was stained with blood. The cattle in the barmkin, detecting the commotion, sensing danger and smelling death in the air, became restless and agitated. I noticed smoke was beginning to rise from the huge gates of the barmkin. At sunrise the raiders had built a fire outside the stockade and lighted arrows had found their mark, igniting the wooden beams. Although their thickness meant it would take some time before any impression was made, the possible breach was a dangerous one. I sensed somebody behind me and turned to find Lady Alice at my shoulder.

"Dost thou really want to watch such bloodshed?" She sounded downcast and I was about to shake my head when suddenly she looked me straight in the eye and with a strange expression on her face continued, "But of course, thou ar't looking for Anselm." She touched my forearm. "Fear not for he is safe. My husband has taken him up to the watchtower. From there they can oversee events." Had she guessed my feelings for Adam or did she think my concern merely that of a cousin? "No harm should befall them on the roof – given that they shelter behind the battlements, and I cannot see my Robert being foolhardy, 'tis not in his nature." She turned her gaze towards the window and settled herself on its stone seat. "We shall know the outcome soon enough – pray to God those murderers do not prevail. Still, if they are successful 'twill be only the cattle we shall lose, and perhaps one or two possessions from the old hall, which is neither here nor there. The tower is impregnable – providing the outer door and grille remain shut, we are secure." Closing her eyes she rested her head against the embrasure. "If only our men are safe, all else matters not."

I continued my vigil, although I must admit I felt much easier, knowing Adam was safe. By now the light was improving and I took stock of the scene. Little had changed in the courtyard with the exception of the barmkin gates where the fire was beginning to take hold. And then I noticed him: my gaze was drawn to a figure hurrying back and forth between the gates and the smithy. Could that person be Tom? I looked more intently, yes I believed it was. He was carrying a pail of water in either hand and with each journey he attempted to douse the fire at the gate. His was an uphill struggle made worse when the supply of water in the smithy ran dry. He moved to the well in the centre of the courtyard but the milling cattle slowed his progress and repeatedly knocked against his buckets causing spillage of the precious contents within. Back and forth he went, until his arms were surely numb with pain. But he was winning the fight: the flames were dying down and the wood was beginning to smoulder.

Suddenly one of the reivers was over Tom, descending from the wall-walk to knock him to the ground. The man was slighter than Tom, quick and lithe and had drawn his dagger before the other could regain his feet. He lunged at his opponent but Tom was swifter than his bulky form suggested and with a neat side step avoided the knife by inches. The man came back at him and a glancing blow to Tom's upper arm produced a large swathe of red to the sleeve of his shirt. He was momentarily off guard and the other pressed his advantage, knocking Tom to the ground once more with a shoulder charge to his midriff. But the larger man still had a lot left in him and a savage kick to the reiver's shin caused him to double up in pain. Tom grabbed him by the shoulders, pulling his body down into the mud of the courtyard. They wrestled back and forth, the reiver's dagger sometimes visible, sometimes hidden between the writhing bodies. My heart was in my mouth, hoping against hope that Tom would survive the marauder's blade. Somehow Tom managed to rise to his knees and was about to stand when his adversary made yet another sweeping arc with his knife. It almost connected with Tom's chest but not quite for, catching the blade in his right hand he managed to keep the lethal stroke at bay. Bringing his left hand up to the reiver's chin he forced the man's head back, further and further, as slowly he extended his reach, pushing with all his might in a continual application of pressure. The man struggled to dislodge Tom's grip but I could sense that gradually his efforts were weakening. I tried to tear my eyes away but found it impossible to stop myself from watching, with a gruesome kind of fascination. The reiver's back was arched out of all proportion but suddenly his body went limp.

Whether his head or back had broken I do not know but as his head rolled limply onto the right shoulder and Tom relaxed his grip, the lifeless body slumped to the ground. The incident was over.

A deep sob interrupted my preoccupation and I turned to find a group surrounding me. All had witnessed the fight and it was Margery's cry I had heard. Her knuckles were white with tension, scarred by the imprint of her teeth where she had bitten down in a struggle to stop herself from calling out.

Lady Alice was comforting her. "There, there lass, thou need not worry. He will be fine. He fought well and hast won through." She rubbed Margery's back. "Why, single-handedly he has quenched the fire and prevented their entry. Thou must be very proud of him." Margery was too emotional to reply. With the fight over she had crumbled under the strain and was crying softly.

I turned back to the window. Tom had relinquished his hold on the dagger and even from that distance I could see his hand was covered in blood. He staggered back towards the smithy and disappeared inside.

The fighting continued for some time but the worst was over. The reivers had suffered heavy casualties and knew they would fail to take the Hall. One by one they limped away. No doubt they would marshal forces, take stock and continue with their raids – but not at Raisgill. We had routed them.

Adam accompanied Sir Robert on his return from the roof and I longed to be able to rush to him and feel his arms about me. It was not to be and I had to make do with a meaningful look and the trace of a smile. Permission was given for the tower door to be opened and Margery was the first to leave heading straight for the smithy, eager to nurse her wounded husband. She was followed closely by several of the other women, each one ready to tend the injured and also check the condition of her own spouse.

Once again Raisgill's inhabitants slipped into gear in an effortless fashion, duties being undertaken and necessities carried out without any hesitation. Nobody was in charge or even oversaw matters but all knew instinctively what was required of them and got on with it. The casualties were brought into the hall and, thankfully, most of the injuries were minor ones: when Sir Robert undertook a final head-count he was pleased to report we had lost only one man.

"'Twas provident we decided to leave Jack Johnson on watch and 'twas that which gave us the upper hand," Sir Robert explained as we sat listening to him over a late breakfast. "'Twould normally be three or four days afore Black-Lock Willie and his men returned but on this occasion the old rogue tried a new ruse, hoping we would be lulled into carelessness. They must have doubled back in an attempt to catch us out. Well his manoeuvre has failed!"

"Jack spotted them?" asked Matthew excitedly, for all the children were present, eagerly devouring not only the food but also each word Sir Robert uttered.

"Aye lad, he did." He turned to face them. "Luckily Jack was alert and at first light he heard their voices outwith the barmkin," he dropped his own voice to match the mood of his tale, "whispering across the marshes. No doubt they hoped to climb the walls without detection then wait in silence for the tower door's opening."

"Would they have murdered us all, Sir Robert?" Matthew's direct question crystallised our thoughts.

"Well," Sir Robert paused as he considered his answer. "Were thou to put that question to the Carletons I daresay they would profess innocence, say their only desire to be plunder. Suffice it to say we should be thankful 'twas not put to the test. Jack's early warning meant we were ready for them and those villains found us more than a match!" The children cheered and leaving the table began fighting a mock battle. Sir Robert's voice took on a more serious note, "Had Tom failed to douse the fire at the gate 'twould have been a very different matter. Although we should have been safe in the tower, those outside would not have been so fortunate. Many a man owes his life to Tom."

The man in question was at the other end of the hall where Margery was fussing over him like a mother hen. In his usual self-deprecating manner he played down his role in Raisgill's survival, readily colouring whenever praise was forthcoming. His right hand was badly gashed, the open cuts extending to the bone where he had gripped the well-honed dagger firmly. Margery had applied liberal amounts of Lady Alice's salve and as the wounds were clean and swiftly dealt with it was hoped they would heal without further infection. However, in the short term he would require alternative work, for to wield a blacksmith's hammer at the moment was certainly impossible.

"What took thee out into't yard?" was a question repeatedly asked.

"Polly was in foal," one of the horses we had brought with us from Overthwaite, "and as her time was due I felt as how I should be there for her ... it being her first, eh? Reivers or no, when any o' my girls needs me, there I shall be, eh?" Glancing up at his wife Tom gave her an imperceptible wink.

By the end of the day life had returned to near normality at Raisgill. Sir Robert's tenants would remain at the Hall for a few days longer, until all threat of a further attack had passed. Adam had decided, however, the time had come for us to leave, as it was now becoming imperative that we set off for Canterbury. We departed on the following morning.

CHAPTER SIXTEEN

It was early evening and a long day in the saddle had checked our conversation. But tired though we were our spirits were lifted at sight of our goal: Canterbury lay below us in the valley of the Stour. The massive bulk of the cathedral Church of Christ dominated the town. As we drew near we could see the Abbey of St. Augustine and beyond, prominent on a rise, our destination – St. Martin's church. We spurred our horses forward, eager to rest for the night.

Our journey from Cumbria had been a straightforward one. We followed the same route as on our previous journey and with favourable weather conditions made good progress, notwithstanding Adam's desire to spare the horses. By Towcester we were three full days ahead of our expectations and once again opted for the road by-passing St. Albans. Adam had decided, for safety's sake, that we should avoid the capital and consequently south of Barnet we joined the Great North Road for a brief spell before turning east just short of London. Dropping down to the river we rested overnight at the abbey in North Woolwich, taking the ferry first thing the following morning.

As we left the shoreline Adam pointed out that the crossing was an old one. "Prithee Edward take note for thy forebears have passed this way oft times before. This ferry hath borne Kings and the like for one hundred and fifty years, and more."

Edward looked impressed but also thoughtful as he gazed around him, taking in our surroundings. I wondered what was passing through his mind and once again reflected on the way he was prepared to give up his inheritance without the slightest murmur. But then, what choice did he have?

At the beginning of our travels we had left Raisgill early heading straight for Shap Abbey. Edward was overjoyed to see us and not surprisingly, in view of his long confinement, I sensed an air of excitement about him. It was several years since he had been to the south of the country and although we had previously talked to him of our trip to London, as we travelled Edward questioned Adam ceaselessly, eager to learn each and every detail of our meeting with his sister.

He was also intrigued about the man who was willing to accept him as his son: what kind of a person was Sir Richard Guildford? Before setting out from Shap Abbey, Adam had again quizzed Edward to ensure he understood the commitment he was about to make. But the boy was adamant he had spent many hours in contemplation and assured us he had relinquished all claim to the throne and desired nothing more than a calm, contented life. Heartened by his words and convinced of his sincerity, Adam felt able to proceed with the next stage of the plan.

We found decent lodgings within the city walls and early the following morning Adam left for St. Martin's church hopeful that John Browne, his old acquaintance was still the priest there. Returning late morning he confirmed that Sir Richard and his son had arrived in Canterbury.

"They have been within the city for some time and Sir Richard has visited St. Martin's on several occasions, hopeful of our arrival. John has provided me with details of their whereabouts and I feel it only right to go there immediately."

"Shall I accompany thee?" Edward sounded nervous now that the appointed hour had arrived.

"Nay, not on this occasion. I think it best that I go alone and see the lie of the land."

Again we awaited Adam's return on tenterhooks: I tried to appear calm and collected while Edward chattered away to hide the tension he must be feeling inside. By mid afternoon he had shed all attempts at nonchalance and was stationed at the window, eagerly scrutinising each passer-by.

"Here he is!" Edward cried at last and was down the stairs in a flash. Adam was smiling as he entered the room, due to a satisfactory meeting and not amusement at Edward's behaviour I hoped. My hopes were confirmed as Adam recounted his discussion with Sir Richard.

"He is still of like resolve, all the more so in view of his son's worsening state. Despite several visits to the shrine of St. Thomas I fear the boy is close to death." The words were spoken in a matter-of-fact way and I realised that now Adam's only concern was Edward's future, to the exclusion of all compassion. I felt a sad twinge inside but reminded myself that the man I loved was from an entirely different way of life, another world – almost literally!

"When shall I meet them?" Again Edward's manner was tense.

"On the morrow, Edward. On the morrow thou wilt meet the man who is to become thy father. The man with whom, I feel sure, thou wilt form a strong bond." Adam gripped the lad by the shoulder and smiled a reassuring smile.

In order to keep a low profile Sir Richard and his son were lodged in a tavern on the outskirts of Canterbury, well away from the main thoroughfare of the city. As we made our way there, on that bright July morning, the butterflies in my stomach were working overtime. Adam had explained my presence to Sir Richard the day before and obtained his agreement to my attendance at the rendezvous – when all was said and done, what threat could a relation of Adam's prove to be? Especially a mute relation and a woman to boot! But my nervousness was not for myself: it was on behalf of Edward. This young boy whose life, once again, was to take a dramatic change of course: this young boy walking silently beside me.

We were soon at Sir Richard's lodgings and I was eager to meet the person who was to play such an important role in this saga. Although Adam had described him to me he had failed to convey the vitality or enthusiasm of the man; even under the present strained circumstances I sensed these two characteristics immediately. With his warm friendly greeting he ensured Edward's ease within the first few minutes of our arrival. Sir Richard turned towards me, an intent look on his face and lifting my hand, lightly brushed his lips across the skin. I felt the stirrings of a blush and quickly lowered my own gaze to try to diffuse the butterflies that had returned, for a different reason, without warning. He was charm personified but also, as I reminded myself, a married man.

Although the hostelry was small, father and son had taken two adjoining rooms which were quite spacious and more importantly, in view of the boy's illness, relatively clean. The room was chill: certainly not due to the mild weather conditions, more by virtue of the sickness within. We heard Sir Richard's son before we saw him. He was lying on a truckle bed in the corner and our entrance must have roused him. His father rushed to his side, eager to tend the small, emaciated figure swaddled within the bedclothes. Edward made to follow but I caught his wrist and gently shook my head – unaware of the extent of knowledge of contagious diseases at that time. I wanted no risks to be taken. As I fumbled for my handkerchief, Adam seeing my gesture and appreciating my actions slowly backed away from the bed. Edward and I joined him by the window, to stand watching helplessly from a distance.

"I fear there is no hope," Sir Richard sounded resigned. "The physicians tell me that they have no further remedies to offer. He has been bled on several occasions – each at the most propitious time, after reference to the astrological charts – and his humours were balanced prior to our journey. All to no avail." He spoke as though to himself, totally engrossed in caring for his dying son.

Even from this distance I could see the ashen colour of the inert body on the bed and the beads of sweat covering the skeletal brow, diligently mopped by the loving father. The boy's breathing was laborious and was accompanied by a distinct rattle at each intake but a comforting sound to Sir Richard, no doubt, acknowledging that life still remained.

The poignant scene and thoughts of the boy's ordeal suddenly moved me to tears and I felt I could stay no longer. I hurried to the adjacent room and steadied myself by the table. Adam followed me and I turned towards him, burying my face in his chest. His arms were about me as he whispered words of endearment to try to stem my weeping.

"Thou must not take on so, Emma. 'Twill soon be over and the boy will be at peace." He guided me to a bench and gently bade me sit. "Stay here until our discourse is done."

I nodded and with a gentle squeeze of the hand he returned next door. It must have been a good half-hour before the three of them emerged but from the looks on their faces I judged the meeting had gone well.

"Pray forgive my lack-wittedness," Sir Richard was contrite. "My good lady is forever chiding me on my want of feeling. But please do not upset thyself, Edward's earthly suffering will soon be at an end and He will look graciously on such a one as my son." I held his hand and hoped my eyes conveyed the compassion I felt within.

That evening, whilst Edward was sleeping in the other room, Adam related to me the details of the morning's discussions.

"I feel sure Sir Richard formed a liking for the lad. They spoke at some length on events of the past three years and Edward's heartfelt openness cannot have been lost on Sir Richard. Time and again he questioned the boy on his aspirations and belaboured the consequences of harbouring ambitions beyond his reach. But Edward held firm to his principles and swore he was sincere."

"And did Sir Richard believe him, do you think?" I whispered, ever cautious in case Edward should awake.

Adam nodded, "Eventually, having acknowledged that Edward's resolve could not be whittled away."

"And judging by Edward's chatter on the way back he liked Sir Richard?"

"Oh, undoubtedly, that much was evident within the first few moments!" Adam smiled and added thoughtfully, "The lad will have a good life, of that I am assured."

I had refrained from asking too many questions of Adam on our return from London in case the plan failed to get off the ground but now I was eager to learn the next stage. "So what happens next?"

"The morrow I shall return to St. Martin's to make the necessary arrangements with John. 'Twill not be necessary to divulge too much information in view of the Queen's missive although certainly he is a trustworthy fellow. I shall merely inform him that 'twould appear Sir Richard's pilgrimage has been unsuccessful and request that when his son departs this world, his remains be interred in the consecrated grounds of the church."

"And then?"

"Sadly, we must await the demise of Edward Guildford." He paused. "For the nonce I must enquire of John how Archbishop Bourchier fares – 'tis many a year since we last encountered one another and to renew our friendship would be pleasing."

However, Adam was destined not to meet his old acquaintance for he learnt that Thomas Bourchier had died the previous April: four days later we received notification of another death, that of Edward Guildford.

John Browne had arranged for the body of Sir Richard's son to be collected from the lodgings and transported to the church. So it was that on a sombre July morning Adam and I made our way to St. Martin's to pay our last respects to Edward Guildford.

The church was compact with attractive walls of flint and rough brickwork. We entered by the west door, beneath the squat, rectangular tower and immediately to my left, about two feet above floor level I espied an unusual opening: later Adam informed me this was a lepers' window. The plain interior was broken only by a large rood beam, which spanned the church between nave and chancel. Resting on the timber were saintly images and a large crucifix, before which hung the perpetually burning light of the Holy Cross.

I shivered: perhaps somebody had walked across my grave. The solemn tone of the day had permeated the fabric of the church creating a dark and drear atmosphere. Through the haze of the burning incense a lonely figure knelt on the cold, stone slabs silently offering up prayers for his recently departed son. We joined Sir Richard, adding our own prayers to his and hoping in some way to provide a measure of comfort to the grieving father.

Outside, in the gently tiered graveyard, the mortal remains of Sir Richard's son were committed to the cold Canterbury earth but not under his own name – for Edward's sake how could they be? Instead he was interred as Edward de Pympe: taking the maiden name of his mother.

The manor of Iham was situated in the town of Winchelsea built high on a peninsula of sandstone. The land beyond fell away steeply to the sea and from our high vantage point we had a magnificent view of the coastline stretching far into the distance. Sir Richard reined in his horse abruptly.

"See Edward," he pointed east, out towards the sea, "yonder, nigh on one league hence, the old town of Winchelsea once stood. But some two hundred years past great storms devoured the township – they do say the sea flowed twice without ebbing!"

"And the village was swept away? Oh, 'tis here then that my forefather King Edward, first of that name, saw to its rebuilding on firmer ground." At times he could sound precocious. However, I reminded myself that, after all, he had been born a Prince.

"I see thy studies have served thee well, Edward," Adam chaffed.

"Aye, father required that we maintain knowledge of our forbears," Edward replied seriously, unaware Adam's remark had been made tongue-in-cheek.

"Well, *I* shall expect thee to acquire some knowledge of thy new surroundings," Sir Richard clapped Edward on the shoulder and continued with a smile, "for *this* is now thy future, Edward. *This*," he swept his arm in a large arc, "shall be thy inheritance."

Winchelsea was laid out in grid formation and much to my amazement was a thriving town full of hustle and bustle on that bright morning in late July when we arrived. For some reason I had been expecting a sleepy village but, as Sir Richard proudly informed us, Winchelsea was a member of the Cinque Ports and was constantly ready to provide ships for the King's service. The town's activity was a blessing, for as we passed along its unbending roads our little group went unnoticed: a situation otherwise unavoidable with Sir Richard's well groomed figure contrasting sharply to Edward's hunched and muffled state. We had thought it a necessary precaution to swaddle him in blankets in order to set the scene and provide some measure of camouflage for his arrival at Iham. He appreciated his 'recovery' would take several months during which time the less he was seen, the better.

We made our way to the manor house, situated to the north of the town and close by the church. The building was reasonably sized and Sir Richard's improvements were evident to see. On one side he had installed arcading which gave access to an open lower floor and on the opposite side of the building a flight of stone stairs directed our steps to a first floor doorway. Immediately upon entering the upper storey my breath was taken away by the impressive roof beams towering above our heads.

"'Tis all new," Sir Richard had seen my gaze and gestured towards the ceiling. "'Twas in dire need of repair but the local shipwrights have done me proud, have they not?"

Before Adam could answer, the steward and his wife hurried to meet their new master. Sir Richard introduced us to Andrew and his wife Martha, vaguely describing us as distant cousins who, in his absence, would care for his ailing son. They were a pleasant couple and although concerned, were not overly inquisitive about Edward's infirmity once they had been informed his illness might be contagious. Sir Richard stated that his son should be confined to his room and that the nursing be carried out wholly by me and Adam.

We settled Edward in his chamber and what meagre possessions we had in our own rooms, before enjoying a wholesome meal, hastily prepared by Martha. Sadly Edward was unable to appreciate her excellent cooking for the invalid was considered to require only a small amount of broth: a situation that was to continue for some weeks!

Sir Richard remained only one evening, leaving for Rolvenden early the following morning. In addition to pressing business he was eager to return to his wife for she knew nothing of the outcome of his trip to Canterbury. He promised to return with his good lady in order that she might become acquainted with her new son but was uncertain as to when that might be. Adam had advised him we could remain with Edward for a month or so and had been assured that the Guildfords' return would be within that timescale: we dearly hoped so for our departure could be delayed no later than the beginning of September.

So began our brief spell at Iham. Our time there was pleasant with warm sunny days when we would leave the manor house, heading out along the coast or up towards the Romney Marshlands. The pretence of Edward's recovery continued. Initially he remained in his chamber reading, not daring to converse with Adam for fear of the steward and his wife overhearing animated voices. But inevitably he grew restless and Adam decided something must be done.

Through Andrew we discovered that one of the outbuildings contained a small cart that looked to be road-worthy. Decking it out with blankets and pillows, Adam informed him, "Our charge appears much the better today helped no doubt by the nourishment of thy wife's excellent cooking! Time spent in the fresh air may improve his wellbeing and aid his recovery somewhat."

That was the first of many excursions: times when Edward could let off steam and give vent to his pent-up emotions; times when his chattering never ceased. On our journey south from Canterbury Sir Richard had talked about the Guildfords, providing names and details of the family Edward was entering into. Although he appreciated this would inevitably be a gradual process, "One may never begin too soon!" were his words, and in a steady, determined way began the coaching of his newly acquired ward.

Adam's excellent memory was a boon for he had remembered the details and was able to step into Sir Richard's role of tutor. Many a time we sat in the cart, overlooking the sea, eating a lunch packed for us by Martha – the only chance Edward had to consume any food other than invalid fare – whilst the boy recited names and dates he had learnt by heart.

It was a time when I grew close to Edward, experiencing maternal instincts I never knew existed. A time when we laughed together; heard his fears for the future; and his sorrows from the past. He was an endearing boy and I hoped with all my heart this plan would succeed and his future would be secure.

True to his word, Sir Richard returned with his wife during the last week of August. Late one afternoon we returned from an outing to find them taking refreshments in the main hall.

As we hurried Edward up to his chamber Martha, as usual, provided a hot posset – or poshoote as she pronounced it – for the convalescent: this, she swore, would cure much more than a cold! Returning to the hall we joined Sir Richard and Lady Anne by the hearth for, although still August, it was a cold day and a fire had been lit to welcome the lady of the manor on her first visit. Because we had been presented to the steward and his wife as relations of Sir Richard, no introductions were made to Lady Anne at that first meeting. Consequently the conversation was stilted but the wine soon warmed us as much as the fire and gradually the tension eased. Only when the Guildfords made a move to visit their 'son' did I realise the true reason for the tension. Lady Anne was extremely nervous. As she stood to leave, her hand shook and she steadied herself on the arm of the chair. Merely a momentary display but in that instant I understood some of the emotions this woman must be feeling. She had nursed her sick son for weeks; very recently she had been informed that when he died his place was to be taken by the bastard son of the late King; her son had died only one month previously; and now she was to meet the boy who would call her mother for the rest of his life. No wonder she was tense!

Adam and I remained in the hall during Sir Richard and Lady Anne's absence which lasted, probably, half an hour but seemed a lot longer. Upon his return Sir Richard motioned us towards Edward's chamber, his face giving nothing away. But my pounding heart need not have worked overtime for as we entered the room the look on the faces of Lady Anne and Edward dissolved any fears I might have had.

"Thy guidance and teaching have reaped benefits, Anselm." She was seated by the bed and reaching out to take Edward's hand continued in deep, mellow tones, "Worry not on behalf of thy charge for he will be safe and sound in our care."

Her voice was at odds with her appearance for she was small and slight and her hair, visible through the transparent gauze of her headdress, was of the palest ivory. I had read that Elizabeth Woodville's hair had been of the same hue and I wondered whether this woman, in some way, reminded Edward of his mother. He had never spoken of her in my hearing: whether or not he was close to her I didn't know. But whereas by all accounts his mother had been a hard, scheming woman, Lady Anne's nature mirrored that of her husband: she was genuine and warm-hearted.

Edward was grinning from ear to ear. "I have informed Sir Richard of Anselm's daily inquisition to ensure that I am now fully versed in the details of my new family!"

"Verily, 'twas not so bad, Edward?" Adam laughed.

"My good lady shall now take up the reins and if thou thought that Anselm was a hard task master, thou had better prepare thyself for the worst!" Sir Richard too was laughing.

"I have also learned something of my future, Emma," excitedly Edward addressed me. I looked enquiringly towards Sir Richard.

"'Tis requisite for me to begin in a somewhat oblique fashion but bear with me, I pray thee, for I *shall* come to the point." Looking towards his wife he smiled, "The Lady Anne is once again with child and the babe is due in the spring of next year. As I have begat only girls of late, I'll trow this one turns out in likewise fashion. That being so, my wife has a mind to name her Mary." He paused for breath. "What, says thee, has this to do with Edward's future? In some ways, naught. Nonetheless …" he paused for effect, a true storyteller, "… I am at present commissioned by the King in the building of a ship. Work is underway and the vessel should be completed some time after the birth of the babe. Provided all goes well, I have decided 'twill be a good business to name the ship the 'Mary Guildford' and …" again he broke off briefly, "… 'tis here that Edward comes in to the tale – for he shall accompany me on the vessel on her maiden voyage!" Edward's eyes were shining as Sir Richard continued, "Be that as it may, ere the Mary Guildford I am due to set sail for Flaundres on the King's business within the next month and intend to introduce Edward to the pleasures of sailing at that time. He shall accompany me!" Although he was already privy to this knowledge, Edward could hardly contain himself. Turning to Adam Sir Richard added, "Whilst I am there I have a mind to pick the brains of these Flemings' for they are past masters in the art of land drainage."

Adam turned to Edward and surreptitiously gave him a wink for had he not mentioned the selfsame thing when apprising him of his future with Sir Richard? "Thy future appears bright, Edward. Let us hope thou findest thy sea-legs!" Again we all laughed.

"If not, perhaps there will be another course left open to us," Sir Richard added in a conspiratorial tone. "I have heard whisper that the King intends to grant me the office of bailiff of Winchelsea – none too onerous a position and rewarding to boot!"

The light-hearted conversation continued for some time, with Lady Anne talking about the family and Sir Richard more intent on the forthcoming voyage. Already I could see Edward was becoming enwrapped in his new family and felt certain he would be happy and contented with them.

Our last evening at Iham was a lavish affair. Although we numbered only four – Edward still being confined to his room – Lady Anne had instructed Martha to provide a sumptuous meal, and it was just that. I felt like royalty as we sat at the large wooden table, eating off pewter dishes with elegantly carved horn-handled spoons. Even fine green-glazed pottery had been brought out for the occasion. The food was excellent and as I sat back listening to the pleasant, carefree conversation the heady wine must have caused my mind to wander. I looked around, at this lofty hall and my thoughts turned to the north. This was a much grander affair than either Overthwaite or Raisgill, with its high quality Arras wall hangings and expensive Italian rugs. The Borders were a much more severe part of the country whereas here, little touches were made to soften the surroundings: deerskins were draped over benches and storage chests covered with tapestries. Once again I lifted my gaze to the hall's impressive roof but as I did so my eyes turned to the lighting above the table. Over the past month we had managed with tallow dips but this evening expensive candles suspended in prickets on a large wooden hoop had been lit for our benefit.

It crossed my mind that, should anything go wrong and I fail to return on time, I would much prefer to live with the luxuries of the south than threats of reiving raids and the harsher conditions in the north.

The following morning, before our departure, we said our farewells to Edward. It was a sad occasion for we both knew we would never see him again. That knowledge, however, must remain secret for Edward was unaware of our future. I checked myself. Did *I* know what the future held in store, or more specifically what Adam's future might be? Although he had hinted and made one or two ambiguous remarks, still I awaited confirmation that he would be accompanying me through the door. I vowed that as soon as we were on our own I must settle the matter once and for all: if he had decided to remain, I must know.

Edward put on a brave face, braver than mine, for my eyes were pricking and tears ran down my cheeks. I turned away, leaving Adam to his goodbyes. As I did so I noticed Edward's comb on the chest and on an impulse hid the item in my pocket. Suddenly the words of Catherine's narrative came into my head and I remembered she too had taken Edward's shirt on an impulse before her return. Perhaps I had more in common with my aunt than I realised.

After leaving Edward we bade farewell to the Guildfords and were soon on our way. Adam was silent for the first few miles and I decided not to disturb him for I guessed he was thinking of Edward.

However, when the silence persisted I could wait no longer. "Penny for them?" Adam looked at me quizzically. "Tell me what you're thinking." My vocal chords had been little used for several weeks and it felt good to be exercising them again.

"Of how I shall miss the lad. Although 'tis only over the past three years that I have had aught to do with him, he has stolen his way into my heart." Forcing himself to brighten he added, "Nonetheless, I must be thankful that his future is assured. Against all odds we have achieved our goal, Emma."

"I'm sure he'll be fine. He seems to have taken to the Guildfords and they to him."

Adam nodded. "Sir Richard and his wife will look after the boy."

A thought suddenly struck me. "Does the Queen know that the plan has succeeded?"

"Assuredly, for Sir Richard told me he had informed Elizabeth and she was much relieved. Perchance in years to come brother and sister may be reunited. For the sake of them both I hope so." He turned to face me. "Now, enough of the past, I fear I have been far too preoccupied of late. 'Tis time to attend to our future."

I reined in my horse and, surprised by my action, Adam did the same. "Adam, I can't wait any longer. I have to know. I didn't want to bother you while your mind was on Edward but now I *must* know ..." the words came out in a tumble. "Do *we* have a future? Are you coming back with me through the door?" I held my breath for what seemed like an age.

"Yes."

It was said simply and that one word caused the defences I had placed around my inner feelings to crumble in an instant. "Oh, Adam ..." his name caught in my throat.

"There. Do not upset thyself." He had moved his horse close to mine in his concern. "Surely 'tis a time for rejoicing not sorrow?" he teased. "Come." Taking the reins of my horse he led us towards a tree where he helped me to dismount. We perched on a smooth rock beneath its branches and, with our hands entwined, turned to face each other.

"Had I but known thou were on tenterhooks I would have spoken ere now. 'Tis indefensible to use Edward as the cause, nonetheless this whole episode hath taken over my life. Even whilst I nursed Catherine I could think of naught but returning and trying to save the lad." He sought my hands. "Regardless, I should have been more sensitive of thy feelings. Wilt thou forgive me, my love?" I nodded – my emotions raw, I doubted the ability of my voice.

Tenderly Adam placed a kiss on the centre of my forehead, on the tip of my nose and, for the first time, covered my lips with his own. This kiss bore no resemblance to the light caress he gave me on our first night at Overthwaite. This kiss was a passionate fulfilment of all that had passed between us. I had waited an eternity but the wait was worthwhile: a rainbow of colours filled my head and I felt that my chest would burst. At last we broke and I rested my head on his shoulder whilst my senses came back to earth. He gazed down at me and I knew he felt the same. We kissed again and although on this occasion some of the urgency had gone, the passion remained. I could have stayed there all day but Adam's soft voice broke my reverie; his simple words filled me with joy.

"Assuredly, we *shall* be happy." He straightened and pulled away. "Now, 'tis five weeks until the first day of October. Five weeks in which to return to Overthwaite." He paused before continuing thoughtfully, "In all honesty we should not leave our arrival too late. We must ensure a margin of at least one week, preferably longer. But that still leaves ample time for what I have in mind." I wondered what he was about to say. "I should dearly love to show thee the places of my boyhood, where I oft wandered with my father – dearly love to revisit Ludlow for one last time." His eyes were shining.

"I can't think of anything I would like better," I uttered, my voice thick with emotion.

CHAPTER SEVENTEEN

Our days around Ludlow were halcyon. For the first time we had an opportunity to be alone together and the insight I gained into Adam's character added a sense of deep devotion to my feelings of love for him. Following on from that first kiss I had wondered whether, or even hoped, we might share a room but no mention was made when we stopped for the night. Presumably his pious upbringing forbade such things until we were married!

It was good to visit his hometown and I felt sure the experience helped him to lay various ghosts to rest, for it was the first time he had been there on anything other than official business for almost thirty years. We viewed the castle from the outside, not daring to venture into a residence now owned by Henry Tudor. I was surprised the buildings had changed relatively little and said as much to Adam.

"I was not aware that thou wert acquainted with the place."

"Well I wouldn't go so far as to say acquainted, but I've certainly been there," I replied. "It's ruined now of course, and there are different buildings in the outer bailey. But the inner parts are pretty similar. Just one or two extra structures put up, by the Tudors I think."

"'Tis a pity I cannot take thee inside for I have fond remembrances of the place." He was quiet and I wondered whether, in addition to childhood memories, his thoughts had turned to Edward's time spent there.

We were blessed with a spell of glorious weather lulling us into a state of unreality where time stood still and we felt safe and secure. Long days were spent in the saddle exploring the countryside and revisiting Adam's favourite haunts. But time was passing and we realised we had stayed longer in Ludlow than we had intended. We set off for Worcester.

The cathedral was visible from a great distance and dominated our view as we approached the city. A look of fond appreciation entered Adam's eye and I knew he would have wished to pay a call there but as he had already explained, "'Tis best we do not take the risk. Had Bishop Carpenter still been resident I should not have hesitated but Alcock is a different matter."

John Carpenter had been the Bishop in charge during Adam's time there but he had died several years previously. John Alcock followed him – a staunch Yorkist supporter and president of young Edward's council. Hence Adam's reticence in meeting with the man, for he had no desire to be quizzed on the past, no desire to answer awkward questions about Edward. In addition, with Adam's recent absence he was unaware as to whether Alcock still held the position in Worcester or whether a new Bishop had been installed there. There was certainly no point in taking that gamble.

"Besides," he continued, "'tis unlikely that any of my former companions still dwell within."

We remained only fleetingly in Worcester and although the more direct road was to the west, for safety sake we opted to cut across country and pick up our outward route towards the north. Consequently our arrival at Overthwaite was well before the end of September: we were later to learn that on the same day in London, Elizabeth had given birth to a son, Arthur.

During the journey Adam had expressed the need for caution upon our return. "We must have a care for Hugo may be resident." Hugo – I had forgotten all about him! "Perchance we had better enquire at the Abbey," Adam continued, "before deciding our course of action."

Thankfully we were informed by Brother Norbert that Hugo was absent from the Hall, neither was he expected in the near future for rumour had it he was abroad, fighting.

Catching our first glimpse of Sleadale I was reminded of the day when I viewed this valley for the first time. Could it have been less than nine months ago? Surely not, for much had happened since then. As we rested our horses and drank in the view I sensed a strong feeling of coming home. Whether home to Overthwaite or a subconscious thought of returning to my own time I do not know.

Whatever the reason I felt a warm glow, deep inside and turned to Adam. "It's good to be back."

"Indeed." He smiled. "I, too, have formed an attachment to these wild dales."

Spurring the horses on, we set off on the last lap of our return to Overthwaite, thereby completing the journey we had begun some five months previously.

The Hall bore little resemblance to its former self. At my last visit I had been aware, in view of Lady Margaret's death, that the place lacked the energy I had found evident in Catherine's narrative. Now, however, with only Stephen and Sarah present the building was lifeless and empty: Hugo's disinterest in the Hall had permeated the fabric of the walls. I decided October 1st and our return could not come too soon.

Our visit was a welcome diversion and nobody queried our stay. Adam passed his time either in the company of Stephen or with his nose in one of Sir Anthony's books – at least Hugo had left his brother's 'library' untouched. Inevitably I had lapsed once more into silence and the days were interminably long. Had it not been for the arrival of Margery I felt I should have gone mad. She and Tom had returned from Raisgill soon after our departure for Canterbury as Margery's mother was ill and it was necessary for Margery to nurse her.

The poor girl was run off her feet trying to balance this extra work with looking after her own family and, most days, still undertaking some work at the Hall. I enjoyed listening to her gossip, even though little had happened since we were last together. Life had returned to normal at Raisgill with the absence of further border raids; Jonathan had asked Jane to become his wife and she had accepted, to the delight of all concerned; and since Margery's return, word had reached Overthwaite that Lady Alice had been brought to bed of a healthy baby boy. All in all, life was good there. At Overthwaite, however, with the deaths of Sir Anthony and Lady Margaret life had changed once and for all. For the likes of Margery who had enjoyed serving a good master and mistress, Hugo's advent heralded a miserable future. I pitied them.

Time was passing and with the approach of our 'journey' I could feel myself becoming increasingly tense. Would everything go smoothly? Would the door actually open? These and a thousand other questions revolved around my head. I ticked off the days on my fingers: only two more to go. The following morning Hugo and Alan rode into the barmkin.

It transpired they had missed their ship after a heavy night's carousing and in typical fashion had decided on a whim to return to Overthwaite.

Hugo was intrigued by our presence. "Ah, 'tis *Master* Anselm, that strange man of mystery," he turned towards me, "and his pretty mute of a cousin. To what do we owe the honour of thy visit?"

"We are merely passing through. On our way to thy kinsfolk at Raisgill to be exact," Adam answered casually. "We thought not that hospitality would be denied us."

"Nay, Overthwaite's welcome hath not diminished since the sad demise of my brother," his voice was thick with sarcasm and I wondered whether he knew the irony of his remark. He continued in the same vein, "I trust thy needs have been catered for during thy stay. But pray forgive me," he feigned recollection, "our wine stock is depleted." He pointed to Alan, "'Tis this drunkard, draining the barrels on his last visit. What say thee fellow? Hast thou a mind to replenish the stock?"

"God's wounds, thou canst go to hell!" This, then, was Jane's brother, the man about whom I had heard much. I could see no family resemblance: where Jane was slight and mousy, Alan was tall and of muscular build; his eyes were steely grey and his blonde hair was cut short. Although his features were pleasing, as with Hugo his manner was sardonic and an aura of baseness hung around him like a cloak. "Ah, 'twas only I who drank the barrels dry was't? Thou lying whoreson!" His voice possessed a menacing quality and all his remarks were spoken with little involvement of facial muscles.

"Aye, drank them like a fish! Come, let's away to town afore our guests have a mind to complain." Sweeping past me Hugo paused and elaborately patted my behind with his gloved hand. "Cheer up, my pretty one, things are about to improve. This *gentleman* and I shall entertain thee upon our return!"

I knew his words and actions were only intended as a goad but unfortunately Adam rose to the bait. "I warned thee at our last encounter to leave Emma alone. Must I repeat myself?"

"Now now, Anselm, I meant no harm," his tone was mocking. "*Surely* thou canst see that I only play the considerate host? For, if I remember aright, when last we met I did promise to pay thy cousin some heed at our next encounter." Passing close to Adam he hissed through clenched teeth, "And I promised *thee* that I would uncover the true reason for thy sudden appearance in my brother's household." He frowned. "But what of thy nephews, Anselm? 'Tis many a long day since I set eyes on the pair. Am I not right in saying they were not with thee when last we met? Where art thou hiding them?"

Adam gave a small start at Hugo's remark but quickly camouflaged his action by murmuring, "The lads are dead. They burned with the fever but God was merciful and their suffering was short. They are now both at peace." He crossed himself.

Reluctantly Hugo did likewise. Still suspicious, nevertheless he was unnerved by Adam's devout manner and, thankfully, had lost his desire to delve further. "Aye ... well ... come Alan, 'tis time we were away." He clapped his comrade on the shoulder. "We lose valuable drinking time!" The pair left without more ado.

They had failed to return the previous evening and as the morning of October 1st dawned I hoped against hope they might remain absent for a further twenty-four hours. Early morning I sought out Adam and we climbed to the roof, alone on the wall-walk in order to speak without fear of being overheard.

"Oh God, I hope they don't return before we go." As soon as the words were out I could have bitten my tongue. I told myself I must stop blaspheming in front of him.

"Whatever the outcome, we must remain calm. We must give them no indication that aught is afoot." He was quiet for a moment, thinking through the evening's preparations. "We must be in the hall well afore nightfall, ready for the appointed hour."

"Two minutes past eight, right? I'll keep an eye on my watch late afternoon ... but then, if we're in the hall at dusk there's no real need is there?" I realised I was wittering: presumably nervous tension.

"Providing we are in good time nothing will go amiss," he squeezed my hand gently, hoping to give reassurance. "Ensure thou hast all thy belongings with thee and I shall do likewise. There is a small niche behind the arras by the door ..."

"Oh yes, I remember Catherine mentioning it," I interrupted. "Funny to think she went through these same motions."

Once again Adam caressed my cheek with his fingers. "We are nearly there, Emma. Dost thou think thou can assume a semblance of normality for our last few hours?" His comment was rhetorical: he knew that the answer was 'with difficulty'.

Early evening I took out my bag and packed my few possessions, thinking as I did so of the night six months previously when I had done the selfsame thing. At that time I was unsure as to whether I would return; neither had I cared, for my only desire was to be with Adam. Now we were to return together, to spend our life together: my pulse raced at the thought. I struggled to bring my mind back to the present, or should that be the past! I retrieved Edward's comb from its hiding place, carefully packing the memento between the folds of my dress. I was ready.

As I tiptoed down to the hall all was quiet and, slipping towards the old door, I pulled the hangings away from the wall to reveal the niche. His things were already there. Hearing a noise behind me I turned quickly, fumbling with the tapestry but was relieved to see only Stephen bringing in more logs for the fire. I breathed deeply, trying to calm my nerves and moving towards a chair picked up a piece of embroidery with which I had been filling my time over the past few days. I knew there was still over an hour to go.

Now that my return was nearing I took the time to reflect on my visit. It had been no bed-of-roses, for coming to terms with ancient ways and amenities (or should I say, lack of them) had been difficult. But stepping back into history certainly had its compensations for these minor discomforts. Yes, I had enjoyed my time in medieval England.

The minutes ticked by. I was having difficult concentrating on my needlework. Where was Adam? I wandered towards the window, hoping to see him. Instead, to my horror, I spotted two figures on horseback heading towards the hall. Please God let this not be Hugo and Alan! The nearer they came, the more certain I became that my plea had gone unanswered: they had returned. Turning, I was relieved to see Adam behind me. He had been in the chamber above and had heard the arrival of horses in the barmkin.

"Remain calm, Emma, and all will be well. Let us pray they are sober or else desirous of sleeping off their inebriation." He spoke urgently in hushed tones. "Come what may, we must remain here ever ready for the appointed hour. And when that time arrives, move with all speed. Let naught get in thy way."

Hugo burst into the hall, followed closely by Alan – it was obvious they had been drinking heavily. I moved away from Adam, trying to concentrate on my embroidery.

"What a touching scene! *Please*, let not our arrival disturb thee. Pray continue."

"Our business is done," Adam replied curtly and ambling towards a chair occupied himself with a book.

"*'Our business is done'* " mimicked Hugo, making straight for my chair. Hovering over me, unsteady on his feet, he added, "*Our* business would not be done so quickly, my sweet." And reaching out, he was about to take my chin when Adam sprang to his feet. Hugo held his hands in the air, palms facing outwards in a mock gesture of atonement, "Forgive me. I meant no harm with thy cousin, *Master* Anselm," his voice was heavy with sarcasm. Catching my eye he gave a surreptitious wink before turning away. "Now, my fellow imbiber, what says thee? More drink?" Alan belched. "Well said!" Hugo tossed Alan the wineskin I had noticed on his shoulder as he entered the room. The other drank greedily, nearly draining the sac in one drought. "Have a care!" Hugo snatched the pouch from him, spilling wine down the front of Alan's shirt. "What of our guests?" Then checking himself he continued, "Certes, what ails me? Such like is not good enough for a *lady*." He marched across to the old door and pulling it open shouted across the barmkin, "Sarah … Sarah!"

He was extremely drunk and I could see his body swaying from side to side. Suddenly, to steady himself, he made a grab for the wall hangings and my heart missed a beat: frightened he might discover our belongings in the niche. But the moment passed and Sarah soon arrived. Releasing the tapestry, Hugo placed his hand on her shoulder in order that she might guide him towards the bench. "We have a mind for wine, my girl. Bring a flagon and some cups." He gestured towards Adam and I, "Our friends wish to join us."

"But Master Hugo, all the cheap wine's been drunk. Only t'good stuff's left."

"Then bring *'t'good stuff'* … quickly." He slapped Sarah's bottom as she turned to go and, with a gentle laugh, she glanced back provocatively over her shoulder. Adam and I sat quietly, not wishing to become involved in this drinking spree but sensing our intervention might be necessary in order to keep Hugo at bay.

Sarah soon returned and placing four goblets on the table poured a generous measure into each. She passed one across to Alan whose head had begun to drop but the smell of the wine roused him and he snatched the cup from her hand. Hugo had been fumbling in his pocket and as Sarah proffered his wine I realised why. He was holding a groat between thumb and forefinger and as she bent invitingly towards him he flipped the coin, aiming it at her cleavage. He was a good shot – no doubt had had much practice – for the coin reached its mark.

"Prithee, take that for thy trouble," he scoffed. Sarah made to retrieve the coin but Hugo was quicker and had his hand at her décolletage in an instant. "Let me!" He made a lunge for the groat but his action pushed the coin further down her kirtle and his hand followed eagerly. In his enthusiasm he tipped some wine down the front of her bodice and the liquid, soaking through the material of her kirtle, highlighted the shape and firmness of her nipples. "Is't the wine or my action which excited thee? Let us see!" Hugo had placed his wine on the table and with both hands free he faced his prey. In one deft movement he had ripped open Sarah's bodice and his hands were poised on her kirtle. Adam was already on his feet, for although the incident had taken only a matter of seconds he anticipated Hugo's next move.

"Desist from thine actions, Sir! Cans't thou not find a whore in town who will quench the appetite without despoiling one in thine own household?"

"Please, Master Hugo!" wailed Sarah, finally aware her teasing had placed her in danger.

"Have done!" spat Hugo. "Remember that thou art a guest in my household, Sir. I'll have none of thy monkish preaching here." Suddenly his dagger was at Adam's throat. "Indeed, if thou canst not hold thy tongue perchance I shall have cause to cut it out. We would then have two mutes in our midst!" His laugh was deep and evil and I held my breath. Sarah had taken this opportunity to slip away but before she had reached the door Hugo spotted her and bellowed across the room, "I didst not give thee leave to go! Alan ...," he gestured to his comrade to stop her.

Throughout this scene Alan, worse for wear with the amount of wine he had drunk, had been dozing at the table. Hugo's bidding brought him to his senses and he rose swiftly from his chair: rather too swiftly for he staggered and with a dazed look weaved his way towards Sarah, catching her by the shoulder. Entwining the thick locks of her long hair around his fingers he wrenched back her head and for the first time noticed her open bodice and dampened kirtle beneath. Sarah tried desperately to cover her undergarment.

"Gods wounds, I have missed much whilst I slept! Here, let me help thee." Leaning over her shoulder, with his free hand he wiped away the wine splashes from her chest ever nearing her exposed cleavage.

"Nay, fellow, do not get thy hopes up for she is mine!" Hugo spoke with a sneer. "Perchance *thou* couldst escort Master Anselm back to his seat for I fear the proximity of this wench excites him in great measure." Dragging Sarah across the room Alan handed her to Hugo and with his dagger at the ready, manhandled Adam back to his seat. Meanwhile, Hugo had resumed his actions prior to Adam's outburst. With one hand firmly pinioning Sarah's wrists behind her back he traced the edge of her neckline with his free hand. Lower and lower he ventured, exposing more and more of her white flesh until, grasping the material, he pulled down sharply to reveal a firm, white breast and coral, rosebud nipple. "Christ and His saints thou art fair! I fancied thou wert hiding a treasure but ne'er suspected one so rich." He could resist the temptation no longer and dropping his head made a sudden lunge for her breast, devouring the flesh with his mouth and taking her nipple between his teeth.

Sarah cried out and struggled fiercely; at the same moment Adam sprang from his seat. "For pity's sake, Hugo ..." but he got no further for, with a backward lash of the wrist, Alan knocked him savagely to his knees. I longed to do something but remained powerless, knowing I would receive the same treatment as Adam or even Sarah.

Hugo looked up. He slowly shook his head, "Wilt thou not take heed? Restrain him."

Pulling Adam by the collar of his gown and roughly seating him in the chair Alan produced a leather thong from his belt. "Have a care, whoreson, or thou shalt feel the steel of my blade!" His dagger remained at Adam's neck giving the latter no option but to allow his wrists to be bound behind his back. This, however, was no easy task for Alan in his inebriated state. Swaying from side to side behind Adam's chair he fumbled with the strap, taking some time to achieve his objective. "What of this one?" Alan nodded in my direction.

"Aye, 'twould be a good business and thwart any ideas she may harbour of freeing *Master* Anselm. Besides, once bound she will be easy prey when we have had our fill of this wench and are ready to move on." Looking across at me he laughed his vile laugh before returning to Sarah. I shuddered and searched for Adam's face but Alan was between us, blocking my vision.

"Fear not, Emma. They dare not harm thee." I suspected Adam's words were a fervent, empty hope: this pair dared all.

Hugo confirmed my misgivings. "Brave words Anselm but who will stop us? Certes not thee. And have a care …" he paused, "… one more outburst and I shall have thee gagged."

Alan was by me, fulfilling his 'master's' bidding. Having no further restraint, he had removed the kerchief from around his neck and once again was having difficulty in securing the bonds. Satisfied, he returned to the table and his wine, seemingly more interested in imbibing than in Hugo's amorous exploits.

Sarah's struggles were increasing and she at last succeeded in freeing one of her hands. Beating Hugo's chest she tried desperately to release herself but with one deft blow to the head, Hugo sent her reeling. "Desist, wench! What ails thee? Art thou not versed in the pleasures of the flesh? Does that man of thine not satisfy thee?" Sarah lay sobbing on the floor. "Mayhap he is impotent!" Hugo roared with laughter at his suggestion. "Alan! Fetch the wench's husband."

In Alan's absence Hugo resumed his drinking, sniggering under his breath at the accusation he had made. Soon the sound of footsteps could be heard and a bewildered

Stephen preceded Alan into the hall. The sight that greeted his eyes must have appalled him and he rushed to comfort his wife. Despite the wine Hugo retained his speed and kicking Stephen to the floor, bloodied his nose in the process.

"Nay Stephen, she does not need thy help. She has been more than happy with my attentions." He gave a mocking snort. "And besides, she tells me that though art incapable of serving her. That thou art not a man!" he let his empty goblet droop in an unambiguous manner. "What say we find out?" He gave an imperceptible nod to his comrade and I suspected the two had played out this scene before for Alan had returned not only with Sarah's husband but also a length of rope. Grasping Stephen by the scruff of the neck he righted him and proceeded to secure his hands, not as I would have imagined behind his back but in front of him. I was soon to understand why. Hauling him across the room Alan threw the rope expertly over one of the wall sconces, hoisting Stephen high so his toes barely touched the ground then secured the tether in a firm knot. Sarah gasped and I felt my own pulse quicken. Whatever did this evil pair have in mind?

Dragging Sarah over to her husband Hugo threw her down against the wall and taking his dagger he deftly sliced open the laces fastening Stephen's codpiece. I tried to look away but was mesmerised by the horrific thoughts swirling through my mind and found my eyes transfixed on the scene. Under the circumstances it was only to be expected that once exposed Stephen would be flaccid and shrunken, a fact Hugo found highly amusing.

"Christ on his cross I was not wrong! 'Tis no surprise thy wife is more than ready for some lovemaking. Aye, and from one whom can satisfy her." Letting out a raucous laugh he rubbed his own codpiece in a lewd gesture and turning to Sarah began to unlace himself. Already he was half aroused and taking her head in his hands it became evident what his intentions were. Sarah fought like one possessed, resisting his advances and finally managed to rake the back of Hugo's hand with her nails before breaking free.

"Thou little hell-cat, thou shalt pay for thine actions!" His voice was menacing as, wiping his hand roughly against his breeches, he removed the blood where it had begun to form on the grazed skin. Moving across to Stephen he unsheathed his dagger and with a blade honed as sharp as his own tongue Hugo traced the tip slowly along his captive's pubic hairline. A thin trail of blood appeared and although Stephen made no sound I could see, clearly etched on his face, the pain he was struggling to control.

Hugo turned to Sarah, "Take care wench," his voice was frightening, "for his fate rests solely in thine own hands. Shouldst thou continue in this frenzied manner I shall be forced to transform thy husband into a eunuch ... cut off his cods ... shorten his manhood. Dost thou understand?" Reaching for Sarah he turned her to face Stephen. "See how he bleeds for thee." Taking the edges of her kirtle in both hands he wrenched it from her shoulders in one swift movement, pulling the garment down to reveal her breasts. "Feast thine eyes, for it may well be thy last stirring." Looking up at Stephen he paused. "Enough? Come, wench, 'tis our turn, let's view thee fully this time." He spun her round to face him. "God but they are beauties! Now ..." grabbing a handful of Sarah's hair he forced her head down, between his legs, "for thy husband's sake, perform!"

Hesitantly, she did as she was bid. Soon Hugo was fully aroused and, propelling her swiftly across the hall, he steered her towards the table. She fell backwards onto its surface, a look of terror contorting her features. Hugo was upon her, keen to slake his desire. He threw back her skirts, revealing plump, ivory thighs, and pinning her arms above her head forced himself inside her, thrusting and thrusting, time and again in a torrid, frantic rape. At last he was spent and withdrawing casually, left Sarah prostrate on the table.

"I have readied her for thee," he called indifferently over his shoulder to Alan.

Throughout the assault Alan had been watching idly, no trace of emotion visible on his face. He sauntered across to the table and after unfastening his codpiece took up where Hugo had left off. "God's teeth, this cunt is sappy. Certes thou hast made her juices flow Hugo," he was becoming breathless, "'twill not take me long."

It was soon over and having satiated one of his desires, Alan was intent on quenching his thirst for he returned to the table and resumed his drinking greedily. Hugo wandered over to Sarah's husband. "Thou hast a fine wench there, Stephen. Methinks thou should take greater care of her – she will then have no cause to look elsewhere. Tell me, how is she when taken from behind? No doubt she has a fine arse." Once again he held the dagger ominously near his captive. "Perchance I should venture where none has ere gone – given that thou art not a sodomite!" Laughing, he turned to his comrade. "What says thou, Alan? Shall I plough that furrow in readiness for *thy* seed sowing?" Again he found great amusement in his own pun.

"Nay, such is not to my liking but *thou* didst always enjoy a tight rut!" This time it was Alan's turn to snigger.

"Touché," acknowledged Hugo. "But first, some wine." Pouring himself a large measure he downed it in one before again turning his attentions to Sarah. Although distracted by her ordeal she had understood the meaning of Hugo's intentions and as he approached she dragged herself across the table, recoiling from her attacker. "Have I not told thee wench? Dost thou hold thy husband's manhood in so little esteem?" Slapping her fiercely across the face he continued, "Do not shrink from me or 'twill be worse for thee in the long run. I *will* have my way with thee! Perchance a drink may sweeten thy mood." He turned and retrieved the goblet. "But see, 'tis empty." Returning to the flagon he found that it too had been drained. "Alan, go fetch more wine. I wouldst oblige but I fear my hands will shortly be full!" Again we heard his sickening laugh.

Alan stumbled from the hall and Hugo resumed his progress towards Sarah. She screamed: a deep, bestial scream in anticipation of her impending fate.

"For pity's sake, Hugo, canst thou not have mercy on the girl? Leave her be." Hushed and pleading, Adam's words cut through the air.

"Ah, thou hast found thy voice at last. Wouldst thou prefer I take the mute instead?" My blood ran cold.

"Nay, leave the women. Untie these bonds and live up to thy manhood. I challenge thee to fight." Again my blood ran cold for Adam was dicing with death.

"A good try Anselm but not good enough. Nay, thou shalt not mar my sport. In the meantime," he carried Alan's goblet over to Adam, "perchance some wine might stem thy wordiness." Forcing open Adam's mouth with his left hand he held the cup high with his right and, slowly, tipped the contents down onto Adam's forehead. As the ruby liquid splashed into his captive's eyes and trickled over his face, Hugo laughed loud, amused by his childish actions.

Throughout Sarah's violation I was aware Adam had been attempting to free his bonds but although Alan's efforts had been affected by drink, the thong was still securely fastened. My ties, however, were less effective. Alan's neckerchief was small and my hidden struggles had begun to loosen the knots. With Hugo's back towards me I took advantage of the lull. Twisting my hands to-and-fro I felt the kerchief give. Without a moment's thought I was on my feet and, quietly retrieving Hugo's empty goblet from the table, crept close behind him. He must have heard a noise for he started to turn but in that instant I had raised the heavy cup above my head and, with all my might, brought the tankard down in a crashing blow to his skull. He suffered only a glancing blow but the impact was enough to fell him and as the realisation of my actions dawned, I stood dumfounded, staring at his inert body where it lay by my feet.

"Quickly, Emma, for he may merely be stunned!" Adam's urgent words brought me from my reverie. I ran to untie him and as I did so, noticed the raw weal marks where the leather had bitten into his skin. "Pray, tend to Sarah." I moved quickly towards the table where she lay, still cringing, and tenderly helping her down, pulled her dishevelled clothes back into place. Adam had turned his attention to Stephen and was engaged in carefully lowering the rope when I heard a noise behind me: Hugo had roused and was making his way unsteadily towards the pair.

"Adam, watch out!" I shouted. My cry was enough, not only to alert Adam but also to startle Hugo: he reeled and faced me, a look of utter astonishment transforming his features.

Adam pressed his advantage and was on him in a trice, thrusting his forearm around Hugo's throat in a tight grip. But the latter was a seasoned fighter and, twisting round, he brought his own hands up to Adam's throat in a fierce strangle hold. Although of similar height, Adam's build was more solid than that of his younger adversary and he utilised his weight in slamming Hugo against the wall, momentarily winding him in the process. However, Hugo recovered quickly, dealing Adam a powerful blow to the midriff. It was now Adam's turn to be out of breath and Hugo who took the upper hand. Knocking Adam to the ground and sitting astride his body, once again the younger man gripped his throat in a tight clamp. Managing to grasp his dagger, Hugo brought the deadly instrument close to Adam's neck. I watched in dread, unsure as to whether any intervention might be help or hindrance. In that fraction of a second, whilst I pondered, the old oak door began its momentous journey: the familiar creak, the sudden change of atmosphere, our route back was ready and waiting. The door acted like a magnet – all eyes were drawn to it.

As he turned Hugo slackened his grip slightly, enough for Adam to regain his breath. "Go, Emma, go." Automatically I moved to the door, knowing I had no choice but still reluctant to leave. I turned and looked beseechingly at Adam. "There is no time. Do not hesitate. Just go!"

I retrieved by bag from the recess and swiftly crossed through but could not resist one last look. As I turned, in that final moment when the door began its preordained regress, my eyes witnessed a terrible sight. Resuming the struggle, the two men had reversed positions and Adam was now lying on top of Hugo. As Adam pushed himself onto his haunches I wondered fleetingly why Hugo was still. I was soon to learn, for Adam's movement revealed the hilt of Hugo's dagger protruding from its owner's doublet: as the two had rolled, the steel blade must have embedded itself in the centre of Hugo's chest.

CHAPTER EIGHTEEN

Pushing Hugo away, Anselm knelt over the inert body. Did his adversary still live? He listened carefully: slow, laboured breathing was faintly audible.

"He lives," Anselm said, calling across the chamber to Stephen. *Rising swiftly he moved to the steward and untied his bonds.*

"Thee must go, Master Anselm ... afore t' other un returns," Stephen urged.

"Nay, I cannot leave thee to face him alone."

"*Thee* must!" Stephen insisted. "Ne'er fret. We shall be fine now that that," he nodded towards Hugo, "is no threat. Besides, Mistress Emma will be awaitin' thee." *Cautiously he added,* "Did I hear a'right, did she speak?"

"Indeed," Anselm *thought on his feet*. "Presumably 'twas brought about by fright – an imbalance of humours, you understand, for she has always possessed a sanguine temperament." *Stephen looked duly impressed, though understanding barely a word of Anselm's smoke screen.* "I have an idea where she will be and thou art right, Stephen, I must go to her. I shall return two days hence ... shall seek out Tom, lest Alan still be resident ... perchance by then we shall know more." *Reclaiming his possessions from behind the wall hanging he moved to the door and, with hand on the latch,* turned, "Pray to God thou canst prevail upon Alan to see sense." He left.

As Stephen approached his wife she shrank from him.

"Nay, nay lass, do not be afeard." He held out his arms to her. "Come. I place no blame on thee." Sarah ran to him and was enfolded in a warm, secure embrace. For the first time throughout her ordeal she gave vent to her emotions: large tears coursed down her cheeks and violent sobs racked her body. "There, there. Tha knows th' art safe wi' me." Gently he rocked her back and forth until the crying ceased.

Suddenly the corner door banged and Alan burst in. "Christ and all His saints thou hast a hellhole down there. 'Tis no wonder thou sent me down ...," seeing the couple Alan paused. "What's amiss?" Further into the chamber he spotted Hugo's body and dropping the flagon on the floor ran to his comrade's side. "God's wounds how comes this?"

"He lives still," said Stephen defiantly, belying his innermost feelings. Alan spun round and was at the steward's side in an instant. Sarah shrank back, dreading the consequences but Stephen retained his bravado.

Grabbing the man's collar Alan demanded, "I asked how comes this, is't thy doing?" Stephen remained silent. "Answer me!" He dealt the steward a heavy blow to the face with the back of his hand. He turned and, realising both Anselm and Emma were absent, continued, "It is the work of Anselm! Tell me I am right!" A second, third and fourth blow rained down on Stephen in quick succession. A cut appeared below his right eye and blood trickled from his nose.

"Tell him, Stephen!" his wife implored.

"Aye, tell me, or I shall beat the answer from thee," Alan threatened malevolently.

"'Twas self-defence. Master Hugo had his knife at Anselm's throat and was stabbed in t' struggle," Sarah was taking no chances. Stephen glanced at his wife, emotions of both censure and pride visible in his face.

"So, I was right! Should Hugo die, I shall bring that whoreson to the gallows, make no mistake," again he spat out the words through clenched teeth. "But for now, give me a hand with him."

Alan and Stephen lifted Hugo's body and, carefully, carried him to the upstairs chamber. Meanwhile, Sarah was despatched to the village in search of Aggie Bowman: on the one hand, for Anselm's sake, hopeful of her master's speedy recovery but on the other, wishing him a swift demise.

Upon leaving the Hall Anselm's sole objective was to distance himself from Sleadale. Once Stephen had assured him that Alan would be confronted, Anselm acknowledged the danger he was in: although Hugo's injuries had been sustained in an attempt at self-preservation, Alan was hardly likely to be open-minded about the affair.

The night air was cold but a cloudless sky aided Anselm in his passage to the stable. He was soon mounted and on his way, musing on Emma's departure: or rather, Stephen's concept of it. From his position by the wall the steward was unable to see beyond the oak door and had assumed Emma was merely stepping outside. Sarah, in her confused state, had failed to grasp the significance of what lay beyond even though she had had a good view. Hugo, alone, may have noticed the bizarre 'addition' to the Hall but was hardly in a position to concern himself with such details.

"Where should I go?" Anselm asked himself. Not too far, but far enough, lest Alan attempt to follow. He decided on the Abbey at Shap. There he could obtain provisions for a day or so and intimate his intentions of travelling south in order to throw any pursuer off the scent. He was unconcerned at the thought of lying low in the short-term and felt sure he could locate some place of refuge until he returned to Overthwaite. But what were his long-term plans? Despite all that had gone before, his mind was clear on that point: he was determined to return to Emma. He only hoped the 'door' would be available to him in six weeks time.

Events went according to plan. Brother Norbert was only too happy to provide essentials for his 'journey south', details of which Anselm elaborated at length. Leaving the Abbey precincts Anselm headed north, making for Carlisle and found an out of the way tavern where he spent two days. On his departure he took pains to supply the innkeeper with particulars of his intended journey over the border. Feeling reasonably secure he had covered his tracks he made his way back to Overthwaite.

The weather had taken a turn for the worse and a fierce autumn wind drove the icy rain through his garments, drenching him after only ten minutes in the saddle. He had timed his arrival at Sleadale for dusk but the going had been slow and by the time he neared Overthwaite the night was as black as pitch. However, Anselm welcomed the fearsome weather for it meant few were out journeying. Nevertheless, he thought it prudent to tether his horse some distance from the village and make his way on foot to Tom and Margery's home.

Anselm received a warm welcome and was instantly drawn in to the close, family atmosphere.

"Ee, Master Anselm, tek off them wet things or tha'll catch tha death o' cold," Margery fussed around Anselm, pushing him towards the fire. "Will, fetch a bowl an' ladle some pottage fer our guest."

The cottage was small and simple, typical of its day but spotlessly clean and tidy. Anselm was soon cosy and dry, hastily dressed in Tom's spare clothing. The pottage was warming and extremely tasty and he realised what a good cook Margery was: such a different person from that young girl, bending over the straw effigy, all those months ago.

Once fed, Anselm was eager to hear the news. "So, Tom, pray tell. How goes it?"

"I 'ave ter say not good, Master Anselm, not good, eh?" He breathed deeply and continued, "Master Hugo died yestere'en an' t' other un's out fer tha blood, eh? Gone straight off ter Lord Dacre, he 'as, sayin' he'd get a warrant fer tha's arrest, eh?" Staring at Anselm, Tom shook his head slowly from side to side.

"Wicked, that's what it is, if yer ask me!" Margery spoke up, busily tending the baby.

"So, I must needs continue to evade apprehension," Anselm was thoughtful.

"Aye, but Stephen's left fer Raisgill, eh? Bent on tellin' Sir Robert t' true tale, after what happ'nd t' his wife an' all, eh?" Tom bowed his head in consideration of Sarah's ordeal.

"He reckons if it weren't fer thee, well, the Lord alone knows what would 'ave happ'nd, eh?" Again he shook his head gravely.

"If yer ask me," Margery chipped in once more, "Master Hugo got what was comin' t' him!"

"Aye, well ...," Tom's agreement was implied, "... Stephen hopes as how Sir Robert'll mek his Lordship see sense, eh? But what wi' Lord Thomas's ways an' Master Hugo's loyalty ter the new King – if that's what yer can call it – well, who knows which way his Lordship 'll jump, eh?"

"Let us hope that justice prevails, Tom." It was Anselm's turn to sit quietly, shaking his head.

"And fer the nonce, what'll tha do, eh?"

"Worry not, for I know where a refuge lies," Anselm assured him. "I shall keep the whereabouts secret for 'tis best for thee if thou art unaware of my domicile. Now," he stood, "I must ready myself to leave."

"Tonight, Master Anselm? Can tha not stay just the night?" Margery enquired.

"Nay lass, 'tis best if he gets on his way, eh? Fer t' other un's still at th' Hall an' tha niver knows when he might cum a-callin', eh?"

"Tom is right. I should dearly love to remain and receive more of thy generous hospitality but I fear I would be placing not only myself at risk by doing so. And I should never forgive myself were that to happen." Anselm smiled warmly at his hostess. Donning his partially dry clothing he was soon ready to depart. "I shall return a few weeks hence. Let us hope that God hears our prayers and thou wilt then have some good news to impart."

It was Anselm's intention to journey to the Abbey at Hexham. His knowledge of Rowland Leschman had convinced him to throw himself on the Prior's mercy and relate the sequence of events in full. The journey could well have been a hazardous one, keeping as he did, well away from the major roads and utilising the lesser-known tracks wherever possible. But luck was on his side and the only perils came from the cold, wet weather, generating terrible conditions that hampered his travels greatly.

At last the Abbey was in sight and his enquiries produced the glad news that the Prior was in residence: God had answered his prayers. Ushered through the corridors of the Abbey, Anselm recalled his days at that other Benedictine house. He had enjoyed his time there but the cold, draughty passageways were a reminder of the harsher aspects of monastic life: one feature he had been pleased to leave behind. Reaching the warming house he quickly divested himself of his wet outer garments and awaited the arrival of the Prior. By-and-by Leschman arrived and was delighted to greet his old acquaintance.

"Anselm, 'tis really thee? I could hardly believe my ears when informed of thy name. What brings thee here on such a foul night?" He was a large, genial man with a distinctive, adenoidal voice and he added in a guilty aside, "But first, lets away to the Abbot's lodging. 'Tis warm there, for I had a fire prepared earlier."

"Is the Abbot in residence?"

"Nay, he is away on business. We will have the place to ourselves." As though to justify his actions he lowered his voice and added, "I felt sure the Lord would forgive my weakness for on such a night as this my joints do ache so." He rubbed the arthritic knuckles of his left hand. "The warmth provides some little ease."

The pair chatted deep into the night, each man keen to learn the fates that had affected the life of the other. Anselm had first met Rowland Leschman during his time at Worcester and the two had cemented a firm friendship. However, during the intervening years they had seen little of one another and although he had no cause to distrust his colleague, Anselm was cautious when talking of his years with King Richard. Conversely, he described in detail the incident at Overthwaite leading to his flight from the Hall.

"'Tis clear these men would benefit from instruction to curb their self-indulgences. As St. Benedict says 'Humility is not to love having our own way, nor to delight in our own desires'."

"Indeed. Hugo's late brother informed me that his father had ever indulged him." Anselm sighed, "So, thou canst see my predicament. This malefactor, this ally of the dead man is sure to convince Lord Dacre of my guilt." He paused and held out his hands in supplication, "What should I do? Do I confront Lord Thomas and take my chance? Can I trust that he will be impartial should he learn of my association with Richard?"

"What choice dost thou have in the matter?" Prior Leschman replied. "I cannot imagine thee persona non grata, living the remainder of thy life outside the law." He placed his hands on Anselm's shoulders. "Pray to the Lord and he will give thee guidance. Put thy trust in Him and he will show thee the right course."

Unable to relate his future intentions to his friend, Anselm merely nodded in agreement.

Anselm had little difficulty in reverting to monastic lifestyle. As Prior Leschman had suggested he attended the offices of prime and compline regularly, praying for divine direction. He also spent many an hour in silent contemplation weighing the pros and cons of attempting to clear his name. He dearly wanted to return to Emma but as a man of honour the accusation rankled with his conscience. Afternoons were spent assisting with the abbey workload and were a welcome diversion for Anselm. At those times he cleared his mind of all distractions, turning his energies instead to manual labour until his body ached with the physical exertion: his inner self, however, felt a tranquillity he had failed to experience in years.

The days passed and soon it was time for him to set off on the return journey to Overthwaite. He said goodbye to his friend and thanked him for the sanctuary the abbey had afforded. "It hath been good to renew our friendship after all these years."

"Aye, perhaps when next we meet I shall outmanoeuvre thee at chess!" the Prior joked but becoming more serious he added, "My thoughts will be with thee. Go with God, Anselm, go with God."

Once again Anselm tethered his horse outside the village and made his way to the cottage on foot. At least on this occasion he was dry, although the night was bitterly cold and crisp. A clear sky had made his journey from Hexham a straightforward one and he now trod carefully, amid the ruts of frozen mud, his way clearly illuminated by moonlight.

Moving swiftly inside, he was greeted by the same warm welcome as on his last visit. "Come in, Master Anselm, come in. Settle thiself by t' fire an' t' lad 'll bring thi summat t' eat, eh?" Tom motioned to his son and Anselm was soon feasting on a customary bowl of tasty pottage. Inevitably the conversation turned, almost immediately, to the events that had led to Anselm's present predicament.

"Things 've moved on apace, Master Anselm. Wi' t' warrant and Lord Thomas an' t' like, eh?" Tom advised. "But a thinks it's best as Stephen tells thi 'imsel', eh? Will," he addressed his son, "run to th' Hall an' fetch steward."

Whilst his son was away Tom informed Anselm that Alan had departed for pastures new. "He soon left when Lord Thomas ruled as how th' Hall should be restored ter Master Matthew, eh?"

"Good news then. At least his Lordship has seen fit to right one wrong," Anselm said. "Who will take charge of Overthwaite until he comes of age?"

"Sir Robert's son, Jonathan," Margery was eager to contribute to the conversation, especially on a point of romance, "and he's soon ter marry Jane!"

"Ah yes, I seem to remember that there was previous talk of a union."

"By all accounts t' lad's had a deal ter do wi' t' runnin' o' Raisgill, eh?" Tom was keen to take over the tale. "An' Sir Robert thinks runnin' t' place on his own'll be t' mekin' of 'im, eh?"

Stephen and William soon returned. Stephen's greeting to Anselm was sincere, no doubt reflecting his appreciation for Sarah's rescue.

"'Tis good to see thee again, Stephen. And Sarah, how fares she?"

"She's copin', Master Anselm." He was silent for a few moments, his sparse words in themselves conveying the true depths to which Hugo's treatment had affected his wife. In a matter of fact manner, he continued, "But I'm not here to talk about Sarah. I know Tom told thee I'd gone to Sir Robert, 'as he told thee owt else?"

"Nay, a thowt a'd let thee do it, eh?" Tom chipped in.

Stephen related his journey to Raisgill and his plea to Sir Robert to intervene on Anselm's behalf once he had apprised him of events on that dreadful night at the beginning of October.

"Sir Robert took no swaying for he knew Hugo's nature," Stephen explained, "an' thought it a good idea for me to go wi' 'im to Dacre. There I repeated mi tale t' 'is Lordship an' Sir Robert spoke up for thy character. I'll give 'im 'is due, Lord Thomas took some time to think on t' matter an' then says he wants to see all persons ..." he ticked them off on his fingers, "... me, Sir Robert, Alan Vescy an' thaself Master Anselm. He wants us all before 'im, to give our accounts, an' then he'll mek a decision. He says until that's 'appened he'll not submit t' case to t' next assize."

Anselm had been listening intently to Stephen's words and now all faces were turned towards him. Silence had fallen on the room: all awaited Anselm's response. He gazed ahead, in deep reflection. Finally he spoke. "An intriguing notion and much food for thought." Bringing the tips of his fingers together he continued, as much to himself as to the other occupants of the room, "But what to do? Do I throw myself on Lord Dacre's mercy? That is the question. I must think long and hard on the matter."

It was now the beginning of November and Anselm had only ten days to decide on his course of action. He had, once more, removed himself to the Abbey at Shap and had spent many hours in deliberation. On the one hand he wished profoundly to clear his name but to do so would mean trusting to Lord Thomas's impartiality and of that he was unconvinced. On the other hand he could leave matters in abeyance and merely return through the door to Emma and a virtually *unknown future. The arguments filled his head every waking hour of the day. He could return to Overthwaite and be in position by the old oak door at the appointed hour ten days hence; for he knew that in Alan's absence the way was clear. This, however, would leave an indelible slur on his family's name and he had been raised a man of honour. Or should he put his trust in God, thereby risking incarceration or an even worse fate for a crime not of his own making?*

He must make a decision.

A cold dread flooded my body as the significance of what I had witnessed fully dawned. Instinctively I grabbed the handle and pulled with all my might but I was merely going through the motions for I knew the door would remain firm. How long I remained there I cannot say for I was in a state of shock. My mind and body were frozen. Eventually I must have found my way to the bedroom, must have lain down, must even have slept – I do not remember, all was a haze. The days passed and still I wandered through the house in my zombie-like state. I could neither eat nor drink: my mind filled with the horrific image of Adam suspended over Hugo's body.

By the end of the week I had decided I must pull myself together. I could do nothing for Adam and moping around the house would certainly not achieve anything. I told myself things would work out. Hugo would recover and Adam would return on November 11th. I must simply fill my time for the next five weeks. Suddenly I was struck by a chilling thought which for some unknown reason had not occurred to me earlier: suppose Hugo died. Where would that leave Adam?

Trying to keep calm I made my way to the living room and once again retrieved the brown envelope containing the Rutherford family tree. My hands shook as I emptied the contents onto the table. I sifted through the papers until the relevant one was in view. The date leapt off the page – October 1486. Hugo had died in October 1486; he *had* died in October 1486; had died at the hands of Adam. I began to panic. What would he do? Had Alan returned and found him? Or even worse, killed him? And if not, even had he managed to get away, what would happen to him? These and a hundred other questions besieged my brain. But the most important one returned again and again throughout the following weeks: would I ever see Adam again?

I tried to fill my days. The weather was mixed but I felt indifferent towards it. I walked the fells, content to allow the elements to take their course, to cleanse my body and free my mind of torment. But the respite was only temporary: each evening, back at Overthwaite, inevitably my thoughts turned once more to Adam and the future.

One week to go.

I had done little housework since my return and decided that even though it was November I would 'spring-clean' the Hall: to be honest, it was as much for therapy as for any great desire to have a clean and tidy house.

I worked my way through the rooms and had reached my own bedroom when my toe touched against something soft under the bed. I bent down and realised the item was my bag. On the night I had returned through the door I must have nudged the bundle inadvertently out of sight and there it had lain for over a month. I undid the fastenings and took out the contents. Instantly my senses were overwhelmed by the sight and smells of the objects, evoking memories of those months spent with Adam and the people I had come to think of as friends. A flood of nostalgia swept through my body and I sank to the bed, gripping the dress tightly to my breast. With eyes closed I could see Overthwaite as it was all those years ago – as it was a mere five weeks ago. I shook myself from the reverie: I must get on.

Opening the bottom drawer of the tallboy I placed the clothes and other contents of the bag carefully into the empty space, smoothing the folds of the dark blue woollen dress with thoughtful tenderness. I picked up Edward's comb, running my fingers along the intricate, bone engravings. Some of his hair was still lodged between the teeth and again my mind went back to the past. How had he fared? What had become of him? I dare say I would be able to find out details of the life of

Edward Guildford, perhaps I should at some time in the future. It was strange to think I knew the outcome of the fates of the Princes in the Tower: knew the answers to all the speculation about Richard III's actions. The germ of an idea began to form in my head.

Why should I not make the facts known? As evidence for my revelations I had Edward's comb and more than that, his shirt – the one Catherine had brought back with her. But how could I prove these were royal possessions? Suddenly an image of Guy flashed into my head. He had not crossed my mind for months, so why now, when I had been thinking of something entirely different? There must have been a reason for my subconscious to turn in his direction. I concentrated but the harder I tried, the more obscure it all became and I was about to return to my work when realisation dawned: DNA. During my time with Guy I had learnt several things about the subject and one was that DNA could be obtained from the collar of a garment and also from the root of a hair follicle. I had both.

I was becoming excited and tried to arrange my thoughts in order. The shirt was from 1484/5, well after the date of the supposed deaths of the Princes; and the comb had been used in 1486, long after Bosworth and Richard's death. Proof positive he had not had his nephews killed! I wondered what to do next. As I was still on amicable terms with Guy I could ask him to conduct a test on the two objects. Perhaps a descendant of Edward Guildford could be traced, a DNA sample obtained and comparisons made to those of Prince Edward. My mind was working overtime until it occurred to me that my reasoning had one fatal flaw: how could I hope to prove it? Although a match might be obtained what did it mean? I could hardly authenticate the objects: who would believe I had travelled back to the 15th century. Even though I had the proof it was no proof at all.

At last it was November 11th. The intervening days had seemed like a lifetime: I had merely been treading water. This day, however, was the longest of my life; also the worst. Again I took to the fells. The weather had improved and in fair conditions I walked for miles; walked until my legs ached although I hardly felt the pain. At home I tried to relax in a hot bath then realising I had eaten nothing since breakfast, arranged some bread and cheese on a plate in the kitchen. But I had no appetite. My stomach churned with emotion: I was too nervy to settle to anything. The hours ticked by.

Five o'clock – only three hours to go. By now darkness had fallen. I wandered across to the kitchen window. Behind the house stood a large oak tree and through its bare branches I caught sight of a pale, watery moon floating in a sea of cloud. Was Adam looking at this same moon, I wondered? Perhaps not – perhaps he was dead. I clenched my fists and told myself not to think in such a way. Be positive: he *would* return; in a few hours I *would* be with him once more.

The clock registered 19.45 and I positioned myself on the landing. As the minutes passed my mind re-lived all we had gone through: those early days when I grew to love Adam; the months spent together in *his* time; those last gruelling hours leading to the death of Hugo. Once again I imagined the awful fates which could have befallen him and my body felt empty and lifeless.

Now it was too late to think; too late to ponder on what fate held in store. With a vibration that shook the whole fabric of the building the door began its momentous swing. I closed my eyes, not daring to look, waiting for the blast of cold air to cease. An eternity passed in a matter of seconds and when all was still I knew I could avoid the outcome no longer.

The rush lights cast their eerie shadows down the hallway and my eyesight took a moment to adjust. I held my breath. A figure emerged, silhouetted in the doorway: a figure whose outline I would know anywhere. I steadied myself for my legs were like jelly and a sob of relief caught in my throat.

Crossing the threshold, Adam took hold of my outstretched hand, pulled me towards him and nuzzling his face in my hair whispered, "I have come home."

BIBLIOGRAPHY

Aslet Clive, 'The Story of Greenwich' (London, 1999)

Bagley J.J., 'Life in Medieval England' (London, 1960)

Brunskill R.W., 'Vernacular Architecture of the Lake Countries' (London, 1974)

Cheetham Anthony, 'The Life and Times of Richard III' (London 1972)

Fraser George MacDonald, 'The Steel Bonnets' (Great Britain, 1971)

Hindley Geoffrey, 'England in the Age of Caxton' (London, 1979)

Jennings Charles, 'Greenwich' (London, 1999)

Lawson J. & Silver H., 'A Social History of Education in England' (London, 1973)

Sheppard Francis, 'London – A History' (Oxford, 1998)

Sim Alison, 'The Tudor Housewife' (Stroud, 1998)

Southern R., 'The Medieval Theatre in the Round' (London, 1957)
'The Staging of Plays Before Shakespeare' (London, 1973)

Stretton E.H.A., 'Dacre Castle' (Kendal, 1994)

Willett C. & Cunnington Phillis, 'Handbook of English Mediaeval Costume' (London, 1952)

Williams Neville, 'The Life and Times of Henry VII' (London, 1973)